"Newcomers and loyal fans alike w... .... adventure in Hyderabad, India, told in Lauren Willig's signature mix of historical richness and whimsical humor."   —*The Newark Star-Ledger*

"*The Betrayal of the Blood Lily* will delight readers with its vivid historical detail, deeply honorable characters fighting against truly wicked villains, and a plot filled with baffling mystery and heart-pounding danger."   —*BookPage*

"The latest sure-to-please installment to the popular Pink Carnation series transports the action to colonial India.... Willig hasn't lost her touch; this outing has all the charm of the previous books in the series."   —*Publishers Weekly*

"Willig brings colonial India to vibrant life through Penelope's eyes, and the sparks flying between Penelope and Alex generate plenty of heat. By taking the story to India, Willig injects a new energy in her already thriving, thrilling series, and presents the best entry to date."   —*Booklist*

"Reading the sixth book in Willig's Pink Carnation series ... is like getting a plate of warm-from-the-oven chocolate chip cookies; it's hard not to eat them all at once, but you also want to savor every bite."   —*Library Journal*

The Temptation of the Night Jasmine

"Jane Austen for the modern girl ... sheer fun!"
                                     —*New York Times* bestselling author Christina Dodd

"An engaging historical romance, delightfully funny and sweet ... a thoroughly charming costume drama.... Romance's rosy glow tints even the spy adventure that unfolds ... fine historical fiction ... thrilling."   —*The Newark Star-Ledger*

"Another sultry spy tale.... The author's conflation of historical fact, quirky observations, and nicely rendered romances results in an elegant and grandly entertaining book."   —*Publishers Weekly*

continued ...

"Honor and romance again take the lead in nineteenth-century England, as yet another flower-named spy continues this high-spirited and thoroughly enjoyable series."   —*Kirkus Reviews*

The Seduction of the Crimson Rose

"Willig's series gets better with each addition, and her latest is filled with swashbuckling fun, romance, and intrigue."   —*Booklist*

"Handily fulfills its promise of intrigue and romance."   —*Publishers Weekly*

"There are few authors capable of matching Lauren Willig's ability to merge historical accuracy, heart-pounding romance, and biting wit . . . continues Willig's trend of making each installment even better than its spectacular predecessor."   —*BookPage*

The Deception of the Emerald Ring

"History textbook meets Bridget Jones."   —*Marie Claire*

"A fun and zany time warp full of history, digestible violence, and plenty of romance."   —*New York Daily News*

"Heaving bodices, embellished history, and witty dialogue: What more could you ask for?"   —*Kirkus Reviews*

"Willig's latest is riveting, providing a great diversion and lots of fun."   —*Booklist*

"Smart . . . [a] fast-paced narrative with mistaken identities, double agents, and high-stakes espionage. . . . The historic action is taut and twisting. Fans of the series will clamor for more."   —*Publishers Weekly*

The Masque of the Black Tulip

"Clever [and] playful. . . . What's most delicious about Willig's novels is that the damsels of 1803 bravely put it all on the line for love and country."   —*Detroit Free Press*

"Studded with clever literary and historical nuggets, this charming historical/contemporary romance moves back and forth in time."   —*USA Today*

"Willig has great fun with the conventions of the genre, putting up obstacles between her lovers at every opportunity . . . a great escape."　　　　　　　　—*The Boston Globe*

"Willig picks up where she left readers breathlessly hanging. . . . Many more will delight in this easy-to-read romp and line up for the next installment."　　*—Publishers Weekly*

The Secret History of the Pink Carnation

"A deftly hilarious, sexy novel."

　　　　　　—Eloisa James, *New York Times* bestselling author of *A Kiss at Midnight*

"A merry romp with never a dull moment! A fun read."

　　　　　　—Mary Balogh, *New York Times* bestselling author of *A Secret Affair*

"This genre-bending read—a dash of chick lit with a historical twist—has it all: romance, mystery, and adventure. Pure fun!"

　　　　　　—Meg Cabot, *New York Times* bestselling author of *Insatiable*

"A historical novel with a modern twist. I loved the way Willig dips back and forth from Eloise's love affair and her swish parties to the Purple Gentian and of course the lovely, feisty Amy. The unmasking of the Pink Carnation is a real surprise."

　　　　　　—Mina Ford, author of *My Fake Wedding*

"Swashbuckling. . . . Willig has an ear for quick wit and an eye for detail. Her fiction debut is chock-full of romance, sexual tension, espionage, adventure, and humor."

　　　　　　—*Library Journal*

"A juicy mystery—chick lit never had it so good!"　　　　　　—*Complete Woman*

"Willig's imaginative debut . . . is a decidedly delightful romp."　　　　—*Booklist*

"Relentlessly effervescent prose . . . a sexy, smirking, determined-to-charm historical romance debut."　　　　　　　　　　　　　　　—*Kirkus Reviews*

"An adventurous, witty blend of historical romance and chick lit . . . will delight readers who like their love stories with a bit of a twist."　　　　—*South Bay's Newspaper*

"A delightful debut."

　　　　　　　　　　　　　　　　　　　—Roundtable Reviews

ALSO BY LAUREN WILLIG

The Secret History of the Pink Carnation
The Masque of the Black Tulip
The Deception of the Emerald Ring
The Seduction of the Crimson Rose
The Temptation of the Night Jasmine
The Betrayal of the Blood Lily

The Mischief of the
MISTLETOE

LAUREN WILLIG

 NEW AMERICAN LIBRARY

NEW AMERICAN LIBRARY
Published by New American Library, a division of
Penguin Group (USA) Inc., 375 Hudson Street,
New York, New York 10014, USA
Penguin Group (Canada), 90 Eglinton Avenue East, Suite 700, Toronto, Ontario M4P 2Y3, Canada
(a division of Pearson Penguin Canada Inc.); Penguin Books Ltd., 80 Strand, London WC2R 0RL,
England; Penguin Ireland, 25 St. Stephen's Green, Dublin 2, Ireland (a division of Penguin Books
Ltd.); Penguin Group (Australia), 250 Camberwell Road, Camberwell, Victoria 3124, Australia (a
division of Pearson Australia Group Pty. Ltd.); Penguin Books India Pvt. Ltd., 11 Community
Centre, Panchsheel Park, New Delhi - 110 017, India; Penguin Group (NZ), 67 Apollo Drive,
Rosedale, Auckland 0632, New Zealand (a division of Pearson New Zealand Ltd.); Penguin Books
(South Africa) (Pty.) Ltd., 24 Sturdee Avenue, Rosebank, Johannesburg 2196, South Africa

Penguin Books Ltd., Registered Offices:
80 Strand, London WC2R 0RL, England

Published by New American Library, a division of Penguin Group (USA) Inc. Previously published
in a Dutton edition.

First New American Library Printing, November 2011
10 9 8 7 6 5 4 3 2 1

REGISTERED TRADEMARK—MARCA REGISTRADA

New American Library Trade Paperback ISBN: 978-0-451-23477-3

THE LIBRARY OF CONGRESS HAS CATALOGED THE HARDCOVER EDITION OF THIS TITLE AS FOLLOWS:

Willig, Lauren.
The mischief of the mistletoe/Lauren Willig
1. Women teachers—Fiction. 2. Girl's schools—Fiction. 3. Austen Jane, 1775–1817—Fiction.
4. England—Social life and customs—19th century—Fiction. 5. Christmas stories. I. Title.
PS3623.I575M57 2010
813'.6—dc22 2010011703

Set in Granjon
Designed by Leonard Telesca

Printed in the United States of America

For my Tweedos
(You know who you are)
&
For all of you
who asked for a book about Turnip

A note for readers of the Pink Carnation series: the action of this book begins after The Seduction of the Crimson Rose, *but before* The Temptation of the Night Jasmine.

The Mischief of the
MISTLETOE

Miss Jane Austen to Miss Arabella Dempsey

My dear Arabella,

Your letter took me quite by surprise this morning. I believe I drank too much wine last night; I know not else how to account for the shaking of my hand today, unless it be the shock of your news. You will kindly make allowance therefore for any indistinctness of writing by attributing it to this venial error.

We are all delighted at the prospect of having you again among us, but under such circumstances! What has the world come to when elderly aunts are so profligate of their fortunes as to squander them on half-pay officers? It saddens me to see you disappointed in your expectations, however much you may *claim you expected nothing of the sort. A pretty piece of work your Aunt Osborne has made of it!*

Mr. Hoare straightaway said that a woman should not be trusted with money; that your aunt ought to have settled something on you as soon as her husband died. To my remark that that would have been to trust you with money, and you a woman, too, he had nothing to say. . . . But I must say no more on this subject.

What must I tell you of your sisters? Truth or falsehood? I will try the former and you may choose for yourself another time. . . . Margaret you will find assiduously courting all accomplishments except that of good humor. As for Olivia, I suspect she does not exist; every time I call, her head is in a book, leaving only a set of limbs sprawled on the hearth rug. I have hopes for Lavinia, who goes on as a young lady of fifteen ought to do, admired and admiring, but for a certain boisterousness of spirit that time and care will cure.

Your father was to have dined with us today, but the weather was so cold he dared not venture forth.

You deserve a longer letter than this, but it is my unhappy fate to seldom treat people so well as they deserve. God bless you! And may God speed your journey to Bath.

Yours very affectionately,
J. Austen
Everybody's love.

Bath
December 1803

" 'So Emma,' said he, 'you are quite the stranger at home. It must seem odd enough for you to be here. A pretty piece of work your Aunt Turner has made of it! By heaven! ... What a blow it must have been upon you! To find yourself, instead of heiress of eight or nine thousand pounds, sent back a weight upon your family, without a sixpence.... After keeping you from your family for such a length of time as must do away all natural affection ... you are returned upon their hands without a sixpence.' "

— Jane Austen, *The Watsons*

" 'Poverty is a great evil, but to a woman of education and feeling it ought not, it cannot be the greatest. I would rather be a teacher at a school (and I can think of nothing worse) than marry a man I did not like.'

'I would rather do anything than be a teacher at a school,' said her sister."

— Jane Austen, *The Watsons*

Chapter 1

"I am for teaching," announced Miss Arabella Dempsey.

Her grand pronouncement fell decidedly flat. It was hard to make grand pronouncements while struggling uphill on a steep road against a stiff wind, and even harder when the wind chose that moment to thrust your bonnet ribbons between your teeth. Arabella tasted wet satin and old dye.

"For what?" asked Miss Jane Austen, swiping at her own bonnet ribbons as the wind blew them into her face.

So much for grand pronouncements. "I intend to apply for a position at Miss Climpson's Select Seminary for Young Ladies. There's a position open for a junior instructress." There. It was out. Short, simple, to the point.

Jane screwed up her face against the wind. At least, Arabella hoped it was against the wind. "Are you quite sure?"

Sure? Arabella had never been less sure of anything in her life. "Absolutely."

Jane hitched her pile of books up under one arm and shoved her ribbons back into place. "If you rest for a moment, perhaps the impulse will pass," she suggested.

"It's not an impulse. It's a considered opinion."

"Not considered enough. Have you ever been inside a young ladies' academy?"

Arabella made a face at the top of Jane's bonneted head. It was very hard having an argument with someone when all you could see was the crown of her hat. Jane might be several years her senior, but she was also several inches shorter. The combination of the two put Arabella at a distinct disadvantage.

Six years older, Jane had always been as much an older sibling as a playmate, telling stories and bandaging bruised knees. Arabella's father had been at one time a pupil of Mr. Austen's at Oxford, when Mr. Austen had been a young proctor at St. John's. Back in the golden days of childhood, Arabella's father's parish had lain not far from Steventon, and both books and children had been exchanged back and forth between the two households.

This happy state of affairs had continued until Arabella was twelve. She remembered her head just fitting on Jane's shoulder as she had cried on it that dreadful winter, as her mother lay still and cold among the gray sheets on the gray bed, everything hued in ice and shadow. She remembered the clasp of Jane's hand as Aunt Osborne's carriage had come to carry her away to London.

"And what of your aunt Osborne?" Jane added. "I thought you were only visiting in Bath. Aren't you to go back to her after Christmas?"

"Mmmph." Arabella was so busy avoiding Jane's eyes that she stumbled. Flushing, she gabbled, "Loose cobble. You would think they would keep the streets in better repair."

"How singular," said Jane. "The cobbles are perfectly stationary on this side of the street. Why this sudden desire to improve young minds?"

That was the problem with old friends. They saw far too much. Arabella developed a deep interest in the cobbles beneath her feet, picking her steps with unnecessary care. "Is it so unlikely I should want to do something more than be Aunt Osborne's companion?"

"You have a very comfortable home with her," Jane pointed out. "One aging lady is less bother than fifty young girls."

"One aging lady and one new uncle," Arabella shot back, and wished she hadn't.

Jane looked at her, far too keenly for comfort. But all she said was, "It is final, then?"

"As final as the marriage vow," said Arabella, with an attempt to keep her voice light. "My aunt and Captain Musgrave were married last week."

"But isn't he . . ."

"Half her age? Yes." There was no point in beating around the bush. It had been all over the scandal sheets. "But what are such petty things as numbers to the majesty of the human heart?"

Jane's laughter made little puffs in the cold air. "A direct quotation?"

"As near as I can recall." Arabella hadn't been in a position to memorize specific phrases; she had been too numb with shock.

Captain Musgrave had made a pretty little speech out of it, all about love defying time, all the while holding Aunt Osborne's jeweled hand in an actor's practiced grip, while she fluttered and dimpled up at him, her own expression more eloquent than any number of speeches. In the half-dark dining room, the candle flames created little pools of light in the polished surface of the dining table, oscillating off Aunt Osborne's rings and the diamond pendant in her turban, but nothing shone so bright as her face. In the uncertain light, with her face lifted towards Captain Musgrave, tightening the loose skin beneath her chin, one could almost imagine her the beauty she once had been. Almost.

Even candlelight wasn't quite that kind.

One of her aunt's friends had dropped a wineglass in shock at the announcement. Arabella could still hear the high, tinkling sound of shattering crystal in the sudden silence, echoing endlessly in her ears like the angry hum of a wasp. Arabella had made her way through the wreckage of shattered crystal, spilled claret staining her slippers, and wished them happy. At least, she assumed she had wished them happy. Memory blurred.

He had never made her any promises. At least, none that was explicit. It had all been done by implication and innuendo, a hand on her elbow here, a touch to her shoulder there, a meeting of eyes across a room. It was all very neatly done. There had been nothing concrete.

Except for that kiss.

"It would make an excellent premise for a novel," said Jane. "A young girl, thrown back on her family after years in grander circumstances . . ."

"Forced to deal with carping sisters and an invalid father?" The wind was beginning to make Arabella's head ache. She could feel the throb beginning just behind her temples. It hurt to think about what a fool she had been, even now, with two months' distance. "If you must do it, at least change my name. Call her . . . Oh, I don't know. Elizabeth or Emma."

"Emma," said Jane decidedly. "I've already used Elizabeth."

Arabella smiled with forced brightness. "Did I tell you that I finished a draft of my novel? I call it *Sketches from the Life of a Young Lady in London*. It's not so much a novel, really. More a series of observations. Sketches, in fact."

Jane ignored her attempts to change the subject. "Your father said you were only home until the holidays."

"I was. I am." Arabella struggled against the wind that seemed determined to wrap her skirt around her legs as she labored uphill. What madman had designed the streets of Bath on a nearly perpendicular grade? Someone with a grudge against young ladies without the means to afford a carriage. "Aunt Osborne expects me back for Christmas. I am to spend the twelve days of Christmas with her at Girdings House at the express command of the Dowager Duchess of Dovedale."

The invitation had been issued before Captain Musgrave had entered onto the scene. An invitation from the Dowager Duchess of Dovedale was something not to be denied. The Dowager Duchess of Dovedale possessed a particularly pointy cane and she knew just how to use it.

Arabella's aunt attributed the invitation to her own social consequence, but Arabella knew better. The house party at Girdings was being thrown quite explicitly as a means of marrying off the dowager's shy granddaughter, Charlotte. The dowager needed to even the numbers with young ladies who could be trusted to draw absolutely no attention to themselves. After years as her aunt's companion, Arabella was a master at the art of self-effacement.

She had been, to Aunt Osborne, the equivalent of a piece of furniture, and to her aunt's friends something even less.

The first person to have looked at her and seen her had been Captain Musgrave.

So much for that. What he had seen was her supposed inheritance. His eyes had been for Aunt Osborne's gold, not for her.

"And after Twelfth Night?" Jane asked.

She wasn't going back to that house. Not with them. Not ever. "What newlyweds want a poor relation cluttering up the house?"

Jane looked at her keenly. "Has your aunt Osborne said as much?"

"No. She wouldn't. But I feel it." It would have been so much simpler if that had been all she felt. "It seemed like a good time to come home."

Except that home wasn't there anymore.

When she thought of home, it had always been of the ivy-hung parsonage of her youth, her father sitting in his study, writing long analyses of Augustan poetry and—very occasionally—his sermons, while her rosy-cheeked sisters tumbled among the butterflies in the flower-filled garden.

To see them now, in a set of rented rooms redolent of failure and boiled mutton, had jarred her. Her father's cheeks were sunken, his frame gaunt. Margaret had gone from being a self-important eight-year-old to an embittered twenty. Olivia had no interest in anything outside the covers of her books; not novels, but dusty commentaries on Latin authors dredged from their father's shelves. Lavinia, a roly-poly three-year-old when Arabella left, was all arms and legs at fifteen, outgoing and awkward. They had grown up without her. There was no place for her in their lives.

No place for her in London, no place for her in Bath. No place for her with her aunt, with her father, her sisters. Arabella fought against a dragging sensation of despair. The wind whistled in her ears, doing its best to push her back down the hill up which she had so laboriously climbed.

Absurd to recall that just three months ago she had believed herself on the verge of being married, living every day in constant expectation of a proposal. It was a proposal that had come, but to Aunt Osborne, not to her.

A lucky escape, she told herself stoutly, struggling her way up the hill. He had proved himself a fortune hunter and a cad. Wasn't she better off without such a husband as that? And she wasn't entirely without resources, whatever the Musgraves of the world might believe. She had her own wits to see her through. Being a schoolmistress might not be what she had expected, and it certainly wasn't the same as having a home of one's own, but it would give her somewhere to go, something to do, a means of living without relying on the charity of her aunt. Or her new uncle.

Uncle Hayworth. It made her feel more than a little sick.

"She must not have been able to do without you," said Jane.

Arabella wrenched her attention back to her friend. "Who?"

"Your aunt." When Arabella continued to look at her blankly, Jane said, "You hadn't heard?"

"Heard what?"

Jane shook her head. "I must have been mistaken. I heard your aunt was in Bath. A party came up from London. There's to be an assembly and a frost fair."

"No. I—" Arabella bit her lip. "You probably weren't mistaken. I'm sure she is in town."

Captain Musgrave had expressed a desire to go to Bath. He had never been, he said. He had made serious noises about Roman ruins and less serious ones about restorative waters, making droll fun of the invalids in their Bath chairs sipping sulfurous tonics.

Jane looked at her with concerned eyes. "Wouldn't she have called?"

"Aunt Osborne call at Westgate Buildings? The imagination rebels." No matter that Arabella had lived under her roof for the larger part of her life; Aunt Osborne recognized only certain addresses. Pasting on a bright smile, Arabella resolutely changed the subject. "But Miss Climpson's is within easy distance of Westgate Buildings. I'll be near enough to visit on my half days."

"If you have half days," murmured Jane.

Arabella chose to ignore her. "Perhaps Margaret will like me better if she doesn't have to share a bed with me." She had meant it as a joke, but it came out flat. "I don't want to be a burden on them."

It was as close as she could come to mentioning the family finances, even to an old family friend.

Jane made a face. "But to teach . . ."

"How can you speak against teaching, with your own father a teacher?"

"He teaches from home, not a school," Jane pointed out sagely. "It's an entirely different proposition."

"I certainly can't teach from my home," said Arabella tartly. "There's scarcely room for us all as it is. Our lodgings are bursting at the seams. If we took in pupils, we would have to stow them in the kitchen dresser, or under the stove like kindling."

Jane regarded her with frank amusement. "Under the stove? You don't have much to do with kitchens in London, do you?"

"You sound like Margaret now."

"That," said Jane, "was unkind."

Arabella brushed that aside. "If I ask nicely, perhaps Miss Climpson will agree to take Lavinia and Olivia on as day students."

It was a bit late for Olivia, already sixteen, but would be a distinct advantage for Lavinia. Arabella, at least, had had the advantage of a good governess, courtesy of Aunt Osborne, and she knew her sisters felt the lack.

"It will not be what you are accustomed to," Jane warned.

"I wasn't accustomed to what I was accustomed to," said Arabella. It was true. She had never felt really at home in society. She was too awkward, too shy, too tall.

"It is a pretty building, at least," she said as they made their way along the Sydney Gardens. Miss Climpson's Select Seminary for Young Ladies was situated on Sydney Place, not far from the Austens' residence.

"On the outside," said Jane. "You won't be seeing much of the facade once you're expected to spend your days within. You can change your mind, you know. Come stay with us for a few weeks instead. My mother and Cassandra would be delighted to have you."

Arabella paused in front of the door of Miss Climpson's seminary. It was painted a pristine white with an arched top. It certainly looked welcoming enough and not at all like the prison her friend painted it. She could be happy here, she told herself.

It was the sensible, responsible decision. She would be making some use of herself, freeing her family from the burden of keeping her.

It wasn't just running away.

Arabella squared her shoulders. "Please give your mother and Cassandra my fondest regards," she said, "and tell them I will see them at supper."

"You are resolved, then?"

Resolved wasn't quite the word Arabella would have chosen.

"At least in a school," she said, as much to convince herself as her companion, "I should feel that I was doing something, something for the good both of my family and the young ladies in my charge. All those shining young faces, eager to learn . . ."

Jane cast her a sidelong glance. "It is painfully apparent that you never attended a young ladies' academy."

Chapter 2

*T*hey were everywhere.

Girls.

Young girls. Very young girls. Even younger girls. Not a surprising thing to be found in an all-girls' school, but Mr. Reginald Fitzhugh, more commonly known to his friends and associates as Turnip, hadn't quite thought through all the ramifications of placing nearly fifty young ladies—using the term "ladies" loosely—under one set of eaves. They thronged the foyer, playing tiddlywinks, nudging one another's arms, whispering, giggling. There was no escaping them.

And someone had thought this was a good idea?

Turnip dodged out of the way of a flying tiddlywink, wondering why no one had warned of the hazards involved in paying calls on all-girls' academies. Come to think of it, this must be why his parents had been so deuced eager to foist the job of delivering Sally's Christmas hamper off on him. He might not be the brightest vegetable in the patch, but he knew a dodge when he saw one.

At the time, it had all been couched in the most sensible and flattering of terms. He was already planning to visit friends at Selwick Hall in early December; it would be only a short jaunt from there to Bath. It would give him an opportunity to test the mettle of his new matched bays, and besides, "Sally will be so delighted to see her favorite brother!"

Favorite brother, ha! He was her only brother. It didn't take much school learning to count to one.

And where was Miss Sally? Some sign of sisterly devotion, that, thought Turnip darkly, leaving him stranded in a wilderness of young females armed with projectiles. If she wanted her ruddy Christmas hamper that badly, she could at least come to collect it.

He didn't even see why she bally well needed a Christmas hamper. She would be home for Christmas. What was so devilish imperative that it couldn't wait the three weeks until Sal hauled herself home for the holidays? She didn't seem to be the only one, however. Among the bustle in the hallway were what appeared to be other siblings, parents, and guardians, bringing their guilt gifts of fruit, cake, and fripperies to their indulged offspring. The only one Turnip recognized was Lord Henry Innes, bruising rider to hounds, terror in the boxing ring, also lugging a large hamper.

According to his parents, there was a regular black market in Christmas hamper goods at Miss Climpson's seminary and Sally didn't like to be behindhand in anything. It was, his mother explained, the female equivalent of debts of honor, and he wouldn't want Sally to welsh on a debt of honor, would he, now?

His mother, Turnip thought darkly, had neglected to mention the tiddlywinks.

"Mr. Fitzhugh?" A harried-looking young lady lightly touched his arm. From her age and the fact that she was tiddlywink-free, Turnip cunningly surmised that she must be a junior mistress rather than a pupil. On the other hand, one could never be too sure. Deuced devious, some of those young girls. After years of Sally, he should know. "You are Mr. Fitzhugh, are you not?"

"The last time I checked!" said Turnip cheerfully. "Not that names tend to change about on one that much, but one can never be too careful. Chap I knew went to bed one name last week and woke up another."

Poor Ruddy Carstairs. He had gone about in a daze all day, completely unable to comprehend why everyone kept calling him Smooton. It had taken him all day to figure out it was because his uncle had stuck in his spoon and left him the title. It made Turnip very glad he didn't have any uncles, or at least not ones with titles. He'd got rather used to being Mr. Fitzhugh. It suited him, like a well-tailored suit of clothes. He'd hate to have to get used to another.

"*Ah, bon,*" said the young lady, looking decidedly relieved, as well as more than a little bit French. Odd thing, nationality. She looked just like everyone else, but when she opened her mouth, the French just came out. "I would have recognized the resemblance anywhere. I am Mademoiselle de Fayette. I teach the French to your sister. Will you come with me?"

Turnip hefted the Christmas hamper. "Lead on!"

"Miss Fitzhugh waits for you in the blue parlor," said the French mistress, leading him down a long corridor dotted with doors, through which various odd sounds could be heard. Someone appeared to be reciting poetry. Through another, rhythmic thumps could be heard.

"Dancing lessons," the teacher explained.

It sounded more like something being pounded to death with a large club. Turnip feared for his feet when this new crop of debutantes was let loose on the ballrooms of London and Bath.

The French mistress opened another door, revealing a parlor that lived up to its title by the blue of its paper and drapes. There was, however, one slight problem. Or rather, three slight problems.

"I say," said Turnip. "Only one of these is mine."

The one that happened to be his jumped up out of her chair. There was no denying the family resemblance. Sally's bright gold hair was considerably longer, of course, and she wore a white muslin dress rather than a—if Turnip said so himself—deuced fetching carnation-patterned waistcoat, but they had the same long-boned bodies and cameo-featured faces.

They were, thought Turnip without conceit, a very attractive family. As more than one would-be wit had said, they were all long on looks and short on brains.

It was only fair, really. One couldn't expect to have everything.

Sally gave him a loud smack on the cheek.

"Silly Reggie!" she said, in the fond tone she used when other people were around. "I wanted Agnes and Lizzy to meet my favorite brother. It's *so* lovely to see you. Do you have my hamper?"

"Right here," said Turnip, brandishing it. "And jolly heavy it is, too. What do you have in here? Bricks?"

"What would I do with those?" demanded Sally in tones of sisterly scorn.

"Build something?" suggested one of her friends, revealing a dimple in one cheek. There were two of them, both attired in muslin dresses with blue sashes. The one who had spoken had bronzy curls and a decided look of mischief about her.

"Oh, Miss Climpson would adore that," said Sally witheringly. Dropping the lid of the hamper, she belatedly remembered her manners. "Reggie, allow me to present you to Miss Agnes Wooliston"—the taller of the two girls curtsied—"and Miss Lizzy Reid." Bronze curls bounced.

Sally beamed regally upon them both. "They are my particular friends."

"What happened to Annabelle Anstrue and Catherine Carruthers?"

Sally's tone turned glacial. "They are no longer my particular friends."

Turnip gave up. Female friendships were a deuced sight harder to follow than international alliances.

"What did they do?" he asked jocularly. "Borrow your ribbons without asking?"

Sally set her chin in a way that her instructresses would have recognized all too well. "I *liked* those ribbons."

"Ah, yes, well. Righty-ho," said Turnip hastily, taking a few steps back. Hell hath no fury like a little sister whose ribbon box had been tampered with. "Good term at school, then?"

"Oh, an excellent one!" contributed one of his sister's new sworn siblings. Bouncing curls . . . this one was Lizzy Reid. Not that it did any good to remember their names. It would be a new set by next Christmas. That is, if Sally weren't already out on the marriage market by then. That was a terrifying thought, his little sister let loose on the world. It was one that Turnip preferred not to contemplate. Ah well, time enough to jump that hedge when he came to it. "Catherine Carruthers was caught exchanging notes with one of the gardeners and was almost sent home in disgrace!"

"It wasn't actually with the gardener," the other one broke in. "He simply carried the notes for her. It was some officer or other on leave from his regiment."

Sally squinted at her. "Are you quite sure? *I* heard that it was an artist and they were going to run away to Rome together!"

Tugging at his cravat, Turnip glanced over his shoulder at the door. Was it just him, or did they keep the school unnaturally warm for December? The French mistress, he noticed, had already beat a hasty retreat. Deuced sensible of her. For a large room, this one felt jolly small.

"Righty-ho, then," he said again. "Jolly good. Rome is lovely this time of year. Wouldn't mind being there myself in fact."

"Reggie!" His sister pulled a horrified face, delighted to be appalled. "It isn't jolly good—it's a terrible scandal!"

"Then why are you all grinning about it?"

The three girls exchanged a look, one of those looks that somehow managed to combine long-suffering patience with a hearty dose of feminine scorn. They must teach those at school along with tromping on a chap's toes during the quadrille.

"Because," said Lizzy Reid, "without scandal, what would there be for us to talk about?"

Turnip suspected a trick question. "Your lessons?" he suggested.

"Oh, Reggie," said Sally sadly.

Blast. It had been a trick question.

"Now," said Sally, getting down to business, "let us discuss my travel arrangements."

"What travel arrangements?" said Turnip warily.

"When you take me home for Christmas, of course," said Sally, as though it were a foregone conclusion. "You can call for me the morning of the twentieth. That should leave plenty of time to drive up to Suffolk."

"Oh no." Turnip wasn't falling for that one. He folded his arms across his chest. "Can't be done, I'm afraid. The Dowager Duchess of Dovedale is having a house party. Wouldn't want to cross the Dowager Duchess."

Even Sally wouldn't want to cross fans with the Dowager Duchess of Dovedale. The woman had a tongue of steel and drank the blood of young virgins for breakfast. Well, the blood-drinking had never been proved. But she could be jolly nasty when she chose, and she usually did choose. That cane of hers left quite a welt.

"Pooh," said Sally. *Pooh?* Turnip regarded his little sister incredulously. When had it come to this? "Parva Magna is on the way. You can drop me off home and then go on to Girdings. Do say yes," she wheedled. "We'll have such fun along the way. You can buy me lemonades and tell me all about your latest waistcoats."

Turnip wasn't quite sure why buying her lemonades was meant to be a privilege, but Sally clearly viewed it as such, so there was no point in arguing.

"Didn't the mater and pater make other arrangements for you?" he asked suspiciously.

Sally wrinkled her nose. "Yes, to travel with Miss Climpson! But she's a regular antidote. It will be *deadly.*"

"A fate worse than death!" chimed in Agnes Wooliston, loyally rushing to her friend's support.

"Doing it a bit too brown there," said Turnip frankly. "Death is death and there's no getting around that."

"That," said Lizzy Reid, "is because you haven't yet met Miss Climpson. If you had, you would understand. She's *ghastly.*"

Turnip rubbed his ear. What was it about young ladies and italics? It was deuced hard on the hearing, having all those words pounded into his head like so many stakes into the ground.

"Ghastly and deadly," he said weakly. "Sounds like quite the character."

"Yes, but would you want to spend four days in a covered conveyance with her?" demanded Sally. "You couldn't possibly wish that on anyone."

Agnes Wooliston assumed a thoughtful expression. "What about Bonaparte?"

"Well, possibly Bonaparte," allowed Sally, making an exception for the odd Corsican dictator. Her blue eyes, so very much like Turnip's, only far more shrewd (or so she liked to claim), narrowed. "Or maybe Catherine Carruthers."

"Really liked those ribbons, did you?" commented Turnip, and regretted it as three sets of female eyes turned back to him. "Never mind that. I'll think about it. It's only the beginning of the month now. Plenty of time to come to an agreement."

His little sister favored him with an approving smile. "Excellent! I'll expect you the morning of the twentieth, then. Do try to be on time this year."

"Just a minute, now." Turnip did his best to look stern, but his features had never been designed for that exercise. "I never said—"

"No worries!" said Sally brightly. "I wouldn't want to keep you when I'm sure you have other things you want to do today. We'll have plenty of time to catch up in the carriage together."

"About that—"

"Here." Getting up, she grabbed something off the windowsill and pressed it into his palm. "Have a Christmas pudding."

"A—" Turnip squinted dubiously down at the muslin-wrapped ball in his hands.

"Christmas pudding," Sally contributed helpfully.

She was right. It was indubitably a Christmas pudding, if a small one, roughly the size of a cricket ball, wrapped in clean muslin and tied up with pretty gold and red ribbons with a sprig of mistletoe for decoration.

"What am I to do with a Christmas pudding?"

"Throw it?" suggested Lizzy Reid. "One certainly can't be expected to eat them."

Interesting idea, that. Turnip hefted the pudding in one hand. Nice fit, nice weight. It would make a jolly good projectile.

Good projectile or not, it didn't make up for four days on the road, fifty-two stops for lemonade, and an endless refrain of "But why can't I hold the reins this time?" When he thought about what had happened the last time he had let Sally drive his grays . . . It was the reason he no longer had grays and now drove bays. The grays had been so traumatized by the experience that they had to be permanently rusticated to a peaceful pasture in Suffolk.

Turnip juggled the pudding from one hand to the other. "I say, frightfully grateful and all that, but . . ."

"Think nothing of it," said Sally firmly, looping an arm through his and leading him inexorably from the room. "It's the least I can do. To thank you for being such a lovely brother."

"I think I deserve a bigger pudding," mumbled Turnip as he stumbled out along the hallway, wondering just how it was that Sally had gotten her way yet again.

It wasn't that he didn't love the minx. Of course, he did. As these things went, she was the positive gold standard of female siblings, the Weston's waistcoat of little sisters. That didn't mean he loved the idea of four days in a carriage with her.

With a meditative toss of his pudding, Turnip reached for the door. Unfortunately, someone else was there first. The pudding tumbled to the floor as Turnip collided with something soft, warm, and quite clearly not a door.

Doors, after all, seldom said, "Ooof!"

Chapter 3

Half an hour later, Arabella emerged from the headmistress's office as a newly minted junior instructress of select young ladies.

All around her, the hall had been decked for Christmas, with bright bows of greenery and sprigs of holly. A pair of bright-eyed young girls walked past her, arm in arm, whispering confidences. Arabella forced herself to unknot her hands, taking a deep, ragged breath. It was done. She had done it, persuaded Miss Climpson to take her on, on short notice with no prior experience. It helped that Arabella had enjoyed the tutelage of an excellent governess, courtesy of Aunt Osborne. It also helped that the headmistress had found herself short an instructress with only three weeks remaining to the term. That, Arabella knew, had been the deciding factor, rather than anything inherent to herself.

Whatever the cause, she had accomplished her goal. She was to start on Monday, and if the three weeks before Christmas went well, she could stay on for the following term. Miss Climpson had made no promises regarding Olivia and Lavinia, but she had promised to consider it. Should Arabella prove satisfactory.

Arabella looked around the hall, at the bows and greenery and whispering girls. She could picture Lavinia and Olivia here. It would be good for them. Olivia needed to be drawn out of herself, exposed to the society of, well, society. As for Lavinia, exuberant and endearing, she needed just the opposite. Miss Climpson's would provide her structure and polish.

As for herself . . . well, there were worse fates, no matter what Jane said. Better to be a teacher at a school than a governess, dependent on one family for her livelihood, caught in a strange half-world between the drawing room and the servants' hall. Going back to Aunt Osborne was out of the question. And she had long ago accepted that she wasn't the sort of girl who could expect an advantageous marriage to secure her future and that of her family.

She was, not to put too fine a point on it, average. Not ugly, not striking, just average, with eye-colored eyes and hair-colored hair. Her eyes were blue, but they weren't the sort of blue about which her father's poets sang. They weren't azure or primrose or deepest sapphire. They were just blue. Plain, common, garden-variety blue, and about as remarkable in England as a daffodil among a field of daffodils. Hardly an asset on the marriage market, especially when coupled with lack of fortune, an invalid father, and three undowered sisters.

It was highly unlikely that any gentlemen of large fortune and undiscriminating taste would rush forward to bowl her over.

Arabella staggered sideways as a large form careened into her, sending her stumbling into the doorframe, while something small, round, and compact managed to land heavily on her left foot before rolling along its way.

"Oooof!" Arabella said cleverly, flailing her arms for balance.

This was not an auspicious beginning to her career as a dignified instructress of young ladies.

A pair of sturdy hands caught her by the shoulders before she could go over, hauling her back up to her feet. He overshot by a bit. Arabella found herself dangling in midair for a moment before her feet landed once again on the wooden floor.

"I say, frightfully sorry!" her unseen assailant and rescuer was babbling. "Deuced ungentlemanly of me—ought to have been watching where I was going."

Arabella's bonnet had been knocked askew in the fracas. She was above the average height, but this man was even taller. With her bonnet brim in the way, all she could see was a stretch of brightly patterned waistcoat, a masterpiece of fine fabric and poor taste.

Everyone knew about Turnip Fitzhugh's waistcoats.

Mr. Fitzhugh bent earnestly over her. "Frightfully sorry and all that. I do beg your pardon, Miss . . ."

He paused expectantly, looking down at her, waiting for her to complete the sentence for him, his blue eyes as guileless as a child's. And as devoid of recognition.

"Dempsey. Miss Arabella Dempsey. We've met before. In fact, we have danced together, Mr. Fitzhugh. Several times."

"Oh." His broad brow furrowed and an expression of consternation crossed his face. "Oh. I say. I am sorry."

"Why?" She had never thought she could be so bold, but it just came out. "I don't recall stepping on your feet. You ought to have emerged from the experience unscathed."

In fact, she was quite a good dancer. But did anyone ever notice? No. If she looked like Mary Alsworthy or had five thousand pounds a year like Deirdre Fairfax, they'd all be praising her for being as light on her feet as thistledown, but she could float like a feather for all any of them cared, or sink like lead. At that rate, she ought to have stomped on a few toes. At least that would have been one way to leave an impression.

"Wouldn't want you to think . . . I never meant to imply . . . That is to say, what I meant was that I'm not much of a dab hand at names, you see. Or faces. Or dates."

Arabella smiled determinedly at Mr. Fitzhugh, and if the smile was rather grim around the edges, hopefully he wouldn't notice. "It is quite all right, Mr. Fitzhugh. You're certainly not the first to have forgotten my name. Or the date of the Norman Conquest," she added, in an attempt to inject a bit of levity.

It didn't work. Instead of being diverted, Mr. Fitzhugh just looked sorry. For her. "I won't forget it again," he said. "Your name, that is. I can't make any promises about the Norman Conquest."

"Thank you, Mr. Fitzhugh. You are too kind."

"Didn't think there was such a thing," Mr. Fitzhugh mused. "As too much kindness, that is." Peering down at her, he added, as though the thought had just struck him. "I say, I didn't mean to detain you. Or knock you over. Might I, er, see you anywhere? My chariot is at your disposal."

"Oh, no, that's quite all right. I'm joining friends for supper just across the street."

"That's all right, then," Mr. Fitzhugh said with evident relief. "Shouldn't like to leave you here by yourself. Not after knocking you over and all that."

Arabella's smile turned sour. "Think nothing of it," she said.

With a tip of his hat, he strode jauntily out the door. Gathering her scattered wits together, Arabella made to follow, but her booted foot struck something hard and round, half hidden under the hem of her walking dress.

Bending over, she picked it up. While slightly the worse for her stepping on it, it was unmistakably a Christmas pudding, small and round and wrapped in white muslin, finished off with jaunty red and gold ribbons.

"Mr. Fitzhugh?" she called after him, holding the small, muslin-wrapped parcel aloft. "Mr. Fitzhugh! You forgot your pudding!"

Blast. He didn't seem to have heard her. Lifting her skirts, Arabella hurried down the short flight of steps. Mr. Fitzhugh, his legs longer than hers, was already some way down the street, making for a very flashy phaeton driven by a team of matched bays.

"Mr. Fitzhugh!" she called, waving the pudding in the air, when the second man in one day knocked the breath out of her by taking a flying leap at the pudding she held in her hand.

It must have been pure stubbornness that caused her to keep her grip, but as the man tugged, Arabella found herself tugging back. Harder.

"I need that pudding!" he growled. "Give it over!"

"No!" gasped Arabella, clinging to the muslin wrapper with all her might. People couldn't just go about taking other people's puddings. It was positively un-British.

"Hey! I say!"

Over the buzzing in her ears, Arabella heard the heavy thrum of booted feet against the cobblestones. With a powerful whoosh, her attacker was lifted up and away from her as a large fist connected with his jaw, sending him sprawling backwards. As the counterpressure was released, Arabella abruptly landed backside first on the cobbles, the wrapper of the pudding clutched triumphantly in one hand. Released from its muslin binding, the gooey ball of mince rolled free, collecting a fine coating of dust, mud, and other inedibles in the process.

This really wasn't shaping up to be a good day. What next? Arabella sat in the gutter and contemplated the scrap of white muslin in her hand. Perhaps she should just stay here. It would save all the trouble of being knocked over again.

For the second time that day, she found herself being hauled up by Mr. Fitzhugh, who lifted her as easily as though she were a lady's reticule. "Are you all right, Miss Dempsey?" he demanded, showing off his newfound command of her name. "Did the cad hurt you?"

"No," said Arabella, forbearing to mention her backside. "Just your pudding."

"Bother the pudding!" said Mr. Fitzhugh.

"I don't think anyone will bother with it now," said Arabella, regarding the gooey ball philosophically. "Although that man seemed to want it rather badly."

That man was lying where he had fallen, making small groaning noises. Now that she was no longer locked in combat with him, Arabella could see that he was only of medium height, slightly built and shabbily dressed.

The man started to lever himself up on his elbows, looked at Mr. Fitzhugh, and thought better of it. "Is 'ee going to 'it me again?" he asked darkly.

"Only if you attack the lady," said Mr. Fitzhugh, looming rather impressively. "That was a jolly rum thing to do."

"I didn't mean to attack 'er. My orders was to get the pudding."

"Orders?" Arabella squinted down at her assailant. "Someone ordered you to collect the pudding from me?"

"There were a lady. There." Struggling to a sitting position, the man gingerly touched his unshaven chin with one hand and pointed to the right with the other, to a narrow alley between Miss Climpson's seminary and the building next door.

There was no lady there now.

"A lady told you to fetch the pudding," repeated Mr. Fitzhugh. "There's a Banbury tale if ever I heard one!"

"I don't know nothing about no Banburies," said the would-be thief belligerently, "but there were a lady and she promised me a guinea for that pudding, she did."

"Delusional," said Mr. Fitzhugh to Arabella, in what he fondly believed to be an undertone, but which carried at least three streets away. "The man's disordered."

The man gave Mr. Fitzhugh a look of pure dislike. "I weren't disordered until you landed me a facer. Although," he admitted grudgingly, "it were a good 'un. Nice and clean."

Mr. Fitzhugh beamed with pleasure. "Much obliged." Belatedly remembering the story was meant to have a moral, he adopted a stern expression. "Only don't let me find you attacking any ladies, or I'll land you more than a facer."

Arabella's backside still hurt and unless she was much mistaken, she had mud in unfortunate places upon her person. And all for a little pudding. Discounting his absurd story, she could only imagine that the man must have been driven to it by hunger. Arabella looked dubiously at the wrapper. Extreme hunger.

Something caught her eye, something odd.

Arabella scraped at the brown spots with one gloved finger, but they didn't come off. It wasn't mud or pudding splotch, as she thought, but rather a particularly untidy script.

Someone had gone to the trouble of writing on the inside of the muslin wrapper. Whoever it was had used a brown ink that, when the pudding was wrapped, would not show through the fabric. The message was written in uneven letters, slightly smeared now with pudding goo, but still legible. Legible and . . . French? Arabella squinted at the muslin. Yes. French.

"Mr. Fitzhugh?" she said sharply.

Looking somewhat sheepish, her rescuer studied her. "All right there?" he asked solicitously. "Feeling quite the thing?"

"Mr. Fitzhugh," she said, dangling the muslin in front of him. "Were you aware that your pudding speaks French?"

Mr. Fitzhugh blinked at her, confused but game. "My puddings generally don't speak to me at'all," he said, before adding gallantly, "But if a pudding were to speak, can't see why it wouldn't *parle* the *français*, if it took the mind."

The thief looked at him as though he were quite crazy. In fact, he looked at both of them as though they were quite crazy. Arabella couldn't blame him.

"Forgive me," she said hastily. "That's not what I meant. What I meant was that there seems to be a message written inside your pudding. And it's in French. See?" She thrust the muslin towards him.

Instead of taking it from her, Mr. Fitzhugh bent over her shoulder to peer at the muslin. "I say! You're quite right! Can't think why that should be there."

"It's not for you, then?" said Arabella.

"Not that I know of. Can't think of anyone who would correspond with me via pudding." Making one of those masculine grunting noises that passed for ratiocination among the other half of the population, Mr. Fitzhugh leaned over the pudding wrapper, saying in puzzled tones, "It seems it wanted someone to meet it at Farley Castle tomorrow afternoon."

It was, Arabella realized, a perfectly accurate translation. Her own French was limited, but she spoke it well enough to be able to read, "Meet me at Farley Castle, tomorrow afternoon. Most urgent."

Chapter 4

Turnip snapped his fingers. "There's a frost fair at Farley Castle tomorrow! Knew I had heard that name before."

"A frost fair?" Miss Dempsey echoed.

"Like a big picnic, but colder," Turnip explained. "Outdoor entertainment among the castle ruins, with mulled wine and all that sort of thing. Huh." Turnip turned the scrap of fabric around. "Deuced funny coincidence."

"It's too coincidental to be a coincidence," said Miss Dempsey. There was a slight smudge of dirt on one cheek. "We seem to have stumbled upon someone's assignation. How very . . ."

"Irregular?" suggested Turnip.

To his surprise, her lips turned up at the corners. "I was going to say intriguing, but irregular would suit as well." Turning to the would-be pudding thief, who had levered himself up off the ground, she asked, "Who was it who sent you after the pudding?"

"Dunno. She came running up to me all distressed-like, grabbed my arm, and told me there'd be a guinea in it for me if I got 'er pudding back." He shrugged. "That's all."

"And you never asked why?" asked Miss Dempsey.

The man gave her a look, as if to wonder why she would suggest such a harebrained thing as that. "There was a guinea in it," he repeated.

"Right, of course," said Miss Dempsey, shaking her head slightly. "Naturally."

The man stuck out his hand at Turnip. "Speaking of guineas . . . Care to cross my palm and we'll call it no 'ard feelings about the jaw-box?"

"How about a shilling?" asked Turnip, digging into his pocket.

Miss Dempsey edged around him. "This woman. Where did she come from? What did she look like?"

The man's fist closed around the shilling Turnip dropped into his palm. "Dunno. She promised me a guinea for the pudding is all."

And with that, he touched his forelock and sauntered away.

Miss Dempsey looked at Turnip thoughtfully. "Where did *you* get the pudding?" she asked.

Turnip scratched his temple, displacing his hat in the process. "My sister, Sally," he said. "Can't think why she'd be hiding messages in— Oh."

"Oh?" Miss Dempsey tilted her head quizzically.

"No," he said decidedly, dismissing the idea as quickly as it had arisen. It would be deuced unfair to Sally to go about accusing her of setting up illicit assignations. He had every faith in his sister's moral rectitude. And her ingenuity. If Sally were to arrange an assignation, she wouldn't do it in such an addlepated way. He was the addlepated one in the family, and he was sticking to it. "It ain't like Sal to set up assignations through puddings. She's not the assignating kind."

"My assailant did say a woman," Miss Dempsey murmured. "Perhaps one of the instructresses? Your sister might have got hold of the pudding by accident."

Turnip clapped his hat firmly back onto his head. "Only one way to find out, isn't there? We can ask her."

"We?"

"You will come with me, won't you, Miss Dempsey?" Turnip flashed her his most winning smile. "You can't expect a chap to venture back into that den of females unprotected, can you? No offense meant. Your being a female and all that, I mean."

"How kind of you to notice," muttered Miss Dempsey.

"Nothing against the breed—er, gender," Turnip hastened to reassure her. "Some of my favorite people are females. But it's when you put lots and lots of them together in a room . . . it becomes . . ."

"A bit overwhelming?" Turnip spotted a hint of a smile beneath Miss Dempsey's bonnet brim and knew he was winning.

Turnip nodded vigorously. "The very thing."

"I have three younger sisters," Miss Dempsey contributed. "All of them at home." She didn't need to explain what she meant. Turnip felt for her, right down to the bottom of his waistcoat. There was no saying what younger sisters might get up to.

"Will you come with me?" he asked eagerly.

Miss Dempsey looked at the pudding cloth in her hand and then back at Turnip. "Why not?" she said. "This day certainly can't get any stranger."

It was not exactly a resounding affirmative, but Turnip knew how to seize his advantage when he had it. "Jolly good!" he exclaimed, hustling her forward before she could change her mind. "Shan't regret it! Lovely girl, Sally. Most of the time."

"Most of the time?" repeated Miss Dempsey as she hurried along beside him into the foyer. Turnip pretended not to hear her.

"Right this way!" he said with exaggerated cheerfulness. "Can't think they will have gone far. When I saw them last they were— Ah, right. Here we go."

The three girls were still together in the blue salon, their heads together, cackling like those three hags in that play he had slept through last month. Something to do with a Scotsman.

Miss Dempsey, he noticed, was still limping slightly, undoubtedly from her tumble on the cobbles. Pluck to the backbone, she was, he thought admiringly. Not a word of complaint out of her.

The same couldn't be said of Sally.

"Reggie!" exclaimed Sally, her pearl earbobs swinging as she jumped up. Technically, Miss Climpson's girls weren't supposed to wear earbobs, but Sally was firmly of the opinion that foolish rules were for other people. "What are you doing back so soon? When I told you to be early, I didn't mean this early."

"Oh, ha-ha," said Turnip cleverly. "What's the idea of giving me a pudding with a message in it? Oh, this is Miss Dempsey. Miss Dempsey, my sister Sally and her two most peculiar friends."

"You mean my two most *particular* friends," corrected Sally through gritted teeth. Donning the mask of sweetness she wore in front of non-family members, she dipped into a curtsy. "Miss Dempsey. How did you ever come to be associated with my ridiculous brother?"

Miss Dempsey extended the cloth. "We were brought together by an accident of pudding."

"The one you gave me," Turnip prompted, looking sternly at Sally. "A thief knocked Miss Dempsey over in an attempt to retrieve it."

"Really?" Lizzy Reid's eyes were as round as . . . well, as very round things. "A footpad? How simply smashing!"

"Yes, if you're the pudding. It was quite smashed, and so was Miss Dempsey."

"I wouldn't say I was quite smashed. Just a trifle shaken." Taking the chair that Turnip offered her, Miss Dempsey turned to the girls. "The odd thing about it was that there was a message on the pudding cloth. Would you know anything about that?"

"What sort of message?" asked Lizzy.

Miss Dempsey and Turnip exchanged a look. Turnip nodded slightly, and Miss Dempsey went on. "The message appears to be an invitation to an assignation. It was written in French."

Agnes Wooliston sat up straighter in her chair. "In French?"

Sally ignored the linguistic angle. "That wasn't the pudding you were planning to send to your brother in India, was it? Lizzy has a brother in India," Sally added, turning to Arabella.

"Two of them, in fact," said Lizzy. "But only one gets pudding. The other is currently In Disgrace. No, I already sent Alex's Christmas basket. Who else do you think could be going about sending messages in puddings?"

"I'd say Catherine Carruthers," said Sally authoritatively, "but she's already been found out and put under house arrest. Besides, I think her artist was English, not French."

"It was a half-pay officer," corrected Agnes. "And he was quite definitely English."

"I can assure you, brother mine," said Sally, "that I have not been arranging assignations. The pudding was here in the parlor when we came in. Wasn't it, Agnes?"

"Ye-es . . . ," said her friend, scanning the room as though trying to fix in her memory where she had seen it. "On the windowsill, there. That was how you came to pick it up. You were standing next to it."

"And you'd not seen it before?" asked Miss Dempsey quietly.

The three girls looked at one another. They all shook their heads.

"There is such a lot of Christmas pudding going about right now, you see," said Agnes apologetically, "with everyone getting their Christmas hampers. It's hard to remember every one."

"Except for the one with the live chickens," put in Lizzy Reid helpfully. "That was a very memorable hamper."

"Do. Not. Mention. The chickens," said Sally darkly.

"She has an unaccountable fear of fowl," explained Turnip to Miss Dempsey in an aside.

"They are nasty, they are smelly, and they *peck*," said Sally passionately. "Does anyone else have anything more to say on the matter?"

"What about eggs?" There was a glint of mischief in Lizzy Reid's eye. Turnip began to understand why she had been sent back from India. India probably didn't know what to do with her.

"Eggs," said Sally repressively, "grow into chickens."

"Could the message in the pudding be a prank?" interjected Miss Dempsey, intervening before the eggs hatched into full-blown fighting cocks. "You *do* have pranks here, I take it?"

"Oh, don't they!" contributed Turnip feelingly. That had been his last visit. He had been forced to endure a very trying hour with the headmistress, trying to explain why Sally's tying another girl's corset ribbons to a drainpipe was nothing more than a case of girlish high spirits and not a cause for sending Sally home. Fortunately, the other girl hadn't actually been in her corset at the time.

"Traitor," said Sally, but in a very perfunctory way. She turned back to Miss Dempsey. "This hasn't any of the . . . the . . ."

"Properties?" provided Agnes.

Sally nodded regally. "Thank you. This hasn't any of the *properties* of a proper prank. First, you can't tell at whom it's aimed. Second, none of us has the slightest way of getting all the way out to Farley Castle. It's not like sneaking out the back way to go shopping for a bunch of ribbons, you know."

Turnip looked suspiciously at his sister. "About this back way—"

"And third," Agnes broke in hastily, before Turnip could ask awkward questions about their illicit extracurricular wanderings, "it's in French! And we all know what French means."

She uttered that last in such portentous tones that Turnip began to wonder if he had misread the text on the pudding. He scratched his head and squinted at the piece of muslin lying open on the tea table.

"I know what that French means," he said cautiously. "It means 'Meet me at Farley Castle.' Doesn't it?"

"That is, indeed, in accord with my translation of it, Mr. Fitzhugh," said Miss Dempsey.

None of the girls paid the slightest bit of attention to either of them.

"But of course!" said Sally breathlessly, just as Lizzy Reid leaned forward in her chair and exclaimed, "But you can't really think . . ."

"Oh, but I do!" said Agnes.

Turning to Turnip, Miss Dempsey said, "Do you think?"

"As little as I can," Turnip replied honestly. "Do you have any notion what they're on about?"

"Chickens?" she provided, in such a droll way that Turnip felt his face break into a broad grin. He might even have chuckled.

Jolly good sport, Miss Dempsey.

Sally directed a reproving look at both of them. "This is far, far worse than chickens," she said with relish.

"Then it must be serious," murmured Miss Dempsey with all due gravity. Only Turnip noticed the corner of her lips twitch.

"Very serious," agreed Agnes Wooliston solemnly. "Who would have thought that even here, one would find . . . spies!"

The announcement had less than the desired impact on the two adults in the room.

"Spies," said Miss Dempsey. "Spies?"

"I wouldn't have thought it," said Turnip bluntly. "In fact, I don't think it."

"Oh, you." Sally waved a dismissive hand. "You never think."

"I still don't quite understand," said Miss Dempsey. "On what are these spies meant to be spying?"

The three girls looked at one another. Clearly, this was not a detail they had considered.

"On . . . something," said Agnes.

Her peers nodded vigorously.

Something was obviously the order of the day, and a commodity for which the French were bound to pay dearly.

"Something," repeated Turnip. He might be the greatest nodcock since the Prince of Wales had ventured into experiments with corsetry, but even he knew a dodge when he heard one.

"Well, think about it," said Sally impatiently. "There must be oodles on which a spy could spy if he wanted to."

"I say, Sal, I've browsed through your journal, and there ain't much there of note."

Sally's eyes shot sparks of fire. "You've read my journal!"

Turnip slunk down in his chair. "I only did it because the mater asked me to. Afraid you were developing a bit of a tendre for that music master of yours."

"Signor Marconi?" This *on dit* was too good to pass by. Lizzy bounced around in her chair. "You must be joking!"

"He had very nice mustaches," mumbled Sally, doing some slinking of her own. Straightening, she gave her brother a look of death. "And I'll thank you to stay out of my private papers!"

Turnip tapped a finger against his forehead. "Word of advice, sister mine. If you want to keep your papers private, don't write 'Private' on the cover. It set the mater right off. It was all I could do to stop her sniff-ing around like some great sniffing thing."

"Hmph," sniffed Sally.

As a sniff, it wasn't quite up to the maternal standard, but, to be fair, their mother had had years more of practice. Put a little more air into it, and Sally would be bang up to the mark in no time.

"I don't think he's a spy," said Agnes thoughtfully, bringing the dis-cussion back where it belonged. "Signor Marconi, I mean."

"What about the new French mistress?" suggested Sally spiritedly, bouncing in her chair as she turned to her peers for confirmation. "She is awfully French."

"Do you mean just because she speeeeeek lak zees?" contributed Lizzy, with an innocence belied by the wicked sparkle in her brown eyes.

"It's a nice idea, but Mademoiselle Fayette does make rather a fuss about her brother's head being chopped off," Agnes pointed out. "That might make one rather less inclined than otherwise to cooperate with the current regime."

"But how do we know whether she actually liked her brother?" said Sally, with a relish that made Turnip clutch protectively at his own neck. "That might be nothing more than a . . . than a . . ."

"Cunning ruse!" supplied Lizzy triumphantly.

"Not so cunning if one can see through it," said Agnes, disgusted by the poor quality of villains nowadays. "If it were really cunning, it would be so cunning we'd have no idea at all how cunning it was."

Turnip's brow furrowed as he attempted to unravel the tangle of cunning.

"How . . . cunning," said Miss Dempsey politely. "But whatever would spies be doing at a young ladies' seminary in Bath?"

"They're everywhere," said Agnes earnestly. As if for confirmation, she added, all in a rush, "My cousin married the Purple Gentian!"

"Did she, by Gad!" Turnip smacked the flat of his hand against one knee as it all became clear. Wooliston . . . ha! That was where he had heard the name before. His friend Lord Richard Selwick, more dramatically known as the Purple Gentian, had married a young lady of half-French extraction who had spent her youth with cousins named Wooliston. Now that he knew who she was, Turnip could see the resemblance in the younger sister.

Ha! Who would have thought to find Selwick's cousin by marriage bosom friends with his own little sister. Small world, that, he thought profoundly. He'd have to let Selwick know and they could have a good chuckle over it.

"The Purple who?" said Miss Dempsey faintly.

Sally tossed back her blond braids. "The Purple Gentian. A terribly dashing spy."

"Not only dashing but terribly dashing, eh, Sal?" Turnip chuckled.

Sally went slightly red about the ears. "Well, a spy in any event," she said in a dismissive tone, addressing herself solely to Miss Dempsey.

"An English one," Agnes Wooliston added hastily, just in case anyone might get the wrong idea. "Not French. He married my cousin Amy last year, so we all know a terrible lot about spies now."

This was obviously a source of both admiration and contention.

Sally shrugged, doing her best to look unimpressed. "There were rumors going about that Reginald might be the Pink Carnation, you know."

Agnes, with all the distinction afforded by a genuine spy-in-law, gave Sally a faintly pitying look. "But he's not."

Sally scrunched her shoulder. "Well, no."

His sister gave Turnip a look that made it abundantly clear that she considered it nothing short of a breach of his fraternal obligations to have been so remiss as to fail to have been the Pink Carnation.

"And a good thing, too!" said Turnip with feeling. "Some of those French spies can be deuced pushy."

There had been the Marquise de Montval, who had invited him for what he believed to be a coffee and a spot of assignation and then presented him with a pistol and three French thugs, all of whom seemed to be named Jean-Luc, all because she mistakenly took him for the Pink Carnation.

It was enough to put a chap right off dalliance. And coffee.

Since then, Turnip had confined his amorous attentions to English ladies. They might lack that je ne sais whatever it was, but at least one knew exactly where one sat.

Turning to the English lady currently seated beside him, Turnip said, "You probably know the Purple Gentian. Lord Richard Selwick. Jolly good chap, Selwick. He made rather a thing of smuggling *comtes* and *ducs* and whatnot right out from under the Frenchies' noses. Brought back some spiffing good brandy, too." Turnip shook his head in regret. "Deuce of a pity he had to retire."

It was his liaison with young Miss Wooliston's cousin that had forced the Purple Gentian's retirement, but Turnip tactfully refrained from reminding her of that bit. Deuced silly of Selwick to go about gallivanting beneath Bonaparte's nose like that, but Turnip supposed that was what love did to one. Cupid's arrows, and all that. He heard they struck a devilishly hard blow.

"Goodness," said Miss Dempsey. "You all live such interesting lives."

The three girls preened. So, he had to confess, did Turnip. But just a little bit.

"Oh, well," he said modestly. "Can't take credit for one's friends. Smashing good chaps, all of them."

"No," said Sally, and there was a gleam in her bright blue eyes that struck her older brother as decidedly dangerous. "One can't take their credit. But one can seize the chance to act oneself when the opportunity arises."

"Even," chimed in Lizzy Reid, obviously catching his sister's drift and running with it, "when the opportunity arises in so unlikely a vessel as a pudding."

Agnes looked at both of her friends. "Are you thinking what I'm thinking?"

As far as Turnip was concerned, there was far too much thinking going on among the junior set.

Miss Dempsey looked at the three girls with all the trepidation he was feeling. "What *are* you thinking?" she asked quietly.

Sally tossed her head, setting her earbobs bouncing. "It's quite obvious. Someone has to go to Farley Castle. To keep the assignation!"

Chapter 5

"Oh, no," said Mr. Fitzhugh to his sister. "Oh, no, no. Don't even think it."

Folding her arms across her chest, Miss Fitzhugh narrowed her eyes at her older brother. "Someone has to go."

"For the good of the country!" chimed in Agnes, who clearly took her spies very, very seriously.

Neither of the Fitzhughs paid the slightest attention. They were too busy staring each other down.

They really did look remarkably alike, thought Arabella, especially now that they were sporting the same scowl. They were both above the average height, both possessed of the same bright gold hair, the same high cheekbones, the same cleanly cut Roman noses. Mr. Fitzhugh might be frequently likened to a vegetable, but there was no denying that he was an extremely attractive man. One could easily imagine him in a short white robe, about to slay the odd hydra or engage in a short concert on the lyre, while his sister would have made an excellent Athena, beautiful, imperious, and entirely aware of both those features.

"If someone has to go, I'll go," said Mr. Fitzhugh, exhibiting admirable brotherly resolve in the face of a decidedly Medusa-like stare.

"How would you know what you were looking for?" demanded his sister.

"How would you?"

Outmaneuvered, Miss Fitzhugh said grudgingly, "Fair enough. But you *will* report back."

"Yes, and take you for ices, too," said Mr. Fitzhugh, generous in triumph.

The ices carried the day. Miss Fitzhugh dropped her arms to her sides. "All right. But if anything interesting does happen, don't forget that it was my pudding!"

"Was that meant to be a good thing?" muttered Mr. Fitzhugh.

"Right now," Arabella pointed out with amusement, "I doubt it's anyone's pudding. Except maybe the rats'. We left the pudding part lying in the gutter."

Lizzy Reid jumped up from her chair, clearly ready to go haring out into the street. "What if there was more inside it? Secret messages!"

"There was a secret message," said Arabella, neatly intercepting the younger girl before she could bolt for the door. This teaching job was certainly going to be no sinecure. Did they bar the school doors at night? She sincerely hoped so. "On the muslin. Why go to the bother of writing another?"

"Oh." Working out the logic of that, Lizzy subsided. She looked more than a little disappointed, obviously having expected nothing short of codes and treasure maps, all buried within one small mix of fruit and suet. "True."

"Still," said Sally brightly, "it couldn't hurt just to be sure. . . ."

"Yes, it could," said Mr. Fitzhugh, snagging his sister before she could get past him. "There's no need. What nodcock would go about sticking messages inside a pudding? They would get all goopy that way."

"What nodcock would put a message *on* a pudding?" Sally countered. "The French are capable of anything."

"Including, but not limited to, flaky pastries," murmured Arabella. Both Fitzhughs looked at her with identical expressions of confusion.

"What?" said Sally, as her brother chimed in with, "I say, what was that?"

"Nothing," said Arabella hastily. "Never mind." Once they got on to pastries, there would be no going back. The girls would probably dismember every brioche in the place, looking for freakishly small spies.

"I mean it, Sal," said Mr. Fitzhugh, looking severely at his sister, or as severely as his genial features would allow. "No running about sneaking out of the school after puddings. I'll go to Farley Castle for you, but only on condition that you stay here. Inside. Where you're meant to be."

"And I will be here to make sure you abide by that," said Arabella. She had spoken quietly, but they all turned to look at her. Now seemed as good a time as any to tell them. She took a deep breath. "I shall be starting here on Monday as a junior instructress."

"Will you? How splendid!"

"Don't worry. We'll show you exactly how to go about! You won't have to fret about a thing!"

"Are you sure you know what you're getting yourself into?" muttered Mr. Fitzhugh.

"No," admitted Arabella. There was no point in pretending, was there? Funny how easy it could be to talk to a man once he had seen you sprawled on the ground, not once, but twice. "But I am committed now. I told Miss Climpson that I would be ready to begin on Monday."

Mr. Fitzhugh looked at her with undisguised pity in his eyes. "Wouldn't want to be in your shoes. I say. You don't start until Monday?"

"Ye-es." Monday did generally mean Monday. It wasn't exactly Arabella's favorite day of the week, but it was what it was. "Why do you ask?"

"I say," Mr. Fitzhugh said hesitantly. "Would you consider— That is, if one were to— What I mean is, this jaunt to Farley Castle. Might I prevail on you to bear me company? That is, if you fancy the drive."

As a pleasure jaunt, the prospect left something to be desired. It was bitterly cold; it would mean hours in an open carriage and then more hours in an open ruin of a castle. If the weather were well inclined, it might simply be frigid cold. Being England, it would probably rain as well. There was nothing like freezing rain to enhance a long drive in an open conveyance with a man who had been nicknamed for a vegetable.

Jane had said that Aunt Osborne was in Bath, part of a party come up from London for an assembly and a frost fair. It didn't seem likely that there could be more than one of the latter. It wasn't the most popular form of entertainment, for obvious reasons. If there was a frost fair, Aunt Osborne was sure to be in attendance.

Aunt Osborne and Captain Musgrave.

"Are you sure you wouldn't mind having me along?" Arabella heard herself saying. "I wouldn't want to be a bother."

Mr. Fitzhugh shook his head emphatically. "You don't know the first thing about being a bother. Takes years of practice to be a proper bother. Just ask Sal."

"I heard that!" chimed in Sally, and turned back to her friends.

"See what I mean?" said Mr. Fitzhugh darkly.

"I don't . . . ," began Arabella.

Mr. Fitzhugh planted the palms of his hands on his knees and leaned forward beseechingly. "You can bear witness to Sal that I really did go to Farley Castle. It might stop her sneaking out in the middle of the night. I hope. Besides, we might find out who set the pudding thief on you."

"Isn't there one slight problem with that?" said Arabella. She hated to ruin their excitement, but there was one fatal flaw with the plan. "The message never reached its intended recipient. And whoever sent it knows it." She should know. Her posterior still ached from the aftermath.

"Details, details," said Sally airily. "Did you see what that message said? Most urgent. If it really is most urgent, she'll find another way to get the message out. I know *I* would."

Turnip exchanged an alarmed glance with Arabella. "Can't persuade you to come along with me anyway, can I? Fascinating place, Farley Castle. Goes back to the Normans, don'tcha know. It's a pleasant drive, when the weather is nice."

In the space of a few days, Farley Castle would be as distant as the moon as far as she was concerned. These pleasant blue-and-white-walled rooms would comprise the whole of her existence, save for those half days when she would be set free to visit with the Austens four houses away or to make the vast journey across the town to see her own family in Westgate Buildings. There would be none of even the milder forms of entertainments, no supper parties, no concerts, no turns about the Pump Room.

There would certainly be no carriage rides with handsome young men.

It didn't matter that he invited her only because he didn't want to drive alone, or because it had been from her hand that the pudding had been plucked, or because he hoped that her presence as witness would satisfy his volatile little sister. It would be one last adventure before the walls of the schoolroom closed about her.

Arabella looked at Mr. Fitzhugh, who was extolling the pleasures of frost fairs, the mulled wine and crisp air, the refreshments and the entertainments. He was, she thought appraisingly, undeniably a fine figure of a man. He was also, despite his nickname, accounted a great catch on the marriage market. Arabella knew it was silly, but there was something very satisfying about the idea of walking into Farley Castle on Mr. Fitzhugh's arm. She might know that their seeming intimacy was a sham, but other people wouldn't.

What would Captain Musgrave think when she strolled in on the arm of Reginald Fitzhugh?

"All right," said Arabella.

"Never know what we might find there! We might— All right?"

"All right," Arabella repeated, smiling across at him. Something about Mr. Fitzhugh's open enthusiasm was infectious. Even if he was a Turnip.

"Splendid!" exclaimed Mr. Fitzhugh, and he sounded as though he really thought it was. "Should be an amusing excursion, even if it is all a mad duck romp."

"You mean a wild-goose chase?"

"That too," said Mr. Fitzhugh airily. "Can't get away from the fowl, it seems."

Sally twisted in her chair, pearl earbobs swinging. "Do *not* mention the chickens!"

"WHAT HAPPENED?" demanded Jane in an undertone. "Did you get the position?"

It was the first chance they had to speak privately since Arabella had arrived, breathless, only moments ahead of the rest of her family.

After supper, the entire party had adjourned upstairs to the drawing room. In the chairs nearest the fire, Papa and Mr. Austen had their heads together over a knotty piece of Virgil. It saddened Arabella to see how old her father looked, how gray and drawn. He had been Mr. Austen's pupil once, but the poor health that had plagued him since her mother's death made him look more his old tutor's contemporary than his junior. Cassandra had taken on the managing of Margaret for the evening, and was speaking to her determinedly of bonnets and trimmings. Olivia sprawled by the fire at their father's feet, her nose buried in one of Mr. Austen's books, while Mrs. Austen busied herself with the tea tray, handing the cups to Lavinia to hand around, an act of extreme faith, given Lavinia's habit of dropping, knocking over, or bumping into things with limbs recently grown too long to manage properly.

Through the long windows that looked out onto the Sydney Gardens, Arabella could just make out the side of Miss Climpson's seminary. Or she could if she leaned and squinted. Odd to think that it would be her home soon, that she would look out onto these very same gardens.

Although, as junior faculty, it was more likely that she would look out onto the service area, up several steep flights of stairs.

"Well?" Jane demanded. "Are you to keep me in suspense all evening? Will you be shaping the minds of the young for years to come?"

"You needn't sound like you hope the answer will be no!"

Jane shook her needlework out on her lap. "I didn't say that."

"No, but it was heavily implied."

Jane rolled her eyes. "Heaven forfend that I should stand accused of imputation. So you did get it, then?"

"Imputation *and* assumption! But yes. I did."

"Ought I to wish you happy?"

"I'm not marrying the school, only working there. Besides," Arabella added hastily, before Jane could say anything too cutting, "I had the oddest adventure along the way. Do you know Mr. Fitzhugh?"

"The one they call Turnip? Possessed of every worldly endowment except intellect?"

"Ouch," said Arabella. "He's not so bad as all that. He's very sweet, really."

Jane furrowed her brow at her. "You're not . . ."

"No! No. He's not a Mr. Bigg-Wither."

Jane pulled a wry face at the reference to her one-day betrothal. "You mean he doesn't stutter?"

"I mean he hasn't offered for me. His sister is at the school. That's all. Well, not quite all." How did one go about explaining about purloined Christmas puddings? "It's a very long story," she finished lamely.

"Those are generally the best kind," said Jane. "Shall I have it in three volumes with appropriate moral interpolations between the chapters?"

"Three sentences is more like it," sighed Arabella. "And I can't think what the moral might be other than to gather one's rosebuds while one may."

Needle poised above her frame, Jane looked at her speculatively. "Precisely which rosebuds are you planning to gather?"

"Only the very lowest-hanging and most innocent blossoms. Mr. Fitzhugh has offered to take me to the frost fair at Farley Castle tomorrow. Not as a sign of partiality," she added hastily. "His sister asked him to examine something for her and he wanted company on the drive."

"And you said yes?"

"Rosebuds," Arabella reminded her. "My last breath of freedom before taking up my new position."

"And who else might be at this frost fair at Farley Castle?"

Arabella shrugged, avoiding Jane's eyes. "I don't know. People. The usual sort of people."

Jane let it drop. "Mind Mr. Fitzhugh doesn't sweep you off your feet," she cautioned drily.

"He already did! He knocked me over in the foyer of Miss Climpson's seminary!" Arabella's eyes caught Jane's over her embroidery frame, lively with amusement, and the two women dissolved into helpless laughter.

"He picked me up again," Arabella gasped. "So the sweeping was only a temporary condition."

"Who picked you up?" demanded Margaret, whose ears were as sharp as her tongue. "What sweeping?"

Her chair had been edging steadily closer, with a scrape and a bump, until she had finally caught some of the whispered conversation that had excited her curiosity.

Cassandra looked at them with a rueful expression, as though to say, *I tried.* So she had. But Margaret was Margaret, and when she wasn't grating on Arabella's nerves, Arabella felt more than a little bit sorry for her.

Not quite sorry enough, though.

"Mr. Tur—er, Reginald Fitzhugh," Arabella replied, still pink with laughter. "He bumped into me earlier today. In the most literal sense."

"Another of your London admirers, I suppose," said Margaret acidly.

Margaret felt very strongly that she ought to have been the one taken off by Aunt Osborne, showered with expensive dresses and courted by London bucks. It was of no use for Arabella to explain that most of her dresses were her aunt's made-over castoffs, or that the London bucks hadn't paid her the slightest bit of attention. Margaret persisted in thinking herself ill used.

"Hardly an admirer," Arabella demurred.

"No," murmured Jane. "Just a low-hanging blossom. Or ought one to say a low-hanging vegetable?"

Arabella kicked her in the ankle. "But he has asked me if I might accompany him to the frost fair at Farley Castle tomorrow. By way of making amends." She looked to her father. "May I, Papa?"

It felt very odd to be looking to her father for acquiescence, when she had been away from his authority for twelve years. Her aunt Osborne had hardly been a disciplinarian. Arabella found herself regretting that she hadn't taken more advantage of that while she had the opportunity.

Her father, hopeless in the face of anything not comprised between leather bindings or on the apothecary's shelf, looked to Mrs. Austen.

"There cannot be any impropriety in a daytime excursion in an open carriage," said Mrs. Austen soothingly. "It *is* an open carriage?"

"Quite open," said Arabella.

"So you will be cold but respectable," provided Mr. Austen, with a slight smile. "Such are the ways of the world. Better an ague than a lost reputation."

"Mr. Fitzhugh did say there was room for another in his phaeton. He said I might take someone with me."

Margaret sat up straighter in her chair, arranging her face along appropriate lines, carefully nonchalant, even mildly scornful, but willing to be wheedled, cajoled, and otherwise persuaded into honoring them with her company.

Lavinia was too young and Olivia indifferent. As the next oldest, it should be Margaret who came with her. Arabella had meant to ask Margaret. Arabella looked at her second sister and contemplated the prospect of a whole day at Farley Castle with her, a day of Margaret sniffing and sniping and training her eagle eye on all of Arabella's interactions with Mr. Fitzhugh in the hopes of finding something to tattle about.

Arabella hastily turned away, so she wouldn't see Margaret's face as she said, "Would you come with me, Jane?"

"A long jaunt in an open carriage in frigid weather? How could I possibly say no?"

Margaret hastily masked her stricken expression with one of extreme scorn. "Farley Castle," she said dismissively, jabbing her needle into the fabric on her embroidery frame. "It's a poky old place."

"How would you know?" demanded Lavinia tactlessly. "You've never been. Oh, I wish I were old enough to go!"

"I wish I could take you all," said Arabella guiltily. "But there is only room for one more in the phaeton."

"I wouldn't want to go," said Margaret. "It's too cold for an excursion. I can't think what your Mr. Fitzhugh was thinking to suggest such a thing in this weather."

Arabella caught Cassandra and Jane exchanging glances with each other over her head.

"Would anyone like more tea?" asked Cassandra.

Chapter 6

"The heroine of *my* story," said Jane determinedly, "shall confine herself only to indoor events." She rubbed enthusiastically at her nose, which had turned the color of holly berries.

"Preferably in summer," agreed Arabella, tripping over a brick as she tried to maneuver her frozen limbs out of the phaeton. It had originally been a hot brick, but like everything else in the carriage it had cooled down considerably over the course of the ride. Farley Castle was a good deal farther than Mr. Fitzhugh had optimistically prophesied.

"Devilish sorry," said Mr. Fitzhugh humbly, handing her down to the ground with diligent care. "Hoped we'd make better time than that."

"There, there," said Jane, shedding blankets as she wiggled her way off the seat. "You certainly couldn't have anticipated the cows."

Arabella choked on a laugh at the memory. A troupe of the creatures, all in malicious conspiracy, had strayed into the road. Deciding they liked it, they had elected to stay there, despite considerable urging, threats, and cajolery. Mr. Fitzhugh had put Drury Lane to shame in his dramatic attempts to persuade the cows to take their leisure elsewhere. The sight of him trying to reason with a large red-and-brown beast, who responded to all his entreaties with a bored "moo," had been one of the highlights of what had been a surprisingly entertaining trip.

Mr. Fitzhugh had spared no effort or expense for their comfort. There had been hot bricks, warm broth in a flask, blankets edged in fur, pastries that smeared sugar across their gloves, and hot chocolate that had solidified into a solid mass before they had crossed into the countryside. Jane, for all her teasing about low-hanging fruit, had taken to Mr. Fitzhugh immediately.

All in all, the ride had passed in a cheerful aura of cold chocolate, squished pastries, and general mirth. Mr. Fitzhugh had regaled them with tales of his sister, while Jane contributed anecdotes from Steventon. The one topic they hadn't broached was puddings.

Puddings and her aunt's marriage.

With the castle before them, Arabella found herself suddenly possessed of a craven wish that the journey had been longer.

"Bingley," Jane murmured to Arabella, as Mr. Fitzhugh handed the reins to his groom. "Quite definitely a Bingley."

"Shall he have a role in your new story?" Arabella asked.

"That," said Jane, "depends on you."

Arabella gave her a look and crossed over towards Mr. Fitzhugh. "We're here now, all in one piece. That's all that matters."

Mr. Fitzhugh slapped his hands together. "Jolly good. Looks rather pleasant, don't it?"

Arabella wasn't sure "pleasant" was quite the adjective she would have used. Opulent, extravagant, whimsical . . . any of those would do. The picturesque ruins of Farley Castle had been turned into a medieval fantasyland for the jaded men and women of the *ton*. Within the ruined castle walls, coal-burning braziers warmed the air to a temperature endurable for picnicking. Fashionably dressed ladies and gentlemen quaffed steaming beverages from silver cups. Musicians in faux medieval livery had struck up their instruments. A man with a droopy mustache was crooning, *"Helas, madame, celle que j'aime tante,"* while his companions struck poses and the occasional chord on the lute. As they strummed, two footmen staggered past, weighted down by two huge pies.

"Mmm. Pie," said Mr. Fitzhugh, looking longingly after them. "Meat in a pastry shell. One of the greatest inventions known to man."

"I had always thought it was the wheel," said Jane.

Mr. Fitzhugh looked meaningfully at Arabella, raising his eyebrows as far as they would go. "Might be an excellent place to find a spot of pudding."

"We can always look," she said, although she rather doubted they would find anything of the kind.

Mr. Fitzhugh raised his hand in an enthusiastic wave. "Look! There's Vaughn."

The man in question, sleekly dressed in a well-tailored black coat, glanced over at the sound of his name. His eyes narrowed. It might just have been the glare of the sun, but Arabella doubted it.

"He doesn't look pleased to see us," observed Jane in an undertone.

"Lord Vaughn never looks pleased to see anyone," Arabella murmured back.

"That's just his way," said Mr. Fitzhugh cheerfully. "Can't take it too to heart. If I had a penny for every time the chap has greeted me with, 'Oh, it's you again. . . .'"

"Yes?"

Mr. Fitzhugh waved a hand. "I'd have lots of pennies. Jolly useful things, pennies. Vaughn, old bean! Didn't think to see you out here!"

"The feeling is mutual," said Lord Vaughn drily. "This party was by invitation only."

"Got the invitation straight from the horse's mouth," Mr. Fitzhugh protested indignantly. "Henry Innes told me to come. Saw him at Miss Climpson's yesterday, bringing parcels to his cousin."

"How delightful," said Lady Vaughn, in a voice that suggested it was anything but.

Arabella took a step back from the glare of Lady Vaughn's rubies. "We didn't mean to intrude upon your party."

"Such a pity, then, that your intent didn't match your execution," said Lady Vaughn, so smoothly that it took one a moment to notice the stiletto beneath the silk. "Miss . . ."

Arabella knew that the former Miss Alsworthy knew very well who she was. Aunt Osborne and Miss Alsworthy's mother had been cronies of sorts. They went shopping together, spurring each other on to ever more egregious purchases. But now that Miss Alsworthy was Lady Vaughn—and now that it was known that Arabella was no longer likely to be her aunt's heiress—Lady Vaughn couldn't be bothered to recall a mere Miss Dempsey.

"It's Dempsey," Mr. Fitzhugh provided for her, looking sternly at Lady Vaughn. "Miss Dempsey. And her friend Miss Austen."

"Dempsey?" Lord Vaughn eyed her lazily through his quizzing glass. "Not Lady Osborne's ward?"

"Her niece," Arabella corrected. Ward implied a status that Arabella no longer enjoyed.

The sun glinted off the serpent scrolled around Vaughn's quizzing glass. "Ah," said Vaughn. "You must be here to see your aunt. How . . . touching."

So they were here. For all her speculations, she hadn't really expected they would be.

Arabella felt her fingers go hot, then cold.

"Oh, no," said Mr. Fitzhugh blithely, immune to nuance. "We're here to see the ruins."

Lady Vaughn looked innocently up at her husband. "Isn't that what you said, Vaughn?"

Her meaning was impossible to mistake. Arabella squirmed, feeling uncomfortable for her aunt, for Jane, for herself. Aunt Osborne's marriage had made all the papers. The scandal sheets had reveled in the ridiculous spectacle of an aging woman marrying an ambitious young man. Arabella had, for the most part, been left out of it, but there had been one or two mentions made of dashed hopes and disinherited relations.

Just so long as no one ever realized exactly which sorts of hopes had been dashed.

"Farley Castle is accounted very picturesque," Jane was saying, when a woman came hurrying out of the castle gates, nearly bumping into their party.

"I do beg your pardon—," she began.

"I say!" Mr. Fitzhugh's face lit up with recognition. "Don't I know you? Met you at Miss Climpson's yesterday. You're the French mistress."

"Mademoiselle de Fayette," said the lady in a soft voice. "And you are Mr. Fitzhugh."

"Miss Climpson's, did you say?" asked Jane, looking meaningfully at Arabella. The young woman, while prettily and warmly dressed, looked harried, her hair escaping in dark wisps from its pins, her bonnet askew.

"Mr. Fitzhugh's sister is a pupil at Miss Climpson's," said Mlle de Fayette. "A most apt pupil too."

She made one of those quick, shifting movements people make as they prepare to excuse themselves, but she was forestalled by Lady Vaughn.

"A Fitzhugh?" Lady Vaughn's laugh, sickly sweet as syrup and just as devoid of any genuine nourishment, grated on Arabella's nerves. "Apt?"

"I shouldn't be too hasty to condemn the entire garden on the basis of one vegetable, my sweet," returned her husband blandly, as though the vegetable in question weren't standing right there. "One never knows where one might find the odd flower."

Lady Vaughn tossed her glossy head, making the crimson plumes on her hat dance. "Why bother with root vegetables when there are roses to be had?"

Lord Vaughn regarded his wife from beneath half-closed lids. "Too humble for you?"

Lady Vaughn's gaze shifted to Mr. Fitzhugh's dangling watch fobs, all decorated with exaggerated enamel carnations. "Too tasteless."

Arabella remembered the hot bricks and the cold chocolate and the solicitude with which Mr. Fitzhugh had tucked blanket after blanket around them in the carriage. When had Lady Vaughn, for all her vaunted good taste, ever performed a kind deed for anyone? Turnips might be plain, but they were certainly nourishing.

"Even humble fare has its advantages," said Arabella defiantly.

"Yes, thirty thousand of them a year," said Lady Vaughn with a knowing arch of her brows. "And all in gold."

Arabella looked at Lady Vaughn, at her crimson-dyed feathers and watchful eyes. "Not everyone counts a man's worth in coins."

Lord Vaughn lifted his quizzing glass. "Who said anything about a man? I spoke merely of cultivating one's garden."

Arabella could feel Mr. Fitzhugh step closer to her, ranging himself protectively beside her. It was a sweet thought, even if misplaced. Lord Vaughn's weaponry was something other than physical.

The French mistress backed away, eager to be gone. "If you will excuse me . . ."

"Ah, Delphine!" Another man joined them, fashionably dressed, but without the ostentation of Mr. Fitzhugh's costume. His voice had a slight French lilt to it, although less so than Mlle de Fayette, whom he addressed in tones of familial intimacy. "Have you found your lost lamb yet? Sebastian, Lady Vaughn," he added, with a nod to the others.

Mlle de Fayette subsided, with a worried look over her shoulder. "Mr. Fitzhugh, ladies. I do not believe you know my cousin, the Chevalier de la Tour d'Argent."

The chevalier directed his smile at Arabella and Jane. "It is a mouthful, is it not? I am Argent to my friends. Nicolas to my very, very close friends."

"And scamp, scapegrace, and limb of Satan to his relations," said Mlle de Fayette. She did not seem to be entirely joking.

"All terms of endearment," explained the chevalier complacently. "It is simply their way of saying 'I love you.'"

"Why not simply say it, then?" suggested Mr. Fitzhugh, with a tinge of asperity. "They could save a lot of bother that way."

"But they would lose so much face," the chevalier returned. "Ladies don't like to make their affections too generally known. Do they, Miss . . . ?"

"Dempsey," Mr. Fitzhugh provided for her, folding his arms across his chest. "Miss Dempsey. And that is Miss Austen."

Ignoring him, the chevalier continued to direct his smile at Arabella, carrying on as though Turnip had never spoken. "What do you say, Miss Dempsey? Have hearts gone out of fashion as ornaments on one's sleeve?"

Arabella glanced away. "I'm sure I couldn't say."

Through the castle gate, she could see the fashionable set milling about. There was Lord Frederick Staines and Mr. Martin Frobisher, both tricked out in the latest of multi-caped coats; Percy Ponsonby and his sister; Lord Henry Innes, Lieutenant Darius Danforth, and a group of their cronies; others she recognized from her many years on the fringes of London's elite.

A dimple appeared in the chevalier's cheek. "Have you no affections, then, Miss Dempsey? Would you, as your poet says, sooner hear your dog bark at a crow than a man say he loves you?"

"The problem has never arisen." The crowd shifted, blocking her view. "I have no dog."

There was a moment of silence and then the chevalier laughed, a genuine, rolling laugh of the sort that made others want to laugh too. "But many admirers, I imagine."

"The chevalier has quite the imagination," Lady Vaughn murmured to her husband.

"Dozens of admirers," Mr. Fitzhugh said stoutly. "Have to beat 'em off with a stick."

"Ah," said the chevalier with amusement. "Due to the lack of a dog. You might want to invest in one. It would save the wear and tear on the trees."

"I thank you for your advice, Monsieur de la Tour d'Argent."

There he was, Captain Musgrave, standing near the refreshment table, a silver cup in one hand. Arabella could see the steam rising off it in long curls, framing his face like a picture carried in a locket.

The chevalier grinned at Arabella. "Why not just call me 'limb of Satan' and have done with it?"

"Because some people, Nicolas, have manners," said the chevalier's cousin.

There were clusters of people on either side of Captain Musgrave, but not with him. He stood alone between the chattering groups while Arabella's aunt gossiped with a nearby matron. As Arabella watched, he looked up, his eyes meeting hers across the clearing, across a divide of two months and one ring.

"Is that what you teach?" Arabella heard Jane ask Mlle de Fayette, dutifully making conversation. "Deportment?"

"Teach?" repeated Lady Vaughn, as though the word were unfamiliar to her.

The crowd moved again and he was gone, blocked out. Arabella looked abruptly away, forcing herself to focus on her companions. Act naturally, she admonished herself. The point was to look as though she were enjoying herself.

"I teach French," said Mlle de Fayette. "It is a logical subject for me, no?"

"Oh, yes!" agreed Arabella enthusiastically. Too enthusiastically. Jane gave her a strange look.

"Do you like it?" asked Jane. "Teaching?"

Mlle de Fayette exchanged a wry look with her cousin. "It was not entirely a matter of choice, but it has its compensations. Today, however . . ." Leaning forward confidentially, she said, "There is a situation of the most awkward. A student of the school is here today, against all prohibitions."

"A former student of the school. Asked to leave for conduct unbecoming young ladies," chimed in the chevalier, in his nearly accentless English. "Who knew that an all-girls' academy could be such a very interesting place?"

"It is not supposed to be," said his cousin severely. "That is the point. It was very sad for Miss Carruthers and her family. Miss Climpson has allowed her to stay until the end of term, but after that . . ."

"Carruthers? Not Catherine Carruthers?" inquired Mr. Fitzhugh.

"I take it you know her, Fitzhugh?" said Vaughn.

"Not like that!" Mr. Fitzhugh's ears went red. "Used to be friends with m'sister. Sally."

"Ah," said Mlle de Fayette, placing a hand confidingly on his arm. "Then you know the story. If you will excuse me. I must ask Signor Marconi if he has seen her. I must get her back to the school before her parents or others find out."

"How did she get out here?" asked Mr. Fitzhugh. "Girls don't make a usual practice of these jaunts, do they?"

"It is of the doing of the cousin, Lord 'Enry Innes. He says he did not know she was meant to be confined to the school." Mlle de Fayette gave a brisk shake of her head. "It is of the most uncomfortable. One does not like to offend Lord Henry, but the parents of Catherine were most particular in their instructions. So I must find her and take her back. If you will pardon me?"

This time, no one stopped her. With a curtsy to the group at large, she hurried away, toward the man with the droopy mustaches, who had just moved on from "Helas" to "Flora Gave Us Fairest Flowers."

"Signor Marconi is the music master at Miss Climpson's," explained the chevalier. "Although he also provides entertainment for private parties. He came very highly recommended."

If he sounded slightly dubious, Arabella could understand why. Even to her untrained ear, Flora's flowers were flat.

The chevalier shrugged. "To teach and to practice are two very different things. One may discuss what one might never do." His gaze made a slow circuit of the assembled company. "Just as one might do things one might never discuss."

A kiss, for example, stolen between a dining room and a drawing room, two long months ago.

Captain Musgrave still stood by the refreshment table, his hair sticking out at odd angles under his hat. He had been joined by her aunt, a head shorter, her hand resting familiarly on Musgrave's arm. She wore a coronet of egret feathers, spangled with some shiny substance that glittered in the winter sunlight.

Aunt Osborne started to turn, and Arabella braced herself for the greeting to come, the exclamations, the embraces, the explanations.

But before Aunt Osborne could spot Arabella, Captain Musgrave turned his wife away with a laugh and a light touch on her arm, directing her attention to the refreshment table. As Aunt Osborne exclaimed over the syllabub, Arabella fell back, the fixed smile frozen on her face.

Her aunt hadn't seen her—that, she was sure of—but Musgrave had.

"Well, jolly good meeting you," said Mr. Fitzhugh jovially to the chevalier, and tugged at Arabella's arm. "Shouldn't like to keep the ladies from the ruins. Early dark in winter and all that, you know."

Entirely unperturbed, the chevalier smiled at Jane. "If ruins you came for, then the ruins you must see. Might I commandeer the humble task of serving as your escort? Ladies? And Mr. Fitzhugh, of course."

Arabella looked away from Musgrave and her aunt.

She put her hand on Mr. Fitzhugh's arm and smiled prettily up at him. She made sure not to catch Jane's eye. Jane saw far too much. As the chevalier had said, there were some things one didn't discuss.

"Yes," she said. "Yes. Let's go see the ruins."

Chapter 7

Turnip tucked Miss Dempsey's arm through his as they strolled through the jagged walls where the Great Hall must once have been, following Miss Austen and the Cheval-whatever-his-name-was.

Deuced silly name, that. Foreigners. Couldn't do anything properly.

"Not that a chap doesn't generally like to give the chaps the benefit of the doubt, but there's something rum about that Cheval-whatever-you-call-it," muttered Turnip.

Not good rum, either. The sort of rum that tasted good in punch but gave a chap a headache the morning after.

"Pardon?" said Miss Dempsey. Visibly collecting herself, she turned her attention to Turnip. "What did you say?"

"Oh, nothing. Just not all that keen on the French chappy. Something deuced dodgy about him."

Being no slouch, Miss Dempsey picked up on his meaning without his having to say anything more. "You don't think the chevalier had something to do with the pudding, do you?"

"He is French," said Turnip. "And his cousin works at the school. Might have been visiting her yesterday, for all we know. Skulking around out back."

"He doesn't seem the skulking sort," said Miss Dempsey, regarding the chevalier with interest. Too much interest.

"You can never tell what a chap might get up to in his spare time. Just because a man doesn't have leaves on his knees doesn't mean he ain't a villain."

"Or a spy?" Miss Dempsey smiled at him. The tip of her nose was pink and her lips were slightly chapped from the wind. "If I were the French secret service, I would try to employ someone a little less obviously French. Even without the accent, his name is a dead giveaway."

"What would you call him, then?" asked Turnip.

Miss Dempsey considered, turning her face up to the sun where it gilded the old gray battlements. The tips of her lashes glittered gold in the sunlight. "Smith," she said. "Or Jones. Something plain and nondescript. Something English."

Sensible, but it lacked a certain panache. Who had ever heard of a hero named Smith? The man would be laughed right out of the Black Mask Club.

"I prefer Fotheringay-Bumblethorpe, myself," said Turnip. "Has a nice ring to it. Rolls pleasantly off the tongue."

"Yes, but can you imagine putting that into code? It would take all day."

"Rather like the Chevalier of Whatever Whatever," conceded Turnip.

"'The Knight of the Silver Tower,'" translated Miss Dempsey. "It is a bit much in English, isn't it? A little too . . ."

"Showy," supplied Turnip.

"I was going to say theatrical. Either way, not necessarily a good moniker for someone bent on illicit activities. It's too unusual. Too memorable."

Hmm. This had all been going well up until that "too memorable" bit. Turnip, for one, found the chevalier eminently forgettable.

The party in front of them turned around a corner, momentarily obscured from view. Lowering his voice, Turnip said, "No matter what Sally and her peculiar friends said, I would lay money that that pudding was someone's private affair. Shouldn't wonder if one of the girls from the school was trying to sneak out to meet someone she shouldn't."

"Like Catherine Carruthers?" said Miss Dempsey.

"Exactly like Catherine Carruthers," agreed Turnip. Over by the musicians, Mlle de Fayette was engaged in earnest conversation with Signor Marconi, who seemed to be disclaiming any knowledge of the errant schoolgirl. "Might even be Catherine Carruthers. Can't imagine a grown man writing a message on pudding, but it's just the hare-brained sort of thing one of Sally's friends would do. According to Sal, that sort of thing goes on rather a lot."

"I agree with you in theory," said Miss Dempsey, "but doesn't Farley Castle strike you as rather a long way to go for . . . um . . ."

"A spot of dalliance?" Turnip provided helpfully.

"Yes. That." Miss Dempsey's cheeks went pink. "The Sydney Gardens are right across the way from the school. Wouldn't that be a more logical place for young lovers to meet?"

"They're not the most logical of breeds, young lovers." He might not be much for book learning, but young love was something on which Turnip could expatiate with absolute authority. There had been that milkmaid the summer he was thirteen. . . . The scent of straw and fresh milk still made him vaguely nostalgic. "Swept away by passion and all that, you know."

"No, I don't know." The words came out like gunshots, cracking in the cold winter air. Flushing, she added, in more normal tones, "But I have read about such things. They generally seem to end badly."

"Only some of them. There are happy endings too."

"But how do you know which it's going to be? How do you know when to sweep and when not to sweep? Or be swept, I suppose."

Turnip grinned. "Always preferred the sweeping myself." She still seemed to be waiting for an answer, so he said, "Never thought about it that much. Happy endings, I mean. A chap's bound to have one eventually. Hunker down on the old family estate, beget some children, scoff down toast and marmalade at the breakfast table, all that sort of thing."

Miss Dempsey looked up at him curiously. "Is that your happy ending? Toast and marmalade?"

"With the odd bit of raspberry jam. What about you, Miss Dempsey? If you could have a happy ending, what would it be?"

"Me?"

"You're the only you I see. Would you choose princes in Spain and jeweled castles? Or was it castles in Spain and jeweled princes?" Turnip couldn't remember.

Miss Dempsey scuffed the toe of her boot against the frost-blasted grass. "I should think jeweled castles would be drafty. And I don't speak any Spanish."

"Then what would you like?" Turnip asked curiously.

She looked away, her bonnet brim hiding her face from view. Deuced annoying contraptions, bonnets.

"To see the ruins," she said lightly. "I've heard the chapel is very fine. I imagine Jane and the chevalier must be there already. We've dawdled."

Had they? It hadn't felt like it. "I rather enjoyed the dawdling," Turnip said honestly.

She was a good chap, Miss Dempsey. Easy on the eyes and the ears. She didn't simper or giggle or slap his arm or say, "Oh, Reggie!" or "Oh, Turnip!" or his least favorite, "Oh, Mr. *Fitzhugh*!" It made a nice change, talking with someone who actually, well, talked to him. No head-shaking, no eye-rolling, no fluttering her lashes and asking coyly after his bank balance.

And he hadn't forgotten the way she had defended him to Lady Vaughn. Not one bit.

"I'm deuced glad I knocked into you yesterday," he blurted out. "I mean, not that I knocked you over—shouldn't be glad of that—but that we bumped into one another."

Miss Dempsey looked at him in surprise.

"Thank you. That's very kind of you." The corners of her lips twitched. "I'm very glad you bumped into me too. Although I must admit I wasn't quite so enthusiastic about it at the time."

"A simple hello would have sufficed, eh?" Turnip grinned back at her, swept up on a wave of good fellowship. "I'll remember that for next time. And I am sorry I forgot your name. Deuced sorry."

There it was again, that downward tilt of the bonnet, as though she were trying to erase her own presence. Turnip was tempted to take the edge of the brim and peel it back.

"It was more than understandable. We occupied different parts of the ballroom."

"Not anymore," said Turnip with feeling. "Next time we see a ball-room, we'll be on the same side of it. Or maybe the middle. The best place for dancing, the middle of the room. Shouldn't like to stand up on the sides. People give one odd looks. So we'd best stand up in the middle. Safest that way."

Miss Dempsey blinked up at him. "Are you asking me to dance?"

"Why, yes. I suppose I am. Not at the moment, of course. But I shall hold you to it the next time we encounter a ballroom. And a band. Bally hard to dance without music, although I suppose one could hum if one had to."

"Or beat time with a stick?" suggested Miss Dempsey.

Turnip liked the way she thought. "Might be a bit dangerous, that, especially in a close-packed ballroom. Wouldn't want one of the dowagers to think you were challenging her to a duel. That Dowager Duchess of Dovedale has a nasty way with a cane. You'd be doing me a favor if you stood up with me. Shielding me from the cranky old dowagers and whatnot."

"Oh, so I'd be the one hit in the ankles, not you?" Miss Dempsey said, smiling. He liked to see her smile.

Through the open windows, they could hear the crunch of dry grass as the others prowled around outside, exploring the remains of the old chapel garden. Inside, the chapel was dark and cool, with bits of old armor hanging from the walls.

"You can fight the dowager off with those," said Turnip, nodding at an old broadsword hanging from the wall.

"Mmm," said Miss Dempsey, craning her neck to stare at the remnants of a painting that had once adorned the chantry ceiling. She pointed up at the shadowy outlines. "Who do you think those are? They must be saints of some sort. The Apostles, maybe?"

They just looked like blobs to Turnip, but then, he had never been much of one for art.

"Most likely," he said amiably, and took her elbow to keep her from tripping over an old slab marking the top of a tomb as they ambled together into the chantry that abutted the chapel.

A large white marble tomb lay in the middle, looking, Turnip thought, incongruously like a bed. Sprawled across it were the effigies of a gentleman in full armor and a lady in a flowing robe, her feet incongruously propped on a small lion.

"Shouldn't like to wake them," he said, nodding at the effigies. At least, that was what he meant to say. The last word came out as a sort of strangled noise.

"Pardon?" Miss Dempsey looked down from the ceiling, blinking.

Turnip jabbed a finger in the direction of the raised tomb. "Look," he said. "Look."

An incongruous splotch of color showed against the white stone. In the marble hands of the effigy lay a Christmas pudding tied with bright crimson ribbons.

Chapter 8

"Good heavens," said Arabella. "What is it doing here? Who on earth is going about dropping puddings all over the place?"

There was something a little macabre about it, the gaily wrapped Christmas pudding so purposefully perched in the cold, marble hands of the effigy. Cold marble hands, cold marble lips, and beneath it all, the bones of the woman who had been, eaten bare by worms and slow time.

It might be decorative, but it was still a grave.

Arabella shivered, and not from the cold. "Is it just me, or do you find this a little . . . incongruous?"

Mr. Fitzhugh tilted his head, taking in the scene from another angle. "Not so odd as all that, when you think of it. We leave flowers on graves, so why not a pudding?"

"I doubt this one was intended for . . . well, whatever her name is."

"Lady Margaret Hungerford," Mr. Fitzhugh provided promptly.

Arabella looked at the tomb and then back at Mr. Fitzhugh. There was no inscription, at least none readily apparent from where they were standing.

Mr. Fitzhugh developed a deep interest in the folds of his cravat. "I read up a bit before we came," he mumbled. "Thought you and Miss Austen might want to know. Let's take a look at the pudding, shall we?"

"Someone has very odd ideas about *billets-doux*," she managed to say, with a suitable approximation of sangfroid, as Mr. Fitzhugh leaned over the pudding.

Mr. Fitzhugh grinned up at her. "If you're going to have sweet letters, why not put them in a sweetmeat?"

"Because it's rather sticky?" ventured Arabella. She looked over her shoulder, very much hoping that no one else would take it upon themselves to visit the chapel just now. She could just picture the expression on Jane's face when she entered to find the two of them avidly dissecting a Christmas pudding in search of secret messages.

Arabella grimaced at herself. If there was anything worse than being caught in an assignation, it was being caught in one that wasn't about assignating.

"The ribbons are the same shade as the last one," Mr. Fitzhugh was saying, leaning in for a better look. "And there's definitely writing on it—whoever it was wrote on the ribbons this time. Guess she didn't like the pudding goo mucking up her message."

"So we assume it is a she?"

Going back to his examination of the pudding, Mr. Fitzhugh said, with great authority, "Looks like a woman's handwriting to me."

Did he see a wide range of women's handwriting?

Arabella strained to see over his shoulder. "What does it say?"

Her shoulder bumped against his. There was no padding there. She could feel the muscles flex beneath his tightly fitted coat as he leaned forward to flip over a ribbon. Arabella edged a little closer. He was so nicely warm, and she was cold even in her long pelisse.

Mr. Fitzhugh squinted at the minuscule writing that nearly blended with the fabric. "Whoever it was wrote in French again. *Il faut que . . .*"

It is necessary that . . . Arabella tentatively tapped him on the arm. "*Il faut que* what?"

His breath steamed in the air as he peered at the ribbon. "Something about a deal. 'It is necessary that the deal be struck at once. The authorities . . .'"

Arabella leaned over his shoulder, intrigued despite herself. "Which authorities?"

Mr. Fitzhugh shook his head in frustration. "The writing's gone blurry. Something *suspicieux.*" He scrolled along the slippery length of the ribbon. "The authorities are suspicious—"

"And this," announced a faintly foreign voice, "is Saint Anne's Chantry."

Arabella's head jerked up like a puppet on a string. Her eyes met Mr. Fitzhugh's. In unspoken accord, they spun around, blocking the pudding with their backs.

Arabella banged into Mr. Fitzhugh's side. Her elbow connected with a rib.

Mr. Fitzhugh smiled manfully and gasped out, "Cheval—um-er! Enjoying the ruins, eh, what?"

"Not nearly so much as you," commented the chevalier blandly, amusement dancing in his hazel eyes. "You seem to have got ahead of me, Fitzhugh."

Arabella hastily righted her bonnet. "Fascinating chapel, isn't it?" she said brightly, her voice a full octave above its normal range. "So many funeral monuments!"

"Yes, indeed," said Jane, wrinkling her brows at her. "One does enjoy a good funeral monument. Always amusing to be reminded of one's own mortality."

"Memento mori and all that!" contributed Mr. Fitzhugh, resting his elbows on Sir Edward Hungerford's marble arm in an attempt to block any view of the pudding.

"Are these all funeral monuments?" Jane asked, looking around curiously.

"Yes, indeed." The chevalier must have been the sort of boy who put frogs in people's beds. His eyes were bright with mischief. "Each one a marker of the mortal remains of your not-so-distant ancestors."

"Well, then," said Mr. Fitzhugh heartily, leaning so far back that he was practically lying across Sir Edward Hungerford's lap. "No point in dwelling here among the dead. Shall we go back to the picnic?"

The chevalier showed no sign of moving. "Have you no interest in the fate of your ancestors, Mr. Fitzhugh? Look at this plaque. It dates to sixteen forty-eight. That was during your civil war, was it not?"

"Don't know about you," said Mr. Fitzhugh loudly, "but there's a pie with my name on it out there."

"It was not a good era for heads, your civil war," said the chevalier.

"Civil wars seldom are," agreed Jane.

"All these chaps seem to have their heads on straight. At least the ones on the walls," said Mr. Fitzhugh in an attempt to redirect the attention of the chevalier. Arabella could feel him shift on his feet as he surreptitiously stretched out his arm, groping for the pudding.

"Well, they would, wouldn't they?" said the chevalier, raising an eyebrow at Mr. Fitzhugh. Mr. Fitzhugh froze. Arabella was reminded of a children's game, one called statues, where the players could move only when the primary actor's back was turned. "One wouldn't want to be preserved for posterity without one's most identifiable feature. Like the Duke of Monmouth."

"The duke of who?" asked Jane innocently.

Arabella gave her a hard look. Jane had written her own, rather mocking, history of Britain. She knew very well who the Duke of Monmouth was. But she would have her fun.

To Arabella's surprise, it was Mr. Fitzhugh who answered. "Duke of Monmouth. He was a, um, er, *child* of Charles II." He tactfully omitted the word "bastard." "Got his head lopped off for treason."

"But they didn't do it right," contributed the chevalier, in thrilling tones. "It took five blows of the ax to sever Monmouth's head. And *that—*"

Mr. Fitzhugh looked anxiously at the ladies. "Don't know if—," he began.

"Is when they remembered that they had forgotten to paint his portrait," the chevalier finished innocently.

"Oh," said Mr. Fitzhugh. "Right."

"You can see how that would be a problem," said the chevalier.

"History, real, solemn history, I cannot be interested in," pronounced Jane. "I read it a little as a duty, but it tells me nothing that does not either vex or weary me."

"How so?" asked the chevalier. Arabella wondered if he suspected that Jane was bamming him.

Jane waved a hand. "The quarrels of popes and kings, with wars and pestilences in every page; the men all so good for nothing, and hardly any women at all. It is very tiresome."

"That sounds like something out of a book," said the chevalier. "Not Dr. Johnson, surely?"

Jane was at her most demure. "No, although no doubt someday someone will lay claim to it on his behalf. I have recently been informed with great authority that Dr. Johnson was the author of *Camilla*."

"Nonsense," said the chevalier blandly. "I have it on even better authority that both *Camilla* and *Evelina* were the works of Voltaire. Operating under a pseudonym, of course."

"Of course," agreed Jane. "And I'm quite sure that the collected works of Mrs. Radcliffe were all written by Monsieur Rousseau. In his spare time. I think I should like some of that pie you mentioned, Mr. Fitzhugh. If you would escort me?"

"I should like nothing better," Mr. Fitzhugh said gallantly, casting Arabella an anguished glance.

It didn't take terribly much intuition to interpret. The moment he moved, the pudding would be exposed to view.

Mr. Fitzhugh babbled on, playing for time. "Hope it's a good kind of pie. Not that there are bad kinds of pie. Amazing thing, the pie! Sheer genius, in pastry form. You can take any type of food and wrap it in dough. Happy consumption and easy transportation, all in one. Doesn't get much better than that."

His fingers glanced off the side of the pudding, sending it rocking on its precarious marble perch. Gathering speed as it went, the pudding went rolling slowly backwards over the side of the monument to fall with a splat on the other side.

"What was that?"

"My reticule. I dropped my reticule," said Arabella, diving towards the ground before they could see that her reticule was still dangling from her wrist.

From this vantage point, Mr. Fitzhugh's boots were very shiny. She could see her own reflection in them.

"You all right down there?" asked Mr. Fitzhugh.

"Yes! Fine! Perfectly all right!"

Arabella made a show of groping around on the floor, scrabbling at the ground with her hands, before popping back up with her reticule in hand. She waved it around a few times so everyone could see that it was, indeed, a reticule.

"These strings are such a bother. I've nearly lost it at least three times today. Shall we? Chevalier?"

She swept forward, bearing the Frenchman along with her. Glancing over her shoulder, she could see Mr. Fitzhugh mime his approval with a little happy dance, which he brought to an abrupt halt as Jane turned to him.

"Are you joining us, Mr. Fitzhugh?"

"I say!" Mr. Fitzhugh made a show of clapping his hand to his head. "Can't think how I came to be so clumsy. Dropped a watch fob, don't you know. Do go on without me. Shan't be a moment."

"Such a rash of falling objects," commented the chevalier.

He led Arabella out into the sunlight, directing her unerringly towards the smell of food and the sound of lute strings being tortured.

"Did you know," said the chevalier conversationally, "that for a time it was rumored that Mr. Fitzhugh was the spy known as the Pink Carnation?"

"That's the silliest thing I've ever heard," said Arabella.

On the other hand, it might take a very clever man to play that much of a fool. But could anyone sustain that kind of act for that long?

"Just because Mr. Fitzhugh wears carnations embroidered on his waistcoat hardly means that he— Oh, I don't know."

"Flies in the face of danger? Sneers at the name of risk?"

"Something like that. I should think that having carnations embroidered on one's stockings would be tantamount to taking out an advertisement that one wasn't the Pink Carnation."

"You question the wisdom of Bonaparte's secret police?" The chevalier's lightly mocking tone invited her to join in the joke at the expense of the French regime.

"If that is the extent of their intelligence, then it's a wonder that Bonaparte wasn't unseated ages ago!" Flushing at her own presumption, Arabella modulated her tone. "What I mean is that Mr. Fitzhugh is a highly unlikely conspirator."

"So was Sir Percy Blakeney in his day," replied the chevalier. "He played the buffoon so well that his own wife did not guess it."

"I hardly know Mr. Fitzhugh so well as that."

"No?" said the chevalier gently, steering her towards a refreshment table, where steaming silver cups of punch had been set out on an equally silver tray.

"No," repeated Arabella firmly. "But I would be willing to wager that he is exactly what he seems."

"A dangerous wager, Miss Dempsey. People are seldom what they seem."

Arabella didn't appreciate being condescended to. She frowned at the chevalier. "Including you?"

Stopping beside the refreshment table, the chevalier abstracted a silver mug from among its fellows, lifting it to his nose to breathe in the hot, scented fragrance of it before passing it over to Arabella. "That, my dear Miss Dempsey, would be telling."

"Telling what?" asked Lord Vaughn, coming up behind them.

"Terrible tales of scandal," said the chevalier, reaching for a second glass and handing it to Vaughn.

Vaughn raised his brows. "Like an old lady by her hearth, enjoying a spot of gossip with her tea."

"I've never known you to balk at scandal, Sebastian," returned the chevalier, unperturbed.

Lord Vaughn looked at him with all the arrogance of two hundred years of semisupreme rule. "I prefer to cause it, rather than discuss it. Other people's scandals are tedious."

"Speaking of which," said Lady Vaughn, "you've just missed your aunt. She left only a few minutes ago."

"She did?" What with one thing and another, with puddings and Pink Carnations, Arabella had almost forgotten about them. "My aunt and my uncle?" She was proud that her voice didn't falter on the last word.

Lady Vaughn shrugged. "At that age, one wants an early night."

Arabella pulled herself together. What had she really expected? That her aunt would fall on her bosom and tell her how much she missed her? That Musgrave would weep tears of remorse?

Fool, she told herself. Three times a fool. She knew Captain Musgrave was false and a cad, so why did she still care what he thought of her, or want so desperately to get his attention?

Habit, she told herself. Habit and wounded pride. He had courted her so assiduously for a time, discovering her interests, praising her prose, pressing her hand just a little too long in greeting. She had wanted—oh, something. Some sort of reparation or revenge. Some sort of acknowledgment.

"It's no matter," she said, with a nonchalance she didn't feel. "I'll be with my aunt at Girdings for Christmas."

Arabella's domestic plans didn't interest the Vaughns. Lifting his quizzing glass, Vaughn let it trail across the shifting groups of people.

"Here comes our favorite vegetable," Vaughn commented languidly. "Looking rather pleased with himself. He must have outwitted a rutabaga."

Looking around, Arabella saw Mr. Fitzhugh striding towards them across the winter-wilted grass, his puce coat a splash of color against the time-weathered walls of the old castle. He had removed his high-crowned hat, leaving it to swing from one hand.

"Is he still dangling after the Deveraux girl?" Lady Vaughn asked her husband in an intimate tone that pointedly cut the others out of the conversation.

Arabella knew Penelope Deveraux. More accurately, she knew of her. It was hard not to know about Penelope Deveraux: She created an eddy of excitement around her wherever she went, a *hiss hiss hiss* of whisper and gossip and speculation that preceded her like the rumble of thunder before lightning.

Like Arabella, Miss Deveraux was tall, but there any resemblance ended. Rather than a dusty blond, Miss Deveraux's hair was a flaming red—true red, no nonsense about red-blond or auburn. Her dresses skirted the edge of impropriety, cut low enough to make a matron blanch, transparent enough to set men hoping and gossips whispering.

In short, she was everything Arabella wasn't. Daring. Bold. Memorable.

Mr. Fitzhugh might have escorted Arabella to the frost fair, but no one would ever believe he had designs on her. Not when there were women like Penelope Deveraux to be had.

He was smiling as he made his way towards them, a smile that lit his face with its own inner radiance. He was, thought Arabella, one of nature's golden children, all light and no dark, happy just to be happy.

He and Miss Deveraux would make an exceptionally striking couple.

Lord Vaughn shrugged. "I make it a point never to interest myself in nursery brangles. Ah, Fitzhugh! We were just talking about you."

"Did you save some pie for me?" Mr. Fitzhugh inquired genially, with a grin at Arabella that made her want to hit him, without quite knowing why.

"We haven't explored the pie yet," said Arabella repressively. "I believe it's on the other side of the keep."

Undaunted, Mr. Fitzhugh held out a hand. "Care to join me for the quest, Miss Dempsey? Shouldn't like to tackle that pie alone."

Arabella set her silver mug down on the silver tray, where it made a distinctly unmusical clanking sound. Discordant. She was discordant, the odd note out in an otherwise coherent symphony.

"Why not," she said. Best to get it over with.

"Splendid," exclaimed Mr. Fitzhugh, and all but dragged her across the clearing, bursting to share his news.

"That was well played in there," he said under his breath. "Deuced cleverly done, getting the chevalier out. *What kind of pie do you think this is?*" he bellowed suddenly.

Arabella rubbed her ears. That had been rather loud.

"*Squab, I think,*" she bellowed back. When in Rome. She lowered her voice, "Did you find the pudding?"

Mr. Fitzhugh tipped his hat to reveal a fleeting glimpse of white muslin and red ribbons. "All right and tight and accounted for. Took another look at those ribbons. That's what took me so long."

He sawed energetically at a venison pie with a silver serving knife. Arabella couldn't remember the last time she had seen so much silver in one place. Silver, like the Chevalier de la Tour d'Argent. Arabella looked at Turnip.

"Did you know that the French secret police think that you're the Pink Carnation?"

An expression of intense irritation passed across Mr. Fitzhugh's amiable face. "Not *that* again. Deuced inconvenient. Not that I don't consider it a compliment, but it's bally irritating, constantly being dogged by murderous operatives all looking to stick a carnation in their caps."

"Has this happened to you frequently?" asked Arabella.

"Oh, once or twice." Mr. Fitzhugh gestured airily with the salver. "Shouldn't think it has anything to do with our pud—oh."

Mr. Fitzhugh looked blankly down at the remains of his pie, which had slid with a splat onto the red damask cloth covering the table.

No. Impossible. No one's acting skills were that good.

"Let me," said Arabella, and took the salver from him.

"Deuced alarming, this pudding," said Mr. Fitzhugh, leaning over her shoulder as she deftly transferred a slice of pie onto a plate. "That bit about a deal. Don't like the look of it at'all. Couldn't make out much more, but one word looked like *guerre*. You know what that signifies."

"Love is war?" suggested Arabella. The pudding was beginning to give her a headache.

Like the rest of the frost fair, the messages in the pudding were nothing more than a game, a diversion for bored aristocrats. The authorities were probably nothing more than the headmistress, the deal nothing more sinister than an exchange of schoolgirl gifts or lovers' tokens. The illusion of intrigue was all make-believe, like the faux medieval livery on the servants, the deliberately aged lute in the hands of the musicians, the bright pennants hanging from the crumbling walls. In a few hours, the coals would be stanched, the silver cutlery would be carted away, the gaily dressed guests would drive home, and the castle would be left as it was, empty, a ruin, all the enchantment gone.

And for that, she had traipsed across half of Sussex on the coldest day of the year.

Not that there hadn't been consolations. She had enjoyed being Mr. Fitzhugh's conspirator—a little too much, perhaps.

"Er, was thinking more of the War Office, myself," said Mr. Fitzhugh gamely. "I had some ideas. Some ideas for our investigation." Mr. Fitzhugh's blue eyes were bright with excitement.

Thrusting the plate at him, Arabella broke in before he could go further. "Mr. Fitzhugh, this has been very amusing, but—"

"You're right." Mr. Fitzhugh nodded emphatically. "This isn't the place for it. Ears everywhere. I'll call on you tomorrow. Safer that way."

For whom?

Margaret would hover, casting suspicious glances from behind her embroidery. Her father would remain firmly planted at his desk, surfacing from time to time to quote obscure Latin lines to no one in particular. And Lavinia would probably drop the tea tray on him.

Knowing Mr. Fitzhugh, he probably wouldn't mind.

But that wasn't the point. The point was that this had been—a lark. A stolen moment in time. Mr. Fitzhugh could afford to go about chasing down puddings for the sheer sport of it, but she had a living to get and a family to care for. She was for teaching.

And he was for Miss Deveraux.

"There's no need for you to call," said Arabella quietly. "I'm sure you were right before. This is just a schoolgirl prank. Nothing more."

Chapter 9

he Middle Ages were called the Dark Ages because they had no windows. In the Renaissance, they discovered glass and everything became light."

Arabella stifled a yawn with the back of her hand. Half past ten, five papers still left to mark, and her mind was already beginning to wander. Arabella squinted at the dense curlicues and ink blots of Clarissa Hardcastle's history composition.

The Middle Ages were called the Dark Ages because they had no windows.

Arabella cocked her pen, trying to think of some tactful way to tackle Clarissa's first sentence. Scratch, scratch, scratch went the nib against the page. *Windows were, in fact, invented as early as . . .*

When were windows invented? A fine instructress she was, Arabella thought, vigorously scratching out the half-written line. Did the Romans have windows? The Greeks? All she knew was that the apertures in Farley Castle had seemed quite sufficiently windowlike to her, thank you very much.

Sitting in the close confines of a small room on the fourth floor of

Miss Climpson's Select Seminary for Young Ladies, she thought Farley Castle seemed farther away than its actual geographic distance. The last few days had passed in a blur of activity, as Arabella struggled to remember names and schedules. Some of the girls had already left for the holidays, but the rest of the school was in a ferment over the annual recital put on by the girls for their friends and family. In addition to her classes, Arabella had coached girls through their lines, soothed hurt feelings, and adjusted hems. Jane had been right about one thing, at least; she hadn't seen the outside of the building since she had entered it.

Even if she hadn't squashed Mr. Fitzhugh's plans, there would have been no way for her to leave the school to take part in them.

Arabella frowned at the shadowy reflection of her own face in the window. Mr. Fitzhugh had looked so confused when she had told him not to call, confused and then hurt, like a puppy being abandoned by the side of the road. He had followed along after her back to the Vaughns, casting her troubled looks from under the brim of the hat he had stuck back on the top of his head.

Well, whatever his hurt feelings at the time, he had obviously gotten over them.

Like the pudding, she had been a two-day diversion, to be forgotten the moment the next, more interesting toy came along. There was nothing malicious about it; it was just the way of the world. Or, rather, the way of the *ton,* England's perpetually bored aristocracy. Arabella had seen it before, the restless shift from diversion to diversion. They wagered on absurdities. They drove their horses too fast. They drank their way into oblivion or gorged their way into ever more ambitious exercises in corsetry.

By now, Turnip Fitzhugh had probably forgotten about both her and puddings and was currently engaged in hopping three times around Bath Cathedral on one foot or trying to balance a rhubarb on his nose.

Reaching for the pile of marked papers, Arabella gave them a brisk shake, making sure all the corners were neatly aligned, all the edges in place. It was for the best—really it was. The casual intimacy of the pudding hunt had been nothing more than the product of the moment, a strange little moment, and very much momentary.

A gentle tap-tap-tapping on the door interrupted her thoughts.

Arabella swiveled in her chair. "Come in!"

Drat. Where had her shoes gotten to? Arabella scrounged desperately for her slippers with a stockinged toe. Arabella's big toe connected with the side of the shoe and sent it skidding even farther under the desk.

"Miss Dempsey?" The door creaked a few inches open, revealing a hem of gray skirt very like Arabella's own.

The hem was followed by the rest of the dress, as its wearer pushed open the portal with her hip, her hands occupied with two cups balanced on saucers.

"I thought you might be in need of some refreshment," said Mlle de Fayette, extending one of the steaming cups in a hand that trembled from the strain of holding it upright.

Arabella blinked stupidly at a curl of steam rising above the rim of the cup. "Oh. Thank you."

The saucer wobbled in Mlle de Fayette's hand. Arabella belatedly launched herself forward to take it from the other teacher. "How kind of you," she said, and wished it didn't sound so much like a question.

"It is of no moment. I was fetching one for myself; it was no bother at all to carry another." Mlle de Fayette set her own cup down on the desk, next to Clarissa's composition. She nodded knowingly at the crumpled piece of paper. "Miss 'Ardcastle?"

Arabella scooted her chair back slightly to make room for the other woman. "Yes. How did you know?"

Lifting her cup, Mlle de Fayette blew gently on her tea. "The blots, mostly. Miss 'Ardcastle has a way with blots."

"Unfortunately, some of the words still got through," said Arabella wryly.

Mlle de Fayette's cheeks creased, displaying a dimple very like that of her cousin, the chevalier. "Not everyone can be clever. With that sort of dowry, I shouldn't bother to be clever either."

"Is Miss Hardcastle an heiress, then?"

It shouldn't have been surprising. Most of the girls in the school came from money of some sort. With a few exceptions, they tended to be the daughters of the landed gentry—untitled, but secure in both their birth and their fortunes.

"Her father is a—what do you call it? A 'cit.'" Mlle de Fayette pronounced the word in inverted commas. "Something to do with the manufacture. He makes the guns. Or is it the cannon?"

"Something that makes loud banging noises and produces smoke," Arabella provided for her. "I can't tell one firearm from the other either. It's what comes of not having brothers."

Mlle de Fayette's fingers stilled on the handle of her teacup. She looked like a lady on a cameo, her profile still and pale in the uncertain light. "I had brothers. Two of them."

Arabella could have kicked herself for tactlessness. What had the girls said that afternoon of the pudding? It had been something to do with their French mistress, and the awful fuss she made over her brother's head being chopped off. Arabella felt a cold chill creep along her spine at the thought. Hard to believe that so nearby, just across the Channel, such atrocities could still occur in their supposedly civilized world, that one could wake up one morning and find oneself bereft of brothers, parents, friends, all with the slice of an ax.

In the sudden hush, she heard herself asking, "What happened to them?"

Mlle de Fayette stared out over the garden, somewhere a million miles away. For a moment, in the unnatural calm of the ill-lit room, it seemed as though she might actually answer.

A light flickered on the grounds—or more likely, thought Arabella, blinking, just the guttering of the candle reflected in the dark glass of the window. Mlle de Fayette turned with an uncharacteristically abrupt movement, sloshing tea over the rim of her cup onto the gray fabric of her dress.

"*Tiens!* How clumsy I am." She scrubbed at the spill with her hand-kerchief. "And tea is so very difficult to get out."

"Here, let me." Crossing the room, Arabella wet her own handker-chief from the washbasin and handed it to the other woman. "I am sorry about your brothers."

Mlle de Fayette dabbed at the blotch with the damp handkerchief, succeeding only in spreading the stain. "I have Nicolas now. He is more trouble than three brothers put together."

"He seems very charming," said Arabella at random.

"The devil charms for his own purpose." Having created a very wide, damp patch with no visible diminution of the stain, Mlle de Fay-ette shook out the handkerchief and handed it back to Arabella. "Your Mr. Fitzhugh has his measure of charm as well. A very different sort of charm, but charm nonetheless."

He wasn't her Mr. Fitzhugh. He had only been borrowed for a little while, like a piece of jewelry taken on loan.

"Sally tells me that charm runs in the family," Arabella said with careful neutrality.

Mlle de Fayette accepted the tacit change of subject. "Ah, she gets far with charm, that one. But do not be fooled. She is charming like a fox."

"A very nice fox," said Arabella loyally. For all her airs, Sally had been kind, taking her under her wing as she had.

"A friendly fox," Mlle de Fayette agreed. Or perhaps it wasn't agreement, after all. Friendly wasn't at all the same thing as nice. "She would be quite clever if she weren't expending so much energy trying to avoid being so."

Arabella perched against the side of the desk, sliding her own teacup aside to prevent further spillage. "What else should I know about the girls?"

Settling herself down on the other end of the desk, Mlle de Fayette contemplated the remains of her tea, and thought better of it. "Miss Anstrue, she has the habit of helping herself to the belongings of the other girls. Only the small things, and she always returns them by and by, but it is of the most awkward."

Sally had warned her of the same, advising Arabella to keep her jewel box locked up. Arabella hadn't liked to tell her that she didn't have a jewel box, only the one strand of coral that Aunt Osborne had given her for her eighteenth birthday.

Mlle de Fayette frowned at her own reflection in the window. "Miss Grandison likes to pretend to the ague so she can spend the day in bed reading novels. Miss Reid copies her sums from Miss Fitzhugh."

Arabella hitched herself up higher on the desk, letting one foot dangle. Gossiping like this, she felt like the schoolgirl she had never been. "I would have thought they both would have been copying from Miss Wooliston."

"Oh no. Miss Fitzhugh, she has the way with maths. Miss Wooliston helps the others with their drawing. Miss Reid cannot draw a straight line."

"That doesn't surprise me," said Arabella. Lizzy Reid seemed to have an endless reserve of restless energy. Her very hair bristled with it. "What about Catherine Carruthers?"

Mlle de Fayette made a face. "I am glad she is yours rather than mine for the rest of the term. She is cunning, that one, and very determined."

"Not so very cunning if she got caught," Arabella pointed out.

"It is not good that Catherine came to Farley Castle," said Mlle de Fayette somberly. "It was to avoid the scandal, you see, that her parents agreed to leave her at the school until the end of term, but only under the condition that she remain under the strictest supervision." Mlle de Fayette lowered her voice, leaning forward. "Catherine is to be betrothed to someone else at Christmas."

"Oh. *Oh.*" Arabella grimaced to show her comprehension. "So if it got out . . ."

"It would not be at all good for Catherine," said Mlle de Fayette solemnly. "Or for the school. Not that she left the school in the first place, nor that she left it again. It would be of the most embarrassing for Miss Climpson and for all of us."

"Does Miss Climpson know?"

Mlle de Fayette shook her head. "Not yet. Lord and Lady Vaughn have pledged themselves to the strictest secrecy—"

Arabella would trust to the word of the Vaughns about as much as she would a snake peddling fruit. But she didn't say that to Mlle de Fayette. The woman looked worried enough.

"As has Nicolas," continued Mlle de Fayette. "But it is of the most imperative that Catherine not be allowed to behave so again. If the scandal were to get out . . ." She spread her hands in a gesture that needed no translation.

To keep the scandal from getting out, that meant they would have to keep Catherine from getting out too.

Catherine was on Arabella's floor. Under her supervision.

A sense of deep foreboding settled deep in Arabella's stomach.

"How did she get out last time?" Forewarned was forearmed, as the saying went.

Mlle de Fayette squinted into the garden. "They say the gardener helped them, by unlocking the garden gate, but this I cannot believe. He is not the helping kind."

Which provided Arabella with absolutely nothing. Sally would probably know, although Arabella doubted the propriety of asking a student to snitch on another student. On the other hand, the impropriety of snitchery would be far less than the impropriety of Catherine Carruthers careering around the countryside.

Arabella sighed.

Mlle de Fayette put out a hand as though to touch her arm. "I am sure you shall do your best," she said.

Why did she find that less than encouraging?

Arabella levered herself up off the corner of the desk. "This really is very kind of you. I can't tell you how much I appreciate it. The advice and the tea." She hoisted her cup in illustration. The surface was beginning to get that vaguely scummy look that served as the universal sign of tea gone cold.

Taking the hint, Mlle de Fayette slithered off the edge of the desk, slippered feet searching for the floor. It was a much farther way down for her than it had been for Arabella. Her feet, Arabella noticed, were tiny. They were Cinderella feet, just made for glass slippers. Mlle de Fayette's skirt brushed against the pile of papers, jostling them all out of alignment.

"It was my pleasure. We must do this again sometime, you and I."

"Oh, yes, certainly," said Arabella, trying not to think about Catherine. Or feet. Just one of her own slippers would make two of Mlle de Fayette's.

As she looked up at the other woman, a glimmer of light caught her eye. It flickered and then went out again, like a firefly. A very large firefly. Arabella squinted around Mlle de Fayette.

"Did you see something?" she asked abruptly.

Mlle de Fayette twisted to peer over her own shoulder. The garden lay dark and still, peopled only by their own shadow images in the window. "See what?"

Arabella pressed her eyes shut. Gold sparkles exploded against the backs of her lids. "Never mind. My eyes are playing tricks on me."

"It is the fatigue," said Mlle de Fayette, retrieving her own cup from the desk. "I remember my first week here. I thought I should drop in my porridge."

"That about sums up my current condition," Arabella admitted. "Does it get any better?"

Mlle de Fayette eyed Clarissa's paper. "The compositions? No. The fatigue? Yes. One grows accustomed."

Something about the way she said it made Arabella wonder what it was that she had been accustomed to before. Something other than this, that was quite sure. Many émigrés had come to England during the Revolution with little more than the clothes on their backs, forced to make their way as best they could. But it did seem rather odd that Mlle de Fayette's cousin was dazzling in town tailoring, chumming about with the likes of the Vaughns, while Mlle de Fayette herself was reduced to teaching her native tongue to the daughters of prosperous squires and socially ambitious cits.

Mlle de Fayette sketched a slight gesture of apology. "It is most unkind of me to keep you when you will be wanting your rest."

"Thank you. Really. I'm so glad you decided to come by." Arabella wondered if the other woman was lonely too. The other schoolmistresses were a closemouthed bunch, and all at least a decade older. The chevalier was very dashing, but he didn't seem the sort to pay regular calls. Immured in the school as she was, Mlle de Fayette couldn't have formed a broad acquaintance in Bath. And, as Arabella was learning, even when one did have the chance to get out, the rigors of the schedule tended to dampen one's ardor for excursions. "The girls are lovely, but I'd forgotten what it is to talk to another adult. And the tea was just what I needed."

Hopefully, Mlle de Fayette wouldn't notice that she hadn't drunk any of it.

Mlle de Fayette smiled at her. "If you need me, I am only one floor down. My room is directly below yours, the third door on the left."

"If I need you, I'll simply stamp on the floor," said Arabella, getting into the spirit of it. "Two stamps for 'Come up for a chat,' three stamps for an emergency."

"Er, yes. Quite. The very thing." Mlle de Fayette backed towards the door. "Good night, Miss Dempsey."

"I wasn't really going to stamp on the floor." Arabella found herself addressing the whitewashed panels of the door.

Too late.

Oh well. That was what came of actually saying the odd things that popped into her head. She had been much better at holding her tongue at Aunt Osborne's. Be grateful, they had told her. Be quiet. Be obedient. And so she had, for twelve long years.

And what had that gotten her?

Marking papers at Miss Climpson's, that was what. There was no point in dwelling on might-have-beens; she had work to do. Shoving the teacup aside, Arabella reached for Clarissa's composition. She paused, her hand on the paper, as a twinkle of light caught her eye.

Bracing both hands on the desk, Arabella leaned forward, feeling the edge of the desk cutting into her stomach. Through the floating image of her room and the blob of light that was her reflected candle flame, she could just make out the garden, the high shrubs that bounded the edges of the property, the faint herringbone pattern of the brick walks, the square shape of the gardener's humble habitation.

There it was again. Sparks of light. Flicker. Flicker. Pause. Flicker. Too stationary to be fireflies, too precise to be the wavering of a candle. It looked, in fact, as though someone were drawing the shutter of a lantern open and closed, creating a pattern and then repeating it.

Flicker. Flicker. Pause. Flicker.

Almost as though someone were signaling.

Chapter 10

*A*rabella watched, frozen, as the lights oscillated in the garden.

There it was again, two quick flashes followed by a pause and then a third. There was no doubting it. It was unmistakably a signal, and it was directed from someone lurking in the garden to someone waiting in the school.

Arabella's nose hit glass as she stretched full-length across the desk, squinting for a better view. Her breath fogged the glass, and she impatiently wiped it away. If she tried hard enough, following the direction of the flashes of light, she could almost make out a human figure. It was hard to tell. Whoever it was out there had taken the precaution of wearing dark clothes. The flashes of light were so short and her own candle proved an impediment, casting weird reflections of her own room, in reverse, over the image of the garden, like seeing two pictures one on top of the other.

What if it were meant for Catherine?

Papers rustled as Arabella levered herself upright. Mlle de Fayette claimed that the gardener was rumored to have helped Catherine and her lover by unlocking the garden gate. It seemed like the sort of thing young lovers would do, signaling from a garden. Catherine's room was on the same side as Arabella's, the garden side, just two doors down the hall.

Mlle de Fayette had also said something about a parentally arranged betrothal. If Catherine were to be chivvied into marriage over Christmas, that might be cause enough to drive her to do something desperate. Like an elopement.

Elopements were bad. Very, very bad. Catherine was on Arabella's floor, Arabella's responsibility. If Catherine eloped, Arabella would be to blame. She could lose her position over it.

The light in the garden twinkled again and then went out.

Arabella's desk chair rocked on its legs as she ran for the door. Outside, the hallway was quiet and dark, all the candles in the sconces already snuffed for the night. In the light from the landing window, she could just make out the shadowy outline of door after door, all closed, just as they should be.

Her own breathing was loud in her ears as she stood there, one hand on the doorknob. From behind the ranks of closed doors, she could hear the usual nighttime sounds: the thwack of a pillow being pounded into place, the creak of a mattress, the hushed rustle of a blanket. There was nothing the least bit out of the ordinary. Even the dust lay quiet on the wainscoting.

Arabella applied her knuckles lightly to Catherine's door. "Miss Carruthers?"

No response.

"Catherine?"

Silence.

A bristling shock of ragtag ends popped out from the doorway next door. "Catherine's gone out again, hasn't she?"

It looked like a sea monster, all bristling locks and staring eyes. It was, in fact, Lizzy Reid, her hair done up in rags and her eyes alight with curiosity, like a squirrel scenting a cache of nuts.

"I'm sure she hasn't," Arabella said bracingly. "She must just be sleeping heavily."

Lizzy looked like she believed that just about as much as Arabella did.

Brilliant. She couldn't even fool a sixteen-year-old.

Lizzy wagged her rags. "That was what just Miss Derwent said."

"Miss Derwent?"

"The mistress who was here before you," said Lizzy blithely. "She was asked to leave."

"Because of—" Arabella tilted her head towards Catherine's door.

Lizzy nodded.

Perfect. Just perfect. She should have known something was a little too easy when Miss Climpson gave her the job. There was a word for the position she had filled: scapegoat.

Pity Miss Climpson hadn't specified that in the advertisement.

When Catherine Carruthers's family found out Catherine had gone missing, Arabella would be out on her backside in the street faster than you could say "Christmas pudding."

"She could be asleep," repeated Arabella, with more hope than conviction.

She could feel Lizzy's pitying gaze on her back as she tapped on the door, louder than last time.

"Catherine?"

Still nothing.

So much for the subtle approach. Arabella turned the knob. Unlike hers, the door was well-oiled. It didn't make a noise as she pushed it open. Holding her candle aloft, Arabella ventured into the dark cubicle.

"Catherine?"

She held her candle down towards the lumpy form in the bed. It didn't move. It also didn't look like a human, unless Catherine had spread in some places and shrunk in others.

"Pillows," pronounced Lizzy, scurrying along after her like a one-woman Greek chorus.

"I knew that," said Arabella.

There was a patter of feet in the hall as the rest of the Greek chorus came scrambling in to join the fun, appropriately garbed for their parts in long white nightdresses and bare feet. The only jarring notes were the nightcaps, adorned with an idiosyncratic variety of ribbons and bows. Miss Climpson's dress code extended only to daytime attire.

"Has Catherine snuck out again?" Miss Agnes Wooliston panted.

Like Lizzy, she didn't look the least bit surprised. They had obviously been here before. With Miss Derwent.

"Of course she has," said Lizzy, rag curls bouncing. She didn't bother to whisper. Why should she? The entire hall was already awake, with the sole exception of Annabelle Anstrue, who had already demonstrated her ability to sleep through the advance of a French artillery column, cannon and all. Or at least through Miss Climpson's morning calisthenics, which amounted to much the same thing. "It's Catherine."

"She's probably in the garden," announced Sally, craning around Agnes for a better look at the pile of pillows. Her nightcap boasted a particularly elaborate concoction of pink and green ribbons. "That's where she usually goes."

Arabella felt as though she was rapidly losing control of the situation. Of course, that would be to suppose that she had ever had control of the situation. Was it too much to have hoped to get through to Christmas without major disasters?

"Back to bed," she said, shooing them in front of her. Like geese, they clucked and flapped but didn't go very far. "I'll deal with Miss Carruthers. I'm sure she just went to the necessary."

"You might want to take the back stairs," said Sally, ignoring Arabella's theory. "That's the fastest way to the garden."

"And you would know this how?" said Arabella sternly.

Lizzy grinned at her. "Best not to ask. You really don't want to know."

"You mean you don't want me to know," muttered Arabella, wondering whether there was a gate on the garden, and, if so, whether there was some way to lock it. Not that there would be much use to it. She had no doubt that the girls would find a way to pole-vault over the fence.

"It's safer all around that way," said Sally. "What Miss Climpson doesn't know can't hurt her."

"Or us," chimed in Agnes earnestly.

"Ignorance is bliss!" contributed Lizzy.

Windowless towers. That was what was needed. Highly underrated things, windowless towers. Preferably with moats around them.

"You," said Arabella, "are all going back to bed. Right now. And as far as I know, you know nothing about any back stairs."

Lizzy smothered her in a quick hug. "We love you, Miss Dempsey."

"I should have stayed in London," muttered Arabella, and made for the back stairs.

She was tempted to take the front stairs, just because, but what was the point of cutting off her nose to spite her face? She liked her nose. And the girls were right; the back stairs were faster.

She could hear scratching and scurrying noises as she approached the main floor. Human or rodent? Arabella wasn't sure. Keeping her skirt close to her legs, she let herself through the green baize door into the first-floor hallway. The schoolrooms lay in demure ranks on either side of the neatly papered wall, doors closed on their secrets. The music room, the dance studio, and the lesson rooms all lay shuttered and silent, waiting to be wakened in the morning with the arrival of the servants who lit the hearths and refreshed the ink and tidied the remains of the previous day's debris.

The drawing room door stood open.

Through the open portal, Arabella could hear a rustling sound, like the whisper of a skirt against the ground or the snick of fabric against fabric. Catherine and her lover? It made sense as a meeting place. The drawing room overlooked the garden, low enough to the ground for an enterprising suitor to wiggle his way through the long sash windows, but shielded from view by high hedges that grew on either side.

It was a pleasant room in the daylight, used occasionally for the purpose of receiving family members, but generally ceded to the older girls for use as a sort of lounge, where they wrote letters, muddled their way through lessons, and sprawled before the hearth engaging in imagined affairs of the heart. By night, the bright blue and white paper darkened to a decidedly ominous gray, the ornamental lozenges like staring eyes and open mouths in the gloom.

Squaring her shoulders, Arabella marched smartly forward. "Catherine?"

Her footfalls sounded unnaturally loud against the floorboards. She could see her own reflection in the pier glass over the mantel, distorted and blurred. There was no one else there. There was only the movement of the starched white curtains, which snicked and whispered in the breeze from the open window, snapping back and forth in the December wind.

Arabella came to a halt in the center of the room, flustered and irritated. In the empty room, the curtains flicked out at her. It felt like a taunt.

Oh, Lord. The window. The open window. Catherine. Of course, thought Arabella, disgusted at her own stupidity. Why rappel four flights down from an upper window when one could climb in comfort out of one on the first floor? It was only heroines in novels who went for the grand and impractical gesture.

"Blast, blast, blast," Arabella muttered to herself, making for the window.

Catherine couldn't have gotten far. The light had been signaling not five minutes ago.

Arabella stumbled backwards, clutching at the curtain for balance, as the menacing form of a man leaned forward through the window. He filled the entire aperture of the window, blotting out the feeble light of the moon.

He was huge; he was threatening; he was . . . "Mr. Fitzhugh?" Arabella squeaked.

She hadn't realized her voice was capable of hitting that register. In real life, she was an alto.

In real life, pinks of the *ton* didn't pop out of windows at her at strange hours of the night.

Mr. Fitzhugh didn't look like a pink of the *ton* now. His brightly patterned waistcoat and exuberant cravat had been replaced by a tight-fitting garment in a coarse, dark material, worn over a pair of equally dark pantaloons. Only his boots remained the same, but even those had been matted with soot to destroy their glossy finish. He had pulled a knit cap down over his bright hair, but bits stuck out at the sides, lending him a mildly maniacal look. If Arabella had encountered him in a dark alley, she would have gone running in the opposite direction.

One thing hadn't changed, though. His smile was as exuberant as ever. He appeared completely unconcerned by the fact that she had caught him lurking outside the window of a young ladies' seminary on the cusp of midnight garbed in garments that could, with extreme charity, at best be termed bizarre.

"Lovely night, ain't it?" he said cheerfully, for all the world as if they had run across each other in the Pump Room over steaming mugs of mineral water. He slapped his arms across his chest for warmth. "Stars seem brighter here, don'tcha know."

Arabella rather doubted that Mr. Fitzhugh was lurking in Miss Climpson's shrubbery for the purpose of stargazing.

"What *are* you doing lurking under a window dressed like . . . like . . ."

"Like it?" Rising to his full height, Mr. Fitzhugh executed a half turn.

"No!" Arabella peered left, then right. "You haven't seen anyone come this way, have you?"

"Through this window, d'you mean?" asked Mr. Fitzhugh, as though it were a perfectly logical question. "Not recently. I should have noticed if they had."

"You haven't seen a girl? Possibly with a man? She might have come this way."

"A girl?" Mr. Fitzhugh appeared genuinely puzzled by the concept.

"An adolescent person of the female persuasion," Arabella clarified.

Mr. Fitzhugh considered. "No. None of those. Did see some one of those lurking about through the curtains, but that was inside, not out. If she'd come through here, I would have known."

Arabella frowned at Mr. Fitzhugh. The coast still seemed to be clear, but they couldn't count on that to last. "You can't be here."

"Don't like to beat a dead chicken and whatnot, but I should think that I jolly well am." Mr. Fitzhugh contemplated the ground at his feet, with its cracking pavement and the winter remains of flower bushes, now slightly squished. Looking up, he beamed at Arabella. "Yes. Definitely still here."

There was something ridiculously infectious about Mr. Fitzhugh's smile. Yes, like the plague, Arabella told herself sternly, and forced her lips to stop grinning back. "What I meant was that you shouldn't be here. Someone will see you."

"They haven't so far." Mr. Fitzhugh clasped his hands behind his back, doing his best to assume a modest expression. "I've been out here for four days. Er, nights."

"Nights. Plural. Four?" Arabella wrapped her arms around her chest. "You've been sitting here in the garden. For four nights."

Mr. Fitzhugh twirled a bit of his watch chain around his finger. "Well, five, really, if you count tonight, but since tonight is still tonight, it didn't seem the done thing to add it to the tally. Night not accomplished yet and all that, don't you know."

Didn't he realize it was December? And cold? She was cold just standing at the window. He was lucky it wasn't snowing.

"Haven't been here all night," said Mr. Fitzhugh virtuously. "M'groom spells me. Splendid sort, Gerkin. Always good in a pickle."

Arabella's brain balked at the vision of frozen servants bobbing in brine. "Let's start again. *What* are you doing in the garden? And don't say 'talking to you.'"

"I got to worrying about you," Mr. Fitzhugh said confidingly, leaning his elbows on the windowsill. "I didn't like the looks of that pudding. If there's something rum going on, I want to know what. Couldn't just leave you here to face it alone."

"Oh," said Arabella. "Oh."

She had meant to say something clever and stinging, but Mr. Fitzhugh's response was so entirely unexpected that the words faltered on her lips. He had been concerned about her? All this time when she had been convinced he had been off gadding and gallivanting, he had been huddling in the dirt beneath the drawing room window, waiting to protect her.

It was ridiculous, of course, and utterly mad, but it was still rather . . . sweet.

"Thank you," she said, although the words seemed entirely inadequate to express the sheer magnificent idiocy of his actions. "You really shouldn't have."

"Not in the slightest," said Mr. Fitzhugh airily, although the nonchalant sentiment was slightly marred by the chattering of his teeth. Reaching under his sweater, he extracted a silver flask and took a bracing swig. "Good for the constitution and all that. Nothing like a good English December."

"Yes, but not all night," retorted Arabella. If Mr. Fitzhugh had been outside all this time, then . . . "It might have been your light I saw. Maybe Catherine really was in the convenience."

Lowering the flask, Mr. Fitzhugh wiped his mouth on the back of his hand. "Catherine?"

"Catherine Carruthers." Of course, there was no reason for Catherine to have piled pillows in her place if all she intended was a quick trip to the necessary. "She wasn't in her bed. Your sister thought—"

"That's your mistake, right there," said Mr. Fitzhugh helpfully. "Letting Sally think. Comes up with some deuced odd notions that way."

"*Sally* comes up with odd notions?" said Arabella.

Mr. Fitzhugh had the grace to blush. Or perhaps it was just windburn. "Just wanted to make sure you were safe. And there was a chap lurking about here earlier in the evening. I saw him last night, too. Went around the other side."

"Are you sure it wasn't just your Gerkin?"

"Not a chance of it. Gerkin and I have a signal."

Arabella had a fairly good idea of what that signal might be. "Two flashes of light, a pause, then another flash?"

Mr. Fitzhugh shook his head. "Too obvious. Someone might see the light. Sort of thing schoolgirls would do. No. Our secret signal is the mating call of the two-billed thrush."

"How can a bird have two bills?"

"That's the genius of it!" Mr. Fitzhugh bounced on his heels, all boyish enthusiasm. "They can't. Made it up ourselves."

"Then how can— Never mind." If it wasn't his lantern, whose was it?

Arabella was about to voice that important point when a familiar creaking sound arrested her attention.

"There's someone coming!" Arabella flapped her hands at Mr. Fitzhugh. "Quick! Hide."

"Your wish is my—ugh." Arabella put a hand on his head and pushed. Flailing, Mr. Fitzhugh went down.

She very much hoped he would take the hint and stay down. It was going to be hard enough explaining to Miss Climpson or one of the other mistresses just what she was doing roaming the lower floors at nearly eleven at night without the added complication of the older brother of one of her pupils squatting in the flower bed. There was no good way to explain that. Arabella doubted Miss Climpson would believe that she was updating Mr. Fitzhugh on Sally's progress in history.

Arabella yanked the curtains closed as she turned to face the doorway. They were thin curtains, designed for ornament more than use, but they at least provided the illusion of a barrier.

Arabella took a tentative step towards the door. "Miss Climpson?" she said, peering into the darkness beyond. She held up her candle. "Is that you?"

The footsteps came to an abrupt halt.

So did Arabella.

It wasn't Miss Climpson. Not unless the headmistress had recently taken to wearing trousers.

"Oh," said Arabella, as the candle flame danced between them. "You're not Miss Climpson."

Chapter 11

Turnip popped out of the flower bed just in time to see a dark figure loom up in the doorway in front of Miss Dempsey.

It might have been dark, but it was unmistakably male, which didn't seem at all the thing in an academy for young ladies. As Turnip knew from Sally—and their parents, who had paid close attention to such points—the school was designated a male-free area after dark, with all male teachers and staff packed off back to their respective lodgings. The only man who was allowed to be on the grounds was the gardener, and it seemed highly unlikely he would be in the house when his job was to be active outside it.

As Miss Dempsey held up her candle, the man shied back, flinging up an arm to shield his eyes from the light or his face from view.

Miss Dempsey advanced on the newcomer. "What—," she began.

Whoever he was, he wasn't in the mood to answer questions. Looking left, then right, the intruder summed up his options and charged for the window. There was one slight problem. Miss Dempsey was in his path.

She swerved. He swerved.

Unfortunately, they both swerved in the same direction.

Time to make his daring entrance and charge to the rescue, sweeping away all malefactors with a hey-ho and a heave-to. Turnip flung himself onto the sill, only to find himself tangled in the folds of a white linen curtain that someone had inconveniently drawn across the window. As Turnip struggled against a tangle of curtains, the intruder feinted to the side, trying to make a run around Miss Dempsey. His shoulder banged into her side, sending her flailing for balance, just as Turnip lost the battle with the curtain and went tumbling back into the flower bed. From his semiprone position, he could see Miss Dempsey's candlestick arc through the air, trailing a brief plume of flame like a falling star before winking into darkness.

From the black nothingness came a feminine cry of surprise and distress as Miss Dempsey landed with a thump flat on her rump on the drawing room floor.

"Sorry," mumbled the thief. His accent was pure Yorkshire. "Sorry. Sorry."

Turnip groped for the edge of the window frame, banging his hand on the side of the window in the process.

The man in the room appeared to be having similar problems. There was a crashing noise as a small table went over, taking with it the intruder and several china knickknacks.

Turnip clawed away the curtain, shoving the window up high enough that he wouldn't bang his head on the way through. He had just swung a foot up onto the ledge when a flurry of activity sounded in the hallway. The sound started low, the merest swish and rustle of fabric, like moths battering their wings against a window, and then gained in intensity, with hisses, whispers, and the slap of bare feet against the floor.

Like a cork exploding from a champagne bottle, someone else shot into the room.

"Don't worry, Miss Dempsey! We're here now!" cried an exuberant female voice.

Turnip froze, his foot propped at an uncomfortable angle on the window ledge.

"Each for each, that's what we teach!" caroled another, calling out the school motto. Turnip knew that voice. He knew it far too well. "Ouch! That was my foot! Lizzy!"

"That wasn't me—it was Agnes," protested the first voice.

"Sorry," said Agnes, in a small voice.

"Girls?" ventured Miss Dempsey, from somewhere on the floor. She sounded more than a little bit breathless. Turnip knew just how she felt.

"We've come to your rescue," explained Sally. "We thought you might need us. Ouch!"

"Sorry," said Lizzy, sounding anything but. "That was me this time. Well, it's dark in here."

"Does anyone see the villain?" demanded Sally. "There is a villain, isn't there?"

The villain had very wisely decided to conduct his own exit. Turnip could hear a low scrabbling sound not far from the window, like someone crawling on his hands and knees.

"Quick!" exclaimed Sally. "He's trying to escape!"

As his eyes adjusted to the lack of light, Turnip could just vaguely make out his sister snatching up a notebook off the windowsill and rushing forward, wielding it like a club, only to go catapulting over the same table the intruder had knocked over before. The notebook spiraled through the air, spewing bits of paper, before landing *thwack* on the head of the burglar, who let out a loud curse.

"Oooh, there he goes!" squealed Lizzy, and blundered into Agnes, who reeled sideways and stepped on Sally, who was still on the floor in front of the table.

There was a flurry of feet and the sound of more crockery breaking and a good deal of gasping and stumbling and stubbing of toes and "mind the table!" during which Miss Dempsey made an attempt to call the group to order, Sally was stepped on again as she was trying to get up, Lizzy Reid tripped over the hem of her own robe, Sally and Lizzy banged heads, and Agnes exclaimed, in tones of wonder, "I think I've got him!"

"Quick, quick, tie him up," urged Lizzy, jiggling up and down in place rather than risking the scattered furniture.

"Use my sash! Here!" Sally charged forward, a long strip of fabric dangling from her hand, and promptly tripped over the exact same table. Her disembodied voice rose eerily from the floor. "Who left that there?"

"Not me," said Agnes quickly.

Taking advantage of her inattention, the intruder wrenched himself free from Agnes's grasp, making a dash for the window.

"Not so fast!" yelled Lizzy, and flung herself chest-first at the intruder. He went down hard, landing with a gasp on the floor, Lizzy on top of him.

Turnip winced in sympathy. That had sounded jolly painful.

"You got him! You got him!" exclaimed Turnip's sister, jumping up and down like a little girl on Christmas morning.

Lizzy planted her bottom firmly on the intruder's back. "He's not going anywhere," she said smugly.

"Girls!" exclaimed Miss Dempsey, trying belatedly to exert some control over the situation. "Don't—"

Lizzy gave a little bounce and the intruder made a sound like a dying accordion as all the air rushed out of his lungs.

"—squash him."

"Sorry, Miss Dempsey," said Sally. "Who has the candle?"

"I do," pronounced a new voice.

Light washed over the room. It glinted off shards of broken porcelain, pooled in the folds of white linen nightdresses, limned the sides of fallen furniture, and blared like twin beacons off the spectacles of the woman holding the candle.

Miss Climpson stepped into the room, the starched ruffles of her dressing gown rustling stiffly as she moved. Her graying brown hair was confined beneath a nightcap of truly impressive proportions. From his vantage point on the far side of the window, Turnip was reminded of a large muffin. A decidedly distressed muffin.

Furniture and girls in white nightdresses littered the room, none of it where it ought to be. Bits of white porcelain were scattered across the blue carpet from what had once been a particularly ugly china cupid. A Meissen shepherdess lay headless in the hearth. Sally, still lying where she had landed, sprawled on the floor in front of an overturned table, her nightcap squashed to one side and her braid over one shoulder. Lizzy Reid was sitting proudly on the back of some poor sod while Agnes Wooliston attempted to locate his hands so she could string a pink-edged sash around them.

Lizzy looked decidedly pleased with herself. It was impossible to discern how the intruder looked. His face was pressed into the ground, from which emerged, from time to time, the odd moaning noise.

"Oh dear, oh dear, oh dear," Miss Climpson murmured, surveying the tattered remnants of her domain. "Oh dear. Miss Dempsey?"

Unlike the girls, Miss Dempsey was still fully dressed, but her hair had burst its pins, unraveling down her back in a burst of congealed sunshine. It looked, somehow, more dramatic against the demure gray of her day dress than it would have had she been in a nightdress like the others. Turnip had never seen her hair down before; it had always been ruthlessly coiled away, stuck about with pins, with a bonnet squashed down on top of it for good measure. He had known it was blond, but he would never have imagined it would be quite so exuberant.

But, then, that was Miss Dempsey all over, wasn't it? She pretended to be all shy and quiet, and then there she was, chasing down prowlers in the middle of the night.

At the moment, she was holding a chair up in front of her like a lion-keeper at the Tower, prepared to hold the villain at bay should he make another rush for the window.

She very slowly lowered the chair to the ground as she turned to face the headmistress. "Miss Climpson? I'm afraid we've had something of an, er, incident."

Lizzy Reid giggled.

Sally flapped a hand to shush her.

Miss Climpson blinked behind her thick spectacles, her candle making a slow arc as she took in the scene in front of her. "Is that my china cupid?" she asked first, and then, "Is that a *man* beneath Miss Reid?"

"I am afraid so," said Miss Dempsey.

Miss Climpson shook her head. "Roaming around the school in the middle of the night, breaking objets d'art, sitting on strange men. Girls! What do you have to say for yourselves?"

"The cupid was already broken when we got here?" suggested Agnes.

"Please." Miss Dempsey placed herself between her charges and the headmistress. "Let me explain."

Sally stepped forward in front of Miss Dempsey. "We heard noises, Miss Climpson. So we asked Miss Dempsey to investigate."

"Just to be safe," chimed in Lizzy Reid from her position on top of the prowler. "One can't be too careful in these dangerous times."

"True, true, true," agreed Miss Climpson, her stiff ruffles rustling. "But there is still no call for sitting on him."

"It was only until we could find something with which to tie him." Agnes Wooliston rushed to her friend's defense.

The intruder groaned.

Miss Climpson released a short exhalation of air that might have been a sigh. "Miss Reid?"

Lizzy looked at her with wide, innocent eyes. "Yes?"

"We do not sit on people in this establishment. Settees are for sitting; chairs are for sitting; not—"

"Hideous midnight intruders?" suggested Lizzy helpfully.

"Even those, even those." It was a sign of Miss Climpson's agitation that she said it only twice, not three times. "Kindly remove yourself from that man's person, Miss Reid. Not later, not soon, but right now."

Lizzy scrambled off the recumbent intruder, who seemed considerably flatter than when he had entered. He looked as though he were trying to become one with the carpet.

Miss Climpson wagged a finger at Lizzy. "That sort of thing is dreadful for your posture. You know what I always say. A crooked back makes for a crooked mind!"

"Yes, Miss Climpson," chorused all three girls.

"But, Miss Climpson," ventured Agnes. "What about the intruder?"

Miss Climpson frowned down at the prone man. "I suppose we could ask the gardener to take him out. He doesn't go at all with the rest of the drawing room. He would be very hard to explain to parents when they came to call." Taking up the fireplace poker, which was lying, in the aftermath of the fray, between an overturned chair and the broken shepherdess, she prodded the man gently in the side. "Sir? Sir?"

The man groaned again.

"Now, now," prodded Miss Climpson. "It isn't at all healthy to lie on your stomach like that. It impedes both the digestion and the flow of air to the brain."

It might have been concern for his digestion that got the man moving, or it might have been the tip of the poker being applied to his side. With a little help from Miss Climpson's poker, he levered himself slowly up onto his elbows, shaking his head from side to side as though to clear it.

Beneath the tousled mess of hair, his lips moved. His voice was scratchy and just barely audible. "I can make-a dee explanation."

Everyone stared at him.

"Oh, Lord," gasped Lizzy. "It's the music master."

And so it was. His hair was all about his face and one of his mustachios had come loose in the fray, but it was still, unmistakably, the same man who had been playing the lute at Farley Castle the week before.

Turnip frowned at the music master. It wasn't beyond the realm of comprehension that the music master might be their spy. He had a foreign name, a strange accent, and access to both the school and Farley Castle. But why sneak in at dead of night when he had perfectly legitimate access by day? No one had ever accused Turnip of being a master of common sense—quite the contrary, in fact—but even he could see that.

Miss Climpson waved her candle at the recumbent music master. "Signor Marconi? What are you doing here?"

"Errrrrr," groaned Signor Marconi.

Not much of an excuse, that, but to be fair, he had until quite recently had a well-fed sixteen-year-old perched on his back.

"Miss Dempsey," said Miss Climpson. "Help Signor Marconi to a chair. Proper posture is very important to the workings of the mind. It's all about the flow of the blood."

Miss Dempsey obediently stepped forward as instructed. The music master clutched at the hand she extended, nearly sending them both reeling as he staggered clumsily to his feet. Miss Dempsey yanked him to his feet with less than complete solicitude.

"What were you doing lurking about down here?" Miss Dempsey demanded, with some asperity. "Why didn't you simply make yourself known when you saw me?"

"I came-a for da music," he said in wounded tones. "Den de girls, they jump on me and break-a my bones. It is dee insult to my art." As he spoke, his right mustachio dropped off entirely.

Miss Dempsey folded her arms across her chest. "No one would have jumped on anyone if you had identified yourself when I asked."

"Yes, yes," said Miss Climpson distractedly, waving Miss Dempsey to silence. "You came for your music. Your music?"

"I give-a dee lesson tomorrow morning. I need-a de music." Signor Marconi seemed to have rediscovered his Italian accent.

Even to Turnip's ears, his excuse sounded as phony as his mustachios.

"Where," asked Miss Dempsey, "is this music?"

Signor Marconi looked from left to right, as though hoping that it might materialize of its own accord. "In the music room?" he said hopefully. Belatedly remembering to look aggrieved, he drooped back in his chair. "All I wanted was to fetch-a de music and go, when de harpies, they, er, dey attack-a me, with de tooth and de claw."

"Tooth?" demanded Sally indignantly. "Claw? I never laid a hand on the man."

"I only sat on him," said Lizzy beatifically. "No teeth or claws involved."

Agnes looked at her fingernails. "Mine are too short to be claws."

"Girls," said Miss Dempsey, and they subsided.

"How did you get in, Signor Marconi?" asked Miss Climpson. "The building is meant to be locked."

"Meant" being the operative word. As far as Turnip could tell, the structure was as porous as a hunk of cheap cheese. They could start charging a toll for all the people coming in and out at night and save on the tuition.

Signor Marconi's eyes darted around and caught on the flapping curtains. He flung out an arm, pointing at the window for all he was worth. "Through the—er, *da* window. I came in-a through da window."

Not this window, he hadn't. Turnip could have vouched for that if he hadn't been crouching beneath said window. Of course, if he hadn't been crouching beneath the window, he wouldn't have been in a position to vouch for anything of the kind. It was quite the tangle.

"Why would you do a thing like that?" asked Miss Climpson, in what appeared to be genuine confusion.

"Because da door, it was a-closed."

"I am glad to hear that," said Miss Climpson with great decision. "It would be quite worry-making to think of the doors being accessible after hours. Nonetheless, the window should be locked."

Behind Signor Marconi, Miss Dempsey began gesturing wildly with one hand, flapping at the air in a downward motion, mouthing something Turnip couldn't quite catch. Turnip cocked his head in inquiry.

Down, down, down, flapped Miss Dempsey.

Uh-oh. If she could see him, so could Miss Climpson. And his sister. Turnip wasn't sure which worried him more. He hastily ducked back down behind the curtain, trusting to his dark clothes to blend into the night.

"Miss Dempsey?" said Miss Climpson. "Are you quite all right?"

"Just, er, shaking out my wrist." Miss Dempsey smiled weakly at the headmistress. "I believe I might have sprained it when Signor Marconi knocked my candle out of my hand."

"And your notebook, as well, it seems." Bending down, Miss Climpson smoothed the pages of a notebook that was splayed open next to a fallen chair. "It does look somewhat the worse for the fall."

"But I didn't—"

"Oh, dear, you seem to be losing pages." Miss Climpson handed her a piece of paper that had fallen from the notebook.

Miss Dempsey stuffed the paper in her pocket and tucked the book up under her arm.

Signor Marconi pressed a hand to his chest. "I offer to you dee most-a sincere apologies of my heart." Struck by a sudden inspiration, he added, "I only a-tried to defend-a dee young-a ladies. I thought you were intrrrrrrrruder."

Miss Dempsey eyed him skeptically. "How very noble of you."

"Well, well," said Miss Climpson vaguely. "I'm sure it was all an accident, and an unfortunate one at that. We'll have stronger locks fitted on all the windows tomorrow. Shouldn't the girls be in bed? And, Signor Marconi, I would appreciate if you would confine your visits to daylight hours. Much less unsettling for everyone. Miss Dempsey, if you would latch the window?"

"What? Oh, yes. Of course." Miss Dempsey pulled herself together sufficiently to make her way to the window, blocking the aperture with her body as she reached up to pull down the sash.

It was quite a nice view. Turnip took back all the unkind things he had thought about that gray dress. The simple lines molded themselves to her upper body as she reached up to pull down the window sash that he had pushed up some time before. Since he was taller than she, there was a fair amount of reaching involved. He might have jammed it up there just a little too hard, since the window appeared to be stuck. Miss Dempsey's feminine attributes jiggled interestingly as she yanked at the sash.

Turnip would have helped, of course. But he wasn't meant to be there.

Turnip shifted uncomfortably in the flower bed. Bloody good thing it was quite so cold outside. He wasn't supposed to be thinking these sorts of things about his sister's teacher. He was sure there was some sort of school rule about it. On the other hand, he had known her before she became a teacher—even if he hadn't quite remembered her name—so oughtn't there to be some special sort of dispensation for that?

Catching Miss Dempsey's eye, Turnip grinned up at her and gave a little wave.

Miss Dempsey blinked at him, resting her hands against the sash.

"The world has gone mad," she said out loud. "And me with it."

"Miss Dempsey? Do you need help with that?" It was Sally's voice, at her most butter-wouldn't-melt.

"No, no. Don't! It's just a bit . . . sticky." The window finally gave, dragging Miss Dempsey along with it. The sash slammed into the sill with enough force to make the glass quiver. Miss Dempsey's chest rose and fell as she let out a heartfelt sigh of relief.

From somewhere just behind her, Turnip could hear his sister's voice. "Are you all right, Miss Dempsey?"

"Ask me again tomorrow." He could hear the snick of the bolt sliding into place. "I haven't decided yet whether this is all a very vivid dream."

"I could pinch you," offered Sally. "I'm a champion pincher. Just ask Reggie."

Through the glass, he could see Miss Dempsey look down at him. He nodded emphatically. Sally could pinch for England. Miss Dempsey's lips twitched and she hastily turned away, blocking the window with her back.

"Thank you for the exceedingly generous offer," she said politely, taking Sally's arm, "but I believe I'll just wait it out."

"Sometimes," offered Lizzy, falling in on her other side, "I dream of being a Chinese philosopher pretending to be a butterfly."

"Dear, oh dear." Miss Climpson turned around from the doorway. "Nurse has an excellent remedy for that. Extract of castor oil, bean curd, all mixed into barley water. It does wonders for the cerebral passageways. Remind me to tell her to dose you tomorrow."

Lifting himself cautiously on his haunches, Turnip watched as the ill-assorted procession made its way out of the drawing room. Miss Dempsey took up the rear, flanked by his sister and Lizzy Reid. She cast a last glance over her shoulder before disappearing around the doorway, but she was too far away and the glass too distorted with frost to determine whether she had been trying to tell him anything by it.

Turnip tried the window, but it was well and truly locked. Nice to know that his sister and Miss Dempsey would be safe, but deuced irritating when one needed to get inside. The side doors were probably all locked right and tight, and if they hadn't been, they would be now.

Bother it. He needed to speak to her, and not merely to gloat about having been right about there being something dodgy going on. Oh, all right. Maybe to gloat only a little bit.

Turnip took a step back, scrutinizing the facade of the building. He could see the light move slowly from window to window. Miss Dempsey's room was on the fourth floor. He knew because he'd had Gerkin ask. The school was made out of a rough stone, hung with ivy.

Where there was ivy, there was generally a trellis.

Chapter 12

When Arabella peeked into Catherine Carruthers's room, Catherine was tucked up in bed with the covers pulled over her head.

She had, however, neglected to remove her shoes.

Arabella stood in Catherine's doorway, her candle casting a faint light over the blackened soles of a pair of brown leather boots. They were half boots, the sort that laced on and couldn't be kicked off easily. Not even when one was racing to bed in a hurry with several school-mistresses in hot pursuit.

As Arabella watched, the shoes slowly retreated beneath the blanket.

Arabella contemplated drawing Catherine's attention to the matter of the shoes and then decided against it. In less than a week, everyone would be packed off home to their families for Christmas and Catherine would be someone else's problem. In the meantime, let her enjoy her small victory. She must have snuck back upstairs while everyone was tripping over furniture and bumping into one another in the drawing room. If the blankets had been just a little longer, or Catherine just a little shorter, she might even have gotten away with it.

Arabella backed soundlessly out of Catherine's room, closing the door gently behind her. Tomorrow morning, she would see that a strong bolt was placed on the outside of Catherine's bedroom door, to prevent any such further nocturnal perambulations. It probably made Arabella a bad schoolmistress, but as long as Catherine was back in her bed, not on the road to Gretna Green, Arabella didn't much care what she had been up to. All that mattered was that Catherine remain on school grounds for the next five days, after which she would be her betrothed's problem, not Arabella's.

Poor Catherine. She so enjoyed flouting her schoolmistresses and shocking her friends. She would hate to know that she had been upstaged by a falling mustachio and a crouching Turnip. But really, compared to the rest of the evening's activities, Catherine's were positively mundane.

Arabella wondered if Turnip Fitzhugh was still out there, keeping the school safe from puddings and their perpetrators. Arabella choked on a giggle. Little did Miss Climpson know that Turnip and his faithful groom were on patrol, like a latter-day Don Quixote and Sancho Panza. All that was missing was the donkey.

Arabella paused in front of her own door. Did that make her the donkey? Perhaps this wasn't quite so perfect an analogy as she had originally thought.

What was it Lizzy Reid had said? Maybe they were all just Chinese philosophers dreaming of being butterflies.

Or maybe it was quite late and she should go to bed before she lost what was left of her mind.

"I must have misplaced it in the drawing room," muttered Arabella, and then looked guiltily around to make sure no one had heard her.

Of course they hadn't. Everyone else was asleep. Or at least doing a decent job pretending.

Juggling her candle in one hand and the notebook Miss Climpson had given her in the other, Arabella shoved the notebook up under her armpit. With the notebook clamped against her side, she awkwardly turned the handle of her door, nudging it open with one foot.

Only to nearly drop the notebook.

There was someone in her room. Not just someone. There was a man in her room. A great big man dressed all in black.

He was sitting on her desk—or, to be more accurate, he was sitting on Clarissa Hardcastle's history composition, which was sitting on her desk. His knit cap had come off somewhere along the way, leaving his hair squashed flat on one side and sticking up at odd angles on the other.

"Hullo," said Turnip Fitzhugh, swinging his feet so his heels clunked against the legs of her desk.

Normally, the sight of a man in one's room would be cause for alarm. Consternation, even. It ought to be enough to send her sprinting down the hallway, screaming rape, murder, and everything in between. Not, however, when that man was Turnip Fitzhugh. Arabella found it hard to work up the proper level of maidenly alarm and indignation at finding Mr. Fitzhugh in her bedchamber. He was just . . . Turnip.

Arabella closed the bedroom door behind her. "Are you a Chinese philosopher or a butterfly?"

Mr. Fitzhugh considered the question. "Since I'm not Chinese, does that make me the butterfly?"

"That would explain how you managed to fly up four stories without using the stairs." Arabella realized that she was still holding the notebook and set it carefully down on the corner of her desk not occupied by Turnip. She would figure out whom it actually belonged to later. "Not to seem nosy—purely out of curiosity, you understand—how did you get up here?"

Mr. Fitzhugh indicated the window behind him, which was currently open and blowing cold air straight through her room. "I climbed the trellis."

Naturally. Why hadn't she thought of that? Perhaps because she hadn't even known there was a trellis. And wouldn't have expected strange men to go climbing up it if she had. Her bedroom was not generally high on the list of Sights to Be Clandestinely Visited by the Male Population of England.

"You climbed the trellis. Of course you did." It made as much sense as anything else that had happened this evening. "Do you climb trellises frequently?"

Mr. Fitzhugh gave the matter due consideration. "Wouldn't quite say that. Never climbed one before. Trees, yes, the odd wall, but never a trellis."

Four flights up, no less. That was impressive. Potentially suicidal, but impressive. "And you made it all the way up on a first go? I'm very impressed."

"It did get a bit dodgy at times, but it's not all that different from climbing a wall once one gets the knack of it." And then, since he seemed to feel some further explanation was required, "Seemed safer up here with the Climpson prowling around below. Didn't want her to catch me and dose me with barley and whatnot."

"She has been known to climb the occasional flight of stairs." As Mr. Fitzhugh started to scoot off the desk, taking the top two pages of Clarissa's composition with him, Arabella held up a reassuring hand. "Don't worry. You're probably safe for the moment. She's too busy with Signor Marconi to bother about the odd trellis climber."

"I'm not that odd," protested Mr. Fitzhugh. He looked down at his sweater, and a leaf flopped down onto his nose. He blew it away. "At least not compared to Signor Whatsis."

"Signor Marconi?"

"That's the chap. Shouldn't wonder if he and your Miss Climpson were a while. They're probably still looking for his missing mustachio."

A sound somewhere between a choke and a snort escaped Arabella's lips. She could just see Miss Climpson and Signor Marconi on their hands and knees, crawling around the drawing room floor, searching for the music master's missing facial hair.

"He should have used stronger glue," Arabella agreed, doing her best to keep a straight face.

"If a man can't grow it, he shouldn't wear it," pronounced Mr. Fitzhugh with great decision.

"That would be very aw-aw-awkward applied to breeches." Arabella barely managed to get the words out. The images in her head were too ridiculous. All the absurdity and tension of the evening came bubbling out, despite the hands she clasped over her mouth to try to keep the laughter in. She could see the whole scene in front of her, everyone bumping into one another and toppling over one another and Signor Marconi—Signor Marconi—

"Miss Dempsey?" Mr. Fitzhugh peered earnestly at her. "But don't you wonder what he was doing there?"

"Other than being sat upon by Lizzy? Oh, heavens, the look on that man's face! And then Miss Clim—Miss Climps—" Arabella was laughing too hard to speak.

Mr. Fitzhugh leaned forward, holding on to the edge of the desk, tilting first this way, then that, to try to get a look at her face. "You all right there? Everything tip-top?"

"Oh, qu-qu-quite!" gasped Arabella. "I wasn't the one who was s-s-s-sat on. *Miss Reid! People are not for sitting!*"

At the memory of Lizzy Reid perched on the music master's back, like a cat standing guard over a particularly juicy mouse, Arabella gave up and howled.

Having ascertained that she was in no immediate danger of dying, Mr. Fitzhugh leaned back, planting his elbows on the desk. "It could have been worse. It could have been Sally sitting on him."

Couldn't. Cope. Arabella clutched her stomach, wheezing. Could a person burst from laughing too much? "S-Sally. Not so heavy."

"No, but she's a good head taller than the Reid girl." Mr. Fitzhugh considered. "Less bounce in her, though. Once Sally sits on someone, she stays sat. Like a rock. Or a very large paperweight."

Arabella pointed a shaking finger at Mr. Fitzhugh, laughing so hard that no sound came out of her mouth. She rocked back and forth, trying to get the words out.

Mr. Fitzhugh looked at her quizzically.

"It's you," she managed to gasp out. "Sitting on my papers."

Mr. Fitzhugh jumped up as though Clarissa's composition had burned his backside.

"No, no." Arabella waved a hand. His face swam in and out of focus through the tears of mirth. "Sit, please. No harm done. You make an excellent paperweight. I might even keep you on permanently."

"Don't think Miss Climpson would like that." He settled very cautiously back down on the desk, taking care to push the papers out of the way. The inkwell rocked on its stand and he made a successful grab for it before it could go over.

"Oooh, that hurts," groaned Arabella, pressing her hands to her abdomen.

"Where you fell?" asked Mr. Fitzhugh, all concern.

"No, where I laughed." Wiping her eyes with the back of her hand, Arabella confessed, "I was terrified that someone would see you out there, c-crouching in the bushes. You kept popping in and out." She waved a hand to illustrate. "Like a j-jack-in-the-box. Every time I'd look, there you were again. Up and down and up and down. You took three years off my life, you know."

"Only three?" Mr. Fitzhugh grinned at her. "Didn't want to miss anything. It was better than Astley's Amphitheatre. Never knew who was going to pull which stunt next. All that was lacking were a few ponies in feathers. Although"—Mr. Fitzhugh's face grew sober—"I did feel bad about not being able to rescue you."

"Rescue—what?" Arabella applied a knuckle beneath her eye to try to clear the moisture away. Heavens, she felt tired all of a sudden. Tired in a good way, as a small child who had been playing outside all day in the sun and the wind, ready to go gratefully to sleep.

"When the intruder came in," Mr. Fitzhugh said. "I was all set to charge in and do the knight-in-shining-armor bit. But I got tangled in the curtains."

Arabella gave a surprised giggle that turned into a hiccup. "No, really?"

Not the curtains. She wasn't sure her aching diaphragm could take it. She was all laughed out, hollowed, as though someone had taken a spoon and scooped out her insides. She took a long, deep breath, feeling it tickle at the back of her throat.

The breath turned into a yawn and she hastily covered her mouth with the back of her hand.

Mr. Fitzhugh scuffed his heels against the desk legs. "What if he hadn't been the music master? What if he had been armed?"

Touched by his concern, Arabella reached out a hand to touch his sleeve. The knit weave of his sweater was rough against her bare fingers. "But he wasn't armed."

"That we know of," countered Mr. Fitzhugh.

"What was he going to do? Threaten to affix his facial hair to my upper lip?" Arabella lowered her voice. "It would have been a disaster if you'd come barging in. I might have lost my position over it. At least Signor Marconi had a plausible reason for being in the school. You had none."

"We could have said I was visiting Sally," Mr. Fitzhugh suggested.

"Dressed like that? In the middle of the night? Besides, Sally and her troops carried the day splendidly." Maybe a little too splendidly. Arabella made a rueful face. "I don't envy the maids who have to tidy the drawing room tomorrow morning. I don't think there's a single piece of furniture left standing."

Mr. Fitzhugh tucked his chin into his chest. "All the same," he muttered.

"All the same," said Arabella, tilting her head to look him in the eye. "I appreciate the intention. Really, I do. And it all turned out for the best. Especially that cupid. I never liked that cupid."

Mr. Fitzhugh squared his shoulders. "The whole thing was dodgy, deuced dodgy."

"I would have called it more ugly," hedged Arabella. "A fat, naked baby cast in porcelain is seldom a good idea."

Mr. Fitzhugh looked up at her in surprise. "I was talking about Signor Whatsis. He was lying about the window, you know. I would have seen him if he'd come in that way."

Arabella covered her mouth as another yawn threatened to force its way out. "You or your pickle?"

"Gerkin," corrected Mr. Fitzhugh.

"Gerkin, pickle. Six of one, half dozen of the other." Arabella was light-headed from laughter and vaguely sleepy. "I wonder if he gets teased by the other grooms."

Mr. Fitzhugh contemplated the question. "I shouldn't think so. One of them is named Snufflepuss."

Arabella's eyes met his. "Snufflepuss. As in . . . Snufflepuss?"

Mr. Fitzhugh's lips twitched. Just a little twitch. Then another. And suddenly they were both laughing, helpless with mirth, teeth flashing, eyes crinkling, shoulders heaving, setting each other off every time they caught the other's eye.

"I c-can't look at you," gasped Arabella, waving a hand in Mr. Fitzhugh's direction. "Stop. Please."

Mr. Fitzhugh swallowed hard, his shoulders still shaking. He made a wobbly gesture with one hand. "Your wish is my—blast!"

One minute she saw him; the next minute she didn't. The room plunged into darkness.

"Well," said Arabella unsteadily, "that was one way to stop me looking at you."

"Sorry. Accidentally snuffed the candle."

"I hate it when that happens," murmured Arabella.

It was a very strange sensation, being entirely in the dark. She knew, on a theoretical level, that she was in her own room at Miss Climpson's, standing just a little bit to the left of her desk, while Mr. Fitzhugh was sitting roughly a foot away from her. Given that neither of them had gone anywhere, he probably still was. She could picture him as he had been a moment ago, with his teeth very white against his grimed face and his hair sticking up at odd angles.

No one had moved and nothing had changed, but the room suddenly seemed much smaller and closer. She could smell the loamy scent of leaves and the alcoholic tang of brandy against the more familiar scents of ink and paper and her own lilac-scented soap. It was warmer in the room than she remembered. Arabella inched her hands cautiously up to her cheeks, pressing her fingertips to her cheekbones. It was December, in England. She wasn't supposed to feel this flushed.

"Mr. Fitzhugh?" she ventured.

"Still here." There was a rustling and crunching of papers as Mr. Fitzhugh shifted on the desk. His leg brushed Arabella's skirt. Goodness. It really was close in here. "Here. I'll—oh. Oops."

Something rolled over the edge of the desk, clipping Arabella on the shin before hitting the floor. She could hear the dull bumping noise of a lopsided object rolling across the uneven floorboards.

"That was the candle, wasn't it?" said Arabella.

"Er, yes." She could feel sheepishness coming off him in waves. She might not be able to see him, but she could picture just how he would look. "Somehow knocked it off its stand. Sorry about that."

"I'm just glad it wasn't the inkwell," said Arabella honestly.

The inkwell clinked as Mr. Fitzhugh scooted forward. "I'll get it. The candle, I mean."

"No, no, I've got it. You stay there." Arabella dove for the ground before he could object. Or knock over the inkwell.

Something cracked into her forehead, so hard that she saw stars.

"Owww," she groaned, staggering back onto her heels. "Was that you?"

"No," said Mr. Fitzhugh apologetically. She couldn't make out quite where he was, but his voice was coming from somewhere above her. "I think that was your desk chair."

No. She wouldn't have— Arabella groped in the darkness, her palm hitting something wooden and spindly. It was, in fact, her chair. It was still rocking slightly back and forth.

There was nothing like maiming oneself on a piece of furniture to make one feel like a complete idiot.

Arabella grabbed the seat to steady herself. Maybe she should just stay down here.

"I'd kick it," Arabella said in a small voice, "but I think that would hurt me more than it."

"I'd challenge it to a duel," Mr. Fitzhugh offered, "but it might win, and that would be deuced embarrassing. Never be able to show my face at my club again."

Mr. Fitzhugh's hands found her elbows, hauling her back up to her feet. He did it very neatly. Then again, reflected Arabella, he'd had practice. This wasn't the first time she'd taken a fall in front of him.

"Where does it hurt?" he asked.

"Does pride have a specific anatomical location?"

Mr. Fitzhugh's hands moved up and down her arms in a comforting gesture. It made Arabella want to lean against him, close her eyes, and stay that way.

"That sounded like a nasty crack. I should know. I've had a few in my time. Many of them self-inflicted."

"Oh, it's just my head," Arabella said, wincing, wiggling just a bit. "Nothing important. Not like I was using it anyway."

Mr. Fitzhugh made a light grunting noise and released his steadying grip on her arms. The grunt obviously meant something in the male lexicon, but, having never had any brothers, Arabella was at a loss for an exact translation.

He reached out and touched her cheek, making his way by feel along the side of her face. He had removed his gloves when he had come inside, and his bare fingers were gentle against her skin as he brushed the hair back from her brow. "Is this where you hit yourself?"

Arabella nodded, before remembering that he couldn't actually see her.

"Yes," she said, and was surprised to find that her voice came out hoarse.

She put up a hand to touch his wrist, although whether to move his hand away or make it stay, she wasn't sure. Her fingers met bare skin below the sleeve of his sweater. She could feel the broadness of the bone and a smattering of coarse hairs beneath her fingers.

He went very still as she touched him.

They were, she realized, standing ridiculously close. He had drawn her forward so that she stood between his legs as he sat on the desk. His hand was in her hair, his knees brushing her hips, his chest so close that that she could practically feel the rise and fall of it as he breathed. In the suddenly alert silence, she could hear the heightened tempo of his breathing, no longer ragged with laughter, but uneven all the same. Strange what different things silences could be. A moment ago, they had been comfortably silent together. And now they were . . . uncomfortably silent.

Arabella tilted her head up to the light-colored smudge that was Mr. Fitzhugh's face. She tried to think of something clever to say, but for once in her life she couldn't think of anything at all. She was having the hardest time remembering who she was or where she was or anything beyond the gentle darkness and the scent of brandy and earth and the rough weave of Mr. Fitzhugh's sweater as it rasped beneath her palm.

"Arabella?" he said, and his voice sounded as unsteady as hers.

"That is my name."

"Promised you I wouldn't forget," he said.

She couldn't see the smile on his face, but she could feel it on his lips, lips which were, somehow, brushing hers.

It was entirely unclear how they had gotten there, or who was technically kissing whom, but it seemed the most natural thing in the world to wrap her arms around his neck and kiss him back.

Chapter 13

Turnip hadn't climbed the trellis with the intention of kissing Arabella Dempsey.

In fact, he had made the perilous climb with only the most serious and responsible of motives. Well, all that and avoiding Miss Climpson.

But then there had been all that laughing and the candle had gone out and she had been standing right there, with the smell of lilac in her hair, and kissing her had seemed a jolly good idea, if he had stopped to think about it, which he really hadn't. It had just happened, the way the best things in life generally did, and once it happened, he wondered why he hadn't thought of it before, why he had wasted so many minutes of the evening crouching outside windows and chasing after puddings when he could have been kissing Arabella Dempsey.

Who, it turned out, when it came to kissability, was entirely kissable.

She was just the right size for him, all comfortable curves beneath that very unattractive gray dress. Like her hair, the rest of her was surprisingly lush once one started exploring. It was a bit like being Columbus, landing on what seemed from the water to be nothing more than your average dull beige beach, only to find a verdant forest bursting with glorious and unexpected foliage.

As he mapped out the cartographical angles of the curve of Arabella's hip, Turnip was a very happy amateur explorer. Then she yanked down on his head and he forgot all about metaphors and just went back to kissing her. She scooted in closer, and he gathered her up in both arms, pulling her in as closely as nature and the desk would allow.

Nature was with them, but the desk was proving to be something of a problem. Turnip scooted a bit to the side, trying to make a more comfortable berth for them on the desk. After all, Arabella was three-quarters of the way onto his lap anyway. If he could just clear a little room to the left . . .

Turnip bumped something with his bum. It skidded off the edge of the desk, landing on the floor with a thump. No matter, he thought hazily, helping Arabella with that extra hitch she needed to join him on the desk. Her feet flailed, catching on something, which was unsporting enough to go toppling over with a decidedly jarring crash.

Turnip was inclined to ignore whatever it was and just go on kissing Arabella. After all, it was already down, ergo it couldn't fall down again, so why worry about it? And she was all soft and warm and—

"What was that?" she asked, sliding down off his thigh.

"Nothing," said Turnip, kissing the tip of her nose and the side of her cheek. He liked the side of her cheek, so he kissed it again. "Nothing important."

Arabella wiggled in his arms, turning to crane her neck at whatever it was that had fallen. Turnip made an attempt to kiss her ear and found himself coughing up a mouthful of hair.

"That was the chair," she announced, after a period of brief but concerted observation.

Turnip gave up trying to kiss her and smoothed her hair back behind her ears. He followed the curve of her neck down to her shoulders, giving them a comforting rub. "I'm sure it's all right. It's a chair." Chairs tended, in his experience, to be fairly resilient objects.

Arabella looked at the fallen chair and then back at him.

Then at the fallen chair. And then back at him.

Turnip couldn't make out her expression—those poets who raved about starlight highly overrated its powers as a lighting agent—but he had the distinct impression that she wasn't happy.

"At least it wasn't the inkwell," said Turnip cheerfully, in an attempt to lighten the mood. "That would have been a bother to clean up."

Even without the inkwell, they had made rather a mess, Turnip had to admit. Not quite as bad as the drawing room—no broken cupids scattering porcelain all over the place—but her desk chair lay on its back, legs pointing stiffly out, and a notebook had fallen next to it, belching out paper as it landed.

"Arabella?" Turnip gave her waist a friendly squeeze. When that didn't work, he tried again. "Miss Dempsey?"

Arabella twisted away from him. Her skirt swished against the uneven boards of the floor. "Mademoiselle de Fayette—she lives just downstairs," she said distractedly. And then, when Turnip still didn't get it, "You have to go."

"What?" Turnip's mind was still occupied elsewhere. Turnip reached for Arabella, asking, with his most winning smile, "What was that you were saying?"

Arabella gave him a little shove. "Please. Go. Now."

"Oh. Right." No mistaking the meaning of that. Clear as a bell. By no stretch of the imagination could it be translated as "Take me now."

Arabella made shooing gestures.

Turnip scrambled up on the desk, sending bits of paper scooting left and right. The window was still open, and the trellis appeared to be where he had left it.

He looked back over his shoulder at Arabella, who was twisting her hands together and craning her head towards the door as though she expected a band of outraged Roman matrons to burst in at any moment.

It didn't seem right to leave it this way.

Turnip paused with one foot out the window. "Just wanted to say—"

Arabella jiggled up and down. "Go! Please."

So much for tender expressions of regard.

"Well, good night, then." Turnip lowered himself the rest of the way out the window, feeling for footholds in the facade. That had felt very inadequate, so he added, "Mind the mustachios!"

That didn't strike quite the right note either, but he was now entirely out the window, clinging to the facade of the building, four stories up. Not exactly the best time for crafting the perfect parting phrase. If he had his friend Richard's je ne sais whatsis or his friend Geoffrey's brains, he might be able to pull it off, but he had enough trouble stringing the old words together when his feet were flat on the ground, much less when his extremities—and the rest of him—were dangling several flights up above hard flagstones and some deuced prickly looking shrubbery. And at that, the shrubbery was still preferable to the flagstones.

Turnip lowered himself hand over hand, concentrating on keeping his hands and feet away from the odd icy patch, wishing he'd remembered to put his gloves back on.

Three stories left to go now. The windows were all dark, which he supposed was a good thing, even if it did make feeling for handholds a bit dicier. It would be hard to explain what he was doing clinging to the side of the building in the wee hours. He supposed he ought to have thought of that before deciding to take the trellis. Next time, he was using the stairs.

Next time. A bit of vine stuck itself to his ear, tickling his nose. He hadn't really thought about whether or not there would be a next time. *Please go now* was seldom conducive to next times. On the other hand, *Please go now* wasn't quite the same as *Never darken my trellis again*.

He'd talk to her tomorrow, he decided. And they could sort it all out then. Among other things, there was still that last pudding to discuss. And whatever it was that Signor Marconi had really been doing, stalking the halls of the school by night. That was, Turnip remembered, with a certain amount of surprise, why he had climbed the trellis in the first place.

There was a rustling noise above him and he looked up to see Arabella leaning out the window. He had never noticed before what a nice chin she had. It was, at this angle, all of her he could see. That and her long hair falling out the window on either side of her face, like that storybook princess who used to let down her hair as a ladder.

"Be careful," she called after him.

Turnip raised a hand in salutation before remembering that waving while clinging to the side of a building thirty feet off the ground was probably a very bad thing to do. He concentrated on climbing.

Upstairs, Arabella watched until she was sure Mr. Fitzhugh had safely reached the ground. He staggered a bit on hitting the pavement, then recovered and directed a jaunty salute in the general direction of her window.

Arabella yanked the window shut and latched it. Not that she thought anyone else was going to climb her trellis, but it never hurt to make sure. An ounce of prevention was worth a pound of cure. Arabella contemplated the wasteland of crumpled and ripped papers on her desk, one of which bore the distinct imprint of Mr. Fitzhugh's shoe, and set about mechanically smoothing them flat.

She felt cold without Mr. Fitzhugh's arms around her.

"That's what shawls are for," she muttered, slapping papers into a pile without bothering to make sure they belonged to the same composition.

Shawls couldn't compromise you. Shawls couldn't cause you to lose your position. Shawls wouldn't regret kissing you in the morning.

There had been many grand moments of stupidity in the course of human history—Clarissa's history composition numbered prominently among them—but surely what had just happened in this room had to take pride of place. Arabella yanked her fallen desk chair back into position, plunked the notebook back on the newly cleared desk, and counted the ways. She had (a) kissed Turnip Fitzhugh (b) in her bedroom (c) in his sister's school (d) where she was an instructress.

Burying her head in her hands, Arabella added an extra item: (e) She had enjoyed it.

Somehow, that was worst of all. She wasn't supposed to kiss Turnip Fitzhugh. And she certainly wasn't supposed to like it.

Or want, so very badly, to do it again.

❧

SINCE TRELLISES WERE OF LIMITED UTILITY during daytime hours, Turnip was forced to resort to a more subtle stratagem in his attempt to see Arabella the next afternoon.

Turnip drummed his fingers against his palm as he waited in Miss Climpson's drawing room, now miraculously restored to a semblance of its usual state. Minus, of course, one china cupid.

One didn't just go calling on schoolmistresses, at least not without arousing talk. Given Miss Dempsey's reaction last night, Turnip had gotten the feeling—just a hunch, mind you—that she might object to that sort of thing. On the other hand, there was nothing to comment upon in a chap wanting to see his favorite sister.

Turnip basked in a combination of sunshine and smugness. The plan was so cunning, one could cut it with a weasel.

Turnip hopped to his feet as soon as Sally entered the room.

"Have you seen Miss Dempsey?" he demanded.

"What? No *hello*? No *how are you*?" Turnip's sister seemed less than thrilled to see him. Sally folded her arms across her chest, her matched gold bracelets knocking against each other with a discordant clang. "You come barging in here in the middle of the day without so much as a note, drag me out of French class in the middle of the *passé simple*, and then ask to see my *teacher*?"

"Not as though you were paying attention in class anyway," said Turnip sagely. "Now, where's that teacher of yours?"

"Yes, but I might have done," said Sally, "and now I'll never have the chance. Then, after all that, it's not even me you want to see. Not a bonbon, not a gift, not a single token for your one and only sister. No. I'm just a means to an end to you, aren't I?"

"That was the idea," said Turnip, ignoring the long windup. He knew this prelude. All it meant was that Sally had her eye on something and wanted him to pay for it.

Sally clasped her hands to her breast in a credible imitation of Mrs. Siddons. "Don't you think you owe me an explanation?"

Turnip knew the answer to that one. "No." And then, since that sounded a little harsh, "But I will take you out for an ice later if you like."

Sally narrowed her eyes at him. "Do you really think I can be bribed with an ice?"

"Yes." That usually worked for him. The sweet tooth ran in the family.

"I'm not ten anymore, you know. Make it that blue enamel and seed pearl set in that shop on Milsom Street, and you have a deal. What *do* you want with Miss Dempsey?"

"It's a surprise." Turnip was seized with a sudden inspiration. "Maybe I want to talk to her about you."

Sally made a scornful sound with her tongue and her teeth. Rude, but effective. What were they teaching her in this school of hers? Weren't they supposed to be turning her into a young lady? "She doesn't seem like your usual sort of flirt."

Turnip regarded his younger sister with alarm. "What would you know about that?"

"What wouldn't I know?" said Sally loftily. "I have my ways."

"You mean you peered through the banisters at Mother's parties. Can I see Miss Dempsey?"

"I haven't peered through the banisters in years! It's not my fault that the ballroom balcony is right beneath my bedroom window. You should have thought of that before you took Miss Deveraux out there."

He hadn't taken Miss Deveraux there; Miss Deveraux had taken him. She was a force of nature. Like an earthquake. Or a hurricane. When she pointed to a balcony, a chap followed.

"Mother didn't like it one bit. She says Miss Deveraux is fast."

Turnip swung his hat from one hand. "Are we done yet?"

Sally was only just warming up. "Miss Dempsey, on the other hand, is the antithesis of fast."

Turnip resented that on Miss Dempsey's behalf. "Wouldn't call her slow."

Sally arched an eyebrow. "Oh?"

"I didn't mean like that. You do want that seed pearl set, don't you?"

"Blue enamel set with seed pearls," Sally corrected him. "And don't forget the earrings. Yes?"

"Yes," Turnip agreed. He had been planning to get it for her for Christmas anyway. No need to tell Sally that, though. She was happier if she thought she had the upper hand. "Earrings and all. Miss Dempsey?"

Sally arranged her hands demurely in her lap. "Miss Dempsey is out."

"Out?"

"As in out of the building. Outside. Away. Not here. Since the school is so empty, Miss Climpson gave her a half day to do her Christmas shopping. At least, that was what Miss Climpson said. I think it was really so people would stop trying to ask her what all the hullabaloo was with Signor Marconi last night."

"You couldn't have told me this before?"

"If I had," said Sally logically, "I would have had to go back to French class."

Turnip resisted the urge to bury his head in his hands. He would only crush his hat that way. Sally would still be Sally. And Miss Dempsey would still be out.

"Do you know when she'll be back?"

Sally opened her mouth to say something silly, but some latent sense of self-preservation stopped her. She shook her head. "I don't. Really. But you'll see her at the recital tomorrow. I do assume that whatever this secret matter may be can wait until tomorrow?"

Turnip ignored the sarcasm. "Recital?"

"Reggie! Don't tell me you forgot! The recital. *The* recital. The big Christmassy thing at which you are expected to sit quietly and clap loudly whenever you see me."

"I will, I will. Very loudly." Come to think of it, he had known about the recital. It would be hard not to. He had been dragged to two of them already. It had been a memorable experience, although not necessarily on account of its artistic merit.

"You're not playing a sheep again, are you?"

Sally narrowed her eyes at him. "I'm an angel. The Angel of the Lord."

No wonder those shepherds had been sore afraid. Turnip would have been too.

"Oh, don't look like that. It won't be that bad. And you can see Miss Dempsey there."

But he wanted to see her now.

Turnip's eyes strayed to the escritoire in the corner, supplied with paper, pens, and ink. He could leave her a note, but, not to put too fine a point on it, eloquent prose wasn't exactly his forte. Besides, he didn't trust Sally not to read it. And there really wasn't any way to put "hope you don't mind about that kiss" in code. He couldn't even figure out what he was trying to say in plain English, much less in circumlocutions obscure enough to be opaque to Sally, but clear enough to be understood by Miss Dempsey.

Maybe he had better wait for the recital.

Turnip brightened at the thought. The place would be milling with parents and siblings, all dutifully chewing their way through Miss Climpson's mini mince pies, which had all the adhesive properties and taste of strong glue. If the event ran to form, at least one piece of scenery would fall down over the course of the evening and one of the younger girls would have a strong case of stage fright. Amid all the traditional hullabaloo, there would be plenty of opportunity to sneak away for a private chat.

There might even be mistletoe.

"When is it?" he heard himself asking.

"I don't know why I bother to tell you *anything*," said Sally. "Six o'clock. And by six o'clock, I mean six o'clock. Not half past or a quarter to seven."

"What color enamel was it again?" asked Turnip.

"Blue." Sally went up on her toes to kiss him on the cheek. "Thank you, lovely brother. I'll tell Miss Dempsey you called."

"You do that." He wouldn't want her to go a whole day thinking he had just kissed her and run off. "Tell her . . . well, tell her I called. And that I asked after her. And that I called."

"Reggie?" Sally tilted her head at him. "Are you all right?"

"Perfectly." Turnip clapped something on his head. Unfortunately, it turned out to be his gloves rather than his hat. He hastily switched hands. "'Course I am. Why wouldn't I be?"

Sally looked pointedly at his gloves. "No reason."

Chapter 14

"My brother was looking for you." Sally pounced the moment Arabella walked through the door.

Arabella put down her parcels and applied herself to untying the strings of her bonnet. Why had she never noticed before that the world was distinctly oversupplied with Fitzhughs? They were everywhere.

Arabella had woken this morning with a headache, a nasty taste in her mouth, and the wild hope that last night had, in fact, been a particularly bizarre dream. That was a hope that had been rudely counteracted at breakfast, where all the older girls were buzzing over the brilliant gossip that Signor Marconi had been caught climbing through a window and chased down and wrested to the ground by Miss Climpson, who had battered him into submission with a china cupid.

Fortunately, no one appeared to have seen a large man climbing the trellis.

In an attempt to give herself something to think about other than Turnip, Arabella had fled to the Austen house, commandeering a surprised but amenable Jane for some impromptu shopping. On a superficial level, the expedition could be counted a success. Arabella had found gifts for all the members of her family, even Margaret, but Christmas shopping hadn't been quite the distraction that she had hoped it would be.

When Jane had asked her what she meant to buy for Margaret, Arabella had replied, "A trellis."

Arabella carefully removed her bonnet and gathered up her parcels before turning back to Turnip's sister. "Don't you have a music lesson?"

"No." Sally sauntered along beside her as Arabella made for the stairs. "The harp needs to be restrung. Several strings were broken in the altercation last night."

"The harp wasn't in the drawing room." If she had tripped over it, she would have known. Harp strings left painful welts.

"Wasn't it?" Sally widened her eyes so far it was painful to watch.

"If you stay like that too long, your face will freeze that way."

"People have told me that before. It hasn't happened yet. What do you think he wanted?"

"Signor Marconi?"

Sally rolled her eyes. "No. Reggie."

Reggie. Arabella applied the name to the person and tried to decide if it fit. She had kissed him, but she had never called him by his first name. Or even by his nickname.

She didn't want to think about that. If she were ten years younger, she would have stuck her fingers in her ears and made loud humming noises.

"What do you think he wants?" persisted Sally.

"The answer to that completely eludes me."

Sally wasn't that easily dismissed. "You must have some idea."

"I've sworn off all ideas until after Christmas."

Once upon a time, she had prided herself on her critical judgment, on her ability to step back and take a clear view of her own character and those of other people. But what if it wasn't that her judgment was so good? What if it was just that she had spent most of her life untested, and now, having been tested, failed miserably? It hurt to find that her feet were as claylike as anyone else's.

It wasn't that she didn't like Turnip. She did. She liked him tremendously. She liked his innate decency and his ridiculous sense of humor and—no, she wasn't supposed to be thinking about that bit. In any event, she did like him, and she was fairly sure that he was equally fond of her, but the thought of anything more between them was entirely out of the question. He was Turnip Fitzhugh—and she was Miss Who? Miss What-Was-Your-Name-Again?

As for Turnip, he was made of a different clay than she was—a shinier, more sophisticated clay. She knew his world, even if she wasn't quite part of it, knew it well enough to know that flirtation was just part of the game, and that it was a game for them. Not meant maliciously—she didn't think Turnip could be malicious if he tried—but the stakes were different for him, for all of them who had the backing of fortune and standing.

It was easy enough for him, with no intent to harm, to kiss Penelope Deveraux on a balcony one day, and Arabella the next, never thinking that in the world from which Arabella hailed, the quiet assemblies of the country gentry, a kiss might be taken as more than a kiss. The gilded circle of the elite operated by less rigorous rules than a country parson's daughter.

The best thing for everyone concerned was simply to pretend that the kiss had never happened.

It didn't help that she could still feel the curve of his cheek beneath her fingers and the way the short hairs at the back of his neck had prickled against the palm of her hand. The body, it seemed, had a long memory.

Well, her body would just have to forget. When she saw him, as she supposed she must someday, she would be friendly but distant. Dignified. If she could put it off until she were eighty or so, that would help tremendously. Nothing said dignity like gray hair and a cane.

"Reggie did say he would be at the recital tomorrow night." Sally watched Arabella out of the corner of her eye. She was about as successful at looking sly as her older brother. Their faces just weren't constructed for it.

"Splendid," said Arabella. "Brilliant. Lovely."

She would be the one there with a burlap sack over her head, hiding. Or perhaps she could find a nice potted plant to hide behind. Now all she needed to do was locate a six-foot-high poinsettia and her plan would be complete.

"He's really not a bad sort," said Sally. "When he isn't acting like a complete buffoon, that is."

"Signor Marconi?" It hadn't worked the first time, but it was worth another try.

Sally cast her a reproachful glance. "No. Reggie."

"Good," said Arabella brightly, heaving herself up the last few stairs. "I wouldn't want you getting any ideas about the music master. I doubt your parents would approve."

"Ugh." Sally shuddered. "Those mustachios."

Jumbling her packages, Arabella nodded to her door. "Would you mind opening that for me? I'm afraid I'll drop something."

"Oh, certainly." Sally gave the door a shove on Arabella's behalf. "Did you hear about Signor Marconi and—oh."

She broke off, stopping so abruptly that Arabella nearly tripped over her foot.

Arabella grappled for a sliding package, catching it just before it fell. "What—oh."

She very slowly straightened, still clutching her inconvenient mound of packages, staring openmouthed at the wreckage that had been her room.

"Good heavens," Sally said breathlessly.

Arabella attempted to wrestle her jaw back into its usual position. "More like the other place."

Her room—while she hadn't exactly left it in a pristine condition—had been nothing like this when she left it. The compositions that had been piled on her desk were now strewn about the floor. Black sludge seeped down the side of the desk from the overturned inkwell, puddling on top of Arabella's favorite Kashmir shawl, which was wadded into a crumpled heap. Her best petticoat sprawled wantonly over the splayed legs of the overturned chair, while bits of ribbon, bonnet trim, and gloves littered the floor like the ground after a parade. The wardrobe doors gaped open, the empty drawers sticking out as though the wardrobe were putting out its tongue at her.

Feathers adhered to everything, even the walls. It wasn't hard to tell where they had come from. She could see the burst skin of a pillow, belching yet more feathers. Who knew that such a little pillow could have so many feathers in it? It was positively Shakespearean. Some of the feathers had landed in the ink, turning the color of a crow's wing.

Without waiting to be asked, Sally wandered into the room ahead of her. Paper crunched beneath the heels of her slippers. The coral beads from Arabella's one decent piece of jewelry skittered about underfoot.

"What happened here?" Sally asked in wonder. A stray feather, stirred by her passage, grazed her nose in passing and she sneezed explosively, covering her mouth with her hand.

Whoever it was had even stripped the bedclothes off her bed, dumping them in an untidy mound at the foot. Whoever it was had ripped long gashes into the mattress itself, out of which sprayed a combination of wool and feathers and whatever else it was that people stuffed inside mattresses. It looked as though rats had been burrowing in it. But it wasn't rats. Just one very malicious human.

Mechanically, Arabella reached out and tried to smooth out the bent brim of a bonnet. The straw stubbornly bounced back out of position. Arabella pushed, harder. The bonnet pushed back. Angry tears prickled at the backs of Arabella's eyes.

She hastily dropped the bonnet on top of the pile of Christmas shopping. This was absurd. She was not, not, not crying over a bonnet. She had never liked that bonnet anyway. She was just overwrought; that was all. And tired. And angry. She tried to focus on anger.

"You're very sanguine," said Sally.

"No," said Arabella, keeping her face carefully averted. She reached down and shook out a petticoat. This one, at least, seemed only crumpled, not stained. "Not really. But I applaud your vocabulary."

Sally dropped the remains of the pillow on the desk, where it landed in a pool of ink. "I've seen some pranks in my time, but nothing like this. This is just plain nasty."

"Thank you," said Arabella. Her tongue felt too thick for her mouth, and her throat was so dry she could barely manage the words. "I find that terribly comforting."

"I didn't mean—" Sally bit her lip, the picture of contrition. "Sorry. Shall I have one of the maids fetched up? To clean all this up?"

Arabella stooped down, lifting one of the crumpled pages from the floor. It was a piece torn out of her journal, a description of the carriage ride to Farley Castle. Or, rather, it had been. Now it was nothing more than wastepaper, hardly legible even to her. And she was the one who had written it. It looked as though someone had danced a jig on it. In heavy boots.

"Yes," Arabella said heavily. "I think that would be best."

They might as well shovel the whole lot up and throw it in the dustbin. It wasn't fit for much else.

Arabella methodically lifted a corset from the wreckage. Aside from the ink stains and the feathers, her clothing didn't appear to be damaged, at least any more than could be expected from its having been thrown across a room. Her papers, on the other hand, had been thoroughly ransacked, as though someone had gone through them, looking for something, and had wreaked his vengeance on the offending papers when he hadn't found it.

Which made no sense at all.

"But why would anyone want to *do* this to you?" asked Sally.

Arabella shook her head helplessly. "Maybe someone didn't like the marks I gave her. Maybe Signor Marconi was looking for his lost mustachio. I don't know. Weren't you going to fetch that maid?"

Sally planted her hands on her hips, turning in a slow circle around the room. "It does look as though someone were looking for something."

"In that case, I hope they found it," said Arabella shortly, shaking a shawl free of feathers before folding it and placing it in one of the open drawers. One had to start somewhere.

Cheer up, she told herself. None of it was irreparable. Ink stains could be washed out; linen could be ironed; coral could be restrung. Everything could be put back just the way it was.

Well, mostly.

"Is anything missing?" Sally asked keenly. She was trying so hard to be helpful that Arabella didn't have the heart to tell her to leave.

"I don't have anything anyone would want to steal." Arabella rose painfully to her feet, clutching at the drawer for balance. She nodded at the desk. "Unless someone wanted your history compositions."

"*I* don't want my history composition," said Sally.

Arabella leaned against the open wardrobe and tried to conjure up an image of her room as she had left it this morning. It shouldn't be that hard. Aside from her clothing, which was now scattered all across the floor in varying degrees of dilapidation, she hadn't brought that much with her from Aunt Osborne's house. There had been her coral necklace, now in pieces; four or five favorite books, of no interest to anyone but herself; and her journal, which appeared to have been chewed by a rabid beast before being scattered across the floor.

Otherwise, the contents of the room were only those things that had been given her when she arrived—one coverlet, one pillow, one desk, one chair, one candlestick—and those that she had acquired through her employment—paper, pen, inkwell, three history texts, a pile of half-read student compositions.

Sally had opened the window, to dispel the scent of ink. The curtains fluttered in the wind just as they had last night, when it had been Turnip sitting on the desk. Arabella remembered that horrible moment as the chair had gone over, clanging against the floor. Something else had fallen too.

Squelching her way through the feathers and the papers, Arabella gingerly lifted the ink-sodden shawl that lay next to her desk. Underneath, there was only a half page from Clarissa's history composition and a very old volume of poetry, the cover now stained with ink.

Shooing Sally aside, Arabella scrabbled through the debris on the desk. The remains of her journal . . . more history compositions . . . a broken pen. . . . Nothing. It wasn't there.

Arabella leaned back against the desk, feeling even more confused than she had before.

"What is it?" asked Sally eagerly.

"The notebook," Arabella said in bewilderment. "Someone took the notebook."

Chapter 15

*T*urnip made a point of arriving early at Miss Climpson's on the evening of Sally's recital.

He strolled happily into the auditorium, wading through a shifting sea of family members, searching for Arabella and doing his best not to trample on any small children. He had been looking forward to this all day. Happy anticipation was not a sentiment he usually associated with Miss Climpson's annual Christmas torture. Trepidation, yes. Anticipation, no.

But the thought of Arabella made him smile, in a rather goofy sort of way. He hoped Miss Climpson had stocked up on the mistletoe this year. It would be a bloody shame if she hadn't, especially after last year's fiasco involving the mistletoe and the games mistress, who had all but wrestled him under it. That had not been an experience he wanted to relive.

Ah, there she was. But she wasn't smiling. And she wasn't looking at him. She whisked past so quickly that Turnip could have sworn her dress blurred around the edges.

"Miss Dem—"

Blast. She was gone before he could get her name out.

"Reggie! Over here!" Turnip found himself waylaid by a creature with feathery things attached to both arms and a gilded pancake sticking six inches up from her head. She folded her feathers across her chest. "Took you long enough."

Turnip shifted to look around Sally, searching for Arabella. "Are you supposed to be mingling with the public?"

Sally shifted along with him. Fortunately, she was shorter than he was. He could still see the room through the space between her head and her halo. "We haven't started yet."

"Excuse me." Turnip moved his little sister aside. He had spotted his quarry, all the way at the far end of the room.

He raised a hand and waved it enthusiastically about. She'd have to be blind not to see him this time.

Arabella bobbed her head, favored him with a smile weaker than weak tea, and disappeared behind a large cutout of the main thoroughfare of Bethlehem, which had, apparently, consisted of four mud huts, a seller of fruits and vegetables, and a somewhat anachronistic milliner's establishment boasting the latest in premodern bonnetry, which just happened to look awfully like modern bonnetry.

Well, she wasn't blind. That was good. She also wasn't overcome with joy at his appearance. That was bad.

"Pardon me." Turnip started after Arabella.

At least, he tried. Unfortunately, his sleeve seemed to be attached to Sally's hand. Or, rather, Sally's hand was attached to his sleeve. Either way, he wasn't going anywhere. The Angel of the Lord had a deuced strong grip when she chose to employ it.

A sudden thought struck him. "Did you tell Miss Dempsey I called?"

"Yes," said Sally. "I did. Twice."

"Oh." That couldn't be it, then. Unless she was upset he hadn't tried again? But that would have looked deuced odd and caused people to talk if he had called twice in one day. And he had thought she didn't want people to talk. It was all very confusing.

Turnip could sense the mistletoe rapidly receding from his future.

Where had he gone wrong? Was it the jumping out the window? The cloves he had been chewing?

"Reggie," Sally said purposefully.

"I know, I know. Sit quietly and clap loudly. We've been through this before," Turnip said, giving his arm a shake. Arabella had gone to ground somewhere behind the manger. "Deuced becoming costume, by the way. Vast improvement on last year's sheep getup."

"Thank you. But that's not it. Did you know that Miss Dempsey's room was ransacked yesterday? Ha! Thought that would get your attention."

"And you're only telling me this *now*?"

"You only just got here," said Sally reasonably.

She should have called for him, sent a note. The "she" he was think-ing of wasn't Sally, but Arabella. Why hadn't she come to him?

Turnip looked to Sally in alarm. "Was she hurt?"

She hadn't looked hurt. But who knew what bruises might be hid-den beneath that ugly gray dress. She certainly had been behaving oddly.

"No," Sally said, and Turnip let out his breath in a rush of relief. "It was while she was out yesterday. They made a frightful mess, though."

"Who did?" Turnip made an effort to concentrate on Sally.

"That's just it. We don't know. The only thing that was missing was a notebook." Sally paused for dramatic impact. "A French notebook."

"The one Miss Climpson handed Miss Dempsey?"

Sally looked at him sharply. "How would you know about that? You weren't there."

Blast. "Arabella—er, Miss Dempsey told me."

"Oh, Arabella, is it?" Turnip could feel the tips of his ears go red. "She couldn't have. You didn't see her yesterday. Remember?"

Sally looked at him speculatively. Turnip knew that look. Her wheels were turning. Turnip had to make them stop. He hastily steered his sister back to the main topic. "What about Miss Dempsey's room? What else was taken?"

"Nothing else. Only the notebook. Agnes thinks— Oh, bother."

"Angels!" Arabella was shooing winged creatures out of the audience into the wings. "Angels, backstage!"

"Miss Dempsey!" called Turnip. Well, bellowed, really.

Arabella jumped as though stung. "Yes?"

Not much encouragement there. Turnip smiled weakly. "Hello?"

"Hello to you too. Angels, this way!"

"Blast," muttered Turnip. Bloody angels.

Struck by a sudden qualm, Turnip glanced quickly at the ceiling. No, no lightning bolts. Thank goodness for that. That was the last thing he needed, to have God annoyed with him too.

This news about Arabella's room was damned—er, deuced (Turnip spared another glance for the ceiling) troubling. He remembered the notebook Sally was talking about. It had been on the floor of the drawing room during that melee the other night. He seemed to recall someone hitting someone with it. Or maybe Sally had thrown it? It had been very dark and hard to keep track of what everyone was flinging, bumping into, or tripping over.

He might not be the brightest loaf in the breadbox, but it didn't take the brains of a Newton to figure out that when a series of unusual events occurred one after another, they were most likely related.

It had seemed a lark, at first, playing follow-the-pudding, but this latest turn of events wasn't amusing at all. What if Arabella had been in the room when the intruder had intruded? What if it hadn't just been the notebook he was after?

Turnip didn't like it. He didn't like it at all.

Avoiding the games mistress, who hailed him cheerfully from the direction of the refreshment table, Turnip trotted along after Arabella as she emerged from herding her angels backstage.

"Miss Dempsey! Miss Dempsey? I wanted to—"

"Excuse me." Arabella brandished a book of pins. "One of the wise men just trod on her own hem. Must go fix it."

"—talk to you," Turnip finished weakly. "Blast."

There were other teachers in the school, weren't there? Surely Arabella could be spared for at least three minutes. Turnip looked around. In one corner of the room, Mlle de Fayette was coaching a group of deceptively angelic-looking younger girls through the refrain of "*Il est né, le divin enfant*" while the games mistress was dealing with the morris dancers.

Huh. Turnip had never seen female morris dancers before. They had strapped the bells to their slippers rather than their legs.

One of them landed heavily, squashing her bells. Turnip winced. That hadn't sounded good.

Signor Marconi, now wearing a new and even bushier mustache, was coaching three older girls in what looked like was meant to be an orchestra. Turnip had his suspicions about Signor Marconi. There was no doubt about it—his accent was as phony as his facial hair. Turnip had dallied with enough opera singers to know the difference between a real and a fake Italian accent when he heard one. Perhaps the Italian accent was meant to mask an accent of another sort entirely—a French one. What if it had been Marconi who had dropped that notebook?

In the meantime, the orchestra was beginning to make noises resembling music; Miss Climpson was beginning to herd people towards their seats; and the assorted angels, animals, and extras had mostly disappeared backstage.

Time was rapidly running out.

Turnip ran Arabella to ground in the prompting booth, a makeshift cubicle to the side of the equally makeshift stage. Screens set to two sides shielded the booth from the audience while leaving it open to both the stage and the wings. A lectern had been set up at the front of the booth, for the purpose of holding the script. Assorted props were scattered on the floor around the base of the lectern, as well as several sets of spare morris bells.

There wasn't room for two in the booth, but Turnip solved that problem by lifting the outer screen and moving it several inches to the left.

"That was my booth," protested Arabella.

"It still is your booth," said Turnip soothingly. "It's just slightly larger now. Sally told me your room was tossed."

She still looked mutinous, but she stopped protesting the invasion of her booth. "Sally talks a lot," she said warily.

"Can't argue with that."

Up close, he could see the signs of sleeplessness. Her hair was as neatly arranged as ever, her white collar and cuffs spotless, but there were purple circles under her eyes and the glimmer of humor that he had taken for granted as so much a part of her was entirely missing. There was something naked about her face without it. Unprotected. Vulnerable.

Turnip dropped his usual jovial pose. "Are you all right?"

"Fine. Perfect. Pardon me. I have to get the animals in order."

She wiggled out of the booth on the stage side.

Turnip followed along after her, past two disgruntled sheep and a camel that appeared to be conferring with its own hindquarters. Deuced strange beasts they had in Bethlehem.

What was this all about? This wasn't just about her room. If it were, she wouldn't be treating him as though he were a personal carrier of the Black Death. This was something else. Something personal.

Was she upset about his precipitous exit out the window the other night? Admittedly, *Mind the mustachios* wasn't the most tender of parting lines, he'd been aware of that at the time, but she had been the one flapping her hands at him, using the word "go."

Go generally meant go, unless this was one of those occasions where they—and by they, he meant the other half of the human race—were purported to say one thing but mean another.

"Are you upset because I climbed out the window? Thought you wanted me out the window. That's generally what *Please go now* tends to mean. Well, not the window, but the going bit. Could have taken the stairs, if that would have made you happier, but the trellis was right there."

"Shhhhh!" Arabella hissed furiously. She cast an anxious glance at the camel. "Not in front of the livestock."

She wiggled her way back into the booth.

Turnip wiggled in after her.

"Why won't you talk to me?"

"I am talking to you. See? My lips are moving. Talking, talking, talking." She shuffled the script, dropping half the pages in the process.

"I'll get those!" Turnip dove for the ground, nearly upsetting the screen, which rocked on its base.

"No. Don't. I'll—" Arabella drew in her breath with a hissing sound that Turnip didn't need to be told meant she wasn't precisely happy.

"Here you go." He propped himself up on one knee and offered the pages up to her again. "Not all quite in order, but all here."

There was a tap-tap-tap on top of the frame and the Angel of the Lord shone round about them. "Excuse me. In case you hadn't noticed, we're starting." Sally looked pointedly at Turnip, who was still down on one knee. "That is, if you're quite done with whatever it is you're doing down there?"

"Righty-ho." Turnip struggled up to his feet, trying not to topple over onto the screen. "Good luck. Break a leg—er, wing."

The Angel of the Lord gave him a look and disappeared again over the partition.

Turnip turned back to Arabella, who was very studiously paging through the script, her cheeks bright red beneath the tightly coiled loops of her hair.

"Didn't mean to upset you," he whispered. "Last thing I wanted to do."

"There's no need to discuss it," said Arabella in a low voice. She raised her voice, looking around. "Caesar? Has anyone seen Caesar Augustus? She's meant to be on."

There were the usual rustling sounds and hastily hushed whispers as the audience settled themselves in their seats. Miss Climpson mounted the makeshift steps to the stage, her spectacles reflecting the light of the candles so that they looked like carriage lamps. There were muffled giggles from backstage. Arabella held a finger to her lips and the giggles stopped.

"Friends, parents, neighbors," declaimed Miss Climpson, opening her arms wide.

"And Romans," muttered Turnip, pointing at Caesar Augustus. "Can't forget the Romans."

Arabella's head remained studiously bent over the script. Ha. Turnip wasn't fooled by that. He doubted Miss Climpson's welcome speech had been included in the playbook.

The headmistress clasped her hands together and beamed myopically out over the assemblage. "We thank you for joining us here today. We know some of you have traveled long distances—"

The headmistress babbled on. Turnip let the familiar words wash over him—she gave the same speech every Christmas; half the people in the room could have delivered it on her behalf without missing a single preposition—and directed his attention instead to Arabella, who was very studiously doing her best to pay no attention to him.

Turnip peered over her shoulder. The first part of the program was a dramatic reenactment of the Gospel according to Saint Luke, chapter two, verses one through fourteen, with additional dialogue by the staff of Miss Climpson's seminary.

Turnip tapped a finger against the page. The fact that he had to reach over her shoulder to do it was a bonus. His sleeve brushed the fabric of her dress, making her give a little jump.

"Think I've read that before," Turnip said. "Deuced good page-turner. Shepherds, wise men, mad emperors . . ."

"Augustus wasn't mad." Arabella was back to not looking at him. She addressed herself to the script in a monotone. "That was his—"

"Wife's great-grandson," Turnip provided. "Caligula. Means 'little boots.' He was the son of Augustus's wife Livia's grandson Germanicus. Livia was the one with the poisoned figs, don't you know. Shouldn't have wanted to dine at her house."

Well, that had gotten Arabella's attention. In a why-is-this-madman-babbling-at-me sort of way, but at least she was looking at him. Turnip wasn't picky. He'd take attention however he could get it.

"Nasty little nipper. Chip off the old family block. Caligula, I mean, not Germanicus. Wouldn't believe some of what he got up to." Turnip shook his head at the depravity of the Caesars. "Makes for good reading, though. Nothing like the odd orgy to get a chap learning Latin."

Arabella cast a quick, alarmed look at the rear end of the camel, which was listening with a little too much attention. "I don't think this is the time for orgies. Are you sure you wouldn't like to find a seat? Miss Climpson is just—"

There was a smattering of polite applause from the audience.

"—about to be done."

"If I sit down, will you talk to me after?"

Arabella frowned and held up one hand to signal him to wait. "Romans?" she called. "Romans? Onstage!"

The Roman Senate, consisting of five ten-year-old girls in togas, scrambled onto the stage.

"That's a no, isn't it?" whispered Turnip.

Caesar Augustus strutted onstage, laurel leaves tacked on with hairpins. "All the world shall be taxed!" she piped.

There was wild clapping from the audience, presumably from Caesar Augustus's parents. No one got that excited about taxes. Except, perhaps, Mr. Pitt, who had once tried to talk finance to Turnip during Turnip's short-lived career as Member of Parliament for Dunny-on-the-Wold.

Turnip made a mental note never again to pass out drunk in a rotten borough on the eve of an election, especially when the only other inhabitant of said borough was a dachshund named Colin. Next thing you knew, you were a Member of Parliament and Mr. Pitt was trying to talk finance to you. It hadn't been all bad. He had gotten some jolly good naps on the back benches. Nothing soothed one to sleep quite like twelve hours of unbroken oratory. Nice benches too. Soft. Padded.

Rather like Arabella.

He wasn't supposed to be thinking about Arabella's padding. Curves were also right out, despite the fact that the booth was very narrow and those curves were very much there, right next to him, pressed up against his side. He could feel her breast brush across his arm every time she reached out to turn a page.

The Romans might have known a few things about torture, but even Caligula at his most depraved could never have come up with this. He was watching a Nativity play, for the love of God. Turnip wasn't quite sure, but salacious imaginings during the virgin birth did seem the sort of thing to send a chap straight to brimstone.

Onstage, a very bashful Mary, who couldn't be more than twelve, was being tugged forward on a wooden donkey with wheels. Turnip did his best to stay quiet and quell lustful thoughts, but it was difficult with Arabella pressed up beside him, all warm and round and lilac-scented.

Turnip shifted uncomfortably. This was not helping. He took a deep breath and tried to concentrate on Joseph, who was currently haggling over the nightly rate of a manger. He had always felt more than a bit sorry for Joseph. Must be tough on a chap to get leg-shackled, only to find that your wife was expecting the child of God. Not that it wasn't an honor and all that, but it did rather cut down on the canoodling.

Turnip was very relieved when the manger was wheeled out and the shepherds came on. One couldn't whisper through the virgin birth, but shepherds abiding in the fields were fair game.

"*And, lo,*" proclaimed the narrator, shouting to be heard over the sheep, "*the glory of the Lord shone round about them. And they were sore afraid.*"

The farthest shepherd to the left gave her sheep a sharp crack with her crook as Sally appeared in all her feathery glory.

Ascending a very short ladder, Sally spread her wings and preened. The shepherds cowered before her.

Turnip regarded his sister fondly as she fluffed her feathers and graciously acknowledged the groveling shepherd people. Sally had a bit of Dowager Duchess of Dovedale in her. Not literally—as far as Turnip knew, the families weren't related—but in spirit.

Turnip made sure to clap loudly, as promised, before turning back to Arabella. "Won't you tell me what the matter is?" he whispered in her ear. "Why are you avoiding me?"

"Fear not! For behold—"

Arabella jerked her head away. "I'm not avoiding you. I am trying to prompt a performance."

"BEHOLD, I bring you—"

"Then why did you keep running off earlier?"

"For heaven's sake!" hissed the Angel of the Lord, appearing suddenly over the edge of the partition. "Can't you see I'm being angelic?"

"Wouldn't want to miss that," muttered Turnip.

He turned just in time to see Arabella smothering a grin.

"For behold . . . ," prompted Arabella, nodding to Sally.

Sally tossed her head. Taking leave of its pins, her halo soared out across the audience, like a discus at the Olympian Games. Children shrieked. Matrons ducked.

Arabella buried her head in her hands.

In the finest traditions of the theater, Sally drew herself up on her stepladder, ignored the wires sticking straight out of her head, and carried grandly on. *"For behold, I bring you good tidings of great joy . . ."*

"I need to talk to you," Turnip said urgently.

". . . which shall be to . . ." The Angel of the Lord raised her voice, ruffling her feathers in warning.

Turnip grabbed Arabella's hand. "Outside?" he urged.

". . . ALL PEOPLE! Except my brother."

"That wasn't in the script," objected a sheep.

A shepherd poked the sheep with her crook. Turnip caught a glimpse of bronzy curls beneath her headcloth. "Neither is a talking sheep."

"Miss Climpson!" whined the sheep.

"Oh, for heaven's sake," snapped the Angel of the Lord, snatching up the crook. "They didn't have Miss Climpsons in Judea. I've just brought you good news. Look happy."

"Wise men!" bellowed Arabella. "Wise men, onstage! Angels and shepherds, *off.*"

"Wait!" exclaimed Sally. "I haven't given my tidings yet. Down!"

The sheep cowered.

The shepherd held out a hand. "May I have my crook back?"

"No," said Sally. Turning back to the audience, she held the crook aloft. *"For unto you is born this day, in the city of David . . ."*

Turnip tugged at her hand. "Arabella?"

". . . a SAVIOR, which is Christ the Lord."

"All right," whispered Arabella, snatching her hand away. "All right."

"And this shall be a sign unto you . . ." Sally was rattling right along, determined to get through her piece without further interruptions.

"That was a yes, wasn't it?"

"Ye shall find the babe wrapped in swaddling clothes . . ."

"In the drawing room," muttered Arabella. "Ten minutes."

". . . and lying in a manger."

"I'll meet you there." Did she mean in ten minutes or for ten minutes? Turnip decided it was wiser not to ask. He'd figure it out as he went along.

"And suddenly, there was with the angel," Arabella prompted, and a chorus of auxiliary angels thudded heavy-footed onto the stage. A makeshift orchestra scraped out the first few bars of Handel's arrangement of "Glory to God" as the shepherds and sheep jostled their way offstage.

Even with all their interruptions, Turnip reassured himself, this performance was going better than last year's. Last year, the manger had collapsed in the first scene and wiped out the Friendly Beasts, three of whom had to be brought to the infirmary. Couldn't compete with that.

"Good will; good will; good will towards men," sang the chorus of angels.

Turnip looked at Arabella, but she wasn't looking at him. They would sort it all out in the drawing room. Hopefully she would have some goodwill for him.

Since she didn't seem to want to talk about personal matters, he would start with the pudding and lead up to the kiss. They could get all the serious bits out of the way, and then move on to the dramatic reenactments. As theatrical productions went, a kiss ought to be easier to stage than a Nativity scene. Fewer camels, for one thing. And no sheep.

Under cover of the hosannas, Turnip saluted Arabella and hopped out of the booth. All he had to do was get to the drawing room and everything else would follow from—

"Ooooph." Turnip caught his foot in a shepherd's crook and went spiraling over a camel, landing with a clang on a pile of discarded morris bells.

He blinked blearily up at a very small shepherd.

"Sorry," said Lizzy Reid.

Through the screen, he could see Arabella bury her head in her hands.

"Baaaa," said Turnip.

Chapter 16

Arabella resisted the overwhelming impulse to bang her head into the lectern. Hard.

Onstage, Handel's chorus had reached its final crescendo, although Arabella doubted that Handel would have wanted to lay claim to this particular rendition.

"Excellent job, beautifully played," she called out indiscriminately as the angels thudded past, trooping heavily off the stage. They beamed back at her, still angelic in their white robes and pasteboard halos.

Arabella could hear the rustling from the audience as parents and guests stirred in their seats, beginning to move and talk again, the more adventurous among them making their way to the refreshment table. Sally was still on her ladder, enjoying her place in the heavens too much to relinquish it quickly.

Ten minutes, she had told Turnip.

The Handel chorus had taken up at least five, maybe more. Turnip was probably already waiting in the drawing room. Alone. In the semi-darkness of a single candle.

Thinking about it, Arabella felt an entirely inappropriate tingle of anticipation.

Sally peered over the edge of the booth. "Where did Reggie go?"

Arabella mustered a very unconvincing shrug. "Oh, um, somewhere."

"Hmm," said Sally.

Were angels allowed to look that skeptical?

"He's probably gone to the refreshment table." Lies, lies, all lies. God was going to strike her down any moment now. "I'm just going to, er. Um."

Arabella fled the booth, leaving Sally perched on her ladder like a contemplative stork. If Miss Climpson wanted that ladder back, she was going to have to pry Sally down by force.

The room was thronged with a bizarre mixture of relatives, friends, and livestock. On the far side of the room, Arabella could see Margaret standing with the elder Austens. Jane and Cassandra were talking with Mlle de Fayette, while Lavinia appeared to have made the acquaintance of Lizzy Reid, who was still wearing her shepherd garb, the headdress tossed nonchalantly back over one shoulder.

Arabella had hoped that this would be a good time to introduce Lavinia and Olivia to both the school and Miss Climpson. Arabella looked at Lizzy and Lavinia. From the way Lizzy was gesticulating with her crook, Lavinia was certainly getting an introduction to the school. Lavinia looked absolutely fascinated.

Arabella rubbed her damp palms against the skirt of her dress. She was feeling as nervous as a schoolgirl, tense with a combination of anticipation and apprehension. She had never expected him to seek her out. Certainly not so assiduously. He might merely be doing the gentlemanly thing, apologizing in person, but he didn't have the air of a man about to recant a kiss, all dragging feet and shifting eyes.

Arabella had seen that before.

It had been three months ago, a chance kiss stolen in the dark corridor between the drawing room and the dining room. She had been giddy for days, all optimism and certainty—until he had avoided her at the Selwick musicale. And again at the Belliston ball. It wasn't until a dinner at her aunt's that he had deigned to speak to her of it. It had been a mistake, he had told her, all shifting eyes and dragging feet, an accident. His betrothal to her aunt had been announced that same night.

Mr. Fitzhugh's demeanor couldn't have been more dissimilar. He had seemed . . . well, happy to see her. Not as though he were trying to hide or pretend the kiss had never happened. There had been no dragging or shifting, none at all. Instead, he had made every effort to get as close to her as possible.

Which, in a small prompting booth, was very close indeed.

Taking deep, shallow breaths, Arabella hurried past the refreshment table, which had been set up along the back wall of the dining hall. She was nearly to the door when someone turned away from the table, directly into her path.

Arabella clapped a hand to her mouth in horror as a small mince pie went launching through the air. "Oh dear. I am sorry."

The Chevalier de la Tour d'Argent pressed his now-empty plate to his chest and bowed. "The lady who launched a thousand pies?"

"It lacks the cachet of ships," said Arabella, preparing to pass. "I *am* sorry."

"No. I am sorry. If I had known you had an aversion for pies, I would have flung something else in your path instead."

Arabella shook her head. "I wasn't watching where I was going."

The chevalier flashed his dimple at her. "One ends up in far more interesting places that way."

Arabella looked dubiously at the long board in front of them. "Like the refreshment table?"

The chevalier gave a particularly Gallic shrug, one that encompassed the inevitability of refreshment tables in the great scheme of the world. "Even so." Having resolved the great philosophical issues of life with three syllables and a shoulder wiggle, he turned the force of his considerable charm on Arabella. "Since you are here, perhaps you might settle a question for me."

"Yes?" Arabella let her skirts fall, since she obviously wasn't going anywhere quickly.

Arabella glanced as inconspicuously as possible over her shoulder. The hallway on the other side of the entry hall lay dark, but she thought she could see a tiny glimmer of light all the way at the end.

The chevalier held up another of Miss Climpson's miniature mince pies. "These . . . pies. Are they intended for eating?"

Arabella let out a surprised chuckle. "Intended, yes."

"But . . . ," prompted the chevalier.

"Miss Climpson is my employer and these are made to her own recipe. You really cannot expect me to say anything more."

The chevalier tapped the side of his nose. "Understood. Pity," he added, surveying the refreshment table. "I had hoped there would be pudding."

"Pudding?" Arabella looked at him sharply.

His attention on the table, the chevalier appeared not to notice. "Yes," he said mildly. "The English Christmas pudding is a source of endless fascination to me."

"It is? I mean, is it?"

For heaven's sake. There was no reason to get all twitchy just because he had said "pudding." It was a Christmas party. Discussion of Christmas pudding followed naturally, as the night did the day. Besides, there hadn't been any more pudding appearances since the one at Farley Castle, well over a week ago.

Mr. Fitzhugh would no doubt claim that was due to his vigilance in crouching outside the school. Arabella thought it more likely that whoever it was—presumably a student—had simply grown bored. Or come to the realization that puddings made a remarkably ineffective mode of communication.

The chevalier waxed philosophical. "It is not so much a foodstuff as it is a sort of icon. Think about it. You wish on it. You dress it up in muslin cloths. You adorn it with holly sprigs as if it were a pagan sacrifice."

"And then we eat it," said Arabella prosaically.

"I have heard rumors of such things," said the chevalier, "but I prefer not to believe them."

"Are you ever serious?" asked Arabella, in some exasperation.

"I try not to be," said the chevalier. "I hear it does terrible things to the complexion."

Behind him, Arabella could see a large figure lurking at the other end of the foyer. Shifting from one foot to the other, Turnip scanned the crowd. He put his whole body into the exercise, his entire torso moving as he turned his head first one way, then the other. He was, Arabella realized, looking for her.

Catching sight of her over the chevalier's shoulder, he started to raise a hand in greeting, but dropped it when he saw whom she was talking to. If she didn't know better, she would say he looked hurt.

Arabella broke into whatever it was that the chevalier had been saying. "Will you excuse me, Monsieur de la Tour d'Argent? I have an, er, sheep that needs grooming for the next act."

The chevalier bowed gallantly over her hand. "Fortunate sheep."

Turnip scowled at the chevalier's back. If he had been ten years younger, he would have put out his tongue at him.

"You wouldn't think so if you'd seen the shepherd," said Arabella. "And I hear fleece have fleas."

The chevalier seemed remarkably loath to relinquish her hand. "Not in the Petit Trianon. Nor, one imagines, in Bath."

"No. There are very few sheep in Bath," said Arabella, exerting some pressure to retrieve her hand. In the hallway, Turnip was growing restless. "Other than the sort in the manger scene."

Turnip shifted from one foot to the other, staring pointedly at the ceiling. There was a sprig of mistletoe dangling from the doorway above him.

"On the contrary," said the chevalier. "There are a great many sheep in Bath, but they tend to walk on two legs."

Arabella blinked at the chevalier. Why was he still talking? "Well, I really must be using mine," she said. "All two of them. It was, as always, lovely—"

The games mistress had spotted Turnip beneath the mistletoe. She moved forward. Turnip moved back, looking like an early Christian who had just spotted a very large lion with a taste for fresh martyr.

"Pardon me," said Arabella desperately. "I really must be going—"

"And so must I," the chevalier agreed. "A very good evening to you, Miss Dempsey."

"Happy Christmas!" Arabella called after him and rapidly looked about for Turnip.

There was no sign of him. He had either given up on her, gone straight to the drawing room, or been eaten by the games mistress. Arabella hoped it wasn't the latter. The mistletoe still dangled from the center of the door as Arabella passed under it. It looked rather forlorn up there, and slightly battered, as though someone had tried to knock it down and failed.

All the doors along the hallway were closed, in an attempt to keep the guests out of the schoolrooms. It didn't seem to have quite worked. She could hear amorous murmurs from the music room.

Someone had taken the mistletoe to heart.

At the very end of the hall, the door to the drawing room was very slightly ajar. Arabella pushed it the rest of the way open and stepped cautiously inside.

Aside from the absence of Miss Climpson's beloved china cupid, the drawing room had been restored to almost exactly its prior state after the antics of two nights ago. If one knew where to look, there were some new nicks on the legs of the chairs, and a scratch on the tabletop that hadn't been there before, but otherwise everything had been restored to its proper place. Even the drapes had been drawn demurely down.

Candles had been lit in the sconces to either side of the mantelpiece, but the room appeared to be empty.

He hadn't waited for her.

Arabella looked again at the drapes. They bulged suspiciously in the middle. And they seemed to have sprouted a leg. She knew that leg. It was clad in very tight-knit pantaloons and a very shiny Hessian boot.

"Mr. Fitzhugh?"

As she watched, the drapes underwent a series of odd contortions. After a few moments' battle, Mr. Fitzhugh emerged triumphant. He flung the white linen away from his face.

"I'm sorry I kept you waiting," Arabella said.

"You should be!" Turnip levered himself off the windowsill, shaking off the last of the drapes where the fabric still clung to his shoulder. "That Miss Quigley is an animal! Didn't think I'd make it out of there with my lips intact."

He shuddered dramatically, scrubbing a hand across his mouth.

"Sorry," Arabella repeated.

His hair was sticking up from his tussle with the curtain. Arabella could remember what it felt like beneath her fingers, the softness of the longer hair on top, the prickle of the shorter hairs at the back of his neck.

Turnip stepped closer, sending the light from the nearer candle falling across his face like a beatification. "Are you all right?"

He cocked his head in inquiry, and Arabella remembered what it felt like to be held against him, the warmth and solidity of him, the comfort of his shoulder beneath her cheek.

It would be so easy to cross the old blue carpet, lean her head against his chest, and burrow into that absurdly embroidered waistcoat.

Arabella held herself very straight. "Yes. Fine."

Turnip peered at her with concern. "You don't look fine."

Just because her stomach was hosting a whole colony of butterflies? "Thank you."

"Didn't mean it that way. What I meant was—well, never mind."

"No, I know what you meant, really." Arabella twisted her fingers together, trying not to sound too breathlessly eager. "You wanted to talk to me?"

"Er, yes. I did."

Ducking his head, he paced a few steps forward, narrowly missing the table that had formerly held the china cupid. He looked up at her, shaking his hair out of his face as he searched for words. He looked so painfully awkward and earnest that Arabella's heart clenched.

Turnip looked away, looked at her again, rubbed his hand together, and then tilted his head back to stare at the ceiling. "Er, yes. I did want to talk to you. I wanted to talk to you about—"

Arabella dropped her eyes, staring at the pattern of lozenges on the carpet.

The kiss.

"—that pudding."

Chapter 17

Arabella's head snapped up.

What?

In the meantime, Turnip blithered blithely on. "Think that pudding might be related to what happened to your room. Too much of a coincidence otherwise. Deuced strange goings-on and whatnot."

"You made a scene in the middle of the virgin birth because you wanted to talk to me about puddings."

"It wasn't the middle of the virgin birth," said Turnip, looking virtuous. "I waited until the shepherds."

"Naturally," said Arabella. Because that made such a difference.

"Sally told me about the notebook that was taken. Said it was in French."

"French exercises," Arabella corrected. "French exercises." Presumably written by an English student. In the process of learning French.

Turnip nodded in agreement, although agreement with what, Arabella wasn't quite sure. "Cunning, ain't it?" he said admiringly. "Who would think anything of a notebook full of French exercises?"

"The French mistress who has to mark them?"

"But that was just the thing!" said Turnip triumphantly. "What if the marks weren't marks, but replies? Sitting on the windowsill like that, anyone could reach out from the outside and take it down, read it, reply, and put it back."

"In plain sight of the gardener, the games mistress, and at least a dozen bedroom windows?"

Turnip ignored her and carried blithely on. "Might have been a sort of code. Really quite brilliant when you think about it—people put all sorts of ridiculous things into school exercises, all that rot about borrowing the plume of one's aunt's sister's second cousin twice removed . . ."

Arabella listened to him go on about his inventive and entirely imaginary scheme for smuggling information and felt her fingers clench tighter and tighter into fists at her side. This was why he had shouldered his way into the prompting booth with her? This was why she had risked discovery and disgrace to meet with him in private? So he could talk about imaginary spies?

Clearly, their kiss had been entirely beside the point for him, just one of those little things that happened in between climbing trellises and lying in wait for puddings, nothing to remark upon and certainly nothing worth remembering a whole long two days later. He'd probably forgotten all about it by now.

All that was merely incidental to the more pressing issue of how spies meant to convey information at an all-girls' academy that was obviously the center of espionage for the entire British Empire—no, Arabella corrected herself recklessly, the world. Bonaparte was probably, at this very moment, making plans to produce reams of student notebooks, written in bad schoolgirl French, purely for the purpose of infiltrating Miss Climpson's Select Seminary for Young Ladies. It made perfect sense, thought Arabella flippantly. He must want her recipe for miniature mince pies. Then he could get all the pastry chefs in France to band together to produce them in bulk and deploy them as a weapon of mass destruction against the combined forces of the Allied Army, which would fall into disarray and defeat, their jaws glued together with mismade mince.

Now, *that* was a brilliant plan. Maybe she should suggest it.

". . . could use vocabulary charts as the decoding key. Don't you see? Then . . ."

Arabella could see Turnip's lips moving and his hands rising and falling as he gesticulated, but the words themselves were entirely drowned out by the angry roaring in her ears.

"There are no spies."

Turnip took a step back under the force of her statement. "Pardon?"

"Read my lips." Turnip obediently looked at her lips. Arabella enunciated very carefully. "There are no spies. There are a series of schoolgirl pranks and a mildly mad music master with poor taste in facial hair. But there are NO SPIES."

Turnip rubbed his ear. "Didn't need to read your lips for that. They could hear you in France."

"Good," said Arabella viciously. "I am sick unto death of spies. Your sister and her friends are all spy mad. I don't know why they can't swoon over Drury Lane actors like normal sixteen-year-olds."

Turnip looked at her with interest. "Did you swoon over Drury Lane actors?"

Kemble had been lovely in his tights. She had kissed her copy of *A Midsummer Night's Dream* before going to bed every night for an entire month.

There were some truly gemlike lines in that particular play. But there was one line above all that stood out as particularly apt to the occasion: *Lord, what fools these mortals be.*

Of the two of them, she wasn't sure who was the greater fool, she or Turnip. It was a close-run contest.

"That," said Arabella stiffly, "is beside the point."

"I can understand," Turnip said, very carefully, the way one might to a peppery maiden aunt or a child prone to tantrums, "how this can all be a bit unnerving if you're not accustomed to the idea. . . ."

"I see no need to grow accustomed to the idea," Arabella said through gritted teeth.

"Felt that way myself until I met my first French spy," expounded Turnip avuncularly. "Deuced unsettling experience, that."

"What did he do?" asked Arabella acidly. "Ask you to conjugate irregular verbs?"

"She, actually," said Turnip mildly. "And she pointed a gun at me. Thought I was the Pink Carnation."

"Oh." That took the wind out of her sails.

Turnip followed up his advantage. "Someone might have hurt you, tearing up your room like that. Sally said the mattress was slashed. What if you'd been there at the time?"

"Then I imagine they would have gone away again."

"What if they had come at night?" Folding his arms across his chest, he leaned against the window frame, looking intently at Arabella. "What if you were sleeping?"

It was a more unsettling image than she cared to admit. She could picture her room, entirely dark except for the faint illumination of the moon. She had always been a heavy sleeper. The room wasn't large. It would take only a moment for someone to climb from the desk to the bed. And once there . . .

Arabella shrugged. "I doubt they would have bothered. Not everyone has your penchant for trellis-climbing."

Turnip slowly uncrossed his arms. Straightening from his recumbent position against the window frame, his eyes locked with Arabella's. "That depends on what's at the top of the trellis."

Arabella could feel color flare in her cheeks. For a very long while, they just looked at each other, and she knew he was remembering, as she was, exactly what had happened at the top of the trellis the other night.

Arabella looked away first. She licked her lips, which felt uncomfortably dry. "This is a ridiculous discussion. There is no point to it. Even if there were dangerous spies who for some obscure reason wanted a commonplace notebook full of French exercises, they have what they came for. There's no need for them to bother me again. I'm perfectly happy to leave them alone if they leave me alone."

"What if they don't? What if they think you know something?"

"What? The recipe for the perfect pudding?" Arabella sat down heavily on a blue silk upholstered chair.

It would be easier to stay annoyed with him if he didn't seem so genuinely concerned for her safety. Even if he was being absurd. She felt, suddenly, very tired. She had been on edge all day, the knowledge that she would see Turnip fizzing through her veins, distracting her from her work, making her hands tremble as she pinned hems and put up scenery. She had spent hours rehearsing and revising hypothetical conversations. In some of them, he had been apologetic and she had been gracious; in others, he had been noble and she had been humble. All of her imaginary conversations had one thing in common: In none of them had anyone said anything about spies.

She knew it was foolish, but Arabella felt distinctly let down. So much for her brief career as a romantic heroine. She had been upstaged by a notebook full of amateur French exercises.

Two worried lines indented the skin between Turnip's brows, and there were lines on either side of his lips that had no place on his good-humored face. He leaned over her, planting a hand on either arm of the chair, his fingers digging into the pale blue silk upholstery, and Arabella tried not to think of how those fingers had felt in her hair two nights before, or how much like an embrace it seemed.

His mind, at least, was not on dalliance. "It isn't funny," he said, leaning so far forward that she could smell the cloves on his breath and see the tiny gold hairs in his skin. "You could be in danger."

Arabella looked down and away, staring at the gray fabric of her skirt. There were lines in the twill if one looked closely enough. It was an ugly fabric, heavy and serviceable. Not the sort of thing a Turnip Fitzhugh would ever encounter, but highly appropriate for what she was: a schoolmistress.

"The only thing I am in danger of is losing my position."

As she said it, she knew it was true. Miss Climpson might be an indulgent—one might even say an absentminded—employer, but she could not possibly condone her instructresses cavorting in darkened rooms with the older brothers of students. It set a bad tone, especially in an institution where one of the students had already been caught in similar behavior. A schoolmistress at an academy for young ladies had to be like Caesar's wife, above reproach.

Arabella might, just might, manage to pass their current tête-à-tête off as a consultation between a teacher and a concerned brother—it was a drawing room, after all, and there were candles lit—but their interlude in her bedroom the other night was completely indefensible, by any standard. She ought to have sent him packing the moment she saw him sitting there on her desk. No, more than that. She should have slammed the window when she saw him lurking outside the drawing room.

But she hadn't. She hadn't because she had wanted to see him, because she had been happy to see him, because she had been prepared to ignore all the potential ramifications in exchange for the immediate pleasure of his company, for that ridiculous, face-splitting grin and the absurd and unpredictable things he said and the way he looked at her, really looked at her, not as an adjunct or an addendum or another girl against the ballroom wall, but as if he saw her, Arabella.

And for that, she had been willing to play blind and deaf and dumb to potential disgrace and the failure of all her plans.

Lord, what fools these mortals be.

Arabella shoved her chair abruptly back, retreating towards the fireplace. "This is folly," she said to the mirror over the mantel. "We can't go on doing this."

Turnip followed along behind her. "Doing what?"

He was so close that their noses nearly collided when she turned. Arabella took a few prudent steps back. "Meeting. Together. Alone. People will start to talk."

Turnip's face cleared. "Is that all?"

"All?" It seemed like rather a lot to her.

He looked at her earnestly, his blue eyes searching her face. "I don't mind if they do talk. Do you?"

Arabella frowned at him. Didn't he realize what that meant? That if they were caught together, there would be expectations, consequences?

Then realization hit. No one would expect him to make good for a schoolteacher, a woman of no money and undistinguished family. A woman whose aunt had titillated the *ton* by running off with a man half her age. Bad blood, they would all say. She would be used goods.

And Turnip could go back to kissing Penelope Deveraux on balconies off ballrooms.

"Yes!" Arabella's fingernails cut into her palms. "I do mind."

Turnip blinked at her. He looked . . . hurt? "Oh."

Arabella pushed away from the mantelpiece, her ugly skirts heavy against her legs. She thought of Margaret and the little sisters she had left. She thought of Aunt Osborne and all the years of being quiet and good. "It's all right for you to play at spy-catching," she said, all in a rush. "It doesn't matter where you go or who you're seen with. You'll always have a home to go back to. You don't have to worry about what people think or getting your own living. I don't have that luxury."

"Arabella?"

She nearly weakened at the sound of her name on his lips. Whatever else one said about Turnip Fitzhugh, he had a beautiful voice, rich and deep. It turned her name into a thing of beauty, a jewel in a velvet case. He followed her, looking so confused that it made Arabella's chest ache. She didn't like herself very much right then. But she knew she was right.

"I don't understand."

Arabella gave a wild laugh. "I didn't expect you would."

Turnip looked at her expectantly.

"I am a woman and I am poor." Saying it out loud was harder than she had thought it would be. The words came out raw and harsh, like freshly hewn granite. "Two things entirely out of your experience."

"What does that have to do with anything?"

He meant it too. He really had no idea. Arabella looked at him, at the richly embroidered brocade of his waistcoat, the gold fobs jangling from his watch chain, the boots from Hoby, the coat from Weston, the large cameo embedded in the folds of his cravat.

The waistcoat alone probably cost something akin to her father's annual income, an income expected to house, feed, and clothe four people. Five, if Arabella found herself forced to leave Miss Climpson's.

"I am an employee at your sister's school. I don't have the liberties you have. If we go on like this, I'll only end by getting sacked."

"I didn't mean—"

"It doesn't matter what you mean or didn't mean. And it wasn't entirely your fault." One didn't blame a puppy for chasing after sticks. The fault was with the person throwing the sticks. "I should have known better."

Turnip followed along after her. "I never wanted to make trouble for you. What can I do? How can I help you?"

Arabella moved sharply out of the way of his outstretched hand. "You can help me by staying away."

Turnip stood rooted in front of the mantelpiece, staring at her with a puzzled little frown between his eyes. "You don't really mean that. Do you?"

No, she wanted to say.

"I wouldn't say it if I didn't."

Turnip looked as though she had slapped him. He stared at her, hurt, uncomprehending.

Arabella folded her arms protectively across her chest. "My life was perfectly rational until you came into it. There was no nonsense about puddings and spies. I didn't go lurking around in the dark with strange men or . . . or . . ." She looked away. "Well, you know. The rest of it."

He was still staring at her, as though seeing her for the first time. She didn't want him to look at her like that. She had much preferred the way he had looked at her before. But that had been the very thing she had been complaining about, so how could she complain if he didn't? She made no sense, even to herself.

"Beg pardon," he said stiffly. "Swept away by circumstances and all that. Shouldn't have forced myself on you."

He hadn't, and they both knew it. That just made it worse. He might have kissed her first, but she had been an enthusiastic participant in everything that had followed. And she knew, with humiliating certainty, that if he had made any sort of gesture, showed any inclination in that direction, she would have done so again.

Fortunate for her that he hadn't.

"Under the circumstances," said Arabella, in a voice she hardly recognized as her own, "I think it best our acquaintance be at an end."

"If that is what you want."

"It isn't a question of want." She sounded so priggish that it hurt to listen to herself. "It's a question of conventions. And circumstances."

"Can't argue with circumstances, can one?" He smiled a lopsided smile without any humor in it.

It hurt to look at it.

Arabella's mouth ached with the need to say something, to protest, to argue, to soften the blow, but she couldn't seem to force any words past the large lump that seemed to have formed at the back of her throat.

Instead, she just nodded, a surprisingly tentative motion of her chin.

"I'll leave first." Mr. Fitzhugh—he was Mr. Fitzhugh now, she reminded herself, not Turnip anymore, never Turnip. Mr. Fitzhugh looked at her for a moment, all the light gone from his eyes. She had never seen him like that before. She hadn't imagined he could look so . . . blank. So remote. "Wouldn't want to cause you further bother."

"I—"

But it was too late. The click of his boots against the floor drowned out her feeble attempt at articulation. For a moment, he checked in the doorway, and Arabella thought he might say something else.

The door swung shut, and he was gone.

Arabella waited five minutes before following after him. Staggering their departures had been a surprisingly sensible suggestion on his part.

Why should she be surprised? Arabella leaned an elbow against the mantel, rubbing her face with her hand. So far, of the two of them, it was a toss-up as to who had shown the least sense. It was very easy, she thought, to criticize the actions of others, to upbraid them for folly, and very different when one found oneself in unpredictable circumstances, behaving in ways one would never have imagined of oneself.

Well, she had quite effectively put an end to all that.

The second hand on the mantel clock jerked stiffly up towards the center. One more minute and she could go. She tried to wipe away the image of Mr. Fitzhugh's face, hurt and confused, his hand extended to her, palm up.

She would introduce Lavinia to Miss Climpson, she told herself brightly, pushing open the drawing room door. This would be an excellent time to broach the topic of waiving Lavinia and Olivia's school fees, while the headmistress was still flushed with Christmas feeling and lightly spiked punch. She would introduce Lavinia and laugh over the performance with Jane and forget that there was such a person as Turnip Fitzhugh in the world.

Arabella paused as she passed the door of the music room. Unlike the other doors in the hall, it was open.

She was about to turn, to close it, when someone jumped out from behind the door. She had only a confused impression of the edge of a white robe, like the innumerable white robes she had sewn for the shepherds and the angels and the wise men, before someone grabbed her from behind, hard enough to knock the air out of her.

Arabella staggered, gasping for breath. She tried to push away, but her assailant was too strong for her. Pinning her arms behind her back, he dragged her backwards into the dark of the music room, her heels skidding against the polished wood of the floor as she struggled for some sort of purchase.

Silver flashed in front of her as something narrow and hard was applied to her throat.

"Where is it?" a muffled voice rasped. "What did you do with it?"

Chapter 18

Turnip blundered down the hallway. He felt the way he had, some years ago, when he had taken a tumble out of his tree house and landed on his head. The fingers the doctor had held up in front of Turnip's eyes had blurred and twisted just as the ranks of doorframes to either side of him were doing now.

What had he done?

One minute, she was clinging to his neck; the next she was acting as though he were a Mongol horde who had just personally ravished her village. All he had tried to do was express a concern for her safety, and what had she done? Ripped at him like a whole flock full of harpies.

Why was it suddenly best that their acquaintance be at an end? And all that about her reputation and being a woman and poor and his just not understanding. She was right about one thing: He didn't understand.

Well, fine. He might take a while to get the message, but let no one say that he didn't get it eventually. If she wanted him gone, he would go. If she had any intruders that needed dealing with, she could jolly well deal with them herself.

Not that he wouldn't help her if she came running to him. Turnip contemplated the highly pleasing image of Arabella, in disarray, her hair all down around her back, flinging her arms around his neck, murmuring that she had been wrong, all wrong, and needed him desperately.

Needed him desperately? The image disappeared with a pop. Arabella was about as likely to say that as he was . . . well, as he was to take tea with Bonaparte. And her voice had come out at least an octave too high. She would more likely say something sarcastic and try to deal with it all herself.

"Mr. Fitzhugh," someone said warmly, and Turnip made a manly effort not to jump out of his own skin.

"How nice to see you again," said the woman who had come with them to Farley Castle.

Miss Anselm? No. Arden? Not that either.

"Nice to see you again too, Miss, er . . ."

Arabella's friend tilted her head up at him. She afforded him a long, speculative glance that made Turnip feel a bit like a butterfly on a botanist's table. Turnip tugged at his cravat. "Austen. Miss Dempsey and I were neighbors in our youth."

Turnip felt like the worst kind of a heel. He had only spent several hours in an open carriage with her, after all. "Didn't mean— That is to say—"

"It's quite all right," said Miss Austen. She smiled up at him, her eyes bright with amusement. "I had the advantage of you and used it shamelessly. You appeared to be in a bit of a brown study."

Or just the study, the one down the hall. "Oh, no, nothing like that," said Turnip too jovially. "Just musing about the Nativity. Bethlehem. All that sort of thing."

Miss Austen raised her brows, but forbore to comment. "Will you be celebrating the Christmas season in Bath, Mr. Fitzhugh?"

"Me? No. Just here to fetch m'sister, Sally, and then I'm off to Girdings House."

"Girdings House?" Miss Austen seemed rather struck by the news. Turnip supposed it made sense, one of the great houses of England, and all that.

"Yes, in Norfolk."

Miss Austen regarded him thoughtfully, but all she said was, "That is the principal seat of the Duke of Dovedale, is it not?"

"Never actually met Dovedale—he's been away for dogs' years— but the Dowager Duchess of Dovedale is hosting a big thingummy."

"A house party?" Miss Austen provided for him.

Turnip nodded energetically. "Yes, that's the word."

One of the other chaps had referred to it as a "private showing." It was the Dowager Duchess of Dovedale's last-ditch attempt to shift her granddaughter before the new year. Lady Charlotte had been on the market for three years now, with no significant success. Sweet-natured soul, Lady Charlotte, but not the sort who showed to good advantage in a crowd. Quiet.

If he had ever thought about her, that was how he would have described Arabella two months ago, just another of those girls on the edge of the ballroom. Quiet, shy, unremarkable.

Just went to show what he knew.

It took him a moment to realize that Miss Austen was looking at him as though expecting him to say something and that her lips were no longer moving.

Turnip blinked at her. "Sorry. Pardon. What was that?"

"What will you do there?" Miss Austen repeated patiently.

"Oh, you know. The usual sorts of things." Drinking and dicing with the chaps, dancing and party games with the ladies. "Christmas things."

"We used to have splendid Christmases back in Steventon," said Miss Austen. "My family and the Dempseys."

"Steventon?"

"It is a small town in Hertfordshire. Mr. Dempsey's parish was not far away."

"Mr. Dempsey is a vicar?"

He hadn't known that.

He hadn't thought to ask. He had just assumed that Arabella was like everyone else. And by everyone else, he meant everyone else at Almack's Assembly Rooms, the comfortable scion of landed interests.

Turnip could see Arabella as a vicar's daughter, taking soup to the poor and organizing the local sewing circle. She had that sort of look to her. Sensible. Capable. But one didn't generally find vicars' daughters at balls in London. It had something to do with matters of finance. Vicars seldom amassed enough in the way of worldly goods to keep a debutante in gloves and fans.

"Mr. Dempsey used to be a vicar." Miss Austen looked briefly away. "Unfortunately, for some time now, his poor health has kept him from following his calling."

If vicars tended not to be too plush in the pocket, what happened to vicars without a vicarage?

I am a woman and I am poor, Arabella had said.

It occurred to him, belatedly, that the address at which he had fetched her for their excursion to Farley Castle had not been a fashionable one.

"How did Miss Dempsey come to be in London?" Turnip asked tentatively, not wanting to pry, but needing to know all the same.

"Her aunt took her in as a companion after her mother died," said Miss Austen, seeming to see nothing wrong with the question. "But her aunt is recently remarried, so we have the great pleasure of having Arabella returned to us."

Despite the pretty phrasing, the meaning was quite clear. "Her aunt didn't adopt her, then?"

"No. She only borrowed her awhile." Turnip had the feeling that Miss Austen didn't think much of Arabella's aunt. Neither did he.

Turnip looked around at Miss Climpson's dining hall, at the costumed girls and the platters of miniature mince pies. He hadn't thought about that, either—about why a young lady of means would suddenly choose to abandon the social whirl to direct Nativity plays at a young ladies' academy. With a sense of shame, he remembered teasing her about it.

"Is that why—?"

He had the feeling Miss Austen knew perfectly well what he meant, but she affected confusion. "Why?"

"Why she chose to teach?"

Miss Austen smiled blandly. "Miss Dempsey has a great commitment to the education of young minds." She looked directly at Turnip. "And there is some hope that Miss Climpson will be kind enough to waive the usual school fees for Arabella's younger sisters."

"Oh," said Turnip. School fees. He supposed Sally had them, but paying them had never been in question. It wasn't when one had thirty thousand pounds a year. "But not if she loses her position."

"No," said Miss Austen gently, "not if she loses her position. Mince pie?"

Turnip took the pie. It tasted a lot like penance and a very little like pie.

❧

ARABELLA TASTED FEAR. It rose like bile as the silver sword pressed against what she was fairly sure was an essential part of her neck.

"Where is it?" her captor demanded.

"Where is what?" Her voice came out as a mere thread of sound as she tried to speak without moving her throat.

There would be no use in screaming. The door to the music room was closed and the din created by the assorted guests in the dining hall would drown out any fragment of sound that did manage to scrape through. Any help was too far away, well down the hall. The sword was at her throat. It would be an unequal contest. She was on her own.

The hand holding her wrists twisted, hard. Arabella did her best not to flinch. Flinching would bring the blade closer to her throat. "You know what."

"No, I don't, really."

She could feel the clammy moisture coating her brow and the droplets of sweat beginning to form beneath her arms. It was cold in the music room, cold and dark. The shrouded forms of instruments hulked against the sides of the room like the funeral monuments in the chantry of Farley Castle.

What a wonderful sort of absurdity, if, after all that, Turnip Fitzhugh had been right. Arabella wondered where he was now. Mingling with the other guests? Scarfing down miniature mince pies? Sticking pins into a picture of her?

Something that was half laugh, half sob caught in her throat. All those nights lurking outside the school, popping up outside the drawing room window, climbing up her trellis, and now, just when she had ordered him away, would be the moment she actually needed him.

If there was some divinity that shaped man's ends, it did have a truly malicious sense of humor.

The sword pressed closer to her throat. Arabella could see her captor's knuckles white against the hilt. There was a ring on one finger, set with a single, large stone that glimmered wetly in the dark, the lack of light leeching it of color. It looked black as a sinner's soul. "What did you do with it?"

"With what?"

The sword was curiously curved, fitting around her throat like a collar. Arabella could have done without such adornments. "The list."

"List?" Arabella squinted down at her neck. It wasn't a sword but a scimitar.

"The list," he repeated, pressing with his scimitar.

Who in heaven's name carried a scimitar? Turkish pashas, maybe, but Arabella doubted that she was being held at scimitar point by a Turkish pasha. There were no Turkish pashas in Bath, at least that she knew of. If there were, she imagined they'd have better things to do than run around ladies' academies accosting junior instructresses.

But there were wise men.

Three of them, in fact. In addition to the usual load of gold, frankincense, and myrrh, they also carried swords. Long, curvy, silver swords, fashioned out of several layers of stiffened paper.

The panic that had held Arabella in its grip dropped away as the reality of the situation dawned upon her in all of its full absurdity. She was being held hostage with a paper sword.

"I need the list," he rasped, jabbing her in the jugular with the now-palpably pasteboard scimitar. Now that she was looking, she could even see that it was bent a bit about the edges.

So much for spies.

Now that she no longer feared for her life, Arabella found herself growing angry. Someone—and she presumed it was the same someone who had ransacked her room—must have bribed an older brother or a cousin or some other variety of male relation to come in and give her a scare. Sally had warned her that new instructresses were fair game for pranks, but Arabella had always assumed it would be something along the lines of toads in the bed, not ripped mattresses and being held in a corridor with a paper sword and menaced with vague threats about missing papers.

List, indeed. Pure nonsense. He might at least have come up with a better line. And a better sword.

"Did you know that your sword is pasteboard?" Arabella asked conversationally.

Her assailant went very still. "No, it's not."

Arabella wriggled, trying to pull her wrists away. The paper sword bumped harmlessly against her chin. "Yes, it is."

"How would you know?" her captor demanded breathlessly, trying to keep his hold on her wrists.

"I was the one who made it."

"Oh."

"You could say that," said Arabella acerbically, and stomped down, hard, on his foot.

He was wearing boots and she was wearing slippers, so the effect wasn't all that she had hoped it would be, but he did make a very gratifying yelping noise. More important, he dropped her hands.

Pins and needles tingled in her wrists as blood rushed back through her extremities.

She barely had time to wring them out before something slammed into her back, sending her sprawling forward. As she fell heavily to her knees, her palms scraping painfully against the carpet, Arabella heard the rasp of the door being yanked open, followed by the resounding reverberation of the wood slamming heavily into its frame.

Arabella stumbled clumsily to her feet, tripping on her own skirts.

"Stop! Wait!"

Wrenching open the door, she skidded out into the hallway.

The corridor was empty.

At least, it was mostly empty. There was something shiny lying on the ground not far from the music room door. Arabella didn't need to stoop down to examine it to know what it was. One pasteboard scimitar with a hilt set with imitation jewels.

A few yards farther along, a pile of fabric showed pale against the baseboards. Arabella lifted it with two fingers, holding it in front of her like three-day-old fish. One wise man's robe.

She opened her fingers, letting the fabric slither to the floor at her feet. Her assailant must have yanked it off while she was still trying to untangle her legs from her blasted skirt and then strolled blithely back into the throng of spectators in the dining hall.

There was no way of determining whose robe it was; she had hemmed dozens of the blasted things, making some over from last year's, sewing others from scratch. The school was positively littered with the garments. Anyone could have taken one. She couldn't even identify her attacker by voice. Whoever it was had taken care to wrap cloth around his face, muffling his voice. The only thing she was fairly sure of was that her attacker had been male.

Arabella paused in the foyer, beneath the battered piece of mistletoe she had passed what felt like a lifetime ago, and looked across the entryway into the dining hall. Miss Climpson's students appeared to possess an inordinately large number of brothers, fathers, uncles, and male cousins.

Among them, she spotted Signor Marconi, who appeared to be even more than usually rumpled. He was in possession of both of his mustachios this time, but his hair was tousled and his cravat askew.

Arabella's eyes narrowed on the music master. For all the absurdity of the fake mustaches, he was younger than he tried to appear, not more than a few years older than she was, at a guess. He had participated in all the rehearsals, so he knew about the wise men's robes and the paper scimitars.

There had been no attacks on her room or her person until she had interrupted Signor Marconi in his midnight wanderings around the school.

As she stared at the music master, something else clicked into place. The music room. The attack had taken place in the music room. It wasn't exactly conclusive evidence, but it certainly militated in that direction. Either the music master thought she had seen something he wanted hidden or he was simply holding a grudge for the fact that she had caused the loss of his favorite set of mustachios.

What a tempest in a teapot it had all turned out to be.

When she told Turnip—

Arabella came up short, feeling a bit as though she had run flat into a wall without seeing it coming. She wasn't going to tell Turnip Fitzhugh about this or about anything.

It was a surprisingly lonely feeling.

She would find Jane. She would find Jane, and eat some disgusting mince pie, and plot the revenge she planned to take on Signor Marconi. Perhaps she might even confront Signor Marconi and make him squirm a bit. Arabella flexed her wrists. There were red marks in her skin that would undoubtedly darken to a lovely purple-yellow by morning. Or she could make him squirm a lot.

Rubbing her sore wrists, Arabella set off into the dining hall in search of Jane. Being so diminutive, Jane was always a bother to spot in a crowd, although less so here than usual, with all the short schoolgirls lowering the general height ratio. Arabella finally located her standing near the refreshment table.

Jane was talking to a tall man, a tall man with hair as gold as a wise man's gift and a coat made of crimson cloth that would have looked absurd on anyone else. Arabella stared at them and wished herself back in that corridor with a paper scimitar against her throat. Or in her bed with the covers pulled up over her head.

As she stood there, he looked up. His eyes briefly met hers.

And he looked away.

He looked away as though he had never seen her before and never cared to again. He turned and said something to Jane. Arabella couldn't hear what it was, but it had to be a farewell of some sort, because he was bowing, and moving away, with a celerity that would have been unflattering under any circumstances and was even more so now, because she knew she had brought it on herself.

Arabella wove her way through the crowd of parents and friends to Jane. By the time she reached her, there was no sign of a broadshouldered blond man with poor taste in cravats.

"Was that Mr. Fitzhugh with you?" asked Arabella without preamble.

"Were you looking for him?" asked Jane innocently.

"No," Arabella snapped.

Jane raised an eyebrow.

"What I mean is"—Arabella tried not to follow him through the crowd with her eyes—"I was looking for you."

"How flattering," said Jane, and Arabella let herself hope that would be the end of it, until, "I like your Mr. Fitzhugh."

"Good. You can have him."

"Arabella?"

Arabella pressed her hands to her face. "I am sorry. It has been an exceedingly long evening."

She had meant to tell Jane about Signor Marconi and the attack of the anonymous wise man, but now that she was here, she didn't know how to begin. It all sounded absurd. The only one sure to believe her was Turnip.

The same Turnip whom she had just told to go away and never come back.

Arabella looked up to find Jane looking at her speculatively. "You are still going to Girdings House for Christmas, aren't you?"

"Yes, with my aunt Osborne." At one point, the thought of spending Christmas with Aunt Osborne and her new husband had filled her with trepidation. Now Arabella found it hard to work up the necessary sense of dread. Being held at scimitar-point could do that to one. "Why?"

"No reason." Jane examined a plate of miniature mince pies. "No reason at all."

Chapter 19

The Dowager Duchess of Dovedale had instructed her guests to arrive at Girdings House by noon on the day before Christmas, but not even the Dowager Duchess of Dovedale could control every axle on every wheel on every carriage in the kingdom.

It was full dark by the time Arabella arrived. After seven long days on the road, Arabella felt nothing but numb, from the blue tips of her toes straight through the mud that had somehow gotten in her hair. Her emotions were as frozen as her fingers.

The events at Miss Climpson's seminary already seemed a world away. The idea that she might have kissed Turnip Fitzhugh or chased with him after a pudding through the grounds of Farley Castle was, quite frankly, ludicrous. She was back to her old life again, back to being that quiet Miss Dempsey who was invited to fill out a table, then shuffled off to the side of the room as quickly as possible.

There was no one from the ducal family to greet Arabella and her maid when they arrived at Girdings House. Arabella hadn't expected there would be. Poor relations seldom got the full ducal treatment.

They were informed that the rest of the party were already out in the grounds, collecting holly and ivy with which to deck the halls. A footman, resplendent in the Dovedale livery of green and gold, showed them up a grand staircase decorated with battle scenes portraying the triumphs of long-dead Dovedales, then up a less grand staircase, and finally down a long hallway that grew considerably less imposing as it went on.

He opened the door into a room that Arabella would have considered luxurious by everyday standards, but which was undoubtedly Spartan on the ducal scale of things. Her room had been allotted to her with a delicate understanding of her place in the great chain of being. No room in Girdings could possibly be called mean, but hers was off to the side, with a view of the kitchen garden and some rather workmanlike outbuildings. There was water waiting and a fire in the grate, and that was all Arabella cared about.

"A fine pickle this is," snapped Rose, vigorously beating mud out of Arabella's pelisse as the door closed behind the footman.

"A pickle or a gherkin?" Arabella stripped her gloves off her frozen fingers and wandered to the one window to inspect the view.

Rose bristled, obviously suspecting Arabella of having fun at her expense. "Six of one, half a dozen of the other," she said repressively, "and no question about it. I should have known that coachman was no good. Here. This is as good as I can make it without a proper cleaning."

"Thank you," said Arabella meekly, and let the maid help her back into her pelisse.

Rose wrung out a cloth, applying it vigorously to Arabella's face, much the same way she had when Arabella was twelve and had underestimated the adhesive properties of raspberry jam. Rose had been with Aunt Osborne for a very long time. She had never quite made up her mind as to whether she approved of Arabella. Family was family, but poor relations something slightly less.

That, thought Arabella, was something she missed about Miss Climpson's. It had been rather nice to have a place in the world that she had earned for herself, rather than being allotted it on perpetual sufferance.

She had thought it didn't make a difference, but it did.

Rose narrowed her eyes at her, squinting at Arabella's head with a critical air. "That's the worst of the travel dust gone from your face, but there's no telling what they'll make of your hair." She shrugged with the air of one abandoning a bad job. "Well, it's dark and you'll have your bonnet on and that's the best one can hope for."

"Thank you, Rose."

Nothing like a few compliments to start one's evening off well.

Despite the size of the grounds, Arabella had no difficulty finding the West Wood. More of the ubiquitous footmen, identical in their white wigs and pseudo-feudal livery, had directed her to the gardens, where flaming lines of torches had been set to guide the houseguests through the carefully clipped parterres of the formal gardens through to the artfully designed wilderness beyond.

Through the smoke of the torches, Arabella could just make out the shapes of marble statues, freed from their winter burlap for the company's delectation. A nymph stretched cold arms into the air above a dry fountain while topiary beasts roared from the sides of the path. She couldn't tell whether they meant to protect her or to warn her away.

There was a blaze of light at the end of the path, more torches, this time arranged in a semicircle, as though for a ritual sacrifice. Arabella hurried towards them. They might be planning to put a maiden on the block, but at least she would be warm while they did it. Her fingers were freezing inside her gloves and her legs had lost all feeling several days ago.

A dog darted forward, nipping at her skirts, growling pleasurably as it attacked and killed her hem. There were more dogs underfoot in the clearing, tripping up yet more of the liveried footmen who were passing among the crowd with silver glasses full of a steaming liquid redolent of spices and spirits. A group of men milled just at the entrance to the clearing, quaffing spiced wine and kicking at the dogs, tricked out in fashionable multi-caped greatcoats, their curly-brimmed hats pulled down low over their eyes.

Arabella recognized most of them, although she doubted they would recognize her. There was Lord Frederick Staines, blond and arrogant, in line for an earldom; Lord Henry Innes, younger son of a duke, thick as a post; the Honorable Martin Frobisher, reputed to be anything but; Sir Francis Medmenham, dark and dissolute, but possessed of substantial properties both in England and abroad; Lieutenant Darius Danforth, formerly of the Horse Guards, also son of an earl, although there were rumors that he had been disowned. It had been all the usual sorts of reasons: drink, cards, and, if Arabella remembered correctly, seducing a young lady of good family. The lady's family were clearly influential enough to protect their own; the name had never come out, but the general outline of the story had spread. The girl was rumored to have been all of sixteen, just a year older than Lavinia.

They were a motley lot, but they all had two things in common. All were monied. And all were unmarried.

They clustered around the low, three-legged braziers that had been provided for warmth, like the ones at Farley Castle.

Something pulled painfully in Arabella's chest at the memory of Farley Castle. She felt suddenly, unaccountably alone.

Perhaps because she was.

It was ridiculous to feel nostalgic for something one had never had, or to regret the loss of a camaraderie that had been nothing more than the product of the moment. Even if she hadn't—behaved like a hysterical shrew? her mind provided. Cut up at him like a demented fishwife? Even if she hadn't put a precipitate end to their acquaintance, he would have forgotten all about her by now. He was the sort of amiable person who was sure to find friends wherever he went.

Arabella accepted a cup of mulled wine from one of the footmen and retreated to the shelter of a convenient tree, trying not to look as though she minded standing by herself. Again. There were other women present, but they seemed to be the ones doing all the hard labor of gathering the greenery. Typical. Lord Freddy and his lot wouldn't want to get their gloves dirty. She could see the dowager's granddaughter, Lady Charlotte Lansdowne, industriously piling mistletoe into a wicker basket, aided by a tall man in a cloak that looked as though it had been chosen more for warmth than fashion. Arabella didn't recognize him, nor the man next to him, also travel-stained, talking to Miss Penelope Deveraux.

Who was just as striking as Arabella remembered. The man standing next to her was practically cross-eyed from staring. Put his tongue any farther out and he'd be panting.

Arabella sent Lady Charlotte a quick and unconvincing smile and hastily looked away, pretending to examine the rest of the party. There were some men who had ventured out into the wood, chopping away at the larger bits of greenery, the boughs of evergreen destined to decorate the hall of Girdings. One of them appeared to be attempting to chop down a tree using the wrong end of the ax.

Arabella's hand jerked, slopping spiced wine over the already soiled leather of her glove.

It was dark away from the enchanted circle of torches, but there was enough reflected light to turn his hair to gold. He was very determinedly hacking away, his face averted from her, but there was no mistaking that profile.

Arabella hastily righted her cup before any more could spill, thinking very nasty thoughts about old family friends, the strange workings of Fate, and house parties generally.

Now she knew why Jane had asked about Girdings. And why she had smiled.

She was going to have to spend the twelve days of Christmas with Turnip Fitzhugh.

❧

WHEN TURNIP SPOTTED ARABELLA DEMPSEY, he did the sensible, mature thing. He began sawing at a tree with the wrong side of his ax.

On the long trip to Norfolk, as Sally's mouth continued to move in an endless stream of school-related anecdotes, there had been far too much time for thinking. He had done his best to avoid it. He had challenged other drivers to race him; he had dragged Sally one day out of the way so he could attend a bout held by a much-praised pugilist and his local challenger; he had even paid attention to some of Sally's stories. But that had still left plenty of time to fume and stew and stew some more as he revisited every baffling moment of their encounter in the blue drawing room.

Was it the money? He veered from anger to guilt as he recalled what that family friend of hers, that Miss Austen, had told him about the Dempseys' circumstances. It had never occurred to him that she might need to work for her living or that his—hmm, how to phrase it? His incredibly well-reasoned and sensible activities might prove an impediment to that. In retrospect, she probably could have gotten into a good deal of trouble if he had been caught in her room. It would have been hard to pass that off as a visit to Sally.

It made him ashamed, to think how little he had thought. Not that there had ever been much need for thought before. He had muddled along fairly happily without it. But that had been all right for him, because, as Arabella had so succinctly pointed out, he was a man and he had money. There wasn't any scrape he couldn't buy himself out of, and he had certainly tried his hand at quite a few. Well, death. He doubted he could buy his way out of death, and there were probably some sorts of behavior—although he couldn't think of any—that even thirty thousand guineas couldn't redeem, but he couldn't help but acknowledge the basic justice of her claim.

Someone tapped him on the shoulder. Turnip started, nearly dropping his ax.

"Two things," said Geoffrey Pinchingdale-Snipe. "One. This is the pointy end. Not that. Two. One uses an ax to strike, not to saw. One uses a saw to saw."

"Oh, ha bloody ha," mumbled Turnip, but he reversed the ax. "Why is it that one uses a saw to saw but one doesn't use an ax to ax? Bloody poor planning on the part of whoever wrote the language, I must say."

"I don't believe it was precisely planned."

"Shouldn't attempt a language without having a plan. That's your problem, then, isn't it?" said Turnip, watching Arabella as she accepted a silver cup of spiced wine from a footman and retreated against a tree.

"No," said Pinchingdale with some amusement. "I believe it was your problem."

That wasn't Turnip's problem. Turnip's problem stood halfway across the clearing, wearing a violet pelisse and a bonnet instead of a hood. They were town clothes, not really appropriate for a country outing. Turnip wondered if they were all she had.

She lifted the cup to just below her lips, blowing a trail of steam off the surface of the liquid. It curled like smoke in the cold air.

"What do you find over there to occasion such interest?" asked Pinchingdale.

"Miss Dempsey just arrived," said Turnip, trying to sound casual about it.

"Miss—?"

Turnip found himself feeling defensive on her behalf. "Miss Dempsey. Third tree from the left. The tall girl, standing by herself. Blond hair, bluish eyes."

Not that one could see either hair or eyes. The sides of her bonnet screened her face from view. She kept her head carefully down, from time to time taking a very small sip from the cup in her hand. It was as though she were trying not to be there. This was the Miss Dempsey he had known—or rather not known—in London.

"Ah. That Miss Dempsey."

"Didn't think you knew the others," said Turnip. "Four Miss Dempseys, don't you know."

"No, I didn't know," said Pinchingdale patiently. It was clearly not a piece of information he found essential to his existence. "Do all of them cause you such consternation, or just this one?"

"Which was the pointy end of the ax again?" said Turnip.

Pinchingdale's lips twitched into a smile. "Point taken. Or, rather, not."

"It's not about that sort of thing. Well, it ain't," Turnip said forcefully, although Pinchingdale hadn't said anything at all. He didn't have to. The man had the most bloody expressive eyebrows Turnip had ever had the misfortune of meeting.

Turnip shouldered his ax. "Miss Dempsey teaches at Miss Climpson's. That's all."

"Miss Climpson's?"

"Miss Climpson's Select Seminary for Young Ladies. In Bath. It's where the mater and pater farmed out Sally when the last governess refused to carry on."

That had been one of Sally's more spectacular triumphs. Either that, or her governesses had been a particularly weak-willed lot. Turnip's tutors had shown considerably more staying power, even in the face of determined unwillingness to get past the first conju-whatever-you-call-it.

"I know what it is," said Pinchingdale slowly. "And where it is. The name came to my attention recently in another context. I didn't realize you had a connection to the school."

"Context? What sort of context?"

Pinchingdale just looked at him.

"Oh," said Turnip. "That sort of context."

It wasn't the sort of thing one trumpeted about, but Pinchingdale had gotten into the whole spying business straight out of school, letting on that he was moving to France to avoid his mother—which anyone who had met his mother could well believe. Over there, he had been the brains behind the League of the Purple Gentian, returning only when Bonaparte's Ministry of Police had unmasked the Purple Gentian. There was also the little matter of Bonaparte banning all Englishmen from France, although, somehow, the Pink Carnation, clever devil, seemed to get around it.

Turnip didn't know for sure, but he suspected that Pinchingdale was working for the Carnation these days. When a man asked a chap to stick a carnation in his buttonhole and parade around Dover as a decoy, one did tend to get that sort of idea. Not that Turnip had minded—aside from the small matter of French agents occasionally launching themselves at him, which could be a deuced nuisance, particularly when one had been expecting an assignation and wound up with a stiletto at one's throat instead. But so far, it had all turned out right as rain, and Turnip had been delighted to do his bit for the effort.

He'd run the other odd job or two for Pinchingdale over the years. Generally, it seemed to consist of waylaying or blundering into people. Turnip was very good at knocking people over and making it look natural. Most of the time, it was. Blethering on was also a particular talent, and if he could employ it in the service of England, he was more than happy to do so. Not that Pinchingdale ever told him what it was about. "Talk to Innes for ten minutes," he would say, and then melt into the shadows in that shadowy way he had. Deuced neat trick, that. It had come in jolly handy when they were boys together at Eton, playing pranks on the masters.

"What are you gentlemen doing standing around gossiping when there's work to be done?" Penelope Deveraux swaggered past on the arm of one of the other houseguests, swinging a silver sickle from one hand like a pirate's hook. She wagged her sickle at Turnip. "Deck those halls, young man!"

"Fa-la-la!" Turnip called back.

Penelope's companion snickered and whispered something in her ear, to which Penelope replied by poking him with the nonpointy end of her sickle. Good to see that someone had worked out which end was which. Otherwise, the house party might not last the whole twelve days of Christmas. Deuced daring of the dowager, providing her guests with both brandy and pointy objects. Turnip wondered if there would be a prize for those who managed to survive until Twelfth Night. Knowing the dowager, she had probably done it on purpose, a modern form of the Roman Coliseum, without the lions.

"Shall we join the others?" suggested Pinchingdale, nodding in Penelope's direction. "You might want to try using the proper end of your ax. You'll cut more holly that way."

Arabella had neatly returned her glass to the refreshment table and was methodically using a small pair of garden shears to clip neat bundles of shiny leaves. The glossy leaves and bright red berries reminded him of those he had seen adorning those Christmas puddings.

There are no spies, she had said. And jolly emphatically too.

Turnip turned back to his old school chum. "That context you were talking about," he said abruptly. "Would it have anything to do with puddings?"

Pinchingdale arched an eyebrow. "Puddings?"

Clearly, that bit hadn't yet reached the War Office.

"Never mind. Christmas and all that. Someone was smuggling messages in them." Turnip gave a deliberately casual wave of one hand. "Messages in French. Deuced odd."

Pinchingdale stopped giving him the eyebrow treatment and started paying genuine attention. "What sort of messages?"

Turnip looked innocently at his old school chum. "What sort of context?"

Pinchingdale looked around, checking that they were safely removed from the rest of the party. He did it very subtly and very thoroughly. Turnip was impressed. But then, years in the secret service could do that for one. Turnip wondered if they had classes on it.

"Do you really want to know?" Pinchingdale asked quietly.

For a clever man, Pinchingdale could be deuced thick sometimes. "Wouldn't ask if I didn't. Waste of time and breath and whatnot."

"You know what they say about curiosity."

Something about cats, wasn't it? "My little sister attends that school. She might be more of a threat to the French than the French are to her"—an eventuality that Turnip found highly likely—"but if there's going to be trouble there, I want to know."

"Fair enough." Pinchingdale drummed his fingers lightly against the trunk of the tree as he sifted through his mental dossier, winnowing the details down to a version he found acceptable to tell. "One of Miss Climpson's pupils has a father who is very highly placed in the government."

Turnip nodded intelligently. Nothing too unusual about that. Took a great deal of blunt to keep a girl at Miss Climpson's.

"He came into possession of . . . a very sensitive document."

From the look on Pinchingdale's face, this wasn't going to be a story with a happy ending.

"What happened to it?"

Pinchingdale pressed his eyes briefly shut. "He misplaced it."

"He what?"

"He misplaced it." Pinchingdale's voice dripped with sarcasm. "He can't remember where he put it. He swears he kept it on his person at all times and he can't think what became of it."

Turnip frowned. "Hard to lose something when it's on one's person."

"One would think," said Pinchingdale drily. "Yet, somehow, he managed it."

"Could one of the servants have taken it? My valet's always taking things off for cleaning." Clothes, for example. Sometimes things got stuck in them, like bills or love letters or little notes to himself to remind himself not to leave notes to himself.

"No," said Pinchingdale. "We've had his staff and his laundry checked."

Turnip decided not to ask what the former entailed. It was the nineteenth century, after all, and they were Englishmen, committed to fair play, due process, and, well, all that sort of thing, so he doubted there were racks or thumbscrews involved.

"How does Miss Climpson's come into this again?"

Pinchingdale sighed. "He was visiting his daughter at Miss Climp-son's when the paper went missing. It's not much of a connection, but it's the best we have."

"How long ago?" asked Turnip, with interest.

"About a month ago. The end of November." The corners of Pinch-ingdale's mouth tightened grimly. "He only told us last week. He said he was hoping it would turn up."

"Huh," said Turnip. He might not know much about international espionage—his application for active membership in the League of the Purple Gentian had been repeatedly turned down—but even he knew enough to know that such things didn't generally just turn up. Or if they did, they didn't turn up where one wanted them to.

It occurred to Turnip that his friend had left out one very crucial detail. "What sort of sensitive document?"

Pinchingdale regarded Turnip thoughtfully. Somewhere, in the elaborate mechanism of his brain, levers and pulleys were being ad-justed as weights were moved from one scale to another. Turnip could see him calculating the benefits and detriments of sharing the informa-tion, or, at least some piece of it.

Turnip squared his shoulders and did his best to look trustworthy and close-lipped. And he was. Well, in a manner of speaking. It wasn't so much that he was close-lipped as that he was so open-lipped that no French spy had ever been able to wade through all the verbiage to get to the essential bits. They generally got bored and gave up.

The silence pressed around them.

"A list," Pinchingdale said finally. "A list of Royalist agents in France."

Chapter 20

After a very cold half hour, it was universally agreed that enough greenery had been gathered. This decision was reached largely due to the fact that the footmen had ceased serving refreshments. The Dowager Duchess of Dovedale, wise in the way of men, knew that the best way to move her guests where she wanted them to go was to divert their source of food and alcohol.

Lord Frederick Staines led the way, riding atop the vast Yule log as eight footmen painstakingly hauled it down the path, harnessed with ropes. Lord Frederick waved his hat in the air, exhorting them to move faster, as his friends and the dogs trotted along beside, making indistinguishable yelping noises.

Arabella left the shelter of her tree to fall in with the cavalcade headed back to the house. Behind them, like magic, the torches were being snuffed, the braziers extinguished, the tools collected, the stray ends of greenery swept up. Ahead loomed the immense facade of Girdings House, the windows blazing with candles, the grounds illuminated with torches.

Inside, the festivities would continue, probably well into the night, with flirtation and merriment and gratuitous use of mistletoe. It was an inexpressibly wearying thought. Arabella wondered if it would be considered a dereliction of her duty as guest if she just snuck away and went to bed.

As Arabella detoured to avoid an icy patch at the foot of the stairs, someone jostled heavily into her. Arabella skidded straight into the ice, her stomach dropping sickeningly as she flailed her arms for balance.

"Sorry!" Lord Henry Innes made an unenthusiastic grab for her. He managed to get her reticule instead. As the sky cartwheeled over her, Arabella could hear the string snap and Lord Henry's bored voice drawling, "Beg pardon, Miss—er."

A pair of hands clamped down over her elbows. The sky went right way up again.

"Dempsey," said Turnip Fitzhugh, plunking her upright. "It's Miss Dempsey."

Lord Henry shrugged, as though he considered it something of an irrelevancy. "Beg pardon, Miss Dempsey. Mind the ice."

Mind the ice? She had been minding the ice until he pushed her into it.

He followed his friends into the house, leaving Arabella and Turnip at the foot of the stairs.

Arabella looked at Turnip.

Turnip looked at her.

They stood there at the base of the steps and stared at each other like a pair of mutes.

This was absurd.

"Thank you," Arabella said. Her voice sounded very thin and reedy in the shadow of the great house. Desperately trying to think of something else to say, she blurted, "How is Sally?"

"Well. Sally is well." Turnip cleared his throat. "And your journey?"

"Wonderfully free of cows," said Arabella, and had the satisfaction of surprising him into a smile.

Turnip's face broke into a broad, genuine grin. "Shouldn't fear for my phaeton, then. Should I?" he added, and Arabella had a feeling he wasn't talking about his phaeton. Or cows.

He regarded her warily from under his hat brim, which was, Arabella noticed, slightly crooked. Her fingers itched to straighten it.

She tucked her hands safely away by her sides.

"No." Arabella looked appealingly at him, wishing she had a clue what to say next. *I'm sorry*, might be a start. So easy in her head, so hard to push past her lips. She dropped her head. "I like your boots. They're very . . . shiny."

"Thank you." Turnip looked down at his own toes. "It's m'valet, you know. He shines them."

"Right," said Arabella. Maybe she ought to try speaking in French or Latin. She wasn't doing very well in English. She took a deep breath. "Tur— Mr. Fitzhugh?"

He leaned forward, his hat slipping over his brow. "Miss Dempsey?"

"There you are!"

Turnip stepped back, hit the patch of ice, and went skidding as Penelope Deveraux appeared at the top of the stairs. He landed heavily on his backside with a loud, grunting noise.

Miss Deveraux was unimpressed. "If you're quite through falling down, Mr. Fitzhugh, I was just telling Lord Frederick that you had already offered to help me hang my bough." On Miss Deveraux's lips, the innocent phrase turned into something indescribably suggestive. She strolled over to Turnip, twirling an evergreen bough in one hand. With the tip of the bough, she flipped the edge of his hat. "Haven't you, Mr. Fitzhugh?"

The sharp scent of pine made Arabella's nose itch.

Turnip stumbled awkwardly to his feet. "Yes. Guess I must have."

Twining her arm through Turnip's, Miss Deveraux cast a challenging look over her shoulder. "As you see, Lord Frederick, you'll just have to wait your turn."

Standing in the doorway, Lord Frederick stepped aside to make room for them to pass into the warmth of the hall. "I don't approve of waiting."

Miss Deveraux paused in the doorway beside him, tilting her head up to look Lord Frederick in the eye. "Patience is a virtue, Lord Frederick."

Lord Frederick lowered his mouth to Miss Deveraux's ear. "Vices are far more entertaining."

Miss Deveraux grinned. "Aren't you optimistic." She shoved lightly at his waistcoat. "Do stop loitering in the doorway, Lord Frederick. You're keeping the others in the cold. Come along, Mr. Fitzhugh. No dawdling."

She tugged Turnip along behind her like a child's toy on a string.

Turnip looked back over his shoulder at Arabella. Arabella quickly looked away. She didn't need his charity. And he would obviously not repine for the lack of her scintillating conversation about the shine on his boots.

Maybe she should go upstairs. There were several rather scathing things she wouldn't mind writing to Jane.

"Arabella!" Arabella found herself wrapped in lace and scent as Aunt Osborne flung her arms about her neck. "Did you arrive before us? Such a journey we've had— Oh, child, what *have* you done to your hair? I must speak to Rose."

She had forgotten how tiny her aunt was. The top of Aunt Osborne's green silk turban barely reached Arabella's chin.

Sneezing as the elaborately curled feather tickled her nose, Arabella dutifully embraced her aunt, inhaling the old familiar scents of face powder and rosewater. "Happy Christmas, Aunt Osborne."

Her aunt beamed at her, the makeup she had always applied with a lavish hand looking less foolish on her than it ought. Up close, Arabella could see the powder caked in the wrinkles of her aunt's cheeks, but from a distance, the effect was deceptively youthful.

"Silly girl, it's not Christmas until tomorrow, although I trust it will be a happy one. Goodness, how red your cheeks are. Have you been outside in that wind? It's terrible for the complexion."

"Yes, Aunt Osborne." It was easier to agree than not.

"We'll do something about it tomorrow." By tomorrow, her aunt would have forgotten all about it.

"Hayworth?" Aunt Osborne twisted her head to look at her husband. "Aren't you going to say hello to Arabella?"

"Certainly," said Hayworth Musgrave smoothly.

She hadn't even realized he was there. How odd to think that not so long ago, she had been preternaturally aware of his presence, attuned to his every least coming and going, as attentive to his moods as she had been to her own. Now his presence came almost as an afterthought.

He stood a little way back, watching the interplay between her and her aunt with a slight, superior smile. He was waiting, Arabella realized, for her to come to him. Two months ago, she would have.

With the detachment of two months' distance, Arabella regarded him critically. Captain Musgrave's wasn't the sort of countenance to set debutantes swooning. His face was oddly shaped, with a heavy jaw that made his head seem larger on the bottom than on the top. His mouth was wide, his smile lopsided, his nose crooked. His sandy hair stuck out at all angles, giving him a scarecrow air. He was tall enough, taller than she at any event, with the muscles that came of regular exercise, but after only two months' marriage, the signs of dissolution and discontent were already beginning to show in his countenance, in the softening of the flesh beneath his chin and the lines at either side of his lips. He would be stout by the time he was thirty, jowly by forty. The uniform he had worn before he sold out suited him better than the civilian clothes Aunt Osborne's generosity had bought him. The puce jacket with its gold embroidery was too bright; it made his face sallow by contrast.

Even at the height of her infatuation, Arabella had never deluded herself into thinking him handsome. Charming, yes; handsome, no.

She had told herself that this was a sign of the true depth of her affections, that she was able to value not the inconsequential physical husk, but the real worth of the man beneath.

What a ninny she had been.

When Arabella made no move to come to him, he took a step forward, reaching out to take both her hands in his. "Hello, Arabella."

His grip was light, more for show than substance. Arabella gently abstracted her hands. "Hello, *Uncle* Hayworth."

He winced theatrically. "You make me sound like Methuselah. I'll be counting gray hairs next."

"Call them silver and I'm sure you'll like them much better," Arabella shot back.

Captain Musgrave gave her a quick, startled glance, as though a Watteau shepherdess had just come after him with her crook.

"I trust you had a good journey?" Arabella said hastily.

There was no point in picking quarrels with her aunt. Or her aunt's husband. It didn't matter anymore.

Captain Musgrave looked at her uneasily for a moment, and then decided he must have misunderstood.

And why shouldn't he? She had always been on good behavior with him before, so anxious to please that she had never said anything of interest at all.

Her new uncle shrugged, setting the gold threads in his jacket glittering. "The inns were nothing to brag about, but we managed passably well."

"Passably?" Aunt Osborne flung her arm through his, entangling him in a web of silk fringe. "I should say we got along famously."

A look of thinly veiled dislike crossed his face before he masked it with a smile as fatuous as hers. "Yes, yes, my love." There was something decidedly perfunctory in the way he patted the jeweled hand resting on his arm. "Your company could make the most dreary road bright."

"More economical than candles," said Arabella brightly.

"Pardon?"

Arabella looked at Captain Musgrave's uncomprehending face and wondered, as if from a world away, how she could have thought she loved him. Admittedly, it hadn't been the cleverest comment, but that didn't matter.

"Nothing," she said. "It was nothing."

It was true, she realized, in more ways than one.

She looked across the hall and saw Turnip standing by the Dowager Duchess of Dovedale's litter—an ornate, gilded thing carried by four uniformed footmen. From where she was standing, Arabella couldn't see the dowager herself, but she could see her cane, wagging imperiously as Turnip obediently followed her direction in moving a bough of holly first this way, then that.

The dowager raised her cane in a peremptory summons and Penelope Deveraux strolled over, pausing on her way to poke Turnip in the ribs with the easy familiarity of old acquaintance.

Arabella thought uncharitable thoughts.

"Arabella?" Captain Musgrave's voice was impatient. She was meant to be paying attention to him, not woolgathering.

"Forgive me." Arabella shook her head to clear it. "The fatigues of the day . . ."

Captain Musgrave arranged his features into an expression of understanding. She could see the pity in his eyes, a very smug and satisfied sort of pity. "Of course. You need your rest." He squeezed Aunt Osborne's arm. "Not everyone can be as young as Celia."

Aunt Osborne fluttered. "Oh, *Hayworth*!"

The dowager snapped her fingers at a footman, who stepped forward with a basketful of mistletoe. Penelope Deveraux reached inside, withdrawing a good-sized sprig. Turnip held out his hand for it. Miss Deveraux drew it challengingly back.

Arabella didn't want to watch.

"Good night, Aunt." She flashed a quick, tortured smile at her aunt, who looked at her in some surprise, as though she had already forgotten she was there.

Captain Musgrave cleared his throat.

"Good night . . . Uncle," said Arabella, and fled in the direction of her room and her writing desk.

❧

"YOU'LL PROBABLY HANG IT UPSIDE DOWN," said Penelope, yanking away the mistletoe.

"At least I can reach the doorframe," said Turnip, holding out his hand for it.

"So can a stepladder," said Penelope scathingly, but she surrendered the sprig.

"The stepladder would make better conversation," opined the dowager from her lofty post atop her litter.

"Stepladders can't talk," Turnip pointed out.

The dowager smirked. "My point precisely."

Penelope rolled her eyes. "Just put up the mistletoe. I have plans for it."

"What sort of plans?" asked Turnip warily.

He hoped they didn't involve him. Every now and again, Penelope got bored and dragged him out onto a balcony. Or under the mistletoe. Smashing girl and all that, Penelope, but she wasn't the one he wanted under the mistletoe.

Turnip looked around, but he didn't see Arabella. The people she had been talking to were still there, but she was gone.

"Those sorts of plans." Penelope sent a sultry glance in the direction of Lord Frederick Staines, who was too busy pounding back claret to notice.

"Drink, drink, drink!" chanted Lord Henry and Lieutenant Danforth, banging their fists against their knees in perfectly syncopated rhythm.

Lord Frederick gave an explosive gasp and set the cup down with a clang, claret dripping bright red drops on the stiffly starched linen of his cravat.

Turnip made a face at Penelope. "Might want to watch yourself there, old thing."

Clasping her hands to her bosom, Penelope pivoted to face the dowager. "He cares! How sweet."

Turnip peered past her, at the misrule reigning in the hall. Freddy Staines was passing the cup to Martin Frobisher; Lady Charlotte was diligently tying red velvet bows around sprigs of greenery; and someone had decided to practice sword dancing with axes instead of swords.

There was still no sign of Arabella. Instead, Turnip caught sight of Pinchingdale, who was making his shadowy way towards the stairs.

He had a few questions he wanted to ask Pinchingdale.

"Here." Turnip shoved the mistletoe at Penelope. "You win. You take it."

"No gumption," decreed the dowager and sped him on his way with a well-placed jab of her cane.

Turnip careened into Pinchingdale. "Just the chap I wanted to see," he said, seizing him by the arm and dragging him off into the next room. It was an anteroom, of the sort used for keeping unimportant people waiting until they were duly intimidated by the ducal decorating scheme. "How important is this list of yours?"

Pinchingdale rubbed his shoulder where Turnip had grabbed him and checked to make sure the door was closed. The walls of Girdings were thick enough to withstand a siege; they wouldn't be overheard. "Very."

"Important enough for someone to tear up someone's room to get it?"

"I'd say that's the least of what people would be willing to do to get their hands on it. Why? What do you know?"

"I think," said Turnip, choosing his words very carefully, "that Miss Dempsey might have had it. Or that someone might think she had it."

"Miss Dempsey?"

"We've been through this before," said Turnip irritably. "You know who she is."

"I know I know who she is," said Pinchingdale, and shook his head a little, as though to clear it. "What I want to know is what she would be doing with a highly sensitive government document."

"She teaches at Miss Climpson's. There was—well, long story, but the short of it is that people were blundering about in the middle of the night and Miss Dempsey ended up with a notebook that wasn't hers. Someone tore her room up the next day. The notebook disappeared."

Pinchingdale shook his head. "The document I'm talking about is a single sheet of paper, not a whole notebook. The two incidents are probably unrelated."

"But what if they're not?"

"If they're not?" Pinchingdale looked grim. "Then your Miss Dempsey is in a great deal of danger."

Chapter 21

"I say," said Turnip in wounded tones. "There's no need to go all melodramatic."

"Well, you did seem to be fishing for it," said Pinchingdale apologetically. "I didn't want to disappoint you."

"I was being serious!" said Turnip indignantly.

"And so was I," said Pinchingdale, sobering. "Up to a point. If your Miss Dempsey really did have that document, she would be in grave danger. I, for one, find it highly unlikely. A student notebook is an unlikely means of conveyance."

"The notebook was in French."

"The document wasn't."

"What exactly is this list? How long is it?"

"Long enough," said Pinchingdale gravely. "Long enough to cause a great deal of bother. We have a string of Royalist agents posted between Boulogne and Paris. Most are French. They serve as couriers for both information and people. Without them, a vital link to the coast would be cut."

"That ain't all, is it?" said Turnip shrewdly.

"Isn't that enough?" Pinchingdale tapped his fingers against the green marble mantelpiece. "Bonaparte would give his eyeteeth to get his hands on that list. Having to rebuild that network would set us back months, perhaps years."

"What are eyeteeth?" asked Turnip.

Pinchingdale mustered a tired grin. "I don't know, but they appear to be uniquely expendable. Some people feel the same way about human life."

"You don't need to tell me," said Turnip. "I've met some of them."

He was fairly sure they were both thinking of the same person: the Marquise de Montval, agent of the dread spy the Black Tulip. She was, by all accounts, dead. Turnip wouldn't have believed it if Pinchingdale hadn't witnessed it himself.

The marquise had had a marked fondness for stilettos. She had worn them in her hair, decorated with diamonds, disguised as ornaments. She hadn't been all that particular as to where they landed. Turnip didn't like to think what she might have done to Arabella. The marquise's motto had been stiletto first, questions later.

Where there was one demented French spy, there would be others. They were a bit like bees, thought Turnip philosophically. Swat one and the whole hive came swarming down on your head.

"Why are you here?" Turnip asked. "Why are you really here?"

Pinchingdale tried the eyebrow trick. "To celebrate Christmas?"

"Ha," said Turnip intelligently. Pinchingdale couldn't fool him, not even with that eyebrow. A chap didn't go off to a Christmas party without his wife. "Where's Lady Pinchingdale, then?"

"Letty," said Pinchingdale, "is upstairs sleeping. The trip tired her."

"Oh." It sounded reasonable enough on the surface, but it didn't quite wash. From what Turnip had seen of the new Lady Pinchingdale, she was fairly indefatigable. Unless . . .

"I say!" he blurted out. "Is she . . . ?"

Pinchingdale looked up at the ceiling overhead, which was decorated with several overblown nymphs. "You really do say whatever comes into your mind, don't you?"

"Sink me if that ain't good news!" Turnip pounded his old school chum on the back so hard that Pinchingdale doubled over, coughing. "Splendid, I say! Make a deuced smashing father. Hope you have ten. Not all at once, of course."

"Thank you," said Pinchingdale, when he got his breath back. "I'll tell Letty you said so."

"Why aren't you with her family? Or yours?"

"You've met my mother," said Pinchingdale. "You don't want to meet Letty's mother."

"You're here about the list, aren't you?"

"Worse than fleas," said Pinchingdale, addressing himself to the nymphs. They simpered in sympathy. "Yes. I am. The man who lost it will be attending the party with his wife and daughter. They're due to arrive just before Epiphany. I gather they plan to announce the daughter's betrothal to Lord Grimmlesby-Thorpe."

"So that's what that old sack is doing here!" exclaimed Turnip. "Didn't seem the sort the duchess would want to marry off to her granddaughter."

"No, but there was a scandal about the daughter, and Carruthers is eager to get her off his hands. I gather Grimmlesby-Thorpe was the only one to bite."

"Carruthers? Catherine Carruthers?"

"You know her?"

"She's friends with Sally. *Was* friends with Sally," Turnip corrected himself. He looked at Pinchingdale, struck by a sudden thought. "Arabella—I mean, Miss Dempsey—is one of her teachers."

Pinchingdale's eyebrow went up at that careless use of her first name, but he forbore to comment. He didn't need to. If they could deploy Pinchingdale's eyebrow against the French, Bonaparte would be all rolled up within the week.

"You don't think that Catherine—," Turnip said hastily.

"No one is suggesting that Catherine took the list," Pinchingdale pointed out. "Why would she take it? And what would she do with it?"

"Fair point," said Turnip. "Do you know a chap named the Cheval-whatsis de la Tour de Something-or-Other?"

Pinchingdale took a moment for mental translation. "By which I presume you mean the Chevalier de la Tour d'Argent?"

"So you do know him!"

"Not well," said Pinchingdale cautiously.

"I wasn't asking if you'd ask the chap to stand godfather to your firstborn child," said Turnip impatiently. "But if you're looking for something rotten in the state of Bath, I'd say he's a jolly good candidate."

Pinchingdale shook his head. "Unlikely. Argent is one of the Comte d'Artois's circle—and his father was one of the first victims of the guillotine. He has no cause to love the revolutionary regime."

"That's what they all say," grumbled Turnip. "Well, you can't expect me to believe that Miss Climpson is secretly a French spy, because I won't."

"That's the curious thing," said Pinchingdale thoughtfully. "There may be no French spy. The paper went missing in November. If it had fallen into the wrong hands, we should have had some word of it already. Instead . . ." He spread his hands in the universal gesture of perplexity. "Silence."

Turnip squinted at him. "Which leaves us . . . ?"

"Absolutely nowhere," said Pinchingdale wryly. "Or rather, at Gird-ings House for Christmas. So we might as well strive to enjoy it. I hear the dowager has mummers' plays and morris dancers for us tomorrow."

"Where's my partridge in the pear tree?" mumbled Turnip.

"I think he was stepped on by the lords a-leaping," said Pinchingdale amiably. "I wouldn't worry too much about your Miss Dempsey. I doubt we have any spies on the loose at Girdings. The dowager would never allow it."

DESPITE PINCHINGDALE'S REASSURING WORDS, Turnip did his best to keep an eye on Arabella, who half the time was out of the room, run-ning errands for her aunt, who seemed to have a remarkable propensity for mislaying everything that wasn't actually pinned to her person. Hard to keep an eye on someone who was constantly in and out of the room. Even harder when they weren't officially speaking. They weren't officially not speaking, either. They just sidled around each other, steal-ing glances when convinced the other wasn't, and producing strained smiles when caught. It was all deuced confusing.

On the fourth day of the house party, with the mummers' plays and morris dancers of Christmas Day behind them and the larger festivities for Twelfth Night still to come, the guests broke into their own separate amusements. Some of the gentlemen went off to practice their fencing in the long gallery; the ladies retreated to their writing desks. And Ara-bella went off to fetch her aunt's shawl.

"Not the long one," Aunt Osborne had instructed, giving Arabella's hand an affectionate squeeze. "The one with the silk fringe. The one I gave you to give Rose to mend. She does a much neater job than my Abigail."

Arabella was passing through one of the many interlinked reception rooms on her way back to the gallery, examining the tiny stitches on the shawl, when she looked up to see Hayworth Musgrave approaching her from the far side of the room. They were in one of the smaller drawing rooms, decorated in shades of yellow with accents of rose picked up in the porcelain arranged in cabinets to either side of the room.

"Arabella," he said warmly. "How fortuitous."

The winter sun slanted through the long windows, creating an illusion of warmth as specious as her new uncle's smile.

"Captain Musgrave," she said.

His smile widened. "I like to hear you call me so," he said sentimentally. "It reminds me of . . . old times."

"How nice," said Arabella. "If you will excuse me, my aunt wanted her shawl."

Captain Musgrave moved to block her egress. "We've seen so little of one another since the wedding."

"Mmm," said Arabella, noncommittally, wondering if it would be ridiculously rude to simply walk around him.

Musgrave took her murmur for assent. "I've been wanting a chance to talk to you."

Arabella raised her eyebrows in polite inquiry, but said nothing.

Her silence seemed to fluster Captain Musgrave. He clasped his hands behind his back, puffing out his chest. "This nonsense about teaching at a school—there's no need for that, you know."

"I like it there." She realized as she said it that it was true. She liked the bustle of it and the feeling of belonging. She liked the odd democracy of girls, all sharing the same meals and the same classes. She liked not having to worry about what she said or what she wore or about having to be grateful.

Captain Musgrave made no attempt to disguise his disbelief. "There's no need to put a good face on it. You can come back, you know. We miss you."

Once upon a time, those words from his lips would have set her hands tingling and her heart fluttering. She would have gone hot and cold and thrilled at the memory of them for days to come.

Now they left her with only one of those sensations: cold. She felt entirely cold, detached, as if she were a third party watching the conversation, unrelated to either of the participants.

"Is that the royal We?" she said coolly.

Captain Musgrave blinked. That hadn't been in her script. "I mean, your aunt and I. Both of us."

"How sweet." If her aunt wanted her back, she could tell her so herself. Captain Musgrave might be her aunt's husband, but he wasn't her uncle. On an impulse, Arabella said, "You should ask Margaret for the season."

"Margaret?"

"My next sister. She would be very glad to have the time in town. I believe she and my aunt would get along famously." And they would, Arabella realized. Aunt Osborne would adore Margaret. How ironic to think that she'd had the wrong sister all along. And even if Margaret chose not to come to town, at least it would be her choice. She would have the chance. "Ask her. You'll see."

"I'm sure Margaret is lovely." Brushing extraneous sisters aside, Captain Musgrave hastily returned to his prepared program. "But it's you I'm concerned about."

"How kind," said Arabella.

Musgrave frowned. He wasn't used to interruptions, at least not from her. That, Arabella realized, must be why he wanted her back so badly. He missed the audience, and the adoration.

"You do realize that our home is still your home. My marriage changes nothing."

Arabella smiled brightly at him. "Except that now I have an uncle."

He was even starting to look like one. A few more years and that paunch would be coming along nicely.

"Arabella . . ." Captain Musgrave took a step forward, oozing earnestness and bay rum cologne. "I hope you never thought . . ."

Oh no.

Arabella hitched her aunt's shawl up over her arm. "As a friend of mine likes to say," she said briskly, "I make it a practice to think as little as possible."

"Friend?" Captain Musgrave was clearly put out at being interrupted midscene. "You don't mean that Fitzhugh character?"

The way he said it put Arabella's teeth on edge. She forced herself to say pleasantly, "Yes. I do."

Captain Musgrave made an incredulous face. "I'm surprised to hear you call him friend. Have you heard what people say about him?"

"I've heard what people say about you," said Arabella.

She didn't need to elaborate. Any man who married a woman more than twice his age had to have a good idea of what the rumors were.

Captain Musgrave reddened. "The man's a buffoon!"

Arabella thought of Turnip's many kindnesses and her lips went tight. "The man is a gentleman. In the truest sense of the word."

Captain Musgrave made a very ungentlemanly snorting sound. "With that income, a chimpanzee could be a gentleman."

"Are you volunteering for the attempt?" Arabella didn't wait for him to figure out how he had just been insulted. She swept on, buoyed by a cold anger that prickled like ice. "It's nothing to do with income or properties or anything that can be measured in shillings and pence. It's about character. I am sure you're familiar with the concept."

Captain Musgrave's nose twitched, as though he smelled something unpleasant. "Watch yourself, my dear. From the way you say it, one would almost think you were in love."

"In love? Me?" The idea was absurd. "Me? I—no. No."

Arabella felt like an hourglass that had just been flipped over. Everything she thought she had known looked different viewed the other way around. Time ran backwards, through Miss Climpson's parlor, her own bedroom, Farley Castle, the street outside the school, Turnip grinning, frowning, picking her up off the ground.

Dizzy and disoriented, she shook her head and repeated the one word she seemed capable of remembering, "No. It's . . . No."

Captain Musgrave folded his arms across his chest, eyeing Arabella narrowly. "Everyone says he's planning to marry that Deveraux girl."

Something twisted in Arabella's chest. The last of the sands shifted down, leaving the bulb empty.

"If he does," Arabella said calmly, "I will be the first to wish him happy. He deserves to be happy."

She looked at the man she had once thought to marry. The facile charm that had once dazzled her was still there, but it had begun to peel away at the edges, like an ill-fitting mask. It was marred by the discontented droop of his mouth, by the way his eyes narrowed when she failed to play her proper part in the drama he had scripted for them.

Musgrave might have attained his heart's desire, but he would never be happy. And she, Arabella realized, would never have been happy with him. He had never wanted her for herself, only for the inheritance he thought she would provide.

"If you will be so kind as to excuse me, I must bring my aunt her wrap."

She didn't wait for him to reply. She turned on her heel and walked away without looking back. She realized her hands were shaking beneath the silk of the shawl. She drew a deep breath into her lungs. What a loathsome, venal little man. And how stupidly blind she had been.

"Oh, Miss—er. Hello." Lord Henry raised a hand. He was walking with a pack of the other guests in the direction of the great doors that opened onto the gardens. "We were wondering where you had got to."

Arabella sincerely doubted it, but she smiled politely, wanting nothing more than to be in the privacy of her own room, to pace and think and sort through everything that had just happened.

"We were just about to play blind man's buff in the gardens," drawled Lord Frederick Staines. "If you'd like to join us."

"Oh, yes, of course," lied Arabella. She held up the silky fall of shawl, which she had managed to twist and crush into something resembling a rope. "I just need to bring this to my aunt. Excuse me."

"Here. Let me." Darius Danforth plucked the shawl from her hands, passing it over to a footman. "Give this to Lady Osborne."

"Problem solved," said Martin Frobisher, and giggled. From the scent of his breath, he had already been hitting the claret decanter. He pushed at the glass doors just as one of the omnipresent footmen swung them open, sending him staggering sideways down the shallow flight of steps.

"Since Miss Dempsey was late," drawled Lieutenant Danforth, "she must be the hoodsman."

"I am quite happy to cede the honor to someone else," said Arabella quickly.

She hated blind man's buff. It wasn't so bad being on the hiding end, but her whole spirit revolted at the helpless humiliation of staggering about to giggles and whispers, knowing that the others could all see you, but you couldn't see them. She preferred to be the observer, not the observed.

"Oh, no," said Lieutenant Danforth smoothly. "I wouldn't hear of it."

He exchanged a look with Lord Henry, and Arabella suspected them of having a private joke at her expense. A wager of some sort, no doubt. They had already wagered on how many times Turnip Fitzhugh would walk into the same sprig of mistletoe and whether Penelope Deveraux would be caught in a compromising position, and, if so, with whom.

Arabella didn't like to think what they might wager about her. Nothing salacious, to be sure, but something petty and cruel, like how many times she would fall down while blind and if her petticoats would show when she did so.

"Here," said Lord Frederick, sauntering over to join his friends, "is your hood."

It was a wide strip of purple satin, entirely opaque.

He reached across her face to draw the fabric over her eyes, the red stone of his ring flashing in the winter sunlight. He yanked the fabric tight, tying it in a double knot that was going to take a good deal of doing to undo.

Cold bit through her dress, and the gravel of the garden path was gritty through the thin soles of her slippers.

Arabella took a deep breath, raising her hands to tentatively touch the sides of the cloth. People did this for fun?

"No cheating," drawled Lieutenant Danforth. He was a fine one to talk. Hadn't he been expelled from Brook's for cheating at cards?

"All right!" called out Arabella, trying to look as though she were enjoying herself. "Is everyone ready?"

"Yes," shouted back Martin Frobisher, "but are you?"

There was a chorus of hoarse guffaws, oddly distorted through the material of the hood. Arabella twisted this way and that, knowing how a fox felt as the hounds converged on it, barking. Only she was supposed to be the predator and they the prey. Wasn't she? She had a very bad feeling about this.

Hands grabbed her and spun her around in clumsy circles, again and again, as her slippers crunched on the gravel and her head swam with the motion. "Around, around, around," someone was chanting, and one of them said, "Dizzy yet?"

"Very," Arabella gasped, and they let her go so abruptly that she stumbled into the boxwood. The needlelike foliage scraped her fingers, but it broke her fall.

"Ready, steady, here I come!" she called.

She could hear the shuffle of feet against the gravel, the hissing sound of whispers and muffled laughter coming from all around her as her quarry scattered.

Arabella groped her way forward, hitting another hedge. They weren't supposed to hide behind things, were they? She generally avoided the game, but she was fairly sure it wasn't considered sporting to remove oneself entirely.

There was a slithering noise as someone trod gently on the pebbles of the path behind her. Arabella blundered towards the noise.

Her fingers grazed fabric. Thank goodness. "Got you!" she called gaily.

"No." A hand clamped down on her forearm, swinging her around. Her back was pressed to someone's chest, her arms pinned behind her. "I've got *you*."

She could feel herself being pulled. Gravel skittered beneath her slippers and boxwood plucked at the fabric of her dress.

"That's not the way the game works," she protested, struggling against his grip. "Who is this?"

Her captor yanked her back against him, hard, so hard that she could feel the breath knocked out of her.

"We're playing my game now," he said harshly. She could feel his breath, hot even through the silk of the hood, heavy and rasping. Something sharp pricked against her neck.

Fear trickled down Arabella's spine, colder than the frost on the statues. She didn't need to see it to know that this was no paper scimitar this time. She could feel the prick of steel, real steel this time, against her jaw.

"Where is it?" he hissed. "Where is the list?"

Chapter 22

"Care to place a wager, Fitzhugh?"

Turnip wandered into the masculine province of the red salon, which Henry Innes's lot appeared to have taken over as their personal playground. Henry Innes was sprawled by the hearth, the claret decanter beside him on the rug, along with a plate of cheese and cold meats. Freddy Staines was dicing with Darius Danforth at a table in the corner, while Sir Francis Medmenham lounged with one elbow on the mantel, where the flames could cast a suitably diabolical glow over his attire.

Martin Frobisher had possession of the wager book. He flapped it in Turnip's general direction. "Last chance to place a bet."

"On what?" asked Turnip, without interest.

They had already tried to get him to participate in a wager to see how many times he could hop around the long gallery with a glass of port balanced on his head. Turnip had said no. He didn't particularly like port.

Frobisher smirked. "It was quite the prank, if I do say so myself.

Wish I could take credit, but it was Danforth's idea—or maybe Miss Ponsonby's."

"What was?" Turnip wasn't sure he wanted to hear it. If it had been Miss Ponsonby's doing, it was sure to be mean-spirited.

"Pretending we were going to play blind man's buff. We got one of the ladies—that quiet one—to play hoodsman, spun her around a few times, and left her. Bet you she's still blundering around out there, wondering why she can't find anyone."

Something about the way Frobisher said "that quiet one" made Turnip's shoulder muscles tense. "Which lady?"

Frobisher tapped his pen against the betting book, adding a few blots to the ones already enshrined within its hallowed cover. "Miss, er . . ."

"Dempsey?" Turnip could hardly hear his own voice for the roaring in his ears.

Unaware that his hours on the earth were now numbered, Frobisher looked smug. "That's the one. We're all taking bets on how long it will take her to figure it out." Frobisher consulted the book. "Staines says five minutes; I give her ten. Danforth is down for eight." He paused with his pen poised over the betting book. "What do you say, Fitzhugh?"

Turnip made a low, growling noise. He hadn't known he had it in him to growl. He also hadn't known he had homicidal tendencies. Funny, the things one found out about oneself.

"Was that nine?" asked Frobisher, busily scribbling.

Turnip realized he had two choices. He could throttle Frobisher or he could rescue Arabella. Much as he wanted to, he couldn't do both.

Throttling Frobisher would have to wait.

As he stormed out of the room, he could hear Sir Francis Medmenham's drawling voice behind him, deliberately pitched so he could hear it. "By Jove, I believe the man is charging off to rescue her. Pity no one informed him that knight-errantry is passé."

The temperature had dropped again. Turnip felt the nip of it straight through his linen, all the way down to his skin. His temper smoldered at the thought of Arabella being deliberately stranded outside in it. She would find her way out eventually, but it was cruel—cruel and vicious. He boiled with impotent anger as he marched down the garden steps. Frost crunched beneath his boots.

He heard her before he saw her, a scuffle of footsteps against the gravel, the sound of fabric scraping against the boxwood.

She stumbled into the clearing. There was a piece of purple silk tied across her eyes, tied so tightly that her hair bulged above it. Her glove-less hands were a pale blue with cold, crisscrossed with scratches from the needlelike foliage of the shrubbery. There was a rent in her dress, an odd slice in one sleeve as though the fabric had been parted with a knife. She was tugging at the hood as she ran, skidding on the pebbles and banging into the boxwood as she attempted to yank the fabric up over her eyes.

Turnip winced at the sight. When he got his hands on Frobisher and the rest . . .

Blindly fighting with the hood, Arabella careened into him, banging heavily into his chest.

Turnip's hands automatically reached out to close around her shoulders.

"No!" She struggled against his grasp. "I don't have it! I tell you, I don't have it! Go *away*!"

"Arabella? Arabella!"

He didn't want to let go for fear she would unbalance herself, but it was proving deuced difficult to hold on to her. She was wriggling like a mad thing.

"Arabella, it's me." Turnip raised his voice to a bellow. "Me! Ouch!"

She stopped trying to stomp on his toes and raised her sightless face to his. "Turnip?"

"The very one."

Her reaction wasn't at all what he expected. Instead of pulling away, she sagged against him, body to body, resting her full weight against him and pressing her cheek into his collarbone. "Thank goodness."

"I'm glad to see you too," he said, but he couldn't quite keep the worry from his voice. "What happened? What's wrong?"

Turnip reached for the knots on the back of the hood, but they had been pulled so hard that they might as well have been set in mortar. He gave up and gently tugged the hood up over her head. It had snagged on her hairpins, which seemed to have riveted it into place.

As he worked on freeing her from the hood, Arabella shook her head, burrowing deeper into his cravat.

"He kept asking me where it is," she said incoherently. "But I don't know. I have no idea what he's talking about."

Turnip managed to get the hood off, taking most of her hairpins along with it.

"He?" He stroked back her disordered hair. It had come down the last time too, when she had been knocked down by Signor Marconi. He remembered the tangled mass of it, the way it had felt beneath his fingers as he kissed her.

"The man who grabbed me. He pulled me back behind a hedge. I kicked him and ran." She swallowed hard, obviously reliving it in her thoughts. "I thought you were he."

Turnip's hand stilled as all thoughts of dalliance fled, replaced by other, darker concerns. This was more than just a prank. "Someone grabbed you?"

Arabella jerked her head back, looking at him with wide, frightened eyes. "Turnip, he had a knife. A real knife this time."

"Good Gad." Turnip pressed her head back against his shoulder, holding on to her as tightly as he could. Forget thrashing; he was going to kill Frobisher and his lot when he saw them. "It's all right. He's gone now. It's just me. No one else here."

He leaned his cheek against her tangled hair, breathing in the familiar scent of her, feeling her breathing return to normal, her chest rising and falling against his, when something peculiar about what she had said belatedly struck him.

Turnip leaned his torso back, peering down his nose at a small slice of forehead and a large amount of hair. Her hair brushed his chin. "What do you mean 'this time'?" he demanded.

There was silence from the direction of his cravat.

He squeezed her shoulders. "Arabella?"

Moving very slowly, she stepped back, extricating herself from his arms. When she did, she didn't quite meet his eyes. "Someone grabbed me once before. At Miss Climpson's."

"When? How?" The very thought of it was enough to make him frantic. "Why didn't you tell me?"

Arabella bit her lip, looking away. "It was right after we, er, quarreled. Someone seized me as I left the drawing room. I couldn't see who it was, only that he was disguised in one of the wise men's robes."

"And you didn't come to me?"

"How could I? I had just told you I never wanted to speak to you again. Remember?"

"That wasn't exactly how you phrased it." He should know. He had every word of that interview burned into his memory in a way his Latin lessons never had. Amazing the way a chap could remember things when they really mattered.

"But it amounted to the same thing. I couldn't come running to you after that. And I didn't think it was important."

"Someone assaults you and it's *not important*? Good Gad! It may not be important to you, but it's jolly well important to—well, to the people who care about you."

Arabella gave him a crooked smile, rubbing her hands over her arms. "I'll bear that in mind the next time someone attacks me."

Before Turnip could point out that there wasn't going to be a next time, not if he had to chain himself to her wrist, she added hastily, "I really didn't think it was important. The man used a paper sword, one of the papier-mâché scimitars we had constructed for the wise men. I thought it was someone's brother being bribed to pull a prank."

"There are altogether too many bally pranks," grumbled Turnip, not liking the thought of Arabella being dragged into a dark hallway, even if it was only with a paper sword. "It's not funny."

"I didn't think so either, not until I realized about the sword, and then it just seemed silly. Imagine, trying to scare someone with a paper sword." She frowned, remembering. "He kept saying the same thing over and over. It was the same thing he said today."

Turnip was all attention. "What? What did he say?"

Arabella shook her head. "It made no sense. It still makes no sense."

"Tell me anyway," said Turnip. He had a very bad feeling about this.

Arabella looked up at him, her pale blond brows drawing together. "He kept saying, 'Where is it? Where's the list?'"

"This list," Turnip repeated. "You're sure he said 'list.'"

"Yes, quite sure. After all," she joked wearily, "I heard it several times."

"By Gad." He sat down heavily on a stone bench. *I told you so* had no savor to it. This was one occasion when he would have preferred not to be right.

He looked up to find Arabella looking down at him with concern. "Turnip? Are you quite all right?"

"Sit. Please."

She sat, tucking her tumbled hair back behind her ears. "What is it?"

"That list—it's not nonsense. I know what it is." He drew a long breath in between his teeth. *There are no spies.* "You're not going to like this."

She looked at him, waiting.

"It's a list of Royalist agents in France," said Turnip, all in one breath, "and Catherine Carruthers's father lost it somewhere at Miss Climpson's."

Arabella blinked. "Catherine Carruthers's father?" She seemed to be struggling to put it all together. Fair enough. If he'd just been blindfolded, pulled behind a bush, and threatened with a knife, he wouldn't be feeling all that sprightly either.

"He's something high up in the government. Claims he misplaced it, but he doesn't remember where. Last time anyone saw it, it was floating around Miss Climpson's."

"And someone thinks I have it."

She was taking it better than he expected. Of course, he had also carefully omitted any use of the word "spies." Best not to tempt his luck.

Turnip nodded vigorously. "Looks like it. That would explain why someone tore apart your room."

Arabella's head lifted as though jerked by a string. "That explains why Rose was complaining—" Her fingers curled around the edge of the bench. Turnip doubted she even realized she was doing it. "They did it again. Today. Someone must have gone through my things. Rose thought I had been rummaging."

"And when he didn't find it, he came after you with a knife. A real one," Turnip concluded. "Dead serious, this lot. It's an eyeteeth sort of thing."

"Eyeteeth?"

"As in people being willing to give them. Gather Bonaparte wants that list rather badly. You don't know how dangerous these spy chappies can be."

Arabella looked at him, her expression inscrutable. But all she said was, "You aren't really the Pink Carnation, are you?"

"Er, no. Though it's often quite convenient for people to think I am. Convenient for the Carnation, that is. Deuced inconvenient for me. But one does like to do one's bit. King and country and all that."

"So it's not entirely just a rumor, then. You do have something to do with the Pink Carnation."

Turnip gave a modest shrug. "Not all that much to write home about. I run the odd errand, sow a bit of confusion here and there, all that sort of thing. Nothing terribly important."

"I imagine you shouldn't be telling me all this, should you? If I weren't reliable, it could get back to the wrong people, and then they could use you to get to the right people. Am I wrong?"

"Er . . ." Strictly speaking, the answer to that was no.

"Why are you telling me all this?"

"Because I want to keep you safe," he said earnestly. "Because you won't believe me without an explanation. Because I'm worried about you. Because I trust you."

"Thank you," she said gravely. She tentatively rested her hand on top of his. "I trust you too."

Turning her hand over, Turnip threaded his fingers through hers. "Jolly glad we're agreed on that."

She dipped her head. "I am too."

Turnip gave her hand a little squeeze. "Now, about this chap who keeps grabbing you . . ."

For a moment, Turnip thought she was going to draw her hand away, but she didn't. She left it in his as she looked away, across the rows of ordered boxwood and the empty flower beds.

"I can't say much about him for sure other than that he's quite definitely taller than I am and he wears a large ring."

"You didn't recognize the voice?" He rubbed his thumb reassuringly along the side of her hand.

"No." She looked down at their joined hands. "His voice was muffled, first by a headdress, then by this absurd hood. It might have been nearly anyone."

"And they all wear rings," said Turnip. "Staines, Innes, Danforth, the whole lot of them."

"You think it's one of them?"

"Who else would have had the chance? Unless—" Turnip sat up straighter. Now, there was an idea.

"Unless . . . ?" Arabella prompted.

"Unless that cheval-whatsis followed you here."

"I can't really see the Chevalier de la Tour d'Argent"—the foreign name rolled grandly off her tongue, a symphony of euphonious syllables—"lurking in gardens."

Bloody showy name. " 'Course you couldn't," said Turnip. "You were wearing a hood. That's the genius of it."

"Unlike some people I know, I doubt the chevalier would sit outside my window in the cold for four nights running." Arabella's lips quirked into a lopsided smile. "He probably doesn't have a Gerkin."

He loved that smile. He loved that she found amusement in the oddest things, at the oddest times. He loved that she remembered the name of his groom. He loved her hair and her eyes and that thing she did with the corners of her lips.

Good Gad. He loved her.

It hit Turnip with the force of the proverbial *coup de foudre*. Love. Not just liking, not just lust, but the whole package, all the bits and pieces rolled into one—liking, lust, possessiveness, fear, anxiety, the urge to roll her up into a little ball and put her in a velvet-lined box where he could keep her safe for, oh, the next sixty years or so. He looked at her and he smelled fresh milk and raspberry jam and freshly cut hay.

Cupid had bally strange timing.

If he were a versifying sort of chap, he could say something about never feeling cold when she was around, or how a hundred nights beneath her window would be but the wink of an eye, or something of that nature, but the words refused to string themselves together in his head.

They jumbled and jostled and, in the end, all he came out with was, "Splendid chap, Gerkin."

Sally was right. He was a national disaster.

"So you say. I have yet to meet this paragon." Arabella cocked her head up at him, the wheels moving in her mind, and a good thing, too, because Turnip wasn't sure his mind was moving at all. It seemed to be stuck in one place. "Lord Henry Innes. Isn't he Catherine Carruthers's cousin?"

"Might be," said Turnip, interrupting the thought about sunshine and raspberry jam and long, lazy mornings in the hay . . . "Think he is, in fact. But why? You think . . ."

"It isn't much, but it's an idea," said Arabella. "A connection. And we know he was at Farley Castle."

"Was he at the Nativity play?" asked Turnip. "Didn't notice him there."

"Neither did I," Arabella admitted. "But that doesn't mean he wasn't there. It was a large crowd, and I . . . was a bit distracted."

"You had other things on your mind," said Turnip generously. "Deuced busy evening, what with all those shepherds and wise men and whatnot."

"Among other things." Arabella developed a sudden and intense interest in the gravel at her feet. Turnip watched as she stirred the pebbles in a small circle with her toe, around and around and around. "About that evening . . . ," she began hesitantly.

Turnip knew, deep in his bones, that anything that was said on that topic couldn't possibly turn out well.

It was time for preemptive measures. Briskly patting her hand, Turnip returned it to her as he scrambled up off the bench. "It's all right. Quite understandable. Out of line, climbing through your window and whatnot. Didn't think. Shall we go in?"

Arabella pressed her lips together, looking very far away and more than a little perturbed. The setting sun picked out the brighter strands in her disheveled hair, turning them to silver gilt.

"Sometimes," she said thoughtfully, "I think I would be happier if I thought less."

"Don't follow you there," said Turnip.

Arabella shook out her skirts as she rose from the bench, making a wry face that contained more than a bit of self-mockery in it. "It's nothing. Only that I'm beginning to feel a tardy appreciation for Hamlet. Action 'sicklied o'er with the pale cast of thought.'"

"Pardon?"

Arabella waved an arm in the air. "'Why let I dare not wait upon I would?'"

"That's not Hamlet," pointed out Turnip. "That's Mac-what's-his-face."

"True," agreed Arabella. "Not exactly a good role model."

"Unless you're planning to set yourself up as king of Scotland. Not sure I'd recommend it. Deuced cold country, Scotland."

"I really hadn't numbered that among my ambitions. I assure you, Scotland is safe from me."

"Ah," said Turnip, just because he wanted to keep her smiling, "but are you safe from Scotland?"

She bit down hard on her lower lip. Turnip knew that expression by now; it was the one she wore when she was trying not to laugh. Slumping forward, she covered her face with both hands, making little snorting noises that weren't quite laughter, but weren't quite sobs, either.

Turnip placed a protective arm around her shoulder. "You all right, there?"

Wiping her eyes, Arabella rested her head briefly against his shoulder before, much to Turnip's disappointment, removing it again. She turned towards him and Turnip hastily dropped his arm.

"Thank you," she said gravely. "You make me laugh."

Was that a good thing? Turnip doubted it. In all the annals of romance, it was never the court jester who got the girl. It was always the knight in shining armor, dashing to the rescue in shining breastplate on a snowy white steed.

He hadn't even managed the rescue part properly, he thought broodingly. He had only managed to make it onto the scene after his lady fair had rescued herself, and even then he'd only made it in time for a consoling embrace rather than the requisite fencing match with the villain. Not that he was complaining about the embrace—he'd quite enjoyed it—but patting someone on the back just wasn't the same as sweeping her into one's manly arms after one had dispatched the villain with a *ha* and a *ho* and a *Take that, you cad!*

He didn't even know who the villain was. It was all very lowering.

"I aim to please," said Turnip glumly. "A laugh a minute, that's my motto. Sounds even better in Latin."

"Thank you. Really." Arabella rubbed her hands over her arms to warm them. Turnip would have liked to have done it for her. "I feel much better now."

Funny, he didn't.

"This isn't good. Can't have you being dragged off again and again."

"No," said Arabella reflectively. "I don't much enjoy it. It's very hard on one's hair."

"We need a plan," said Turnip. "And I think I know someone who can help us."

Chapter 23

"It does come as a bit of a shock, doesn't it?" said Lady Pinchingdale kindly.

Arabella was tucked up in the Pinchingdales' suite of rooms, a blanket over her lap, a cup of tea in her hand, and a roaring fire at her feet. Her hair had been brushed and pinned up, the rent in her sleeve had been exclaimed over, and Lady Pinchingdale had clucked and fussed and ordered enough hot tea and biscuits for a small army. Arabella had let herself be hustled along. She was beginning to feel like a chick with not one, but two mother hens: Lady Pinchingdale and Turnip.

Arabella suspected Lady Pinchingdale of sneaking brandy into the tea. She felt curiously floaty, although that might have more to do with her own disordered emotions than any artificial opiate. There was something very bewildering about the shift from cold to warmth, from the monochrome landscape of the December garden to the brilliant gilding and rich crimson brocades of the rooms allotted to the Pinchingdales. It wasn't just the change in her physical surroundings that had her head spinning. After a week of being little more than a shadow behind her aunt's chair, she found herself swamped with solicitousness, overwhelmed with goodwill. She scarcely knew how to react to it.

And then there was Turnip, hovering over the back of her chair, checking the level of tea in her cup, shoveling enough coals onto the fire to burn down a small village. After he had practically set Arabella's feet on fire with his wild jabbing of the poker, Lady Pinchingdale had shooed him away, taking over the operation herself.

She looked at him, at his bare head shining in the firelight. The early-winter dark had already fallen outside the heavy-paned windows, making the light inside seem even brighter in comparison, as it did only on winter days. With his bright head and brighter clothes, Turnip looked right at home among the rich furnishings, among the gilded curlicues and shimmering satins. Cameo fobs dangled beneath the dramatically cut edges of his carnation-patterned waistcoat, their gold casing catching the light as he moved. His coat, more pink than burgundy, was shot through with gold thread, and his cravat, ruffled at the edges with lace, was the last word in cravats—probably because Brummel himself would be rendered speechless at the sheer number of loops and swags. His clothing was just as absurd as the wags always claimed. But on him, they looked just right, a proper casing for his exuberant personality.

Right now, he was not so much exuberant as anxious, drumming his fingers against the mantelpiece, pacing in short, explosive bursts between Arabella's chair and the fire, whipping around every few minutes to peer at her, as though he were afraid that she might disappear again.

He caught her catching him staring at her and gave her a lopsided smile that didn't hide the worry in his eyes.

She smiled back ruefully.

It didn't do to read too much into his concern. He would have done the same for Lady Pinchingdale or Jane or a stray cat that sank its claws into his pantaloons and mewed for milk. That was Turnip, decent to the core.

Arabella tried not to think about what Captain Musgrave had said. Or the very foolish things that she herself had been on the verge of saying in the garden, before he had stopped her. It was good that he had, she told herself. It had just been an impulse, born of the drama of the moment, and she would only have embarrassed both herself and him.

For a moment, when he had twined his fingers through hers, she had thought . . . But that was all nonsense.

Arabella blinked and tried to attend to what Lady Pinchingdale was saying.

"I had no idea what I was getting into when I married Geoffrey," Lady Pinchingdale was saying, as she busily poured more tea into Arabella's cup. Fragrant steam rose from the lip of the spout. "When he first told me about the spies, I thought he was making it up." She set the teapot back down on the tray. "Unfortunately, he wasn't."

Arabella rested her saucer on one blanket-covered knee. "I hadn't realized that spies were such a common household pest."

Lady Pinchingdale made a face. "They're worse than termites. They get into everything."

"Chewing away at the fabric of state?" provided Pinchingdale, smiling at his wife.

"It ain't his teeth I'm worried about. He had a *knife*, Pinchingdale. A knife!" When no one responded, Turnip crossed his arms across his chest and glowered. "Well, he did!"

"He didn't seem to want to use it, though," Arabella said thoughtfully.

Maybe it was whatever Lady Pinchingdale had slipped into the tea, but she felt the tension slipping away from her.

"I wouldn't count on that," said Turnip, pushing away from the mantel. "Deuced dangerous, relying on the goodwill of a scoundrel."

"What strikes me about all of this," Arabella said, taking another long swig of tea, "is how tentative it all is."

"There's nothing tentative about a knife at your throat," protested Turnip.

Arabella wiggled forward under her blankets so that she was sitting properly upright. "Yes, but he wasn't in any hurry to do anything with it. He scratched my arm, but that was only because I kicked him and it slipped. Last time, the knife wasn't even a real one."

"Last time?" asked Lady Pinchingdale. "This happened before?"

"Yes," said Arabella. "I was borne off by a papier-mâché scimitar filched from one of the three wise men."

She said it so drolly that both the Pinchingdales smothered smiles.

Turnip was not amused. "It wasn't papier-mâché this time. Look at the scratch on your arm."

"Are you trying to scare me?" Arabella asked, looking up at him over the rim of her teacup.

"Yes!" Turnip exploded. He dropped to his knees in front of her chair, moderating his tone. "Scare you into staying safe."

"I'm not going to stay tucked away in my room for the next two days," said Arabella. "That would just be silly. Not to mention incredibly dull."

"We could barricade your door," said Turnip, "and tell everyone you're ill. You have the grippe—no, a fever. An extremely nasty, contagious fever."

Lord Pinchingdale coughed on his tea. "Why not just say plague? That would keep the would-be murderers away."

Turnip scowled. "That's not funny."

Arabella tilted her head up at him. He looked very odd from that angle. "You don't find the Black Death amusing?"

"I don't find *your* death amusing. I won't stand here and see you murdered." Turnip's cheeks were flushed with emotion rather than tea.

"No one is going to murder me," said Arabella, with more confidence than she felt. "Among other things, if whoever it is killed me, how would he ever find out where his list is? That's probably a better safeguard of my health than all the goodwill in the world."

Turnip looked unconvinced. "I still say the best safeguard is a few solid locks."

"And some boils?" Arabella hitched up her blanket, which was slipping down over her lap. "It won't work. Locks can be picked and walls can be scaled."

"Not these walls," said Turnip with confidence. "There isn't a trellis. I checked."

Their eyes met and Arabella felt all the heat in the room go straight to her cheeks. "Well," she said, in muffled tones, "that is reassuring."

"I feel like I'm missing something," murmured Lady Pinchingdale to her husband, not quite sotto voce.

"A trellis, apparently," said Lord Pinchingdale. "But you raise an interesting point. As long as our villain thinks you have the list, he has an interest in following your movements."

"Which means," his wife finished for him, her eyes bright, "that we can follow him."

"Oh no," said Turnip, catching their drift. "Don't like it. Don't like it at'all. Won't have Miss Dempsey being used as bait."

"What I don't understand," Arabella intervened, before he could start steaming at the ears, "is why this . . . person persists in believing that I have his list in the first place. Unlike all of you," she added, looking from Lord Pinchingdale to his wife to, at very long last, Turnip, brooding by the mantelpiece, "I have nothing to do with spying or spies."

"You mean you *had* nothing to do with them," contributed Lady Pinchingdale wryly. "I felt much the same way."

Turnip, who had been brooding into the flames, turned abruptly. "It's the notebook. It must have been in the notebook. Everyone saw Miss Climpson hand it to you."

"Everyone being your sister, her friends, Miss Climpson, and Signor Marconi," countered Arabella, ticking them off on her fingers. "Somehow, I doubt that Sally has been augmenting her allowance by running an international spy ring."

A slight grin tweaked one side of Turnip's lips. "Shouldn't put it past her," he said fondly. "But you're forgetting someone. Signor Marconi. No man who wears false mustachios can be up to any good."

"Words to live by," murmured Lord Pinchingdale. "You are right in part. Signor Marconi isn't what he seems."

"Ha!" said Turnip. "Thought I saw him lurking about the place. That third dragon from the left in Monday's mummer play . . ."

"Couldn't have been Marconi," Pinchingdale interrupted him pointedly. "Marconi is, in fact, none other than Bert Marks of Tipton Downs, Yorkshire, and has never been farther abroad than Portsmouth."

"Oh," said Turnip. "How—?"

"He was Henrietta Selwick's voice teacher," Lady Pinchingdale provided on her husband's behalf, snuggling down on the arm of his chair. "Apparently Italians do better as music teachers, just as Frenchwomen do better as dressmakers, so Mr. Marks became Signor Marconi. Lady Uppington had his background thoroughly vetted before allowing him into the house. He's a fraud, but not a traitor."

"At least as far as we know," Lord Pinchingdale qualified. "More honorable men have been known to turn traitor for the right sum. Marks—or Marconi—hasn't exactly shown himself to be of sterling character."

"It needn't have been Marconi," Turnip interjected. "What with the furniture flying and the porcelain breaking, anyone could have marched through that room and no one would have noticed. Half of Bath was climbing in and out the windows of the school that night."

Arabella forbore to point out that he had been one of them. That would only bring up trellises again, and heaven only knew where that would lead them.

Lady Pinchingdale's round blue eyes were even rounder than usual. "What sort of school is this?"

"Not one to which we are sending our daughter," said Lord Pinchingdale. "We seem to be straying from the point."

"One gets to much more interesting places that way," murmured Arabella. Who was it who had said that to her? Oh. The chevalier. That reminded her of Mlle de Fayette's visit earlier that night, and the flashes of lights in the garden that had set the whole bizarre series of events in train. "There was someone else in the garden that night, someone signaling with a lantern."

"By Gad! That's it!" Turnip slapped a hand on the mantel so emphatically that a china vase tottered on its base. "The lantern and the notebook. The chap with the lantern must have come to collect the notebook. It was always on that windowsill."

"It's true," agreed Arabella from her nest of blankets. "I saw it there almost every time I was in the blue parlor. Sometimes it moved about from window to table, but no one ever claimed it."

Turnip's blue eyes were bright with excitement. "Would have been an excellent way to pass on information. So commonplace that no one remarked on it. Deuced clever when you think about it."

Arabella hated to destroy his pretty theory. "There's just one problem. The notebook went missing. I don't have it. If our villain was the one who looted my room, why is he still bothering me?"

Turnip lost some of his glow. "Oh," he said. "Haven't worked that out yet."

Lord Pinchingdale looked from one to the other. "The document that went missing would have been a single sheet of paper, closely written on both sides."

Something snagged at Arabella's memory. Like flotsam in a river, it bobbed briefly to the surface before drifting away again.

"The paper might have been inside the notebook," suggested Lady Pinchingdale practically, wiggling to get a more comfortable purchase on the edge of her husband's chair. "There's no better place to hide a piece of paper than among other pieces of paper."

Lord Pinchingdale shifted to make room for her, sliding an arm around her waist to steady her. She leaned her head comfortably against his shoulder, in a gesture of such affection and trust that it made Arabella's throat hurt to look at it.

As Arabella watched, Lord Pinchingdale absently rubbed a finger along Lady Pinchingdale's arm, a movement too small to be officially called a caress, and yet intimate enough to make Arabella look away. It reminded her of the casual intimacy of Turnip's thumb stroking the side of her hand as they had sat together in the garden, her fingers twined with his.

Clasping her hands in her lap, Arabella hastily cleared her throat. "It would be an excellent way to get messages in and out of the school," she babbled, not looking at anyone. "People were constantly in and out of that room, and no one would have remarked on the window being open. All you would have to do is reach through the window, extract the paper from between the covers, and exit by the garden gate again."

She could see the tassels swinging on Turnip's boots as he paced excitedly back and forth in front of her chair. "The first pudding was by the window too, wasn't it? That's where Sal said she found it. On the windowsill."

"Pudding?" Lady Pinchingdale said warily from the vicinity of her husband's shoulder.

"I'll explain later," said her husband. He looked at her with concern. "Are you all right?"

Now that he asked, Arabella noticed that Lady Pinchingdale was looking very green.

"Um-hmm," she said, her lips pinched very tightly together. "Go on. Please." There was a faint sheen of sweat at her brow.

"All right." He dragged his gaze reluctantly away from the top of his wife's head, looking from Turnip to Arabella. "In short, your villain might have been anyone at the school. We know Mr. Carruthers lost the paper while at Miss Climpson's. It might have been extracted from him by nearly anyone there. We have no idea who took the paper or for whom it was intended."

"We just know that they want it back," contributed Lady Pinchingdale. Her lips had gone very pale. Even her freckles seemed subdued.

Turnip looked seriously at his old school friend. "Do you think if they have it, they'll leave Miss Dempsey alone?"

Lord Pinchingdale raised one dark brow. "So one presumes."

"Right," said Turnip, squaring his shoulders. "Then we just have to give them what they want."

"But I don't have it," said Arabella, to her own knees.

"Don't you see?" Turnip's eyes were blazing with excitement. He looked like a man whose team had just beat Rugby at rugby. "We give them a false list! We change names and places about. We rout the spy, stymie Bonaparte, and keep those demmed knives from your throat!"

Lady Pinchingdale lifted her head briefly from her husband's shoulder. "That's brilliant."

"Two problems," said Lord Pinchingdale. Both his wife and his friend shot him wounded looks. He held up his free hand in a gesture of self-defense. "Don't shoot the messenger. I'm not disputing the desirability of the plan, simply the odds of executing it."

"Care to translate that to English?" requested Turnip.

Lady Pinchingdale rolled her head over just enough to clear her mouth. "He thinks it can't be done," she said, and then rolled her face back into his sleeve.

"Thank you, sweetheart," said Pinchingdale affectionately to the top of her head. "Succinctly put. Our first problem is that we haven't seen the list. He has. He'll spot a fake."

"Not until he has it in hand!" said Turnip hotly. "And by then we'll have pounced."

He made a pouncing motion.

"*Second,*" said Lord Pinchingdale, pointedly ignoring the pouncing, "we run up against our fundamental problem. It's almost tautological in nature."

"English, Pinchingdale?" prompted Turnip.

"If we don't know who he is, how do we communicate with him?"

"Ha," said Turnip, folding his arms across his chest. "I already thought of that. We leave him a pudding."

The mention of pudding proved too much for Lady Pinchingdale. From the crook of her husband's arm, she made a slight gurgling noise.

"Will you excuse me, please?" she said faintly, and half stood, half slid off the side of the chair.

Face averted, she stumbled towards the door that connected sitting room and bedroom. What Arabella could make out of her face had gone greener than her green wool dress.

"Be right back," she mumbled, fumbling at the doorknob. "Carry on without me."

"She has morning sickness," said Pinchingdale distractedly, his eyes following his wife. "And afternoon sickness and evening sickness. Excuse me for a moment."

Pushing himself off his chair, he disappeared into the bedroom after her, leaving Arabella and Turnip momentarily unchaperoned.

Scooching down in her chair, Arabella looked at the gilded frame of the door, all but disguised by the paneling. "She reminds me of my mother. Not physically"—her mother had been tall and big-boned where Lady Pinchingdale was short and plump, fresh faced where Lady Pinchingdale was freckled, straight-haired where Lady Pinchingdale's was curly—"but in spirit."

It was nearly impossible to remember that Lady Pinchingdale was sister to the terrifying Lady Vaughn, scourge of wallflowers everywhere.

During their ballroom days, Arabella had often shared a patch of wall with the former Miss Letty Alsworthy, but they had never done more than exchange a smile and a nod. Arabella wondered why they had never spoken. She rather wished they had. She had been so busy trying to pretend that she wasn't there that she had missed the chance for a friend.

Arabella's teacup listed dangerously to one side. Turnip plucked it from her hand. Lifting it to his nose, he sniffed the contents. "Letty must have emptied half a decanter in here. We'll have to sober you up before tonight." He hunkered down on his knees in front of her chair, looking up at her hopefully. "Unless you'd rather stay in your room?"

Arabella shook her head, making his features swim. "And miss the Epiphany Eve dance? I wouldn't think of it."

Turnip sighed. "That's that, then." Standing, he rested a hand on her shoulder, the only part of her showing above the blanket. "Won't leave your side for a minute. I'll keep you safe. I promise."

For just a moment, Arabella leaned her cheek against his hand, letting herself savor the prospect of comfort and tenderness it offered.

Turnip's hand lingered on her arm, protectively covering the slit in her sleeve. Through the corner of her eye, she could see his face, perturbed, his brows drawn together over his nose. "Arabella, I—"

She knew what he was thinking. "Don't worry," she said, allowing herself, very fleetingly, the luxury of touching his hand where it covered her arm. She could feel the muscles in his fingers contract at her touch. "I'm not in any danger. This is England, not *The Castle of Otranto*. It is silly. The whole thing. Messages being passed in puddings, paper swords—it's something out of farce, not tragedy."

"I hope you're right." Turnip's hand tightened protectively on her arm. "But I'm sticking by your side until we know for sure. Anyone who wants you will have to get through me first."

Chapter 24

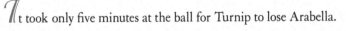

It took only five minutes at the ball for Turnip to lose Arabella.

The event was a small affair by the dowager's standards. "A little entertainment for the country folk," she called it, if a little entertainment could be held to comprise more than two hundred people, all rigged out in their very best. Tomorrow night, the long gallery at Girdings would be mobbed with fashionable folk come up from London, with peers and peeresses glittering with diamonds, but tonight the ballroom was crowded with an ill-assorted mix of the dowager's country neighbors, the rarefied denizens of the house party, and guests come early for the following evening's elaborate Twelfth Night festivities. The country squires, in their old-fashioned wigs and buckled shoes, looked askance at the pinks of the *ton*, with their elaborate cravats and painfully high shirt points, while the London matrons made moues at the heavy, full-skirted brocades and long curls of the country set.

"So last century!" Turnip heard one hiss to another behind her fan. "Do you think someone ought to tell them?"

And they both snickered.

Turnip craned to see over the towering headdress of one of the country ladies, who looked as though she was wearing her hair in memorial of the late lamented Queen of France—or simply had a few birds' nests piled in there. He had seen Arabella settled in her customary place by her aunt's side not five minutes ago, safely tucked away among the wallflowers and the dowagers.

But now she was gone.

The space beside Lady Osborne on the settee was conspicuously empty. Captain Musgrave was still there, leaning over his wife's shoulder, ostensibly whispering something in her ear even as his eyes scanned the room. Lady Osborne herself seemed entirely unconcerned, fanning herself with a feather-edged fan as she gossiped to the lady on her other side.

The villain couldn't have abstracted Arabella from among a ballroom full of people, could he? Not in the first five minutes of the ball?

Turnip shoved and elbowed his way through the crowd, trying not to panic. If only he hadn't let himself be distracted by Lady Henrietta Selwick—er, Dorrington—who insisted on smothering him in an embrace and then mocking his waistcoat.

Ha! There Arabella was. Turnip's breath escaped his lungs in an explosive gasp. For a moment, the relief was so intense that he felt lightheaded with it. There was no one next to her or behind her, no one holding a knife to her ribs or a pistol to her head. She was walking entirely alone and unescorted towards the doors of the gallery.

Alone and unescorted. Turnip's bubble of well-being popped. What was she doing leaving the safety of the gallery?

Where in the bloody hell was Pinchingdale? Probably gone up to check on Letty, who would be having another bout of evening sickness. Which meant that there would be no one else watching for Arabella.

Except, of course, her assailant.

Turnip bolted for the doors to the gallery, skirting around a group of country squires discussing agricultural improvements, knocking over three old-fashioned periwigs and one wooden leg, dodging two lapdogs, and momentarily getting tangled with one ceremonial sword. Fortunately, it was sheathed.

"Sorry, sorry," he said generally, and kept going, leaping over the dowager's small yippy dog to arrive breathless but triumphant at the doors of the gallery only moments after Arabella.

An impassive footman, stiff as a toy soldier in his green and gold livery, opened the door before Turnip could go barreling through.

Turnip skidded to a halt just beyond the door. A series of rooms stretched out enfilade, one opening onto another. The ducal architects had believed in decorating on a grand scale. Among the more conventional pieces of furniture, huge pieces of classical statuary leered down from pedestals; trompe l'oeil panels on the walls created the illusion of alcoves holding vast flowering urns, mirroring the actual urns set across from them.

In short, it was a villain's playhouse. Turnip could feel the hairs on his neck begin to prickle. Even with the candles dripping wax from the great candelabra stationed along the route, there were far too many places for a man to hide, lying in wait. It was making him deuced twitchy just thinking about it.

The rooms ran along the garden front, each boasting a set of doors, some cleverly concealed, others grandly displayed, opening into the same shrubbery into which Arabella had been dragged, blind, just hours before. It would be far too easy for a chap to slip out from behind a statue, clap a hand over her mouth before she had a chance to scream, and back her out through those cleverly concealed doors into the garden. The gallery, with its many balconies, looked out onto the West

Front. The chatter from the ballroom, the pounding of dancing feet, the exuberant playing of the musicians, all would mask any sounds from the acres of garden at the back of the house.

Back to the wall, Turnip slunk along behind, keeping one eye on Arabella's back, the other on the lookout for potential villains. Deuced good thing he had two of them.

He would cling to her like a shadow, follow her like a bad dream, stalk her footsteps like a—well, something else shadowy and intangible. She would never know he was there.

"Turnip?"

Turnip ducked behind a statue of Neptune. Fortunately, Neptune had been a full-figured sort of chap. Tall, too. Especially since he was on a pedestal.

Arabella stopped and turned. "Turnip, I know you're there."

Turnip stepped out from behind Neptune. "Don't mind me," he said airily. "Never know I'm here. Just a shadow on the wall." He thumped the wall for emphasis.

"For a shadow," said Arabella, "you are surprisingly corporeal."

"Shouldn't do you much good if I weren't," he said, flexing one arm. If anyone attacked her, he would show them just how corporeal he could be. "What are you doing out of the ballroom? You weren't supposed to leave the gallery."

"My aunt wanted her vinaigrette. She forgot it in here." Placing her hands on her hips, Arabella surveyed the room, a small drawing room decorated in yellow and rose.

"Ah. There it is." Arabella dove for the ground, getting down on hands and knees to peer beneath a small settee upholstered in pale gold stripes. Candlelight shimmered distractingly off the peach silk lovingly covering the curves of her backside as she wiggled head and shoulders under the settee.

Turnip swallowed hard as the movement caused the rest of her to wiggle too. He inserted a finger beneath his collar.

"It rolled some way," came Arabella's voice, slightly muffled, from beneath the settee. "Ha! Got it."

She backed out from beneath the settee, a small object clutched triumphantly in one gloved hand.

Blinking, Turnip recalled himself to his duty. He was supposed to be protecting Arabella from spies. Not—well.

He looked sternly at her. "I don't care if your aunt forgot her own name. You're not to leave that ballroom. Can't keep an eye on you if you go on wandering about."

Whatever else she wanted—the moon on a platter, the head of John the Baptist, tea and figgy pudding—it would be hers for the asking, but this, this was too important for negotiation. Couldn't bring her heads on platters if she wasn't alive to receive them, could he?

Her eyes fixed thoughtfully on his face, Arabella swiped a dust clump from the shoulder of her gown. "All right," she said.

"It ain't negotiable," Turnip said belligerently. "Don't matter if she forgot her left rib. I— All right?"

"All right," Arabella confirmed. "Until we know who it is, I would have to be an idiot to take risks just for the sake of taking them. There's no point in courting danger unless it gets us something."

Turnip didn't like the idea of her courting danger even then. He had nearly come to blows with Pinchingdale over it, an argument derailed only by Letty's turning a pale shade of green and bolting for the bedroom again. It was, Pinchingdale had argued, the best and easiest way. How else could they get the villain to expose himself, but by giving him the opportunity—a false opportunity, he had specified carefully—to corner Arabella? Turnip's answer to that, but for the presence of the ladies, would have been profane. As it was, it had simply been incoherent.

Turnip's plan, that they put messages in puddings and plant them in various key places around Girdings House, had been universally voted down.

In the end, they had compromised. Arabella wasn't to be exposed to unnecessary danger, but neither was she to be locked up in her room with a guard at her door (Turnip's preferred plan). Instead, they were all to go about their normal activities, with someone keeping watch at all times, ready to catch the villain if he pounced.

Or, as Pinchingdale put it, when he pounced.

"If your aunt needs anything, *I* can get it," declared Turnip grandly, before remembering that that, too, would rather defeat the purpose. Couldn't keep an eye on her if he wasn't there. "Stay where I can see you! And no more vinaigrettes."

Arabella lifted the vinaigrette to him in salute and turned her back. She wore a thin silk shawl looped over her elbows, and he watched the gentle sway of it as she walked briskly back down the long line of rooms.

Turnip waited five minutes before following her. It felt like a great deal longer. When he returned to the gallery, it was to find the long room even more crowded than before. A set was just about to finish in the area that had been cleared for dancing, boasting a line of twenty couples. He could smell the reek of strong perfume, sweat, and the ale the dowager had provided for her country guests warring with the more familiar sickly sweet scent of champagne.

As he threaded his way through the room, looking for a good vantage point from which to keep watch on Arabella, he passed a mutinous-looking Catherine Carruthers, standing with her parents on the edge of the dance floor, wearing a dress as flounced and frilled as current fashion would allow. Her light brown hair had been twisted into curls that bounced on either side of her small-featured, oval face.

She would have been pretty enough but for the sulky expression that drew down the corners of her mouth, turning her otherwise pleasantly featured face into something one wouldn't want to run into in a dark alley.

Although her betrothal to Lord Grimmlesby-Thorpe had already been officially announced in the papers, her parents were obviously taking no further chances with her. One stood to either side, flanking her like gaolers guarding a prisoner.

As Turnip passed by, he could hear her high-pitched, slightly nasal voice saying, "At least *I* didn't elope with the music master."

What was that about the music master? Turnip came to an abrupt halt. "Beg pardon?"

Mr. and Mrs. Carruthers gave him strange looks, but Catherine took his rude intrusion into their conversation with the peculiar sang-froid known only to sixteen-year-old girls.

She gestured to Turnip in a world-weary way, showing off the very shiny gold bracelet fastened over her glove. "This is Sally Fitzhugh's brother, Mama. You remember Sally Fitzhugh? The one I visited at Parva Magna last winter."

"Oh, yes." Mrs. Carruthers totted up the cost of Turnip's clothes and decided to forgive him for his breach of etiquette. "How nice to meet you at last, Mr. Fitzhugh. Your sister is a charming girl."

"She puts on a good show when she has to," agreed Turnip. Mrs. Carruthers looked mildly startled, but he barreled on. "What's that about the music master?"

"Oh," said Catherine, looking superior, "didn't you hear? He ran off with Clarissa Hardcastle just before Christmas. Apparently they had been meeting by night in the music room. *Disgusting.*"

It was unclear whether the adjective referred to the location or the event.

"Frightfully bad *ton*," complained her mother, who looked more like a Pekingese than a Pekingese, "eloping with music masters."

"Bad idea eloping at all," said Catherine's father, looking stern. If Mrs. Carruthers was a Pekingese, Mr. Carruthers was an elderly bloodhound. He had a long, narrow face, made longer and narrower by the fact that his cheeks seemed to have slowly slid straight off the side of his face to dangle on either side of his jaw, like the droopy jowls of a tired old dog.

"Wasn't intending to," Turnip said hastily. "Wouldn't dream of it. Deuced hard on the shins, climbing down bedsheets and all that."

The Carrutherses, parents and child, gave him strange looks, but Turnip didn't notice. So that explained what the music master had been doing, blundering about the school in the wee hours.

"An heiress, I take it?" said Turnip.

"Yes," said Mrs. Carruthers, as though the word soiled her mouth. "Her father does something in the city. Something with guns. *Frightful*. I don't know what Miss Climpson was thinking."

About the music master or munitions heiresses? Turnip decided not to ask. He was spared the necessity by the arrival of Catherine's intended, Lord Grimmlesby-Thorpe, who was tricked out in a getup nearly as brilliant as Turnip's, with a canary yellow waistcoat sewn with brilliants and a pair of breeches so tight they creaked when he walked.

The creaking sound might also have been the corset that he, like his great friend the Prince of Wales, wore to contain the embonpoint attendant on too much port and game.

Grimmlesby-Thorpe set his hand on Catherine's half-bared shoulder. "There you are, my dear."

He was the only one who didn't notice the way Catherine flinched away from his touch. The expression on her face reminded Turnip of a half-broken horse he had once seen. The horse had rolled his eyes and bared his gums in just the same way—right before dumping his rider, stomping on his knee, and jumping three fences and a small brook before he was finally caught.

Turnip had never liked Catherine—she had pulled one too many supposedly friendly tricks on Sally during the duration of their intimacy—but, at this moment, he felt sincerely sorry for her. It wasn't right marrying a young girl like that off to an old bon vivant like Grimmlesby. No matter how many half-pay officers she had tried to run off with, it just wasn't right.

On the other hand, from the look Catherine was giving her intended, she fully planned to get her own back. Turnip didn't envy Grimmlesby-Thorpe his half of the marriage bed either. If ever he had met a junior Lady Mac-whatever-it-was in training, Catherine was it.

Speaking of marriage beds . . . Turnip peered across the couples on the dance floor to make sure that Arabella was still with her aunt. She was, although she had been ousted from her seat on the settee by the Dowager Lady Pinchingdale, forced instead to stand beside the settee, her back against the wall. She didn't see him. She was watching the dancers in the center of the floor, her skirt moving almost imperceptibly as her foot tapped in time to the music. There was a wistful look on her face as she watched the couples move through the patterns of the dance. Then her aunt tapped her on the arm, demanding her attention, and her face cleared and her foot stilled. The patient mask was back in place.

Turnip was suddenly reminded of a conversation they had had a very long time ago, in the ruins of Farley Castle, something about inhabiting opposite sides of the ballroom. And he, carelessly, had promised that the next time they found themselves in the ballroom, they would meet in the middle, to dance.

He had failed in his promise so far, but there was still time to redeem it, and to the devil with all French spies and interfering aunts.

Mrs. Carruthers was saying something to him, but Turnip couldn't have vouched for a word of it.

At the front of the room, the master of ceremonies was banging his long stick and calling all couples to line up for the Fairy Queen.

"Excuse me," he broke in on a startled Mrs. Carruthers. "Must go. Debts of honor and all that, don't you know."

"The *impertinence!*" he heard her say, but he was already halfway across the room, making for the spot where the dowagers sat.

He must have looked rather fearsome, because Arabella looked at him with an expression of mingled inquiry and alarm.

He grinned at her to set her at her ease, a big, silly grin that expanded straight through to both his ears, a grin so big his face hardly had room to contain it.

He grinned and held out a hand that was, considering his bounding joy, surprisingly steady.

"I say," he said. "Don't I owe you this dance?"

Chapter 25

"*P*romised you we would dance together. Remember?"

For her aunt's benefit, Arabella said primly, "I shouldn't want to hold you to the obligation should you no longer wish to discharge it."

Turnip held out his hand, palm up. "Dance with me."

Heaving a sigh, Arabella surrendered her hand to his with feigned reluctance. "If you insist. But I want it on the record that it was under duress."

"Bullied you into it and all that," Turnip agreed, tucking her hand into the crook of his arm. It looked nice there, like it belonged.

"What's all this?" demanded Captain Musgrave, leaning over the back of the settee.

Turnip thought it was a bit rich, the man turning all guardianish when he couldn't be much older than Turnip himself, if that, but Arabella got there first.

"What one does at a dance," Arabella said, and there was a peculiarly militant light to her eye. "Dance."

"Oh dear," said Lady Osborne, hunting through the folds of her shawl in a preoccupied way that Turnip had seen time and time before. "I believe I left my—"

Turnip saw the shades of the prison house fall across Arabella's face and felt all his instincts for knight-errantry rise to the fore. Might not be precisely in the accepted heroic model, but dragons came in all shapes and sizes. Just look at the Dowager Duchess of Dovedale.

Taking Arabella's arm, Turnip propelled her shamelessly away. "Set's filling up! Must go or we'll lose our place! Coming, Miss Dempsey?"

"Did I have a choice?" asked Arabella breathlessly. He looked down to see the corners of her eyes crinkling with amusement and something else. If he weren't a modest man, he might call it admiration. It made him feel about ten feet tall.

"Can't let Cinderella miss all the ball," he said jovially, swinging her into place at the bottom of the set just as the initial strains began.

Arabella sank into a curtsy as he bowed. "Is that how you see me?" she asked, as their hands came together in the first figure. "Cinderella?"

Turnip rather suspected that this was one of those trick questions females seemed always to be asking. He only wished he knew what the answer was. He suspected that it wasn't yes, but if he told her how he really saw her, it would scandalize the people on either side of them and probably get him summarily evicted from the dowager's ballroom.

"The only woman I want to be dancing with," he said extravagantly.

Arabella gave him a look of mingled pleasure and skepticism before skipping off down the center of the aisle.

Of all the women he knew, she had the hardest time accepting a compliment. Maybe, he thought, watching her as she circled Darius

Danforth, who was partnering Lucy Ponsonby, that was because she hadn't received very many of them.

Men were idiots. Himself included.

If he had ever bothered to ask her to dance, all those years ago, he might have observed how enthusiastically she moved to the music. It wasn't just that she was a good dancer—anyone with a proper sense of rhythm and time with a memory for the movements could be a good dancer—but that she was a joyful one, dancing not just with her feet, but with her whole body, putting herself heart and soul into every twirl and skip, every turn and dip. There was an innocent sort of abandon to it, all the walls she built so carefully around herself momentarily abandoned in the wordless execution of the dance.

How did everyone else not notice?

It was an energetic dance, with lots of twirling and circling and galloping about. Arabella's cheeks were pink, her forehead shiny, and her lips very red from the exercise. Her hair, which had been so modestly smoothed down and pulled back, had escaped in little wisps around her face, clinging to her cheeks and forehead.

Turnip could feel himself growing short of breath, but not from the exertion.

As he clasped her right hand with his left, prancing in a circle with Danforth and Lucy Ponsonby, she smiled up at him and unself-consciously gave a little puff of breath to blow a stubborn lock of hair out of her eye.

It was the most unconsciously seductive thing he had ever seen. Turnip nearly lost his footing.

Of course, at this point, she could debone a kipper with a fish knife and he would find it seductive, he was that far gone.

Well, maybe not a kipper.

As the dance drew to its close, Turnip snuck a glance at Arabella as they retreated to opposite sides of the line for the final bow. The filmy white lace that edged her décolletage clung damply to her skin, calling attention to the curve of her breasts beneath the fabric.

No wonder some puritan sects frowned on dancing. Turnip had always thought it a fairly innocent sport until now.

As the set disintegrated, some going off to find other partners, others heading for the refreshment tables, Arabella self-consciously fanned her flushed face. "It is rather warm in here, isn't it?"

Warm didn't even begin to describe it.

Turnip seized on the excuse. "Shall we take the air? It will be cooler outside on the balcony."

If he had had a club on him, he would have banged her over the head and borne her off to his cave. Being a supposedly civilized nineteenth-century gentleman, the best he could do was a balcony.

In Norfolk. In January. Not exactly the most romantic gesture in the world, shivering in the frigid cold. Perhaps that was why Shakespeare had set so many of his comedies in warm climates, and only the tragedies in cold ones. Wouldn't be much of a romance with Beatrice and Benedick both succumbing to pneumonia before the end of the second act.

Arabella looked to the corner where her aunt sat, gossiping with the Dowager Lady Pinchingdale. "My aunt doesn't seem to need her left rib yet."

"If she does, her husband can get it," said Turnip, tucking Arabella's hand beneath his arm before she could change her mind. That hadn't been precisely a yes, but Turnip felt secure in taking it as one. "That's what they're for. Husbands, I mean, not ribs. Jolly useful things, husbands," he added. It was never too early to set the groundwork. "Or so I hear."

As they walked through the French doors onto the balcony, Arabella surveyed the breadth of the veranda, a curious expression on her face. "So this is what a balcony looks like by night."

"Much as it does by day. Doesn't move about much, you know. Attached to the house and all that."

"I always used to be"—she hunched her shoulders self-deprecatingly—"a little bit envious of those women who slipped off to balconies during a ball. I know one is supposed to disapprove, but . . ."

She looked up at him and shrugged, acknowledging the inevitability of human frailty.

Turnip was feeling pretty bally frail just about now. The fall of man had never made more sense than it did now. His only regret was that he had wasted so much time. There had been so many ballrooms and so many balconies that they could have shared.

"Well, here you are! Nothing like making up for lost time."

Arabella wrinkled her nose at him. "There's no need to mock."

"Wouldn't think of it," Turnip assured her, scanning the balcony for a properly secluded spot, someplace near enough to the door for warmth, but far enough away for privacy. "Not a mock on me. Entirely mock-free."

"Just because you've been out on dozens of balconies . . ."

"Yes, but never one so nice as this. Shan't look at another balcony ever again." Turnip pointed to a nice little area about three feet over, near enough to the door to still be considered respectable, but nicely out of view. "I say, that's a charming patch of balustrade over there. Let's go lean on it."

"Oh," said Arabella, her eyes bright with amusement, her cheeks flushed with cold and exertion, "is *that* what one does on balconies?"

"That and play tiddlywinks," said Turnip giddily, putting his hand on the small of her back to guide her. Her hair brushed his cheek as she turned her head, and he smelled soap and lilac.

"I'll warn you," said Arabella, looking up at him. "I'm a fierce tiddlywink player."

Turnip touched a hand to her cheek, admiring the messy wisps of her hair, the reddening tip of her nose, the remains of a dust smudge on her chin.

"I wouldn't expect anything less," he said tenderly.

She looked at him with wide, uncertain eyes, knowing as well as he that they weren't talking about tiddlywinks anymore. But she didn't say anything. And she didn't pull away. Beyond them, the parkland stretched out in all its winter barrenness, but Turnip could have sworn he smelled flowers blooming.

Arabella's lashes fluttered down to cover her eyes.

And abruptly popped up again as the balcony door banged open.

Turnip hastily moved to shield her with his body; he wasn't even sure why or from what; it was just an automatic reflex.

A girl in a white-and-silver dress came tumbling through the door, her brilliant red hair caught high above her head, threaded with matching silver ribbons, her every move a challenge as she gestured back over her shoulder at the man following close behind her.

"Too cold for you, Freddy?" she demanded, her voice husky. Turnip could feel Arabella stiffen beside him at the sound of it.

"Is that a challenge?" Lord Frederick Staines asked, sauntering through the ballroom doors. He stood silhouetted in the light from the ballroom, hands in his pockets, the picture of aristocratic boredom.

Already at the bottom of the steps, Penelope tilted her head up at him. Neither of them seemed to have noticed the couple in the shadows on the side of the balcony. Or if they had, they didn't care. "It is if you choose to take it as such."

Lord Frederick laughed, a low, arrogant sound that made Turnip think of the horns blown to signal the beginning of the hunt. He bounded down the steps, catching Penelope around the waist. "I'll take whatever I like."

She twisted away, lithe in the moonlight, part hunted, part huntress. "We'll see about that."

They disappeared into the shadows, Penelope's slippers soundless, Lord Frederick's booted feet crunching on the gravel.

"Not good," Turnip said. "Not good at'all."

"No." He looked down to find Arabella watching him, all the humor that had animated her face a moment ago gone. She looked weary and more than a little bit unhappy. "I'm sorry," she said, and the words seemed to cost her an effort.

"So am I," agreed Turnip. Not that he should talk, having inveigled Arabella out onto the balcony, but there was a difference. He knew his intentions were honorable. Staines wouldn't know honorable if it bit him in the backside. Penelope might be a bit of a wild thing, but she was a good soul at heart. She deserved better. "Staines is a rotter."

Stepping away from him, Arabella placed both hands on the flat surface of the balustrade, leaning her weight on her palms as she gazed out over the thickly planted shrubbery. "Perhaps if you said something?"

"Doubt old Pen would thank me for going jumping over the balcony and disturbing her fun."

For that matter, he wasn't entirely thrilled with old Pen for having disrupted his. One minute they had been laughing with each other, a whisper away from a kiss, and now Arabella was as distant as the moon.

Turnip didn't understand it. He didn't understand it at all. Did she want him to go rescue Penelope? Was that it?

Arabella appeared to have developed a deep interest in the urn on the side of the balustrade. Not that it wasn't a perfectly nice urn, but it had the unfortunate effect of turning her face well out of his view.

"Did you ever think to declare yourself?" she asked the urn.

"Declare? Declare what?"

Arabella waved her hands helplessly. "Your feelings. For her."

Feelings?

Turnip looked sharply at Arabella, who was very pointedly not looking at him. "You didn't think that Penelope—? That I—?" It was too absurd to articulate. "By Gad, that's a good one."

"I don't see how it's funny," said Arabella stiffly. "Everyone keeps saying you mean to marry her."

"Pen is—well, she's a chum."

More than a chum if one counted those interludes on balconies, but Turnip deemed it wiser not to go into that. Penelope took something of a male approach to things like balconies, but Turnip didn't think Arabella would quite understand that.

"We've known each other since I was in dresses. But marry her?" Turnip shuddered dramatically. "She'd have me for breakfast."

"With or without raspberry jam?" Arabella asked suspiciously.

"Without," Turnip said with authority. "Pen is more a marmalade sort of girl. More tart than sweet, don't you know."

"No, I wouldn't know," said Arabella crankily. "But I do know that it's very cold out here."

She pushed away from the balustrade, making as though to go to the door, but Turnip moved to block her. "You're jealous, aren't you?"

She blinked at him. "I beg your pardon?"

Hmm. Maybe he oughtn't to have said that aloud.

"She's not the flavor of jam I want," he said hastily. "Never has been. Didn't mean to give anyone that idea, least of all you."

Arabella hastily shook her head, not looking at him. "You don't need to explain yourself to me. Really."

Turnip took her chin in his hand, raising her face to his. "Yes, I do. Wouldn't be able to live with myself if I didn't." More important, he wouldn't be able to live with her. "Your good opinion matters to me. It matters a lot."

He wasn't doing a very good job of this, was he? At least she had stopped trying to wiggle past him.

She bit her lip, as though unsure what to say. "Thank you. I value your good opinion too."

They sounded like a couple of Oxford dons exchanging commendations. Bother, bother, bother. Next they would be shaking hands and saying things like "value and esteem," which were about as passionate as a glass of warm milk.

Turnip planted his hands on the balustrade on either side of her, effectively boxing her in. "What I'm trying to say is—" What was he trying to say? "You don't have a handkerchief, do you?" he blurted out, playing for time.

Now he understood why chaps generally liked to have a ring about them when they proposed. Whipping it out bought a chap time to figure out what he was trying to say. The shinier the ring, the longer the reprieve.

Confused but game, Arabella fumbled at the side of her skirt, looking for a pocket that wasn't there.

Rolling her eyes, she laughed nervously. "You see how unfashionable I've become. We had pockets in our dresses at Miss—"

She broke off, her face frozen. Her mouth was slightly open and her eyes were fixed in a glazed sort of way on something just past Turnip's right shoulder. Turnip glanced back, but he didn't see anything other than the stone wall of the house. Not so much as a caterpillar.

"Arabella?" Turnip waved a hand in front of her face. "Hallo? All right there?"

Arabella grabbed his hand, face glowing brighter than all the candles in the ballroom. "Turnip! I've got it!"

Well, that was a relief. That would save him trying to explain it.

"If you mean my hand," he said, giving hers a squeeze, "yes, you have. And while we're on that topic . . ."

"Turnip! Don't you see?" She gave a little hop, taking his hand along with her. She clapped her other hand to her face. "Oh, Lord, how stupid I've been! It's been here all along."

Turnip didn't mind the clinging to his hand—he had rather hoped for that bit—but he was beginning to feel that he had lost the thread of the conversation.

"What has?" he asked cautiously.

Arabella tossed her head back, looking him straight in the eye. She crackled with excitement, like an explorer looking for the first time on a long-awaited shore.

"Don't you see? I *do* have it. The list! Turnip, I know where to find the list!"

Chapter 26

$\mathcal{T}$urnip blinked down at her in confusion. "The list?"

Arabella belatedly realized that she was clinging to Turnip's hand. Blushing, she dropped it.

She covered her consternation by waving her hands about just a little too enthusiastically. She probably looked like she was about to take flight. "I can't believe I didn't think of it before. What an idiot I am!"

"I never thought you were an idiot."

There was something about the way Turnip looked at her that made Arabella look away. "You may change your mind when I tell you where it is," she said, only half-jokingly. "It was right under my nose the whole time, and I never knew it was there. Oh, I'm sorry. Were you about to say something?"

Turnip sunk his chin into the depths of his cravat. "Nothing. Nothing at'all. Carry on."

"There's not much carrying to do. It's really embarrassingly simple. Mystery solved, adventure over. And just in time for the end of the house party."

"Not quite over yet," said Turnip hastily. "We still have one more day. And night."

A line from a Milton piece whispered through Arabella's memory: *What has night to do with sleep / Night hath better sweets to prove.* The night beyond the balustrade seemed redolent with all sorts of dangerous prospects. Even the rustling of the wind in the shrubbery had a sensual sound to it, like clothes crumpling at a lover's embrace.

Arabella clasped her hands tightly together at her waist. "The sooner we get the list to the proper people, the better," she said, in her most schoolmistress-ish voice. "I don't like to think of it just sitting there."

Turnip nodded emphatically. "Good thinking. Let's go get it."

Before they could suit action to words, a long shadow fell across the door to the balcony. "Fitzhugh?" called a bored voice. "Are you out here?"

Turnip quickly stepped in front of Arabella, blocking her from view. "Just came out for a bit of air and all that."

"You're going to get a great deal more of it," said Darius Danforth, stepping into the fall of light from the ballroom door. He was modishly dressed in a tight-fitting dark blue coat, cut high at the waist and long in the back, his hair styled in the windswept style made fashionable by the Prince of Wales. He prowled out onto the balcony, an advertisement for all that was fashionable and dissolute. "The duchess wants us all out in the West Wood."

"What for?"

Danforth shrugged, showing off the excellence of his tailoring. The material didn't so much as ripple. "Some Epiphany Eve ritual involving guns, ciders, and a band of overexcited yokels."

"Think I'll skip it this time, thanks all the same," said Turnip amiably.

His tone was casual enough, but Arabella could see the tension in the set of his shoulders. In fact, his shoulders were all she could see. They were very broad shoulders, seamlessly outlined by the set of a coat that clung to his form as though it had been painted on.

There was really something to be said for London tailoring, thought Arabella inconsequentially.

"Oh no," said Danforth, leaning languidly against the doorjamb. "There will be no skip. The dowager has made it quite clear that every able-bodied man is to join in shooting away the evil spirits. No exceptions. And you know how the dowager gets when she's thwarted."

"You mean she'll shoot us," said Turnip glumly.

Danforth didn't bother to deny or confirm. He simply looked at Turnip. "You can't think I'd be freezing my balls off in the cold with a bunch of bloody farmers if it weren't for the threat of imminent death?"

Turnip made a sharp, alarmed motion at Danforth's foul language.

"Oh, I am sorry," drawled Danforth, with an innocence that was anything but. "Do you have someone with you?"

Turnip's ears turned red around the edges.

"If you have, best return her to the ballroom before the dowager does it for you, Fitzhugh," Danforth advised in world-weary tones. "Shouldn't want to find yourself leg-shackled."

Danforth turned and sauntered back through the doorway.

Turnip's fists opened and closed at his side. "That—that—"

"Person?" suggested Arabella.

A reluctant smile broke out on Turnip's face. "Don't know if I'd go that far. Toadstool is more like it."

So this was it, then, was it? The end of her one and only rendezvous on a balcony. Only she, thought Arabella wryly, would manage to spend a good fifteen minutes on a balcony, freezing her shoulders off in the January cold, without so much as a kiss.

Arabella pasted a fake smile on her face. "You'd best be going, hadn't you? You wouldn't want the dowager to start shooting."

Despite the increasing bustle from the ballroom, Turnip made no move to go anywhere. He looked at her with concern, his brows drawing so close together they practically met in the middle. "Don't do anything until I get back. Anything dangerous, that is."

"I'm not the one shooting at evil spirits," Arabella pointed out. "Your mortality rate is likely to be higher than mine."

Turnip was not mollified. "Stay with the others. Don't go wandering off by yourself. That bally list can rot where it is, for all I care, so long as you're safe." His eyes brightened as he was seized by a sudden inspiration. "Stay with Lady Henrietta. Deuced good chap, Lady Henrietta. Got me out of that pickle with that Black Tulip person last spring. She'll see you right."

"Fitzhugh," called Danforth. "The sooner you move, the sooner we all get this over with."

"Don't worry," said Arabella softly. "I'll be fine." With all the men outside, any threat was radically reduced. Her assailant, on both occasions, had quite definitely been male. "Only two more days to go."

Turnip was unconvinced. "All the more reason for the chap to get desperate."

Inside, someone accidentally fired his pistol. There were shrieks and the sound of clattering crystal.

"My point, I think," said Arabella. "You'd best be going."

Turnip still didn't look convinced, but he nodded anyway. "You go in this door. I'll take the other." He indicated another door into the ballroom, farther down the balcony. "Wouldn't want to give Danforth ammunition."

"I thought the dowager was planning to do just that," said Arabella lightly, but Turnip didn't smile. "Turnip?"

Something was bothering him. He cocked his head to one side and shifted from one foot to another, opened his mouth to say something, thought better of it, closed it again, narrowed his eyes in an expression of great concentration, shook his head, and finally gave up.

"Oh, bother it," he said, then grabbed her by the shoulders and kissed her.

Having made up his mind, there was nothing the least bit tentative about Turnip's kiss. One minute Arabella was peaceably standing beside the balustrade; the next she was half bent over the balustrade, clinging to Turnip's neck for dear life, while little specks of light exploded against the backs of her eyelids like the royal fireworks during a particularly rousing performance of the Hallelujah chorus.

Arabella gave a silent hallelujah of her own, wrapped her arms more firmly around his neck, and kissed him back. Through the open ballroom door, she could hear violins playing, singing out a high, sweet strain.

"I've been wanting to do that all evening," said Turnip with satisfaction, setting her back on her feet. He thought about it for a moment. "All week, actually."

"Oh," said Arabella, which was about the most she could manage. Her knees didn't seem to want to work properly anymore. She held on to Turnip's shoulders for balance. She blinked up at him, searching for the scattered remains of her wits. "You waited until *now*?"

Turnip grinned and butted his nose against hers. "Sorry. Bad timing."

"You could say that," agreed Arabella, although the word "bad" no longer really had a place in her lexicon. That had been quite good, actually. More than good. Would spectacular be going too far?

"Fitzhugh . . . ," drawled Danforth.

"I could learn to dislike that man," said Arabella.

"I already have." Dropping one last kiss on the top of her head, Turnip released her and stepped back. "I'll be back as soon as I can. Don't do anything reckless."

"Mmmph," said Arabella. It seemed like a perfectly reasonable response at the time.

Arabella floated back into the ballroom on a wave of euphoria, sparing one last glance for the shadowy balcony behind her, with its broad stone balustrade and ornamental urns.

So that's what a balustrade is for, she thought, and experienced a very silly urge to giggle.

Inside, the ballroom looked more like a scene of an impromptu siege than a country dance. Red-faced squires were lovingly loading ancient fowling pieces, while the young bucks nonchalantly dangled expensive dueling pistols from gloved fingertips. The musicians were packing up their instruments, carting them away to make room for the London musicians who were to take their places for the following night's far larger and grander ball. In the center of the room, where the dancing had been, Martin Frobisher and Percy Ponsonby were comparing the sizes of their pistols, Frobisher insisting that his was bigger. Freddy Staines, red-faced from windburn, was called in as referee.

Arabella wondered if her face had the same telltale flush. Probably. But she couldn't bring herself to care. She couldn't seem to stop smiling. She smiled at the old gentlemen sifting powder into their muskets, at the musicians hauling away their stands, at the young daughters of the local gentry, with their unfashionably long curls and last season's clothes, goggling at the magnificence of the London gentlemen in their tight breeches and extravagant cravats.

One smiled back at her, shyly, and then quickly ducked her head. Arabella realized, with amusement, that they had marked her down as one of the London ladies, grand and full of her own consequence. Her heart was too full to mind.

A few feet away, Lady Charlotte Lansdowne, the duchess's grand-daughter, was attempting to explain the martial preparations to the new duke, who was looking with a distinctly unenthusiastic eye at the fire-arms being paraded around what was, at least in theory, his ballroom.

"It's an old country tradition," Lady Charlotte was saying, in that earnest way of hers. "On Epiphany Eve, the gentlemen gather round the biggest tree on the estate—or at least the most convenient big tree—to scare away the evil spirits."

The Duke of Dovedale, who was more a stranger in his own home than most of his guests, looked dubious at the prospect. "How does one go about doing that?"

Lord Henry Innes clapped him on the shoulder in passing. "You shoot them, man. What else?"

He was a big, bruising man, Lord Henry, with thick features and a pugilist's physique. There was an air of barely suppressed physicality about him.

It would have been ridiculously easy for him to haul her back into the bushes. But once there, Arabella couldn't see him resorting to the refinement of a knife, or the subtlety of threats. Those large hands would have fit far too easily around her throat.

Behind Lord Henry, Turnip jerked his head to the side like a bird having an epileptic fit.

Arabella made an inquisitive face.

Turnip mimed something. If they had been playing charades, Arabella would have guessed "squirrel." Or maybe "chipmunk." "Stealthy chipmunk"? Ah, right. Stealthy chipmunk appeared to be aimed at Lord Henry's back. In other words, Turnip was going to shadow Lord Henry while they were outside.

It was gallant and absurd and probably pointless. Arabella looked across at her very own Don Quixote, all pleased at his own cleverness, and felt such a rush of affection that it was a wonder that they couldn't light the ballroom with it.

"Arabella." It took a few moments for the name to filter through to Arabella's consciousness. She was too busy beaming at Turnip like an idiot. Or a woman in love. Which, when one thought about it, were probably much the same thing. *"Arabella."*

The name caller sounded distinctly displeased at having to repeat himself.

It was with the utmost reluctance that Arabella dragged her attention away from Turnip and forced herself to focus on Captain Musgrave, who was buzzing away, like a particularly large fly, somewhere in the vicinity of his left shoulder.

She looked at him and felt . . . nothing. Not make-believe nothing, the sort of nothing one pretended to salve a wounded pride, but genuine nothing.

"Yes?" she said.

Captain Musgrave was still sulking over having been ignored. "Your aunt was looking for you," he said.

Musgrave looked at her gravely, waiting for an explanation, an apology. Once, Arabella might have felt duty-bound to provide one, to justify her dereliction. But the world had changed.

"Where is my aunt?" she asked lightly.

It wasn't what he had been expecting. "Upstairs," he said brusquely. "In her room." In a belated attempt to recover the ground he had lost, he added, "She'll be wanting to see you."

That was pure nonsense. The only things Aunt Osborne wanted to see after a party were her maid and a large glass of ratafia.

"I'll take you to her," volunteered her new uncle.

Arabella dodged his outstretched arm. "I'll go to her by and by," she hedged. "Excuse me."

Captain Musgrave moved to block her. "She wants to talk to you now. About your behavior. With Fitzhugh."

Arabella's serene expression was beginning to crack around the edges. "My behavior," she said dangerously, "is no longer my aunt's concern. Or yours."

Musgrave's mouth opened, but whatever he had been about to say was drowned out by an exuberant cry of "To the tree!" that seemed to rattle the very chandeliers on their chains.

"To the tree! The Epiphany tree!" was taken up all around the room.

The floor quivered with the pounding of masculine feet as the gentlemen grabbed up their guns and thudded for the doors, ready to repel an armada of trees.

"Every able-bodied man to his post! No shirkers!" barked a ruddy-faced gentleman in a too tightly buttoned coat, the master of the local hunt if the stentorian quality of his voice was anything to go by. He gave Musgrave a shove that sent the younger man stumbling several feet forward. "No lagging, man! To the tree!"

"The tree!" echoed the horde behind him, and Musgrave was swept up in the mob, pouring out through the double doors, past the offended statuary, down the marble hall, out the wide-flung doors and down the garden steps, where torches had been set out to light their way, and the men whooped and shot into the air for the sheer glee of it in the cold night air.

With all the men gone, the gallery felt much larger. Large and empty and suddenly cold. Arabella wrapped her shawl more firmly about her shoulders, regretting that it was only a wispy thing of silk and fringe, designed for fashion rather than warmth. Some of the ladies remained, chattering in small groups, but the majority appeared to have retired for the night, ceding the remainder of the evening to the gentlemen and their pursuits.

"—will have to be carried upstairs again," one matron sighed to another. "Singing vulgar songs and still wearing his boots."

"It's that *cider,*" said her companion, pronouncing the word with distaste. "I can't think why the duchess allows it."

"It is Epiphany Eve," said the first, apologetically. "It's a tradition."

"It's pagan—that's what it is!" snapped the second, whom Arabella belatedly recognized as Mrs. Carruthers. "Nothing more than an excuse for the men to enjoy low drink and vulgar company. I can't think what they see in it."

"Boys will be boys," said the first, a little ruefully. "And they do like their cider."

"Disgraceful," said Mrs. Carruthers.

Rolling her eyes, Catherine assumed an expression of intense boredom, every particle of her body language pronouncing her entire indifference to the conversation, the ballroom, and everyone in it.

Arabella ignored Turnip's instruction to find Lady Henrietta. Lady Henrietta had retreated with Lady Charlotte into a curtained alcove, and Arabella could hear giggles and exclamations through the blue silk. They wouldn't thank her for intruding.

She would be perfectly safe in her own room, particularly now that all the men had been chivvied out of the house by the duchess. The only men who had been excused were the footmen, silent and statue-like in their white wigs and green and gold livery.

Two were stationed at the foot of the stairs, like human gateposts. Arabella passed between them as she made her way up the silent stairs. Funny how empty a house, even a grand mansion such as this, could feel with half the population removed from it. The duchess scorned the more economical practice of leaving candles on a table by the stairs for the guests to light their way upstairs; candles had been lit in sconces at intervals along the walls, creating patches of light and shadow that fell in striations along the stairs.

If she was right, the list, this ridiculous list about which everyone was so concerned, was in the pocket of her gray school dress.

It had been such a small detail, such a minimal moment in a hectic night, someone—she couldn't even remember who now, whether it had been Miss Climpson or Lizzy or Sally—thrusting a piece of paper at her, something fallen out of the notebook. She had remembered it only when she reached for a pocket that wasn't there and experienced the sudden, tactile memory of crumpling a piece of paper into another pocket on another night.

It might not be the list. It might very well just be someone's French exercises or a laundry list, like the sheaf of paper Jane's foolish heroine discovered, but Arabella's steps quickened nonetheless, until she was practically running along the last stretch of hallway.

She let herself into her room, closing the door firmly behind her. Rose had left candles burning. Arabella's nightdress was laid out across the foot of the bed and her tooth powder had been set out on the dressing table along with a basin and ewer. A proper lady's maid would have waited up for her, but Rose had always been somewhat lackadaisical in her attentions, deeming Arabella too unimportant to complain.

In this instance, Arabella was glad of it.

The gray dress wasn't in the wardrobe with her other gowns. Arabella tracked it down at the bottom of her trunk, along with two others of which Rose disapproved, tucked out of sight where Arabella wouldn't be tempted to wear them.

Lifting her school dress from the trunk, Arabella surveyed it critically. It did look nearly too dilapidated to wear, with an ink stain on the skirt and something sticky—mince?—on the bodice. The fabric was a mass of wrinkles, the skirt distended by a strange lump on one side.

It made a very satisfying crinkling sound as Arabella slowly rose to her feet, lifting the dress up as she went.

A slow tingle of excitement began to spread from Arabella's fingers to her palms, making the skin on her back prickle, catching at the breath in her throat. It was still there, whatever it was that she had put into her pocket on that ridiculous, hurly-burly whirlwind of a night. That didn't mean that it was what she thought it might be, Arabella told herself as she draped the dress over the back of a chair, groping for the pocket. Paper crackled beneath her fingers.

A single sheet, just as Lord Pinchingdale had said, written front and back.

Placing the paper flat on her dressing table, Arabella smoothed out the worst of the wrinkles. It was closely written, in a small, neat hand. The first line read "Boisvallon, Abbeville, 150 L.," followed by, on the next line, "La Rose, Pas de Calais, 400 L.," and so on down the line. It looked a bit like a laundry list, but a laundry list like none Arabella had ever seen. The pattern repeated, straight down the page. Name, place, number. It took Arabella a moment to figure out what the number signified, not a pound sign, but an L.

Louis. Louis d'or, the old French currency. No wonder it looked like an account; it was one. Some foolish soul in the War Office had taken it upon himself to write up a rendering of the amounts being paid to foreign agents, and had, ever so helpfully, included their stations. There had to be at least a hundred names on the list, closely written, front and back, some proper names, others, like La Prime-Rose and Le Mouron, both flowers, quite obviously pseudonyms. Arabella recognized some of the place-names, but not all; from the look of the list, it seemed like the Royalist web had a strand in every village in France.

No wonder someone wanted this so badly. Publish the list and the entire English network from the coast to Paris would be in tatters.

It was rather alarming to think that the fate of the French monarchy might well have rested on Rose's reluctance to press Arabella's gray gown. Whoever had searched her room, not once but twice, had never thought to check the side pocket of a discarded dress.

Which meant, reasoned Arabella, that whoever it was must have seen her take possession of the notebook, but hadn't seen her put the loose page in her pocket. That ruled out Signor Marconi, Sally, Lizzy, Agnes, Miss Climpson, and Turnip.

Who else knew she had the notebook? And how? It had to have been someone outside the drawing room, someone who had seen her walk away with the notebook, but without witnessing the actual events inside the room.

There was a scraping noise behind her as someone opened the door to the room, the wood of the door pushing against the nap of the Axminster carpet. Of course, Rose would choose now to help her undress. Arabella slapped a book down over the dangerous bit of paper.

"It's all right, Rose," she said, keeping a hand on top of the book as she straightened. "I don't need—"

She broke off at the unmistakable click of a pistol being cocked.

"Rose isn't here," said Catherine Carruthers, and leveled her pistol at Arabella's head.

Chapter 27

*C*rack.

The report of a gun echoed somewhere to Turnip's right.

"Not yet, you idiot!" someone shouted, flown on champagne and brandy cakes. "Wait until you see the green of their leaves!"

The duchess's male guests jostled into the forest clearing in a whooping, staggering, gleeful mass. The acrid smell of gun smoke warred with the sickly sweet scents of pomade, cologne, and hothouse fruits. A vast bonfire sent sparks flaring into the sky, turning the faces of the laughing, shouting men into something out of primitive history. They might have been their own ancestors, charging forward to cut down a Roman brigade, rather than a few tree spirits.

Free of feminine oversight, wigs had been discarded, cravats loosened, waistcoats unbuttoned. Some had liberated champagne from the feast and were chugging directly out of the bottle; others refreshed themselves from flasks. A safe distance from the bonfire, the servants had set out a table, the delicate Irish linen covering the raw boards in stark contrast to the rough pottery casks that had been lined up in two rows on top of the table.

"Cider!" someone shouted, and everyone made a dash for the table, eager to get to the famed Norfolk cider that had been known to lay grown men low.

"Shall we get on?" said the Duke of Dovedale.

Turnip couldn't have agreed more. The sooner they got this over with, the sooner he could get back to Arabella. She had to like him at least a little bit to kiss him back like that. She wasn't a Penelope, to cast her kisses on the wind like bread unto the waters. Penelope. Turnip shook his head to himself, eliciting several funny looks from the people around him. How could she have thought he was carrying a torch for Penelope? He wasn't holding even a very small candle.

Still, if she was jealous, that had to mean something. Rather encouraging, really. Turnip drew in a deep breath. Once they had finished with this ridiculous list, he could put his courage to the sticking point, corner Arabella on a balcony—he'd rather liked that balcony—and make a declaration she couldn't mistake.

It didn't matter that she didn't have a dowry. He had income enough for two—well, for ten, really, if one totted up the numbers and all that, but he didn't want ten; he just wanted Arabella. He could send her younger sisters to school and find her father a nicer spa and give that cranky sister a season and hire half a dozen paid companions to make demmed sure that Arabella never had to fetch another vinaigrette for Lady Osborne ever again.

Turnip circled warily around the tree. "I say, are we meant to shoot at the tree or away from it?"

For all that it was meant to be stuffed full of evil spirits, it still looked like a tree to him.

"At it, I should think," opined Lord Freddy Staines, shining the already shiny stock of his pistol. It was as elaborately designed as a lady's dresser set, polished to a fine sheen and chased with delicate curlicues of sterling silver. "How else are we to kill the evil spirits?"

Good point, that. Turnip nodded intelligently.

The Duke of Dovedale bared his teeth in an unconvincing imitation of a smile. "I'd say shooting at the tree would be a jolly dangerous idea."

"Why?" demanded Lord Henry Innes, joining the group, a jug of cider in one hand, pistol in the other. "It ain't going to shoot back."

Turnip eyed Innes thoughtfully. If Innes were here, he couldn't be in the house. Which meant, in a rather roundabout way, that now would be an excellent time to dispose of that list. From the size of that jug, Innes should be occupied for a good long while. He wasn't going to be dragging anyone off behind bushes anytime soon.

Sir Francis Medmenham delicately reached out and turned Innes's pistol away from the tree. "Ricochet," he said succinctly. "I, for one, have no desire to breathe my last because of a bullet bouncing off a tree."

Turnip didn't wait to hear the rest of the argument.

"Just going for refreshments, don't you know," he said to no one in particular, and began to back away, past the bonfire, past the table with the cider jugs, past another table set out with a variety of hearty foods to sustain the tree hunters on their midnight quest. No namby-pamby lady foods such as were served at the ball, but good, hearty meat pastries, cold meats, the smelliest of cheeses, and hefty loaves of fresh-baked bread. There was also, set out to one side, a neat pyramid of Christmas puddings, each adorned with its own sprig of mistletoe.

Hmm. Struck by inspiration, Turnip snatched up a pudding in passing before bolting back towards the house. It was, he decided, practically a sign. Anyone could bring flowers, but nothing said *I love you* like a slightly squished Christmas pudding.

It made Turnip feel warm inside just thinking about it. It was a pudding that had brought them together, after all. Amazing, the way the rest of one's life could hinge on one little ball of suet and dried fruit.

Turnip looked down at the muslin-wrapped ball in his hand and grinned. He was sure they could find excellent use for that mistletoe trimming too.

The gallery was all but deserted when he entered, save for the silent army of servants sweeping up the last of the feast, scrubbing squished lobster patties off the gleaming parquet floor, setting the room to rights for tomorrow's festivities. Turnip was about to look elsewhere when one of the long silk curtains shading the ornamental alcoves rustled and Lady Henrietta Dorrington wiggled her way out, still speaking to someone in the alcove behind her.

Phew. Turnip let out the breath he hadn't realized he had been holding. Deuced clever of Lady Hen to hide Arabella away in an alcove, he thought, as he strode towards her across the deserted dance floor. Not that he would tell her, of course. She was the gloating sort, Lady Hen.

He raised his hand in greeting as he approached. There was no need to stand on ceremony with Lady Henrietta; he had known her since she was a chubby-cheeked toddler trying to make her brother's friends play dolls. He had managed a bally good falsetto, if he did say so himself.

"Hullo," Lady Henrietta said cheerfully, holding the curtain for someone behind her. "Aren't you supposed to be tree hunting?"

"Spirit hunting," Turnip corrected her, craning his neck to try to see around her. "Is Miss Dempsey in there?"

"No," said Lady Charlotte Lansdowne apologetically, shoving the curtain aside. "Just me."

Lady Henrietta looked pointedly at Turnip's hands. "Why are you holding a pudding?"

Turnip clutched his love offering protectively to his chest. "I like pudding."

"So do I," said Lady Henrietta, "but I don't go around embracing it."

Refusing to let himself be drawn, Turnip fixed Lady Henrietta with anxious eyes. "Thought Miss Dempsey was supposed to be with you."

Lady Henrietta looked at Lady Charlotte, who shook her head. Lady Henrietta turned back to Turnip. "I haven't see her since the Fairy Queen."

"You haven't?" Turnip had heard of blood running cold, but it was the first time his had actually done it. "Do you know where she went?"

"If I haven't seen her," said Lady Henrietta with exaggerated patience, "how could I know where she is?"

If she wasn't with Lady Henrietta, where was she? Turnip didn't have a good feeling about this.

"Thanks all the same," mumbled Turnip, bolting for the doors. "Shan't keep you."

"What is it?" Lady Henrietta called after him. "Is something wrong?"

But Turnip was already gone.

There were only a handful of middle-aged matrons playing whist in the card room, none of whom was Arabella. The footman by the garden doors hadn't seen a girl in a peach silk dress. Neither had the ones napping by the front door, who snapped guiltily to attention as Turnip dashed up to them.

Good Gad, had someone whisked her out through a window? Down a trellis?

The footmen at the foot of the stairs looked exactly like the ten footmen he had already spoken to. But there was one crucial distinction.

These footmen remembered Arabella, and they remembered her going upstairs, not fifteen minutes before.

"Alone?" Turnip asked, bouncing from one foot to the other in his agitation. "There wasn't a chap with a knife, or a gun, or a paper scimitar, or anything like that?"

The footman's impassive mask never altered. "I am sure I couldn't say, sir."

"Her room," he demanded, mangling the pudding in his stranglehold. "Where's her room?"

If the footman deemed it an improper question, he was too well trained to show it. His gaze never deviated from the correct two inches above Turnip's left shoulder. "Two flights up, fourth door to the left, sir."

"Two up, four left," muttered Turnip. "Two up, four left."

How long had it been now? Fifteen minutes? Twenty?

Turnip took the stairs two steps at a time.

⚜

"YOU AREN'T GOING TO SCREAM, are you?" said Catherine. "That would be too tedious for words."

"Catherine?" Arabella stared at her former student, trying to reconcile the conflict between the curls, the frills, the flounces, and the very businesslike pistol in Catherine's hand. It didn't even have silver chasing or mother-of-pearl inlay. It was simply what it was: a highly efficient instrument of death.

And it was pointed straight at Arabella.

"Don't try anything silly," Catherine instructed, her bracelet glinting in the candlelight as she aimed the gun at Arabella's chest. "I can use this. And I will."

Arabella didn't doubt it.

"If this is about your history mark," she said mildly, "wouldn't it have been simpler to have seen me about it before the end of term?"

"There's no use pretending you don't have it. I know you do."

"Have what?" Arabella said, as calmly as she could manage.

"The list." Catherine's voice was clipped and hard. There was a steeliness to her that belied the seeming frivolity of her clothes, the childlike sweetness of her still-round cheeks. There was petulance there too: adult purpose married to adolescent single-mindedness. It was a combination that made Arabella very, very afraid. "I need that list."

Lifting her hand from the book, Arabella very slowly turned the rest of the way around, conscious of the pistol following her every movement.

"Catherine," she began briskly.

"Just because someone invited you to this party doesn't mean you have any right to address me so familiarly." Catherine's nose lifted in an uncanny imitation of her mother's. "From now on, you will address me as Mrs. Danforth."

Danforth. Danforth? Whatever Arabella had expected, it hadn't been that. "As in . . . Lieutenant Darius Danforth?"

As she said it, she could picture him. Danforth, who was friends with Catherine's cousin. Danforth, who had been disowned for dishonoring a young lady of good family. Danforth, who had spearheaded that game of blind man's buff.

"The very one," said Catherine smugly.

A host of disregarded images came belatedly and painfully into focus: Danforth passing close by Catherine, stopping to murmur something into her ear; Danforth and Catherine, exchanging glances across the drawing room; Danforth and Catherine, in collusion.

Arabella licked her dry lips. "Not Lady Grimmlesby-Thorpe?"

Catherine tossed her head. "You didn't think I was going to marry that old sot? No. Darius and I were married by special license in November." She preened. "He does have important connections, you know. Darius is the son of an earl."

The disowned son of an earl, but Arabella deemed it wiser not to point that out while Catherine was holding a pistol.

It had been in November that Catherine had been expelled from Miss Climpson's. "That was when you ran away from the school."

"I didn't *run away*," Catherine corrected her. "I *eloped*."

"Of course," Arabella said quickly. Rule Number One: Don't make the woman with the pistol angry. "My felicitations."

Diving for the pistol wasn't really an option. Arabella wouldn't be surprised to find that Catherine really was as good a shot as she claimed.

There was a rather heavy perfume atomizer on the dressing table. If she could reach behind and grab it, she could throw it at Catherine, duck, and run. Of course, that presumed that she managed to reach it without Catherine noticing, and, once she had it in hand, that she threw true, neither of which seemed highly likely.

"Thank you." Catherine took her congratulations as her due. "But as you can see, this is hardly a social call. You have caused me a great deal of bother since you arrived at Miss Climpson's."

Arabella had caused *her* a great deal of bother?

"I'm so sorry," Arabella said. "Was that your pudding?"

"Whose did you think it was? The Prince of Wales's? You had no business reading it, no business at all."

"You left it on the windowsill," Arabella said slowly, "so Lieutenant Danforth could pick it up."

"Those pedants at Miss Climpson's persisted in watching me to make sure I didn't see Darius. But they didn't think anything of a Christmas pudding left on a windowsill."

"Or a notebook?"

"Clever, wasn't it?" Catherine smirked.

Arabella was still putting all the pieces together. "That night at Miss Climpson's Christmas performance. You were one of the wise men."

"I gave Darius my robe and my sword while Sally and those other angels were still preening themselves onstage. It was easy enough. The robe was too short on him, but you didn't look very closely, did you?"

"One doesn't when one is being dragged backwards in a dark corridor." One by one, the pieces were beginning to fall into place. "You were the one who searched my room."

"Twice. Really, you might think of investing in some new walking dresses. That green one is disgraceful." Catherine shuddered in distaste. If one had to paw through someone else's belongings looking for treasonous documents, they might, in Catherine's view, at least be fashionable ones.

Catherine's snobbery might have been all that had kept her from discovering the paper the first few times; she would never have considered touching Arabella's gray school dress, any more than Rose had. It was an amusing irony that Arabella would be sure to savor at her leisure. If she survived to do it.

"Whose idea was the game of blind man's buff?"

"I came up with the idea, of course"—Catherine was leaving no doubts as to the evil mastermind in this partnership—"but I had to leave it to Darius to execute. Being a gentleman, he didn't have the nerve to do it properly."

Gentleman? Arabella bit her tongue on the acerbic comment that rose to her lips.

Catherine's curls quivered as she contemplated the inefficiency of the opposite sex. "I was appalled when I arrived this morning to find that he had been here two weeks and done nothing! Nothing! I had given him very specific instructions."

Arabella didn't like to think what those instructions might have been. She suspected Catherine's methods of information extraction ran to the rack-and-thumbscrews variety.

"I can't fault him for the delicacy of his nature," Catherine went on, with a pro forma simper. As far as Arabella could tell, Darius Danforth was about as delicate as a goat, but Catherine apparently knew a different, more sensitive man. "His scruples become him, but it just wouldn't do and I told him so."

Arabella knew she should have reported Catherine's midnight escapades to Miss Climpson while she still had the chance. This was what she got for being tolerant and understanding.

"So he got up his game of blind man's buff," Arabella said grimly.

"*My* game of blind man's buff, you mean." Catherine wasn't willing to be cheated out of her credit, even at the expense of her husband. "Those idiot friends of his will do anything if you tell them it's for a wager. By the end, each of them thought it was his own idea. They all find you an utter antidote, you know."

"Lovely," said Arabella.

"After all that, Darius made a botch of it, poor lamb. So here I am." Catherine smiled brightly at Arabella and brought her pistol back up. "Give me the list. Now."

In a novel, the proper sort of heroine would refuse to hand over the list, guarding it to the death.

Arabella didn't want to die.

What good could she do to anyone dead? Other than alert the others to the treason with the sound of the shot that killed her, but, frankly, the walls of Girdings were too thick for that sort of thing. It might, in fact, be wiser to let Catherine have the blasted thing—as least, for the moment. Stranded in Girdings House, Catherine wouldn't be able to get terribly far. While she was savoring her triumph, Arabella could muster the troops and catch her with list in hand.

"All right," Arabella said slowly. "It was yours, after all. I only came upon it by accident. I never meant to interfere with your plans."

It was what Catherine wanted to hear. She laughed happily. "Can you believe Darius even suggested paying you for it? I told him not to be absurd."

Arabella reached behind her for the crumpled piece of paper. "Why do you want it so very badly? I don't see you as a French spy."

Catherine sniffed derisively. "As if I would be in it for that! Darius knows someone who knows someone who's willing to pay good money for the thing. We'll be set for life."

"If you aren't hanged for treason." Seeing Catherine's brows draw together, Arabella said hastily, "You can still put it back, you know. You can hide it among your father's things. He'll think he misplaced it. No one will be the wiser."

"And live in some little hovel until my parents forgive me? No." So much for their hard-won rapport. Catherine's lips curved in a distinctly feline smile. Arabella could all but see her licking the cream off her whiskers. With impeccable logic, Catherine said, "They can't hang me for treason if no one knows about it."

Catherine was going to kill her. Arabella knew it as surely as she knew her own name. It wouldn't have mattered if she handed over the list or not. Catherine had been planning to kill her either way. If there were no witnesses, those nasty events had never happened.

She wasn't mad. It would be easier if she were. One could reason with a madman, suss out his distorted logic and play on it. But Catherine wasn't mad. She was just very, very determined and entirely selfish.

What was the life of a lowly schoolmistress so long as she got her Darius and the money too?

Not to mention all of those other lives, the Royalist agents stationed between Paris and Boulogne, the English agents who relied upon them, the locals who supported them, all the hundreds of individuals whose lives would be forfeit when that list reached Bonaparte's hands.

Arabella could see the carnage stretching out from Norfolk to Paris, life after life, all at the hands of the self-satisfied sixteen-year-old standing in front of her, gold bracelets gleaming on her wrists, all frills and ruffles and deadly self-indulgence.

Jane was right—teaching was a far more hazardous profession than Arabella had ever envisioned.

"How do you explain about the money, then?" Arabella asked desperately.

Catherine widened her eyes guilelessly. "Didn't you hear? The money was a gift to Darius from a very elderly relative." Dropping the pose, she added frankly, "She's senile, you know. She'll never know the difference. She may even think she did give it to us."

Arabella retreated as Catherine advanced. "But someone else does know. That friend of Lieutenant Danforth's, the one who arranged the deal."

Catherine dismissed that with a casual wave of her pistol. "He wouldn't dare tell. He's in it too. You, on the other hand, are not."

"Have you ever thought that he might be a counteragent? Perhaps he's really working for the government and only pretending to sell secrets to the French."

"He's not," said Catherine with terrifying certainty. "You forget. My father is in the government."

"The government might pay you for it!" Arabella's back was against the window. She could feel the latch digging into her spine. "You can tell them you found it. There might be a finder's fee. You would be a heroine. His Majesty would invite you to tea."

"Open the window," said Catherine.

"Pardon?"

"Open the window." Catherine pointed with her pistol. "You are going to have a nice little fall."

Little wasn't the adjective Arabella would have chosen. Her room was three stories up. They were very tall stories. The kitchen garden lay below, but, at this height, Arabella doubted that the winter-gray stalks of thyme and sage were going to do much to break her fall.

Arabella frowned at her former pupil. "These aren't the sort of windows one just falls out of. You won't be able to pass it off as an accident."

Catherine looked smug. "I don't need to. Everyone knows that you've been flinging yourself at Sally Fitzhugh's brother. When he turned you down—who's to say what you might do?"

Arabella eyed her askance. "Killing oneself for unrequited love? Does anyone really do that these days?"

Catherine jabbed the gun in her direction. "As of now, you do. Just think, you can start a whole new fashion." She adopted an expression of mock remorse. "Such a shame that Mr. Fitzhugh didn't return your affections."

"'Fraid there's a problem with that plan," came a voice from the doorway.

Chapter 28

"You see," said Turnip Fitzhugh, "I do. Return her affections, that is. So your little scheme ain't going to work."

Turnip looked entirely at home, lounging in the doorway, his shoulders propped against the frame. Arabella didn't know whether to be elated or horrified.

Catherine swung wildly around, backing up to keep both of them in her sights, her pistol wavering from one to the other.

"Her? You love *her*?"

"Don't see what's so odd about it." Turnip deliberately moved towards the bed, away from Arabella, forcing Catherine to widen her range.

Following his lead, Arabella inched in the other direction, towards the fireplace. There was a poker in the rack beside the fireplace, a poker and a shovel, either of which could be used to whack the pistol from Catherine's hand.

Catherine's face was a study in bewilderment and rage.

"But she's a *schoolmistress*."

"Mistress of my heart, and all that," said Turnip cheerfully, his eyes on the pistol. "Well schooled in affection. Tutored in—"

Catherine put a period to the catalogue by stamping her foot. "Fine!" she declared, flinging up her hands. Arabella instinctively ducked. "You can just die together, then."

Choosing her target, she spun to face Arabella, her finger tightening on the trigger. Arabella flung herself to the ground. In the confused moment of falling, she saw Turnip's arm draw back, and something round and pale fly with astonishing speed across the room, straight at Catherine. A piece of mistletoe fluttered like a lost feather to the floor.

The pudding hit Catherine smack in the side of the head, sending her reeling sideways. As her fingers relaxed, the pistol fell from her limp hand, clattering to the floor.

Catherine went down like a stone.

Flat out on the floor, Arabella could only stare. The pudding, slightly dented on one side, lay next to Catherine's fallen form. What was the cook putting into her puddings? Rocks? Arabella swallowed hard, realizing that a rocklike pudding and the force of Turnip's throwing arm were the only things that had stood between her and a bullet in the gut.

A pair of slightly muddy boots appeared in front of Arabella's line of vision. Turnip's usually immaculate attire was rather the worse for wear. His boots were stained with garden mulch, his hair wrinkled, and his cravat askew.

He had never looked better.

He held out a hand to her. "All right, there?" he said.

Arabella took the offered hand, and felt his fingers close around hers, strong and safe. He smelled of pudding and spilled cider.

"All right," she said, pulling heavily on his hand as she rose to her feet. She looked up at him, at his dear, familiar, earnest face. "That was an excellent toss."

Turnip made no move to release her hand. "Meant it, you know," he said. "What I said to her. About you."

The door was wide-open; a would-be murderess was sprawled on the floor; and a piece of paper that could unsettle half of Europe sat on the desk a yard away. Arabella didn't care about any of it.

"About me?" she echoed.

Darius Danforth skidded to a halt in the doorway. "Catherine, he slipped away from me. I—"

He took one look at his ladylove sprawled out on the floor, then at the murderous expression on Turnip's face, performed an abrupt full turn, and made to flee.

He didn't get very far.

With a suspiciously growllike sound, Turnip flung himself at Danforth, bringing the other man down before he could reach the door. His hat went tumbling into the hallway as Danforth hit the ground with a splat.

Clambering to his feet, Turnip adopted the accepted pugilistic position, fists up and knees bent.

"Get up," he commanded. "Get up and fight like a gentleman."

There was a slight problem with that suggestion. Danforth wasn't one.

Arabella considered pointing that out, but decided her energy could be better spent restraining Catherine. Catherine appeared to be unconscious, but she couldn't be trusted to remain that way. She was the deadlier of the pair.

Extracting a cord from the bed-hangings, Arabella crouched down next to Catherine. Catherine jerked as Arabella reached for her wrists.

"If I were you, I would stay there," Arabella told her. "Your parents aren't going to like any of this."

Catherine went limp again.

Arabella wasted no time in looping the rope around her wrists.

Levering himself painfully to his feet, Danforth backed away from Turnip, his hands held up in front of him. "No need to go to extremes, old thing. Your quarrel isn't with me."

"Isn't it?" Turnip bared his teeth. "'Spose you don't know anything about a certain paper scimitar?"

Danforth flushed. "That was just a prank." He jackknifed out of the way as Turnip feinted a blow to his stomach. "It was paper, man, paper!"

"And that game of blind man's buff?" This time the mock blow was to Danforth's temple. Danforth's head whipped back so quickly Arabella could hear his neck crack. "Just a bit of fun! High spirits, that's all."

Turnip advanced on Danforth. There was no levity in Turnip's expression, none of the jovial bonhomie that usually characterized his amiable features. He was deadly serious and just plain deadly. "What about Miss Dempsey? It wasn't fun for her. Never stopped to think of that, did you?"

"Um—" Danforth's breath was coming fast as he dodged around the bedpost.

"Apologize."

"What?"

"Apologize to Miss Dempsey."

Danforth stared at him before bursting out into incredulous laughter. "Thousands of pounds at stake and you want me to *apologize*? By Jove, that's rich!"

Turnip's expression hardened. "Right," he said, and swung. His fist connected solidly with Danforth's stomach. Arabella winced at the sound. "This is for your manners."

Danforth made a wheezing noise.

The seams of Turnip's coat strained as he dealt Danforth another blow. "This is for the scimitar." A button popped off Turnip's waistcoat. "This is for blind man's buff." Danforth tried to get in a blow of his own, but missed. "And *this*"—there was an ominous cracking sound as his fist connected with Danforth's chin—"is for forgetting her name!"

Danforth's head snapped back. He staggered, eyes unfocused, before falling heavily to his knees. For a moment, he hovered there, swaying. Then his eyes rolled back in his head.

"Bother," he said faintly, and collapsed face-first onto the ground.

"That's that, then," said Turnip, scrubbing his hands vigorously against the sides of his breeches. "Good riddance to bad rubbish. Now, where were we?"

Arabella looked down at Danforth's prone form. "You're really quite good at that, aren't you? That, um, punching thing."

Turnip looked pleased. "Practice regularly, and all that. Gentleman Jackson's." He drew in a deep breath, squaring his shoulders. "What I was trying to say, before the fight and all that, was that I—"

Once again, the door crashed back against the frame.

"Miss Dempsey? Fitzhugh?" Lord Pinchingdale stopped short at the sight of the prone bodies scattered across the carpet. "Good Gad! It looks like the last act of *Hamlet* in here."

Turnip banged his head against his clenched fists, making inarticulate moaning noises.

Pinchingdale gave him an odd look. "I had no idea you felt so strongly about the play, Fitzhugh."

"Too much thinking, not enough action," Arabella provided for him.

"And lots of bally interruptions from extraneous characters," muttered Turnip. "Who needed Horatio?"

"It could have been worse," said Arabella giddily. "It could have been the grave diggers."

And might have been, had Turnip not arrived in time. It was a sobering thought. Extracting the dangerous piece of paper that had started it all from beneath her journal, Arabella held it out to Lord Pinchingdale.

"Here is your list, Lord Pinchingdale. It was in the pocket of my gray school dress." Her lip twisted. "It wasn't fashionable enough for Catherine to search."

"Fashion be damned. You would look beautiful in a sack," declared Turnip, his voice somewhat muffled. Removing his hands from his face, he cocked his head, considering. "Not that I recommend it. Dresses generally more the thing, don't you know."

Pinchingdale started to say something, shook his head, and gave up. Instead, he turned back to Arabella. "Is that Catherine Carruthers on the floor?"

"Catherine Danforth now," said Arabella. "She married Darius Danforth by special license in November. The two of them had a scheme to sell secrets in exchange for enough money to tide them over until their families forgave them."

Lord Pinchingdale wasn't a veteran of three different spy leagues for nothing. "Which would, I imagine, explain why Darius Danforth is also on the floor."

"That was me," said Turnip proudly. "Put him there myself. Catherine too."

"It was an extremely dashing rescue," said Arabella loyally. "And just in the nick of time too. I've never seen a pudding used to such good purpose."

"A pudding?" Lord Pinchingdale spoke with some trepidation. "Do I want to know?"

Turnip never took his eyes from Arabella. "That was one deuced solid piece of confectionary. Shouldn't think why they bother using metal for cannonballs when they could use mince. Save on the national debt and all that, don't you know."

Arabella smiled up at him. "Only if aimed with great precision."

Turnip looked earnestly down at her. "Couldn't let her shoot you."

"I appreciate that," said Arabella gravely. "I shouldn't have liked to be shot."

"Pardon me," said Lord Pinchingdale. Both Arabella and Turnip looked at him in some surprise. It was very easy to forget he was there. "I seem to be missing something. Many things, in fact."

Arabella glanced back at Turnip, laughter in her eyes. "Mr. Fitz-hugh disarmed Mrs. Danforth with a Christmas pudding."

Turnip grinned back at her. "Deuced fond of puddings. Always have been. Never know what use they can be put to next."

Lord Pinchingdale raised his eyes to the heavens. "What did you use on Danforth? A mince pie?"

"'Course not," said Turnip with great dignity. "That would be silly."

Curling himself into a fetal position, his eyes tightly shut, Danforth was making faint moaning noises. Catherine was lying so perfectly still that Arabella suspected she was faking it. She'd had a good deal of practice, after all.

Lord Pinchingdale contemplated them both with distaste. "Needless to say, we can't just leave them here. Catherine will have to be delivered to her father's custody. I imagine he'll want to keep it quiet."

"What about Danforth?"

"I imagine Wickham at the War Office will have one or two questions for him. I can take him into custody until then." Lord Pinchingdale paced around the bodies, thinking aloud. "If we ask the duchess nicely, I imagine she won't mind lending us a footman or two to keep guard. She won't want any of this getting about any more than we do. If anyone asks, Danforth remembered a familial obligation and decided to go home early."

"And Catherine?" asked Arabella quietly.

"That is for her parents to decide. Thank goodness. Although," Lord Pinchingdale added drily, "I doubt she will ever look at pudding in quite the same way."

"Neither will I," said Arabella fervently, looking at the muslin-wrapped ball on the floor.

She looked up to find Turnip looking at her.

"Wouldn't have met you but for pudding," he said in a low voice.

"You would still have met me," said Arabella. "You just wouldn't have remembered me."

Lord Pinchingdale had taken Danforth by the shoulders and was beginning to haul him across the carpet. "Fitzhugh, if you'd help me with—"

Pinchingdale looked up and something in his friend's face caused him to drop Danforth's shoulders and beat a hasty retreat towards the door, leaving both Catherine and Danforth sprawled across the floor. Both were either still unconscious, or doing a fairly good job of pretending to be so.

"Never mind," Pinchingdale called over his shoulder. "I'll get Dorrington to help me. I'll be back in ten minutes, Fitzhugh. Ten minutes."

Turnip's eyes narrowed. Dashing to the door, he opened it and peered both ways down the hallway. Pulling the door firmly shut, he turned the key in the lock.

The click sounded unnaturally loud in the quiet room.

"There," he said, with great satisfaction, pocketing the key. "It's a sad day when a chap can't declare his love without half of Norfolk barging in."

"Is that what this is?" Arabella asked, her heart in her throat. "Love?"

"Well, it's certainly not a toothache." It seemed belatedly to occur to Turnip that he might have somehow botched it. Stumbling over his feet and his words, he said, "Wouldn't want you to feel obligated, if you don't return the emotion, that is. Shouldn't have said anything, but I thought—that is—"

"I wasn't sure if you were saying it just to stop Catherine." Arabella knew she was being shameless, fishing like that, but she wanted the reassurance.

The expression of pure horror on Turnip's face was all the reassurance she needed. That was one of the loveliest things about Turnip, she thought vaguely. One never had to worry about lies or dissembling. Everything he thought or felt was written all over his face in a very large hand.

"Good Gad, no! That day I knocked you over—you remember? Best day of my life. Didn't know it then, of course. If I had, I would probably have thrown a sack over your head and dragged you home with me. Only you might not have liked that."

Arabella considered the prospect. "I wouldn't be so sure of that."

"The sack, I mean," said Turnip.

"Um, yes." Fair enough. "I think we can forgo the sack."

Turnip clasped and unclasped his hands behind his back. "What I'm trying to say is, it's yours, you know. My heart. If you want it."

Arabella felt a great big silly smile spreading across her face. She stepped boldly up to him. "Is it my Christmas gift?"

Turnip rested his cheek briefly against her hair. "Wish I could wrap it in pretty words for you, all shiny and tied up in bows."

Arabella put her fingers to his lips to stop the words. "I like it just the way it is. I like you just the way you are."

Turnip kissed her fingers.

Arabella looked at him and thought of all the flowery things one would say if this were a romance in a book. She had read such speeches—long, elegant monologues rich with classical allusions and clever turns of phrase. They all felt all wrong somehow, not because the emotion wasn't there, but because it was.

Next to the sheer vastness of her love, verbal frills felt superfluous. Silly, even, like trying to deck out a mountain range in lace trim.

So she made Turnip no flowery speeches.

Instead, she took a deep breath, and said, "I love you."

"Really?" Turnip's face lit up.

He looked at her with such tenderness and hope that Arabella had to say it again. "I love you. I want to prowl castles with you and celebrate Christmas with you and get annoyed with you for climbing things. And I'm terribly fond of raspberry jam. Lots of it."

Turnip wrapped his arms around her, his eyes on her lips. "We'll celebrate our anniversary with jam," he promised, leaning forward. "With jam and Christmas pudding."

Struck by a sudden thought, Arabella pulled back in his arms, tilting her head back to see his face.

"One last thing—"

"Anything!" Turnip promised extravagantly.

"Why were you carrying a pudding?"

Chapter 29

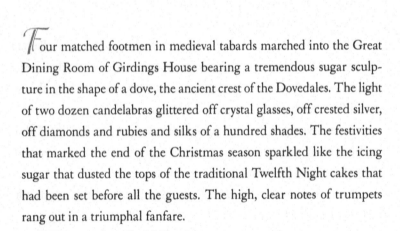

*F*our matched footmen in medieval tabards marched into the Great Dining Room of Girdings House bearing a tremendous sugar sculpture in the shape of a dove, the ancient crest of the Dovedales. The light of two dozen candelabras glittered off crystal glasses, off crested silver, off diamonds and rubies and silks of a hundred shades. The festivities that marked the end of the Christmas season sparkled like the icing sugar that dusted the tops of the traditional Twelfth Night cakes that had been set before all the guests. The high, clear notes of trumpets rang out in a triumphal fanfare.

"I like your dress," said Turnip.

Arabella glanced down at her own décolletage. It was a shiny white meringue of a dress, one of Aunt Osborne's choosing, with lots of frills around the neckline.

There was one thing to be said about it. It bared a great deal of bosom.

"It makes me look like a milkmaid."

"I know," said Turnip happily. "Always liked the dairy, don't you know."

Arabella saw it all through a happy haze, like the world viewed through the side of a champagne glass, everything bubbling and beautiful and tinted with a golden glow. She didn't even mind that the dowager had seated Penelope Deveraux on Turnip's other side, not with Turnip's hand discreetly clasping hers under the tablecloth.

As untitled, and therefore uninteresting, people, both Arabella and Turnip had been seated all the way down at the far end of the table. Turnip hadn't even had to juggle placement to put them together; the duchess in her infinite wisdom had already known. Or, more likely, the duchess had decided that two of her least favorite guests ought to bore each other rather than others.

Turnip had dashed off a letter to his parents, with a special postscript for Sally, and another, shorter letter to her father, formally requesting an interview, but other than that, they had made no announcements. It was still too new and precious to share.

All around them, people were prospecting in their cakes, searching for the tiny golden tokens that would proclaim the two main figures of the Twelfth Night festivities to come: the Lord of Misrule and the Queen of the Feast. In lesser households, it would be a bean and a pea. The dowager used a jester's staff and a miniature golden crown, specially made for the occasion.

Turnip poked about his cake with his fork. "Nothing," he announced. He took a whopping forkful of sugared dough, adding, somewhat indistinctly, "Jolly good cake." Catching Arabella's eye, he grinned. "Better with jam, though."

"Everything is better with jam," said Arabella serenely.

Turnip rocked back in his chair. "There are berry brambles all around the grounds of Parva Magna. We can go berry picking next summer."

"With Sally?"

"And your sisters too, if they like. Shouldn't wonder if Sally takes your Lavinia on as a protégée." He gave an exaggerated shudder. "Heaven help us all."

From the middle of the table came a great roaring noise. "I say!" Henry Innes shouted. "Freddy got the staff!"

There was a great clattering as inebriated gentlemen pounded their appreciation on the tablecloth, making china tremble and crystal jump.

"Hope you put it to good use!" shouted Martin Frobisher, one hand on the claret decanter, followed by something else that Arabella didn't quite catch, but was distinctly bawdy in nature.

Turnip turned red and looked anxiously at Arabella. "It's all right," Arabella said, patting his hand. "I've read my Shakespeare."

Lord Freddy pumped a hand into the air, spraying crumbs across the table and down Lucy Ponsonby's décolletage. The golden staff looked absurdly small in his large fist.

"All hail your Lord of Misrule!" he cried.

"Couldn't have picked a better man for the job," muttered Turnip.

"Except maybe Lieutenant Danforth," said Arabella.

Darius Danforth had been spirited off to London that morning, the folds of his cape hiding the ropes around his wrists.

The Carruthers family had also made a precipitate departure, Catherine all but invisible between the flanking forms of her parents. Mrs. Carruthers had looked like a very angry Pekingese. Arabella hadn't envied Catherine the long carriage ride back to London.

"Do you think they'll get that annulment?" Arabella asked Turnip.

Turnip shook his head. "Shouldn't think so. Marriage was illegal, and all that, but it would be too much of a scandal. Better for them to wait for a time and then announce a match."

Remembering the hard glitter of Catherine's eyes, Arabella shivered. "If I were Danforth's older brother," she said, "I would be very, very careful of what I ate. I would also avoid balconies and open windows."

Under the table, Turnip's fingers tightened around hers. "Lost ten years of my life when I saw her herding you towards that window. New rule: no windows."

"That would get very dark," Arabella pointed out.

Turnip grinned rakishly. "I don't mind the dark. Do you?"

Arabella's blushes were spared by a loud commotion at the head table, where the Duke of Dovedale and his cousin, Lady Charlotte, sat in lonely splendor. She glanced hastily away, all too aware of Turnip's knee bumping hers under the table.

"We have a monarch!" roared out the Duke of Dovedale. "Queen Charlotte!"

"I say, does he mean the real one?" demanded Turnip, craning to look over his shoulder, in case the queen might have entered while he was otherwise occupied.

"Oh, do be quiet," said Penelope Deveraux, whacking him on the shoulder with her fork. Cake crumbled down the front of Turnip's jacket. "It's our Charlotte—*that* Charlotte. Over there."

She pointed with her fork up the table, where Lady Charlotte was blushingly allowing the duke to help her from her chair, gazing up at him as though he were all the knights of the Round Table rolled into one. The duke was a handsome man, to be sure, but there was something about him that Arabella didn't like, something self-contained to the point of secretive.

She looked at Turnip, his mouth wide with laughter, a dusting of multicolored cake sugar glittering on one side of his jacket, and felt like laughing herself. How wonderful not to have to worry about subtexts and secrets and things that couldn't be said; everything Turnip thought or felt was in his eyes and his lips.

"What is it?" he whispered.

Arabella shook her head. "Nothing. Just you."

At the head of the table, the Duke of Dovedale once more called the revelers to attention. "To Her Majesty, our Queen of the Feast—Queen Charlotte!"

All up and down the table, crystal glittered as the houseguests raised their glasses, dutifully echoing, "Queen Charlotte!"

All except Turnip. He didn't lift his glass to the evening's queen.

He lifted it to Arabella, whispering, for her ears alone, "Queen Arabella. Queen of my heart, in any event," he added, in more normal tones, as he set the glass back on the cloth.

"Do you have any pronouncements for your loyal subjects?" shouted out Tommy Fluellen, from Arabella's other side.

Lady Charlotte beamed down from the head table, a gilded crown of mistletoe set slightly askew on her golden curls. "That I do!" she called back, deploying her fan like a scepter. "Go forth and enjoy yourself mightily."

A roar of approval went up from the table as chairs scraped back against the polished floors and inebriated guests staggered towards the conveniences, the gallery, or their own private alcoves. The rest of the guests were already beginning to assemble in the grand reception rooms on the other side of the house, wandering through a wonderland of improbably flowering urns, champagne fountains, and elaborate garlands of holly and mistletoe.

Turnip squeezed Arabella's hand. "I claim your first dance. Rather like the second and third ones too."

"What about the fourth?" Arabella stood as a footman drew her chair back.

Turnip pretended to consider. "Take that one as well. Shouldn't want it to feel left out."

Hand in hand, they joined the giddy crowd making its way out of the dining room. Turnip looked hopefully at the doorframe, but there was no mistletoe there. Tommy Fluellen trailed along after Penelope, who was pretending not to notice Freddy Staines—at least, until he grabbed her by the back of the dress and pulled. Everyone was loose and laughing with wine and feasting, returned to the mores of an earlier, faster era.

Everyone, apparently, but Arabella's new uncle by marriage. He stalked stiffly up to them, his expression rigid. "Fitzhugh," he said in an undertone. "I've been wanting to speak to you."

"Have you? Jolly good of you," said Turnip. "Look forward to it. After the dancing."

"I'm afraid it won't wait until after the dancing," said Musgrave.

Across the room, Aunt Osborne raised a diamond-spangled hand to hail him. Diamond bracelets wrapped around her pudgy wrists and diamond rings sparkled on her gloved fingers. In her too-youthful white and silver gauze, she looked like an aging water nymph liberated from the edge of a fountain.

Musgrave waved unenthusiastically back.

"You shouldn't keep my aunt waiting," said Arabella, enjoying herself just a little too much.

"I came to speak to you on behalf of your aunt," he said, but his eyes shifted as he said it. He turned to Turnip. "She is very perturbed by the way you have been trifling with her niece."

"Oh, for heaven's sake," said Arabella, twining her arm through Turnip's. "Nobody is trifling with anyone. We're quite in accord on that."

"Perfectly in accord," echoed Turnip. "In accord as an accordion."

Musgrave looked at her with concern, and more than a little bit of pity. "You can't think he means to marry you?"

He meant it, she realized. In his own odd way, he genuinely thought he was protecting her honor. Having not wanted to marry her himself, he assumed no one else would. It would have been amusing if it hadn't been mildly insulting.

Lowering his voice, Musgrave addressed Turnip. "You do know she doesn't have a dowry?"

Turnip's deliberately daft smile never faltered. "That's quite all right. I do," he said. Turning to Arabella, he asked, with great seriousness, "Would you prefer it in goats or pigs?"

"Cows," said Arabella, "definitely cows. You can waylay them for me."

"Deuced tetchy beasts, cows," warned Turnip.

"But they make such lovely dairy."

"Always did like dairy," agreed Turnip. "Have I mentioned how much I like that dress?"

"You're both mad," muttered Musgrave.

"Mad with happiness," said Turnip. "True love and all that, don't you know."

Captain Musgrave looked from one to the other, making a belated attempt to regain control over the situation.

"Does this mean that you do intend to marry?" he asked, with difficulty, as though the idea were such an oddity that it pained him to even entertain it.

"A pertinent question," Arabella said to Turnip. "What with one thing and another, I don't believe you ever did officially ask for my hand."

Turnip whapped himself on the head with the flat of his hand. "Blast this deuced absent mind of mine! Could've sworn I had . . . but, oh well, no harm in doing it again. Would you like the grand display or would a small one do?"

"The grand display," said Arabella, her lips twitching. "Quite definitely the grand display."

"I love that about you," said Turnip abruptly.

Arabella looked quizzically at him. "My instinct for drama?"

"The little lip-twitchy thing you do when you're trying not to laugh. It's very high on the list of things I love about you."

"How long is this list?"

"Hard to tell, really. It keeps growing on me. Deuced inconvenient that way."

The two shared a long and extremely soppy look.

Arabella fluttered her lashes at him. "I love the way you hit yourself in the head when you've forgotten something."

"Good," said Turnip, "because I'm deuced forgetful."

"So long as you don't forget me."

Turnip twined his fingers through hers. "Couldn't do that if I tried. You're engraved on my heart, don't you know."

Arabella batted her eyelashes at him. "How very uncomfortable for you."

Captain Musgrave peered over his shoulder, checking to see if anyone had heard. "You're making a scandal of yourself, Arabella," he said in low, urgent tones.

"Good," said Arabella cheerfully. "I've been far too well behaved for far too long."

Shame having failed, Captain Musgrave tried guilt. "If you won't think of yourself, think of your aunt."

"I'm not thinking. I'm acting. No more *Hamlet* for me." Turnip grinned proudly. It went straight to Arabella's head. Turning back to her step-uncle, she said giddily, "If you're not careful, I might invade Scotland next."

Musgrave looked at her with genuine concern. "I know this year has been difficult for you, but I hadn't realized quite how difficult. Maybe you should go lie down. You aren't yourself."

Arabella smiled ruefully at him, thinking how little he knew. "On the contrary, I am most entirely myself. More so than I've been for years."

Musgrave shook his head in determined negation. "This isn't the you I know."

"That's because you didn't know me. You wouldn't have wanted to." It was true. If she had said half the things she had been thinking, it would have scared him to death. Arabella turned back to Turnip. "As for you, Mr. Fitzhugh, didn't you promise me a grand display of the scandalous and embarrassing variety?"

"Do my best." Turnip plopped himself down on one knee where he would be sure to cause the maximum disruption, right in the doorway of the dining room. "Arabella—er, do you have a middle name?"

"Elizabeth." Arabella was enjoying herself hugely. "You do have troubles with my name, don't you?"

"Practice makes perfect." Turnip rubbed his hands together, gearing up for his grand scene. "Right. Here goes. Arabella Elizabeth Dempsey, I adore you. You are the plums in my pudding, the spice in my cider, the holly on my ivy."

"I don't think holly grows on ivy," said Arabella, lips twitching.

"Well, it should," said Turnip forcefully. "More things in heaven and earth and whatnot. Christmas is a season of miracles."

A snorting sound came from somewhere above Arabella's head. It was the dowager, perched high on her litter, wearing a truly alarming headdress of holly and ivy, her sparse gray hair frizzed out like Marie Antoinette's in her heyday.

"Say yes, girl!" commanded the Dowager Duchess of Dovedale. "If he keeps talking, I hold you responsible."

Arabella held out her hands to Turnip, raising him up from his knees. "I love you," she said, "and I would be honored to be your wife."

"You don't mind being Mrs. Turnip?"

"So long as you don't mind Mr. What's-Her-Name."

"Now, that's a name I can remember," said Turnip smugly and swept her into his arms, tilting her back at an improbable and wonderfully dizzying angle. "Happy Christmas, my own Arabella."

Arabella could feel her hair slipping free from its pins in a decidedly wanton way. She smiled up at him. "Aren't you forgetting something?"

Turnip paused, midswoop. "True love, eternal adoration, plum pudding . . . all seems to be here."

"There's just one thing missing." Raising her head slightly, she flapped a hand in the air, calling out, "Does anyone have any mistletoe?"

An excerpt from the Dempsey Collection:

Miss Jane Austen to Miss Arabella Dempsey
Green Park Buildings, 7 March, 1805

My dear Arabella,

Many thanks for your affectionate letter. I should be delighted to stand godmother to baby Jane, although you have quite ruined my plans for The Watsons. *I had intended you for a vicar, not for a wealthy species of vegetable. I refuse to play with puddings and paper scimitars, even for you. You have quite upset my designs, but I forgive you for the excellent diversion your letters provided.*

   [Several paragraphs omitted]

   Thank you for your excellent suggestion regarding the hero in First Impressions. *Can you really imagine I would change his name from Darcy to Parsnip?*

Yours ever truly,
J. A.

Acknowledgments

First and foremost, to Brooke, my little sister, and Claudia Brittenham, the best college roommate in the whole wide world, who both put in massive scads of overtime on this book. Thank you for holding my hand through character conundrums and plot nightmares and for convincing me to retrieve those first six chapters from the recycle bin. I love you both.

To Kara Cesare, my former editor, who cheered me through the beginning of this project, and to Erika Imranyi, my new editor, who valiantly picked it up in the middle. And, as always, to Joe Veltre, my agent, who makes this and all things possible.

To my parents, for being nothing like Arabella's, and to my friends, for reminding me that there was light at the end of the tunnel.

Last but not least, to Miss Austen, who set the tone for generations of novels to come. What would the world be without Lizzy and Darcy?

Historical Note

In the winter of 1803, Jane Austen was twenty-eight years old and living with her family at Sydney Place, in Bath. Biographers agree that Austen was less than pleased with this arrangement. The move from Steventon to Bath in 1800, just after her twenty-fifth birthday, had been much against her wishes. She found Bath, in her own words, "vapour, shadow, smoke and confusion," and the people disagreeable. The Bath years were ones of discontent and dead ends. In December of 1802, Austen received a proposal from a family friend, a man of fortune and property, Mr. Harris Bigg-Withers. The proposal must have been a tempting one, to be mistress of her own household—but Austen, having yielded to worldly considerations and accepted his proposal, immediately thought better of it. She rescinded her acceptance the next day and hastened back to Bath. In another disappointment, in 1803, a publisher accepted her novel *Susan* (later *Northanger Abbey*), but failed to bring it to publication.

Unfortunately, there is little in Austen's own voice to tell us about this period in her life. Due to the destruction of most of her letters after her death, only 160 remain extant. In this period, the period between 1801 and 1805, only one letter survives, written from Lyme in September of 1804.

What we do know is that towards the end of 1803 Austen began work on a new novel. By 1800, when she made the move to Bath, Austen had already written *First Impressions* (later *Pride and Prejudice*), *Elinor and Marianne* (later *Sense and Sensibility*) and *Susan* (*Northanger Abbey*). Her later works, *Mansfield Park*, *Emma*, *Persuasion*, and *Sanditon*, were all written much later in her life, after 1812. The Bath years mark a long, fallow period, broken only by one, incomplete work: *The Watsons*.

The Watsons follows the plight of a young lady who, like many characters in Austen's books, has been wrenched from her family as a young child and sent to live with a wealthy aunt in the expectation of becoming her aunt's heiress. When her aunt contracts an imprudent match to a fortune-hunting army officer, Emma Watson is thrown back upon the bosom of her family: an ailing clergyman father and three unmarried sisters. Critics have commented on the dark tone of this work. In *Jane Austen: A Life*, Claire Tomalin writes that "[t]he conversations [Austen] wrote for the Watson sisters are strikingly grimmer than anything else in her work," while in *Jane Austen: The World of Her Novels*, Deirdre La Faye refers to *The Watsons* as "a bitter rerun of *Pride and Prejudice*," positing that Austen might have dropped it because it "was becoming too sad," the situation of Emma and her sisters and their ailing clergyman father being far too close to home.

I borrowed the basic premise of *The Watsons* for this book, although in Austen's version, Emma is the youngest sister rather than the oldest. Margaret, Arabella's most troublesome sister, is lifted straight out of *The Watsons*, as are the invalid father and Aunt Osborne and the fortune-hunting army officer. Like Arabella, Austen's Emma Watson plays with the idea of relieving the burden on her family by finding work at a school, a notion her sister strongly deplores. There all resemblance ends. There is no indication in *The Watsons* that the aunt's second husband had previously courted Emma, nor are there any French spies or English gentlemen named after vegetables.

Even more telling, Austen's heroine decides not to take up work at a school; mine does. From her own school days at Mrs. La Tournelle's Ladies' Boarding School at Reading, Austen retained a distaste for young ladies' scholastic institutions that came out loud and clear in her novels. The school in which I place Arabella is a larger, more luxurious version of the institutions with which Austen would have been familiar. Like Miss Climpson, Mrs. La Tournelle hired a number of young woman teachers who conducted the actual instruction, while she presided over the institution. For the sake of my story (and since this was a rather more luxe institution than the one Austen attended), I gave the girls private rooms; at Mrs. La Tournelle's they would have slept six to a room.

The haphazard nature of the educational program, however, is true to form. A contemporary of Austen's at Mrs. La Tournelle's described it as a place "where girls might be sent to be out of the way and scramble themselves into an education, without any danger of coming back prodigies." According to Austen's biographers, the curriculum included French, spelling, needlework, deportment, dancing, music—and, surprisingly, theater. The inspiration for the Christmas recital at Miss Climpson's came directly from Mrs. La Tournelle's boarding school, where the girls took part in a number of amateur theatricals.

Biographers have debated why Austen failed to finish *The Watsons*. Her nephew, Austen-Leigh, posited that she abandoned it because her heroine was too socially lowly. Jon Spence, in *Becoming Jane Austen*, attributes it to her recognition of the grim tone of the novel, arguing,

"She had given free rein to the expression of her own bitterness, and it signals her defeat in trying to write *The Watsons*. . . . [S]he did not want to write such a novel." Claire Tomalin believes "a more likely reason" may have been because "the theme of the story touched too closely on Jane's fears for herself." According to Austen's older sister, Cassandra, Austen intended to kill off Emma Watson's father partway through the novel. Deirdre Le Faye posits that the death of Austen's own father, early in 1805, may have been the stimulus for abandoning the book. Far more fun, all around, to pretend that the cause lay in Christmas puddings, French spies, and a man named Turnip.

For those wishing to hear more of Austen in her own voice, there are her letters, reprinted by Pavilion Press (I shamelessly culled phrases from Austen's extant letters for the letter to Arabella at the front of this book), and her juvenilia, compiled in *Catharine and Other Writings*. For contemporary, or near-contemporary, recollections, one can go to J. E. Austen-Leigh's *Memoir* and Caroline Austen's *My Aunt Jane Austen: A Memoir* and *Reminiscences*. Biographies of the authoress include, among the more recent efforts, Claire Tomalin's *Jane Austen: A Life*, Jon Spence's *Becoming Jane Austen*, and John Halperin's *The Life of Jane Austen*. Deirdre Le Faye's *Jane Austen: The World of Her Novels* does an excellent job of situating both the authoress and her novels in cultural context. I also owe a debt of gratitude for the Morgan Library's fortuitously timed exhibit "A Woman's Wit: Jane Austen's Life and Legacy," which provided a rare opportunity to see letters and manuscript pages written in her own hand, books from her library, and contemporary images of people, places, and events that touched on her life.

As a final note, you may have noticed some differences between Christmas as we know it and as Arabella and Turnip experience it. Much of what we associate with a "traditional" English Christmas came over with Victoria's Albert from Germany in the mid-nineteenth century. The iconic Christmas tree was introduced by Queen Charlotte in 1800, but became popular only during the reign of her granddaughter, Queen Victoria. Carols were also a Victorian addition to the Christmas canon. Although I did include some anachronisms (like the Christmas pageant), for the folks at Miss Climpson's and at Girdings House, I tried to re-create the earlier model of Christmas celebration, in which the halls would have been decked with holly—but no tree—and the main celebration took place on Twelfth Night, rather than Christmas proper. Different parts of England had their own regional traditions, including the fascinating Epiphany Eve ritual of frightening away the evil spirits, that I co-opted for my characters.

The Mischief of the
MISTLETOE

LAUREN WILLIG

A Brief History of the Turnip

You knew I didn't mean the root vegetable, right? I'm talking about Mr. Reginald Fitzhugh, more commonly known to his friends and associates as "Turnip." Turnip first blundered into my books as a disposable side character in *The Masque of the Black Tulip*. I had intended him purely for comic relief, but before he had uttered his second "deuced havey-cavey!" I knew he was there to stay.

Turnip emerges from a long literary tradition. Chaucer's naive narrator has a bit of Turnip in him (when the literary critics refer to a man as a good-natured bumbler, you know he's of the lineage of Turnip), as does Jane Austen's beloved Bingley, over whom Mr. Bennett shakes his head for "being so easy, that every servant will cheat you; and so generous, that you will always exceed your income." Fortunately, Turnip's income is quite large. On the distaff side of the bookshelf, you can find Turnip's near relations scattered as comic side characters through the works of Georgette Heyer and her modern imitators. One of my favorite proto-Turnips is the endearing but awkward Nigel from Jill Barnett's *Bewitching*, for whose sake there wasn't a chapter thirteen (bad luck, don't you know!).

For the most part, these lovable bunglers tend to be side characters. People like their heroes to be heroic, and we ascribe to heroism certain qualities of command. It's hard to imagine Henry V at Agincourt stirring up men with, "Today is called the day of Crispin, don'cha know. Er . . . least, I thought it was the day of St. Crispin. More like the afternoon of Crispin, really. Not that there's anything wrong with afternoon and all that—it's a scrumbly good time for a battle!" But there are other forms of heroism, and, as Georgette Heyer shows us with her unknown Ajax, sometimes an unimposing exterior can hide unexpected qualities of leadership and resolve. Despite the usual biases towards the alpha hero, one can find the odd leading man among the Turnip brigade. I had already written Turnip into being by the time I read Loretta Chase's *Mr. Impossible*, but the minute I met Rupert Carsington, I knew him to be a kinsman of Turnip.

All of these are in Turnip's DNA, but his real progenitor, the one to whom I doff my chapeau (or my carnation-embroidered waistcoat) is P. G. Wodehouse's Bertie Wooster. Like Bertie Wooster, Turnip is entirely at home in his own world and his own waistcoats. It takes so little to make them happy: a new waistcoat, a well-mixed drink, a weekend in the country. The Turnip/Woosters of the world are generous companions. They may be thoughtless, but they're never malicious. What they might lack in erudition, they make up for in kindness. As Wooster blunders into scrapes in the attempt to help out one benighted friend after another, just so Turnip can never refuse a friend in distress, even if his cunning plans sometimes turn out to be less cunning than expected. But that's all right too. Wooster has Jeeves to set him straight; my Turnip has his Arabella. In the end, the Woosters and Turnips of the world can always find someone to set the world to rights for them.

A final note on Turnip. Turnip may owe his basic nature to P. G. Wodehouse, but his name comes straight out of the British comedy *Blackadder*. For those of you who haven't seen *Blackadder*, it deals with Edmund Blackadder, a rascally Englishman scheming his way across various eras of British history with more or less success. (If one is looking for proto-Turnips, there are at least two in the *Blackadder* series: Sir Percy Percy of the first and second series and the Thicky Prince, aka the Prince Regent, in the third.) There are certain truths one learns from *Blackadder*: plans must be cunning; sheep are inherently amusing animals; and if one must have a vegetable, there's no better vegetable to have than a turnip. I heard Baldrick is still saving up for his little turnip in the country. I had already used up my share of sheep jokes in the first book of the Pink series, so, when I needed an amusing name for a side character, what better than a Turnip?

Turnip's Wild Raspberry Jam

*I*nspired by Turnip's passion for raspberry jam, I tried my hand at a bit of jam making while I was writing this book. After several "the jelly won't jell!" incidents, one dramatic boil-over, three nasty blisters, and many botched batches, this was the best recipe to come out of my trial-and-error approach to the making of preserves.

> *8 cups wild raspberries*
> *1 apple, peeled, cored, and diced*
> *1 cup sugar (may add more depending on personal taste)*

Remove bugs and twigs from berries. Finely dice apple (in case you're curious, the apple provides the pectin). Combine raspberries, apple, and sugar in medium-sized saucepan. (Optional: you can lightly crush the berries with a potato masher. Good for getting out aggressions, may or may not do anything for the jam.) Bring to a boil. Continue to boil, stirring frequently, for thirty minutes or until mixture appears sufficiently gooey. Pour into prepared mason jars. Yield: two 16-ounce jars.

Works well spread on toast, served over vanilla ice cream, or eaten straight out of the jar with a spoon while stressing out over book deadlines.

Christmas Pudding

To make what is termed a pound pudding, take of raisins well stoned, currants thoroughly washed, one pound each; chop a pound of suet very finely and mix with them; add a quarter of a pound of flour, or bread very finely crumbled, three ounces of sugar, one ounce and a half of grated lemon-peel, a blade of mace, half a small nutmeg, one teaspoonful of ginger, half a dozen eggs well beaten; work it well together, put it into a cloth, tie it firmly, allowing room to swell, and boil not less than five hours. It should not be suffered to stop boiling.

— *Godey's Ladies Book*, 1860, Recipe for
"Old English Christmas Pudding"

By 1803, the year in which this story is set, plum pudding was well established as traditional Christmas fare. Traditions and mythologies abound. Some require that Christmas pudding be made no later than the twenty-fifth Sunday after Trinity, with each member of the household stirring the pudding three times, in tribute to the Three Kings. Likewise, the thirteen ingredients (although some recipes have more and other fewer) are said to represent Christ and the twelve Apostles, while the holly garnish is meant to symbolize the crown of thorns. Other, less religiously charged traditions include making a wish as one stirs the pudding (I've always liked this one) and hiding coins, gold rings, thimbles, buttons, or other items in the pudding, as the Dowager Duchess of Dovedale does with the cakes in this book.

There are a dizzying number of Christmas pudding recipes. While recipes vary, all seem to include the same basic components: suet, raisins, lemon peel, spices, bread crumbs, and brandy or ale. According to one source, plum pudding originated as a medieval dish called frumenty—a soupy porridge made up of boiled mutton, raisins, prunes, spices, and wine. With the addition of eggs, bread crumbs, and dried fruit during the late sixteenth century, the soupy porridge thickened into the glutinous ball recognizable to us as plum pudding. Christmas pudding fell out of favor during the latter part of the seventeenth century but was brought back to the fore by George I, who might not have been able to speak English, but did know a good thing when he tasted it.

King George's Christmas Pudding (1714)

Combine:

1 lb eggs	*1 lb sugar*
1½ lb shredded suet	*1 lb breadcrumbs*
1 lb dried plums	*1 teaspoon mixed spice*
1 lb raisins	*½ grated nutmeg*
1 lb mixed peel	*½ pint milk*
1 lb currants	*½ teaspoon salt*
1 lb sultanas	*the juice of a lemon*
1 lb flour	*a large glass of brandy*

Let stand for 12 hours.

Boil for 8 hours and boil again on Christmas Day for 2 hours.

This will yield 9 lbs of pudding.

Don't forget to make a wish as you stir. . . .

A Note About the Pink Carnation Series

Turnip Fitzhugh first stumbled his way onto the scene as a lovable bumbler in the second book of the Pink Carnation series, *The Masque of the Black Tulip*. For some time now, the e-mails have poured in, asking when Turnip was going to get some lovin' (direct quote, there). For all of you who worried about Turnip's future, this book is for you.

I had vague ideas for a book about Turnip, but I didn't know quite what I was going to do with him until *The Temptation of the Night Jasmine*, at the Dowager Duchess of Dovedale's Twelfth Night dinner, when I saw Turnip seated all the way down at the end of the table next to a wallflower named Arabella Dempsey. And I thought, what if . . . ? "What if" always gets me into trouble.

For those of you who have read the series, you'll have recognized the second half of this book as *Night Jasmine* turned inside out, the same events and characters experienced from the point of view of minor members of the house party, whose focus and concerns are completely different from those of Robert, Duke of Dovedale; Lady Charlotte Lansdowne; and the other primary actors of that book. Ever wonder why Turnip was trying to cut down that tree with the wrong side of his ax in *Night Jasmine*? Now you know.

While I tried not to turn this book into a Christmas reunion special, several characters from the prior Pink books did pop up to make appearances in Turnip's story. As a refresher for those who have read the series, or an introduction for those who haven't, here's the Who's Who of both recurring characters and some new friends and relations of preexisting ones.

Since we've already mentioned Robert and Charlotte, hero and heroine of Book V, *The Temptation of the Night Jasmine*, here's the rest of the gang.

Turnip Fitzhugh: Turnip has been around for several books now, fighting off French spies, spreading good cheer, and tripping over things. He attended Eton with the main characters of the first three Pink books: Lord Richard Selwick (aka the Purple Gentian), Miles Dorrington, and Geoffrey Pinchingdale-Snipe. Lord Richard and Miles were the year ahead, Geoff and Turnip a year behind, which accounts for the strange rapport between the brainy Geoff and scatterbrained Turnip.

Miss Penelope Deveraux: Heroine of Book VI, *The Betrayal of the Blood Lily*. Poor Pen. It's not easy being a femme fatale. In Penelope's first appearance, in *The Masque of the Black Tulip*, she's being scolded by Henrietta Selwick and Charlotte Lansdowne, her two closest friends, for improper behavior on a balcony with none other than our favorite Turnip. Turnip isn't the only man with whom Penelope canoodles on projecting bits of masonry. At that very same eventful Twelfth Night ball, just a few hours after the end of this book, restless and rebellious Penelope manages to get herself into a fix she can't brazen her way out of.

Lord and Lady Vaughn: Stars of Book IV, *The Seduction of the Crimson Rose*. Lord Vaughn is related to absolutely everyone who is anyone, including dodgy French chevaliers. After he spent a decade in shadowy pursuits on the Continent, his loyalty is frequently suspect. His wife, the former Mary Alsworthy, likes to forget her low origins by lording it over people.

Lord and Lady Pinchingdale: Hero and heroine of Book III, *The Deception of the Emerald Ring*. Geoffrey Pinchingdale-Snipe originally served in the League of the Scarlet Pimpernel, rose to second-in-command of the League of the Purple Gentian, and now freelances for the League of the Pink Carnation. Given that Geoff tends to be the mastermind behind the scenes, rather than the man in the black mask swinging from a rope, one assumes that fatherhood won't do too much to curtail his activities for the cause.

Lady Henrietta Dorrington: Heroine of Book II, *The Masque of the Black Tulip*. We don't see much of Hen in this one, because, as readers of *Night Jasmine* know, she's occupied with Charlotte's romantic crises, but she does get a brief cameo. Sister of the Purple Gentian, Lord Richard Selwick, Henrietta likes to have a finger in every pie—or pudding, as the case may be.

Lieutenant Tommy Fluellen: Best friend to Robert, Duke of Dovedale, harboring a painful and unrequited infatuation for Miss Penelope Deveraux (see *Temptation of the Night Jasmine*).

The Dowager Duchess of Dovedale: Terrorizing innocent characters for five books and still going strong. Nothing outlasts the Energizer dragon!

Martin Frobisher, Lord Henry Innes, Sir Francis Medmenham, and Lord Freddy Staines: Men-about-town and members of the same dodgy Hellfire Club, the Order of the Lotus (see *Temptation of the Night Jasmine*).

Sally Fitzhugh, Lizzy Reid, and Agnes Wooliston: We haven't met any of these characters before, but you can bet we're going to see more of them. Sally Fitzhugh is, obviously, Turnip's sister, but the other two are also sibs of Pink Carnation veterans.

Lizzy Reid is the younger sister of Captain Alex Reid, hero of Book VI, *The Betrayal of the Blood Lily*. She's also sister to Jack Reid, the double agent known as the Moonflower.

Agnes Wooliston is first cousin to Miss Amy Balcourt, heroine of Book I, *The Secret History of the Pink Carnation*. More important, she's the youngest sister of Miss Jane Wooliston, aka the Pink Carnation.

Add up three adventurous sixteen-year-olds, two deadly spies, and one very lax headmistress, and you have the potential for a great deal of trouble. . . .

Read on for an excerpt from

The Orchid Affair

a new book in Lauren Willig's
bestselling Pink Carnation series.

Paris, 1804

"Around the back," said the gatekeeper.

Laura scrambled backwards as a moving wall of iron careened towards her face. From the distance, the gate was a grand thing, a towering edifice of black metal with heraldic symbols outlined in flaking gilt. From up close, it was decidedly less attractive. Especially when it was on a collision course with one's nose. Her nose might not have been a thing of beauty, but she liked it where it was.

"But—" Laura grabbed at the bars with her gloved hands. The leather skidded against the bars, leaving long, rusty streaks across her palms. So much for her last pair of gloves.

Laura bit down on a sharp exclamation of frustration. She reminded herself of Rule #10 of the Guide to Better Governessing: Never Let Them See You Suffer. Weakness bred contempt. If there was one thing she had learned, it was that the meek never inherited anything—except maybe a gate to the nose.

"I am expected," Laura announced with all the dignity she could muster.

It was hard to be dignified with raindrops dripping off one's nose. She could feel wet strands of hair scraggling down her neck, under the back of her collar. Errant strands tickled her back, making her want to squirm. Oh, heavens, that itched.

She looked down her nose through the grille of ironwork. "Kindly let me in."

Ahead of her, just a stretch of courtyard away, across gardens grown unkempt with neglect, lay warmth and shelter. Or at least shelter. From the look of the unlit windows, there was precious little warmth. But even a roof looked good to her right now. Roofs served an important purpose. They kept off rain. Blasted rain. This was France, not England. What was it doing mizzling like this?

The gatekeeper shrugged, and started to turn away.

Laura resisted the urge to reach through the bars, grab him by the collar, and shake.

"The governess," she called after him, trying to keep any touch of desperation from her voice. She refused to believe her mission could end like this, this ignominiously, this early. This moistly. "I am the governess."

"Around the back," the gatekeeper repeated and spat for good measure.

Around the back? The house was a good mile around. Would it really have been so much bother to have let her in through the front? What had happened to *liberté, égalité* and *fraternité*? Apparently, those sentiments didn't extend to governesses.

Laura took a step back, landing in a puddle that went clear up to her ankle. She could feel the icy water soaking through the worn kid leather of her sensible boot. At least, it would have been sensible, if it hadn't had a hole the size of Nôtre-Dame in the sole. Laura took a deep breath in and out through her nose. Right. If he wanted her around the back, around the back it was. There was no point in starting off on the wrong foot by fighting with the gatekeeper. Even if the man was a petty cretin who shouldn't have been trusted with a latchkey.

Temper, she reminded herself. Temper. She had been a semi-servant for years enough now that one would think she was immune to such slights.

Gathering up the sodden folds of her pelisse (dark brown wool, sensible, warm, didn't show the dirt, largely because it had already been designed to look like dirt), Laura trudged the length of the street, skidding a bit as her sodden shoes slipped and slid on the rounded cobbles. The Hôtel de Bac was in the heart of the Marais, among a twisted welter of ancient streets, most without sidewalks. During her long years in England, Laura had never thought she would miss London, but she did miss the sidewalks. And the tea.

Mmm, tea. Hot amber liquid with curls of steam rising from the top, the curved sides of the cup warm against one's palms on a cold day . . .

This had been her choice, she reminded herself. No one had placed a knife to her neck and demanded she go. She could very well have stayed in England and done exactly as she had done for the past sixteen years. She could have walked primly down the sidewalked streets, herding her charges in front of her, yanking them back from horses' hooves and mud puddles and bits of interesting masonry; she could have poured her tea from the nursery teapot, watching the steam curl from the cup and knowing that she was seeing in those endless curls a lifetime of the same streets, the same tea, the same high-pitched voices whining, "Miss Grey! Miss Grey!"

She didn't want to be Miss Grey anymore. Miss Grey might have warm hands and dry feet, but she wanted to be Laura again, before it was too late and the stony edifice that was Miss Grey closed entirely around her. It was time to get her feet wet.

Laura looked down at the soaking mess of her shoes. It was a pity Fate had to take her quite so literally.

The gatekeeper was waiting for her by the side entrance. He had an umbrella—which he held over his own head. Unlike the main gate, this one was designed for use rather than show, two thick slabs of dark wood leading onto a square stone courtyard. He opened the gate just wide enough for her to wiggle through, in an undignified sideways shuffle. That was, she was sure, quite intentional.

Rain oozed down the gray stone of the building, seeping through the cracks in the masonry, puddling in the crevices in the paving. Tucked away in a corner, a stone angel wept over the round mouth of a well, raindrops dripping down her face like tears. The long windows were the same unforgiving gray as the stone.

After the bright, modern town houses of Mayfair, the great bulk of the seventeenth-century mansion looked archaic and more than a little threatening.

From very long ago, a whisper of memory presented itself, of the fairy stories so in vogue in the fashionable salons of her youth, of castles under curses, their ruined halls echoing to the fearsome tread of the ogre as a captive princess shivered in her tower.

Laura didn't believe in fairy stories. Any ogres here would have been of the human variety.

One ogre, to be precise. André Jaouen. Thirty-six years old. Formerly an *avocat* of Nantes. Now employed at the Préfecture de Paris under the ostensible supervision of Louis-Nicolas Dubois. Commonly known to be a protégé of Bonaparte's Chief of Police, Joseph Fouché, to whom he bore a distant relation. It was his department through which any word of suspicious personages in Paris would come. It was his job to hunt down and secure these threats to the Republic.

Which meant that it was Laura's job to get the information to the Pink Carnation before he could get to them.

They had dubbed her the Orchid—the Silver Orchid. The Carnation had chosen the name, with her usual perspicacity. It seemed appropriate, thought Laura, for the Carnation to have named her after a flower that drew its sustenance from others, dependent on more firmly rooted flora for its very existence.

Her mission was simple enough. She was to embed herself into the household of the assistant to the Prefect of Police. There, she was to keep an eye out for suspicious behavior and useful information, taking specific instructions from the Pink Carnation as directed.

Just a simple little task. Nothing to write home about. She had nothing to do but outwit a man whose very business was the outwitting of others, with no training but sixteen years of governessing and a six-month course at a spy school in Sussex executed in a way that could only have been called cheerfully haphazard. The Selwicks had taught her to blacken her teeth with soot and gum (just in case she wanted to play a demented old hag); to ask the way to Rouen in a thick Norman accent; and to swing on a rope through a window without breaking the glass or herself. None of these skills seemed entirely applicable to her current situation.

Laura wasn't under any illusions as to her qualifications. The Pink Carnation would have been happier inserting a maid into Jaouen's household, or a groom—someone with more experience in the field, someone less conspicuous, someone with a proven record—but Jaouen hadn't needed a maid or a groom. He had needed a governess, and governess she was.

If there was one role she could play convincingly, it was the one she had lived for the past sixteen years. She just had to remember that.

Laura looked levelly at the gatekeeper, trying not to wince at the rain that blew below her bonnet rim, plastering wet strands of hair against her face.

"Hello," she said, as if she hadn't been forced to walk half a mile in the rain when there had been a perfectly good gate right there. "I am the governess. Your master is expecting me."

The gatekeeper jerked his head brusquely to the side. "This way."

There had been a formal entrance on the other side, equipped with a grand porte cochere designed to keep the rain off more privileged heads than hers. No such luxuries for a potential governess. Shivering, Laura picked her way along behind the gatekeeper across the uncovered courtyard, trying to avoid the slicks of mud where the stone had cracked and crumbled, ruinous with neglect. Whatever equality the Revolution had preached, it didn't extend to domestic staff.

Laura squelched her way down an uncarpeted corridor after the gatekeeper, her sodden shoes leaving damp prints on the floor. If possible, it felt even colder inside than out. Despite the frost on the windows, there were no fires in any of the grates. The Hôtel de Bac was as cold as the grave.

Pushing open a door, the gatekeeper managed to force two full syllables through his lips. "Wait here."

With that edifying communication, he stalked off the way he had come from.

Shaking out her damp skirts, Laura turned in a slow circle. *Here* was a once-grand salon, entirely bare of furniture. Smoke had dulled the once-elegant silk hangings on the walls and filmed the ornate plasterwork of the ceiling. Darker patches on the wall revealed places where paintings had once hung, but did no longer. The gold leaf that had once picked out the frame of a painting set into the ceiling had flaked off in large chips, giving the whole a derelict air. The painting was still in its rightful place, but dirt and wear had given the king of the gods a decidedly down-at-the-mouth look.

Most of the decay was due to neglect, but not all. The coat of arms above the fireplace had been hacked into oblivion. Deep gashes scored the shield, obliterating both the symbols of rank and the ceremonial border around them. Beneath a now lopsided border of plumes, the gashes gaped like open wounds, oozing pure malice and mindless hate.

Laura felt a chill that had nothing to do with the January cold run down her spine. So much for the old family de Bac. She wondered what this new regime did to spies. That particular information had not been part of her training course, and probably for good reason.

Laura caught herself digging her nails into her palms and made herself stop. The gloves were her only pair; she couldn't afford to claw out the palms.

Stupid, Laura told herself. Stupid, stupid, not to have expected this. Stupid to have believed that the Paris to which she returned would have been the Paris of her childhood. It had been seventeen years since she had last been in Paris. There had been a little event called a Revolution in between. That was why she was here, after all.

During her training in Sussex, Laura had memorized the new Revolutionary calendar, with its odd ten-day weeks and renamed months. She had learned which place-names had been changed and which had changed back again. But what was a name, more or less? Nothing had prepared her for the scars the city bore; the bloodstains that never quite came out; the damaged buildings; the air of anxiety in the streets, where any man might be an agent of the Minister of Police, any soldier on his way to foment yet another coup, where the blood might run from the Place de la Révolution once again as it had before. The charming, urbane, decadent city of her youth had become anxious and gray.

Laura gave herself a good shake. Of course it felt gray. It was raining. She wasn't going to let herself throw away a heaven-sent opportunity all for the sake of a little fall of rain. This was her chance. Her chance to do something more, to be something more, to throw off the yoke of governessing forever, even if the only way to do it was to pretend to be the governess she had once been in truth. She only had to prove to the Pink Carnation that she could spy as well as she could teach.

Only, Laura mocked herself. As simple as that.

The door of the salon snapped open, the hinges giving way with a strident squawk that made Laura half trip over the hem of her own dress.

Through the doorway strode a man in a caped coat. Raindrops sparkled in his close-cropped brown hair and created dark patches on the wool of his coat. The fabric made a brisk swooshing sound as he walked, as if it were hurrying to get out of his way.

Laura couldn't blame it. Jaouen walked with the purposeful stride of a man who knew exactly where he was going and woe betide anything that stood in his way.

His clothes were simple, serviceable, of the sort of fabric that lasted for years and didn't show dirt. Whatever he was in this game for, it wasn't for the pecuniary payoff. There was nothing of the dandy about him. His black boots were flecked with fresh mud and old wear. His medium brown hair had been cut short in what might have been an approximation of the Roman style currently in vogue, but which Laura suspected was simply for convenience. Her new employer—her potential employer, she corrected herself—didn't seem the sort to waste unnecessary time preening in front of a mirror. He looked like what he had been, a lawyer from the provinces, still wearing the clothes he had worn then.

Laura was standing, as she always stood, in a corner of the room, her drab dress blending neatly into the shadows. She was an adept at that. It was the reason the Pink Carnation had recruited her, her ability to be neither seen nor heard, to be as gray in character as she was in name. But André Jaouen seemed to have no trouble finding her, even in the gloom of the room. Without wasting a moment, he made directly for her.

"Mademoiselle Griscogne." It was a statement, not a question.

He wore spectacles, small ones, rimmed in dark metal. His dossier had not specified that. Perhaps whoever had compiled it hadn't thought it important. Laura disagreed. The glint of the glass sharpened an already sharp gaze, sizing her up and filleting her into neat pieces, all in the space of a moment's inspection.

"Monsieur." Laura forced herself not to flinch away.

Beneath the twin circles of glass, Jaouen's eyes were a bright, unexpected aquamarine. In contrast to his drab brown cloak and weather-browned skin, there was something almost frivolous about the color, as if it had been an oversight on the part of nature.

There was nothing frivolous about the way the Assistant Prefect of Police was looking her up and down.

There was nothing about her appearance to give her away, Laura reassured herself, fighting to keep the prickles of fear at bay. They had been very careful of that. Her attire was all French-made, from the scuffed half-boots on her feet to the hairpins driving into her scalp. Her real wardrobe, the wardrobe she had worn in her past life as Laura Grey, governess, as well as her small cache of books and personal keepsakes, had been left in Sussex, in a trunk in a box room in a house called Selwick Hall—sixteen years of her life boxed away and reduced to three square feet of storage space. There was no more Laura Grey, governess. Only Laure Griscogne.

Governess.

Ah, well.

Whatever André Jaouen saw passed muster. Well, it should, shouldn't it? French or English, she looked like the governess she was. "Apologies for keeping you waiting," he said. "I can only spare you a few moments."

As apologies went, it wasn't much of one. Still, the fact that he had offered one at all was something. Laura inclined her head in acknowledgment. Servility had come hard to her, but she'd had many years in which to learn it. "I am at your convenience, Monsieur Jaouen."

"Not mine," he said, with a sudden, unexpected glint of humor. Or perhaps it was only a trick of the watery light, reflected through rain-streaked windows. "My children's. The agency told me that you have been a governess for . . . how many years was it?"

She would have wagered her French-made hairpins that he knew exactly how many, but she supplied the number all the same. "Sixteen."

That much was true. Sixteen excruciating years. She had been sixteen herself when she began, stranded and friendless in a foreign country. She had lied with all the efficiency of desperation, convincing the woman at the agency that she was twenty. She had scraped back her hair to make herself look older and ruthlessly scowled down anyone who dared to question it. Mostly, they hadn't. Hunger and worry did their work quickly. By the end of that first, desperate month, she could easily have passed for older than she claimed. Her upbringing might have been unconventional, but it had left her unprepared for the shock of true poverty.

"Sixteen years," her prospective employer repeated. Through the spectacles, he submitted her to the sort of scrutiny he must have given dodgy witnesses in the courtroom, as though he could fright out lies by the force of his look alone. "Think again, Mademoiselle Griscogne."

Laura pinched her lips together. Sixteen years ago, she had learned that the expression made her look older, more reliable. People expected their governess to look like a prune who had just been sucking on a lemon.

By now it came naturally.

She had to succeed in this mission. Had to, had to. Anything rather than face being a governess forever, feeling her face freeze a little more every year into a caricature of herself until there was no Laura left beneath it.

For the next few months, she would be the very best governess she could be, if only it meant—please, God—that she never had to be a governess again.

Laura squared her shoulders beneath her sodden pelisse, steeling herself against the urge to shiver. "I assure you, Monsieur Jaouen," she said frostily, "my experience as a governess is quite as extensive as the agency has claimed. I provide elementary instruction in composition, literature, Scripture, history, geography, botany, and arithmetic. I am proficient in Italian, German, English, and the classical languages. I teach music, drawing, and needlework."

André Jaouen's eyebrows lifted. "All that in the same day?"

Laura's brows drew together. Was he joking? It was hard to tell. Either way, it was always better to ignore such lapses in one's employers. If they weren't joking, they tended to take offense at the assumption of levity. If they were, it was dangerous to encourage them.

The reflection helped settle her nervous stomach. She felt on firmer ground here, putting a prospective employer in his place. She had played this game before.

"I tailor the curriculum to fit the specific needs and interests of the children in my care," she said loftily. "Not all subjects are appropriate in every situation."

André Jaouen made an impatient gesture. "No, of course not. I doubt my son would appreciate your tutelage on needlework. You are free to start immediately?" At her look of surprise, he said briskly, "I wish to have this business dealt with as quickly as possible. Your references were excellent."

Of course they had been. The Pink Carnation employed only the best forgers.

Was it just her nerves acting up again, or had that been too easy? Shouldn't he question her about her references? Ask her more about her teaching methods? Tell her about the children?

"Mademoiselle Griscogne?"

"Yes," she said hastily. "I can begin whenever you like."

André Jaouen motioned her forward, already in motion himself, making short work of the distance to the double doors through which Laura had entered. "I have two children, Gabrielle and Pierre-André. Gabrielle is nine. Pierre-André is almost five. Until now, they have been with their grandparents in Nantes. This is their first time in Paris." He spoke as he walked: direct, economical, no effort wasted.

"And their prior education?" Laura lengthened her stride to keep up, her wet skirts tangling in her legs as she followed him past a wide staircase, the marble balustrade gone a dull gray with grime. An empty pedestal stood on the landing, marking the place where a statue must once have stood. Tapestries still lined the walls, but they hung crookedly, and several bore poorly mended gashes.

"Their grandfather taught them at home."

Laura did her best to suppress a grimace. Fairy stories. Basic reading. Arithmetic. If she were lucky. She would have to start from the very beginning with them. The boy, Pierre-André, was nearly of an age to be sent off to school. She would have to bring him up to the level of other boys his age.

No, she wouldn't. The thought brought Laura up short. If she did her job well, she wouldn't be around long enough for it to matter. She had been thinking like a governess again, falling back into the old patterns.

Jaouen was still talking, words marshalling themselves into neat, economical sentences. Behind the measured cadences, Laura could detect just a hint of a Breton burr. There was no faux-aristocratic ostentation there, no pretense. "Your wages will be paid quarterly. Room and board will be provided to you. Ah, Jean." That last had been directed to the gatekeeper. "Tell Jeannette to find Mademoiselle Griscogne a room. Something near the children."

Jean and Jeannette? His servants couldn't be named Jean and Jeannette. It was too much like something out of the Commedia dell'Arte. Did the still-unseen Jeannette run around in a particolored costume smacking Jean over the head with a big stick, like Pierrot and Pierrette? Perhaps they were spies too. If so, one would have thought they could have come up with better aliases.

"Jeannette is the nursery maid," Jaouen said as an aside to her. Without waiting for them to be handed to him, he scooped up his own hat and cane off a marble-topped table by the door. "Jeannette will see you settled and make you known to Gabrielle and Pierre-André. If you need anything, either Jean or Jeannette will see to it."

With a nonchalant push, Jean the gatekeeper shoved open the door, letting in a blast of damp air. The rain looked as though it were contemplating turning to snow. The icy pellets stung Laura's cheeks as she followed Jaouen to the door. She was still wearing her pelisse, and her pelisse was still just as wet as it had been when she had entered; the entire interview, such as it was, had taken all of ten minutes. Ten minutes to embark on the most dangerous gamble of her life.

A carriage was waiting in the courtyard, plain and black like the cloak draped over Jaouen's shoulders, the horses pawing impatiently at the cobbles.

She had clearly been dismissed. And hired. She had been hired, hadn't she?

Jean the gatekeeper gave her a disapproving look as she followed her new employer out under the porte cochere. Or perhaps that was just his normal expression. "I will need to fetch my things," Laura said desperately. "And settle my account at my current lodgings."

Reaching into his waistcoat pocket, André Jaouen took out a purse and shook several coins out into his palm. He thrust what looked to her untutored eyes like a substantial sum in her direction.

"An advance," he said impatiently, when Laura looked at him uncomprehending. "On your wages."

Laura's back stiffened. "My own funds are more than adequate to settle my current obligations."

He looked at her curiously, then shrugged, returning the coins to his pocket. "Will you bite my head off if I offer you the use of the carriage?"

He cocked an eyebrow, waiting for her reply. There it was again, that glimmer of what might have been humor.

"There is no need, sir," Laura said coolly. "My lodgings are not far and I am more than accustomed to managing for myself."

Jaouen eyed her speculatively, his glasses glinting in the light of the carriage lamps. "I can see that." And then he ruined it by adding, "I wouldn't hire you if I thought it were otherwise. My occupation is a demanding one. I have no time for domestic squabbles."

That had put her in her place. Between fear and relief, she felt almost giddy. "Squelching squabbles is one of my particular specialties."

Jaouen forbore to comment. With the air of someone getting done with a bad job, he continued. "You may be troubled from time to time by my wife's cousin, who persists under the unfortunate delusion that my home is his own. Ignore him."

Ah, one of those, was he? Once, she might have claimed that she wasn't the sort of governess to inflame a young man's lusts. But she had learned the hard way that, after a certain degree of inebriation, all it took was being female, and sometimes not even that. She had also learned that employers seldom took kindly to their elder sons, nephews, or houseguests being hit over the head with a warming pan, candlestick, or chamber pot. Laura appreciated both the warning and the implicit authorization to do whatever she needed to do.

It was comforting to know that the intimidating M. Jaouen had an Achilles' heel, even if that Achilles' heel was only a cousin by marriage. It made him more human, somehow. And human meant fallible. Fallible was good, especially for her purposes.

"I will. Sir."

Jaouen nodded brusquely, her message received and accepted. Hat in one hand, cane in the other, he started for the carriage. At the last moment, just beyond the protective cover of the awning, Jaouen jerked his head back over his shoulder. Laura shot to attention.

"Why did you leave your last position?" he asked abruptly.

"My pupil married." If he had hoped to shock her into an admission, he would have been disappointed. Her pupil had married in June, leaving her once more without a situation. The family had been kind; they had kept her on through the wedding, but there was a limit to the charity she was willing to accept. "She had no need for a governess anymore."

But the Pink Carnation had had need of an agent.

Rain pocked Jaouen's glasses as he treated her to another long, thoughtful look. He held his hat in one hand but didn't bother to put it on, despite the rivulets of rain that silvered his hair and dampened his coat. "An occupational hazard?"

Laura permitted herself a grim smile. "One of the most hazard-ous."

She had never thought much of matrimony herself—her parents had set no favorable example—but it had been distinctly unsettling to make a place for oneself only to be flung out into the world again. And again and again. Some of them, the sentimental ones, sent letters for a time, but those generally tailed off within the first year, as the daily demands of the domestic state outweighed sentimental recollections of the schoolroom.

"You shan't have to worry about that with Gabrielle. Yet."

She wouldn't be around long enough to worry about that.

"Indeed," she agreed. Noncommittal replies were always best in dealing with employers. Yes, sir; no, sir; indeed, sir. It came out by rote.

Jaouen clapped his hat onto his head. "Tomorrow morning," he said. "The children will be expecting you."

Jean the gatekeeper slammed the door shut behind Jaouen as he swung up into the carriage. The horses' nostrils flared, their breath steaming in the cold air as the coachman clucked to them, setting them into motion. Through the rapidly misting glass of the window, Jaouen was nothing more than a silhouette, a blurred image in tans and browns.

That was it. She had done it. She had really done it. Blood surged to Laura's cheeks and fingertips, sending a rush of warmth tingling through her, despite the freezing wind gluing her soaking skirts to her legs. Whatever else came of it, the first step was accomplished; she was a member of Jaouen's household. She was in.

Between the rain and the sound of hooves against the cobbles, Laura could just barely hear her new employer call out his instructions to the coachman.

"To the Abbaye Prison. As fast as you can."

Laura swallowed hard, turning her face away from a sudden gust of wind that tore at her bonnet strings and snatched away the very breath from her throat.

Oh, she was in all right. Way over her head.

Photo by John Earle

Lauren Willig is the RITA Award–winning and bestselling author of seven previous Pink Carnation novels. She received a graduate degree in English history from Harvard University and a J.D. from Harvard Law School, though she now writes full-time. Willig lives in New York City.

Notes

Notes